Dear Bs

M000291318

THE TROUBLED MAN

A Q.C. DAVIS MYSTERY

LISA M. LILLY

Enjoy! Great to see you.

Lisa M. Lilly

SPINY WOMAN LLC

1

What's the one thing you want to do before you die?

That question was printed in neon green chalk at the top of a blackboard hanging just inside Niche's Women's Room. I hadn't noticed it when I walked in, but now I studied the chalkboard as I washed my hands. Ten numbered white chalk lines underneath provided spaces for restaurant patrons to write answers. It was early in the evening, and only one diner had filled in an answer. She wanted to visit the Galapagos Islands.

Despite all the death around me since before I was born, it was a question I never thought about.

"Take a trip to Paris?" Ty said when I rejoined him at our small, square table and told him about it.

"Maybe next summer," I said.

"Or you could set a goal of dodging better in your training sessions." He grinned at me.

"You noticed." My hand rose to my jawline. I had layered on extra foundation and carefully styled my long hair into waves to cover the bruising. Early in the summer I started training with a retired police academy instructor. A City of Chicago detective who owed me a favor had referred me to him to help me learn to better defend myself and avoid danger. "First day we finally get to fighting. I was supposed to be ducking. Obviously, I'm not a natural."

Ty sipped the last of his wine. "The heavy makeup layer gave it away. Not exactly your usual look. Other than in those old publicity shots your Gram showed me."

I was a stage actress as a child and teenager. Spending so much time in makeup and costumes, and being stared at, left me leaning toward a fairly simple look in real life. I use enough foundation to even my olive skin tone. If I'm going to court – now I'm a lawyer – or out for an evening I add some mascara and lip gloss and I'm done.

"I thought maybe the dress would distract you."

I wore a bright red sundress with spaghetti straps, perfect for the heat that day. Most of my clothes double for work and going out, but this did not.

"Oh, it's definitely distracting. Which I appreciate."

"You think Eric will notice the bruise?" I said.

Without asking any questions, Ty had agreed to drive forty-five minutes west of downtown Chicago for dinner so I could meet Eric Ruggirello afterwards. Eric was the son of a man I had been involved with two years before. That man's death led to my meeting the police detective who later suggested some defense training for me. And it led to a friendship with Eric.

"Probably not," Ty said. "He didn't say what he wanted to talk to you about?"

"He's fourteen. He didn't say. He texted. But he did give me a little background." My phone showed seven-twenty-five. "We should go."

Ty slid his chair back. "I just hope it's not about another murder."

"Well –" I said.

It's a far west suburb of Chicago, but Geneva looks more like one of those quaint antique towns that tourists frequent. Not unlike Lake Geneva in Wisconsin, which people sometimes confuse it with if they don't live in the area. Geneva draws people from all over the Chicago area for its seasonal festivals, and during the winter holidays you feel like you're walking through a festive snow globe.

Small restaurants and boutiques with specialty items like candles, gourmet olive oil, or unique jewelry line its downtown streets.

It also has plenty of free parking, another wonder of suburbia. Ty had easily found a spot on the street midway between the restaurant and the chocolate bar where we planned to meet Eric.

During our short walk, I told Ty that Eric had a friend whose mother died a month ago, at the end of July. Today, her dad had been arrested.

"That's why she's staying out here. With her aunt and uncle," I said.

"So she needs a defense attorney."

"Probably. But I already offered a referral. Eric asked if he could talk to me in person."

I handle only civil matters. Which means money is at stake, not anyone's liberty or life. But I share office space with a criminal defense attorney. Eric had met Danielle once or twice and already knew I thought highly of her skills. So it must be something more.

Eric sat at a table near the windows, not far from a five-foot-tall dark chocolate sculpture of a peacock. A girl who must be his friend Alexis sat opposite him, her spine flattened against the back of the booth. He hadn't told me she would be with him.

Her blue-streaked blond hair had been gelled and sculpted to stand straight up from her head. Her eyebrows slashed dark lines over her eyes. Like me, she had olive-tinged skin. Tonight, the areas under her eyes looked almost bruised. Some of her makeup foundation had worn away, showing a rash of acne on her left cheek.

Eric stood when he saw us. It used to make my heart hurt when I saw him. He looks so much like a slimmer teenaged version of his dad. But it had been long enough since Marco's death that now Eric reminded me more of happy memories.

He looked taller than when I last saw him, though it had only been a month ago. And his dark curly hair, so much like his dad's, looked shorter, with no flyaway ends. A few curls hung over his forehead.

He hugged me and introduced Alexis. I adjusted the spaghetti straps of my red sundress, which had slipped partway down my shoulders during the hug, wishing I'd opted for my usual way of dressing. I favor neutrals and clothes that I can mix and match for business or going out. The red dress didn't feel appropriate to talk to a girl in Alexis' circumstances. I told myself she likely didn't care.

Eric and Ty shook hands.

Ty left to get us drinks. Eric slid into the booth next to Alexis, and I sat across from them.

"I'm so sorry to hear about your mom's death," I said to Alexis. "And now about your dad."

"It's just –" She clutched a half-full mug of some sort of frothy drink and stared down into it. "When my uncle picked me up from school today, I kept telling him he had to do something, but he won't. He won't do anything."

"Is there something specific you want him to do?" I said.

"Tell them. The police. Tell them they're wrong." She inhaled through her mouth, a sharp, quick breath that made her chest heave. "Stupid, right? It's not like it would change their minds."

"Probably not. Did he say why the police focused on your dad?" I said.

"Just they always think the spouse did it." Alexis fixed her eyes on me. "Is that true? Eric said you know about criminal stuff."

In the two years of sharing space with Danielle, I picked up a lot. She once told me that fifty-five percent of the time if a woman is murdered, her husband or boyfriend did it. A statistic that wouldn't make Alexis feel any better.

"The police typically look first at a spouse," I said. "But to make an arrest, there must be more than that."

Eric pushed aside his milkshake. "They're saying it was poison. That Ivy – that's Alexis' mom – was poisoned."

Ty slipped into the booth next to me with two glasses of ice water plus a root beer for him and a dark hot cocoa for me. I love hot cocoa no matter the weather, and I love that he doesn't find that weird.

"And is that what the police told you right away?" I said.

Alexis shook her head. "No. Everyone thought complications from stomach flu or something. My mom had a lot of digestive problems."

Not everyone or there wouldn't have been an investigation. "So what changed?"

"I don't know."

"Seems like not many people die from stomach flu," Ty said.

Alexis cleared her throat. "Yeah, probably not. But my mom has – had – a weak stomach. So we all kind of thought it was something like that."

I supposed some type of digestive issues could be fatal, but it sounded to me more like something a detective might have mentioned to give everyone involved the false impression that murder wasn't suspected.

Eric hit a few keys on his phone. "Do you know this lawyer? Is he any good?" He passed the phone across the table to me. It was open to a solo lawyer's law firm website.

"My uncle recommended him," Alexis said.

"I don't." The name was unfamiliar to me, but that didn't mean anything. Through Danielle I knew some of the Chicago area defense attorneys' names, but definitely not all of them. I scrolled through the single-page website. "Wrongful death, contract cases, criminal defense. I can't tell how much of the practice is criminal."

"I compared it to Danielle's," Eric said. "Hers is all criminal defense info. And she has all these links to news articles about her trials."

I sipped the hot chocolate. Not bad, but still a bit too sweet for me. I like bitter dark.

"Well, you know Danielle's who I'd choose if I were ever in trouble. But this attorney might just not be very good at creating a website."

I fired off a text to Danielle asking about the attorney.

She was a prosecutor before she became a defense attorney, and a cop before that – one of the first Black women on the force. She knew most lawyers who practiced criminal law in Chicago. At least she did if they appeared in court very much.

"My uncle says any private lawyer's better than a public defender," Alexis said.

I felt unsure how much information to provide if it might unsettle her more. But I always tried to be up front with Eric. I doubted he would have contacted me if he wanted someone to sugarcoat things. Though it wasn't clear yet what exactly he wanted me to do here.

"That's not always so," I said. "I'm a private attorney. You could hire me to represent your dad, but it would be a bad idea. My eight years of practice have all been civil." Alexis looked at me blankly. "Cases about money. A first-year public defender knows more than I do about criminal procedure. And an experienced one knows all about sentencing and which judges are more likely to grant certain types of motions. And what sorts of things a jury might think about."

Danielle had horror stories about clients who came to her after a friend who was a real estate attorney or corporate lawyer represented them. Or one who handled minor criminal matters but had never tried a case and got hired to defend a murder charge. Unfortunately, most of the bad advice couldn't be fixed after the fact.

Alexis squared her shoulders. "But Eric told me you investigated crimes before. Like his dad's death."

"And for your friend Caleb," Eric said. "And that other time."

"That didn't turn out so well for Caleb," I said. "I think he ended up being sorry he got me involved."

"He nearly got killed," Ty said. "And so did Quille."

I shot him a look. When talking with Eric I downplayed any close calls I had. He'd already lost his dad. He didn't need to worry about something happening to another adult in his life.

"You didn't tell me that," Eric said.

"Ty's exaggerating," I said.

Eric's eyebrows rose.

"Okay, not by much. Which is why I'm doing that training I told you about. So I can protect myself better."

Eric slouched. "Now I feel like I shouldn't have asked you to come here."

"Because?" I said, though I had a guess as to what might be coming. Eric wouldn't have asked me to meet in person just for background on a defense lawyer.

Alexis and Eric glanced at each other. She spoke. "We want you to help us figure out who really killed my mom."

2
___

Ty's grip around his root beer mug tightened. "Murder investigations are dangerous. That's why people leave them to the police."

"The police who decided my dad did it?" Alexis said.

"I know that doesn't sound like a great option," I said. "But if there is another killer, either of you getting in that person's sightline isn't going to help anything. Would your dad want you taking a chance like that?"

Her shoulders slumped. "No." She mumbled the word, staring at the table.

"Just because they arrested him doesn't mean they'll stop investigating, does it?" Ty said.

I thought about it. "It really isn't my area of law. But post-arrest investigation might be more about gathering evidence to bolster the case. Not chasing down other suspects."

"What about this defense attorney?" Ty said. "Or Danielle, if she got hired. Wouldn't one of them do that?"

"The goal is to show reasonable doubt," I said. "Sometimes that means showing someone else could've done it. But not always."

"My uncle says my dad's not coming home for a long, long time." Alexis puffed out her chest as she spoke.

"There can't have been a bond hearing yet. So he doesn't know how long it'll be. If your dad, or his family and friends, can raise money for a bond, he'll be out while the case against him moves toward trial."

"My uncle says there's no money for a bond," Alexis said.

This uncle had a lot of opinions.

"But there's money for a lawyer?" Ty said.

Alexis rubbed her fingers over the tarnished silver chain she wore around her left wrist. "He says it's one or the other."

"Defendants in criminal cases do sometimes have to make that choice," I said. "Your uncle – on your mom's or dad's side?"

"He's my mom's brother."

That could explain his negativity. If I thought my brother-in-law killed my sister, I wouldn't be rushing out to make things easy for him.

"Well, there's no way he knows how much the bond will be," I said. "The judge will decide."

Eric frowned. "But it won't be low, right? For a murder charge."

"It won't be low," I said. "But he'll likely need only ten percent of it in cash, not all of it. A bondsperson usually guarantees the rest. For a fee."

All the same, ten percent might be a lot. A half-million-dollar bond meant $50,000. Not many people have that lying around.

"But he's supposed to be innocent unless he's proven guilty," Alexis said. "Why does he have to pay to get out of jail?"

"That's why a lot of people who are arrested don't have bonds anymore," I said. "But for murder, judges worry a defendant might disappear. Or hurt or kill someone else."

I asked what her father did for work.

"Drives a truck. In Chicago. He started that a couple years ago. Before that he was over-the-road."

If that change meant he was with a new company he wasn't likely to have a lot of paid time off coming. Putting him in an even worse financial position. But truck driving paid reasonably well. Maybe he could afford both a bond and an attorney.

"Does he own a house? A lot of people borrow against their homes to pay the bond."

"My mom owned the house – well, it's like part of a house. She was getting it in the divorce. My dad and I live in an apartment now."

I was curious about what part of a house meant. But the mention of divorce raised my antennae. I took out a small notebook I carry. While I could take notes on my phone, it makes a lot of people uncomfortable. They think I'm texting or checking email instead of paying attention to them. Also, writing by hand helps me remember things more than typing does.

Ty glanced at my notebook and frowned. Probably correctly guessing I was trying to figure out what I could do for Alexis.

"Your parents were separated? For how long?"

"Almost two years now. Since I started eighth grade. But they got along really good."

I scribbled a note. "But they were planning to divorce?"

"It would have been final, like, three weeks ago I think."

"Which is when in relation to when your mom died?" I asked.

"A week after? Maybe less," Alexis said.

I carefully kept my face neutral, not wanting to signal my reaction.

But they were both smart kids.

"That doesn't mean her dad killed her mom," Eric said.

"No," I said. "But it might be why the police focused on him."

Especially if the mom was getting the house or other assets, leaving the husband in a bad financial position.

Ty nudged my arm. My phone was buzzing with a text from Danielle about the lawyer:

only ran into him a couple times – as they say, he doesn't belong above the first floor

I frowned.

"What?" Eric said.

Usually I don't like to comment negatively about another lawyer's experience. But this could make a big difference.

I showed Eric and Alexis the text. "The first floor is where the early stages of a criminal case are handled at 26th and California. Chicago's main criminal courthouse. Bond hearings, preliminary hearings. The trials are on the upper floors."

"So it means he shouldn't handle trials?" Ty said.

"Shouldn't or doesn't."

"But don't all criminal lawyers try cases?" Eric said.

I shook my head. "Not all. Maybe thirty or forty percent never do. A lot of criminal cases never get to trial. They're plea bargained out. If the case heads for trial, they might bring in someone like Danielle who has a lot of experience. Or wing it. The problem is, prosecutors know who tries cases and who doesn't. They don't make as good an offer to an attorney they know won't try the case."

"Why would my uncle suggest someone like that?" Alexis said. "Does he want my dad to stay in jail?"

"Most people don't know the difference," I said. "Like all of you did, they assume all criminal lawyers do pretty much the same thing."

"So what does Danielle charge?" Eric said.

"It depends on how involved the case is, but let me see if she can give me a ballpark." I sent another text.

I knew Danielle's fees were more than reasonable compared to high profile defense attorneys, the ones you see on the news all the time. But tens of thousands of dollars isn't cheap from most clients' perspectives. Which was the exact reason many criminal defendants charged with felonies paid attorney's fees rather than paying the bond.

"If my dad can't pay, could she do it as a favor?" Alexis said. "I mean, I know it's her job, but what if he can't pay?"

"It's not that Danielle wouldn't want to help a friend of mine. She would. But a lot of cases come through friends who are lawyers. If she worked as a favor every time, she'd be out of business in a month. But usually part of the fee goes to the lawyer who referred the case. Which here would be me. So if your dad decides to hire her, I'll ask her to discount her fee by the amount she would have paid me instead."

"We can't ask you to do that," Eric said. "It's how you make your living too."

"I make mine through my civil cases, not on referrals. It'll be fine."

The referral fee would help my bottom line, which was shaky after a quiet summer. But I couldn't take a fee where Eric was involved.

"Thank you," Alexis said. "Really."

My phone buzzed.

Depends but at least $12,000 or $15,000 to start maybe double or triple that later depending how far case goes. Less if you're skipping your share.

I told them the general price range.

Alexis excused herself to visit the restroom. When he stood to let Alexis out of the booth, I noticed Eric's pants looked too short, barely grazing the tops of his shoes. Not quite an adult and no longer a kid. And, like me at his age, already too much experience with death.

"Alexis – your girlfriend?" Ty said.

Eric's eyes twitched as if he were about to roll them, but he stopped himself and straightened his shoulders. "Uh, no one says that anymore."

"But if they did she might be?" Ty said.

Eric creased the edge of his napkin. "Maybe."

"Do you know anything else?" I said to Eric. "About why the police suspect her dad?"

"Alexis said her dad stopped at her mom's place a lot, including the day before she died. He was one of the few people who had a key."

"And he told the police that?"

"Probably."

"And her dad talked to the police?"

"Everyone did."

"Without a lawyer, I'm guessing."

"I told Alexis maybe her dad should have one. But that was back when everyone thought it was the flu, and the police said they just wanted to establish a timeline or something. We had kind of a fight about it. She kept saying her dad didn't do anything wrong, he didn't need a lawyer." He stared at his hands. "I should've tried harder."

Eric seemed to shrink as he spoke. His dress shirt bagged at the shoulders.

I covered his hand with mine. "It wasn't your call. Or Alexis'. It was her dad's."

"Yeah, but –"

"A lot of people feel like bringing in a lawyer makes them look guilty. Or they think they don't need one."

A few years before, Danielle had defended a cop accused of murder who answered questions without a lawyer. He really should've known better. But his fellow officers questioned him and he thought they were trying to help him. I told Eric about the case, hoping it would make him feel better, especially because Danielle had still gotten a not guilty.

I returned to my notes. "Do you know if Alexis' parents argued about anything? Right before she died?"

It struck me as odd the police felt so sure about the ex-husband when the method was poisoning. I didn't know much about poison, but Alexis' dad couldn't have been the only person with access to her food or drink.

"Not that I heard." He drained the last of his milkshake. "But Alexis' mom was unhappy about Alexis living with Santiago. That's her dad."

"How long has she lived with him?"

"Not sure. I think Alexis lived with her mom at first. After her sister went away to school."

Alexis returned from the Women's Room. Her lips looked dry and cracked. "So will you help?"

"I'm not sure how I'd do it. People aren't likely to want to talk to me."

"You got people to talk to you other times," Eric said.

"When I had an official reason – like with your dad, where I was involved with him and the executor of his will – or where someone who knew me very well made the connections for me."

"I can do that," Alexis said.

"Yes. You don't really know me, though. Your family and friends will be suspicious of this new person in your life. Wonder about my agenda."

"You don't exactly come across as a scary person or a con artist, Quille," Ty said.

"Thanks." I smiled at him, glad that his concerns about me didn't keep him from understanding how much helping

Eric mattered to me. "But if I were Alexis' relatives, I might worry about this lawyer coming around randomly asking questions. Though if you think they'd take your word for it –"

Alexis sagged back against the booth. "No. Not my aunt and uncle. Or my sister. Or anyone probably."

I squeezed her hand. "Let me think about it. There might be some way."

Alexis squeezed her eyes shut. "Think hard. Please? I need my dad."

3

"Do you need to get people to talk to you?" Ty said as we got in the car. Night had fallen. The stores along Third Street were closed. The restaurant across the street was still lit, but the three tables along the windows stood empty. "If Santiago hires Danielle, you'll have access to a lot of information."

"Yes and no. More than if it were a defense lawyer I didn't know. But anything Santiago tells her will be confidential."

Ty turned onto Roosevelt Road. "Isn't it usually women who poison? I think I read that somewhere. That could make it more likely Santiago didn't do it."

We drove over a bridge above the Fox River. The water reflected light from the gas streetlamps along the river's edge.

"Sounds right to me, but it's not something I've ever looked at."

I took out my phone and did some searching.

"So?" Ty said after a few minutes.

"The Bureau of Justice has a lot of statistics. Putting it together, it looks like if women kill, they're more likely to use poison than a more violent method like a gun or knife. Men use poison, too, but eight times less often than women. And if a woman is killed, like with any other murder of a woman, it's most likely a man did it. A man she knew."

"Not good for Santiago."

"No," I said. "But I'll do more digging when I'm in my office."

The wind coming through the windows felt perfect on my face. Not quite cool, but warm enough to relax me. A relief after the hot day.

"You're okay with me doing this?" I said.

"If by okay you mean I won't try to convince you not to, yeah, I'm okay." Ty squeezed my hand. "But doesn't this raise issues for you?"

"Issues?"

"A parent falsely accused of murder? Two girls more or less abandoned by both parents?"

As the car accelerated, wind whipped my hair into my face. I fumbled through my purse for a ponytail holder and twisted my hair into it. "The investigation, my sister's death, it was all before I was born."

"Right, but it's hung over your whole life."

"I wouldn't say hung over."

"Quille, they named you for your dead sister."

"Yeah, that was awful. But my parents didn't exactly abandon me. I could have gone with them to Edwardsville. I wanted to stay with Gram. Keep acting."

"They at least could have stayed until you were eighteen."

I shrugged. "All that would have changed is living one apartment down. I already spent more time at Gram's. Is there some reason you're asking about this?"

"I thought maybe your issues with your parents are why you don't want me to meet them."

"What? Of course I want you to meet them."

"Each time I suggest driving there for a weekend you put me off."

I remembered Ty mentioning it once early in the summer after I met his parents. They'd come into Chicago to see him. I shifted in my seat to face him. "Did I?"

"Three times."

"I didn't realize that. But you met Gram. And you know Carole." Carole was a Frenchwoman who ran the café in my neighborhood. She was more like a real mom to me than mine was. And the café, on the ground floor of the building where I have my law office, was a second home.

"Your other friends know your parents," Ty said.

"Only the ones who met them when they lived here."

"Joe's gone to Edwardsville with you. He mentioned it."

Joe sang in an a cappella trio with Danielle and me. I had first met her through Joe, long before I went to law school. But Joe hadn't been around much lately. I couldn't think of any time he and Ty would have talked alone.

"Is this – are you – you're not jealous of Joe?"

Ty merged onto the expressway. "He's known you decades. I've known you less than a year. I kind of feel like I'm playing catch up."

"It's not – Joe's like a buffer when I see my mom. Makes it easier to cope. That's why he came with me a few times."

"I can be a buffer. I've got good practice at it."

Ty's a real estate developer. A lot of his job includes wining and dining people. He's one of the most fun people I know to be around, so I didn't doubt my parents would enjoy meeting him.

"I know you can. Mom might even crack a smile."

"Is it because I'm Black? Are your parents not comfortable with that?"

"No. They won't care."

"You're sure. Ever brought a brother home?"

"No, because I've brought hardly anyone home. Anyway,

Edwardsville isn't home for me. It's more like a shrine to the original Q.C. Davis."

"That bad?"

"It's not my favorite place to be. But I do want you to meet them, and it'd be good to see my dad. Let's plan a weekend. Defining weekend as arriving late Saturday and leaving early Sunday."

"Works for me. After that I'll see if I can pry you away from the office for a trip to Maine when the leaves turn."

"One trip at a time."

Ty flipped a button and a mix of summer hits played through his speakers. He didn't know the words, but he could carry a tune. When he got stuck, he made up his own lyrics. Sometimes with our names in them.

I reached over and squeezed his hand. And promised myself that looking into Alexis' dad's defense wouldn't interfere with either trip he wanted to take.

4

Danielle twisted a tuning peg on her guitar. "There's a strong chance her dad's guilty."

We sat on counter stools at my kitchen island. The glass doors to the deck stood open. Warm, humid August air drifted over me, making me feel a bit too lazy for practice, but we had a job tomorrow morning.

Her words made me sit up straight. "What?"

"Statistically speaking, that is. I want you to be prepared." Danielle plucked the fifth string and a warm, near-perfect A reverberated. It lowered as she turned the peg. "The police, the prosecutor, they're not always right. But in a murder case, ninety-five percent of the time, the person who gets charged is the person who did it."

"How do you know? I thought you don't ask if your clients are guilty," I said.

"I don't. At the start I tell them whatever they say about what happened, that's what I'll believe. No changing the story later. But some tell me they did it. Others, based on what adds up and what doesn't, I'm pretty sure are. But I can still put them on the stand if I need to."

I nodded. It's a key principle for any lawyer. Your job is to represent the client to the best of your ability. Which means you're allowed to present the best possible arguments and evidence even if you personally have doubts. But a lawyer can't put a client on the witness stand to lie. So if her client admits to a crime to her, Danielle can't put that person on the stand to deny it.

I hoped that wasn't the case with Santiago. Because Alexis clearly wanted not just her dad out of jail but to know he didn't do it.

"Can I help you with the defense? If Santiago hires you?"

He and Danielle had spoken briefly by phone that morning.

"I've got an idea for a different way you can help Alexis. But it could be complicated, so let's practice first." She pointed to the list of songs on her iPad. Our trio, known as The Harmoniums, was singing at a Sunday brunch fundraiser tomorrow morning. Joe had emailed this morning to say he couldn't make it, so we needed to switch out our set list at the last minute.

"Simple Gifts to start?" I said. "Easy to transition it to a duet."

"Sure. Folks might like a little gospel on a Sunday morning."

I nodded, and she plucked an E on her guitar to give us a starting note.

Danielle's religious. Joe and I are not, but we all love harmony singing, which most gospel songs and hymns are great for. Plus we were singing for a Chicago Catholic Women's Group. Mostly they liked our mix of sixties and seventies pop/folk songs, but they appreciated a little nod to faith as well.

Half an hour later we had a solid forty-five-minute set.

One that should work well enough to avoid disappointing the ladies who had paid for a trio.

Danielle set her Martin D18 into its case and flipped the locks while I got out a corkscrew and a bottle of Pinot Noir. Neither of us likes to drink alcohol while practicing. It dries the throat.

But after we almost always open a bottle.

"So when is Joe going to crawl out of his hole?" Danielle took two clear green wine glasses out of my upper kitchen cabinet. "Break ups are hard but I never thought he was that invested in that relationship."

Joe and his long-time girlfriend had split up the previous Valentine's Day.

"I'm not sure that's all it is." I poured taco chips into a green glass bowl that matched the wine glasses and opened a jar of medium-hot salsa.

"Then what?"

"Lauren told me a while back she thought Joe might be interested in me. And that's why he was snarky to Ty when they met."

Plus in the brief moments they'd talked, he'd apparently told Ty he'd met my parents. Why bring that up if not to tweak Ty?

"Huh." Danielle balanced the two glasses of wine in one hand and opened the sliding door to my deck. "Could be. But I never thought Joe saw you that way."

I followed her outside. The wind had shifted, and it felt cooler than in my condo. You can't see Lake Michigan from my deck – at eight stories it's not tall enough to see over the skyscrapers. But the breeze reached us all the same. After an exceptionally cold winter and spring, the lake stayed much chillier than the air all summer.

"Me either." I set the chips and salsa on my table. "But I've hardly heard from him since I started seeing Ty."

"I say ask him." Danielle settled at the wooden bench nearest my neighbors' row of outdoor plants. "Turn up at his door if you have to. Clear the air. I like duets, but I miss that three-part harmony. And my friend."

"I miss him, too." I sat across from Danielle. "So what's your idea about Alexis?"

Danielle sipped her wine. "She could hire you to bring a wrongful death suit."

I paused with a chip midway to the bowl of salsa. "Against Santiago? How would that help?"

"No. Against whoever might be responsible who's not Santiago. You can't file a lawsuit right away because you don't have a defendant. But if Alexis hires you, you've got a built-in reason to ask questions. Get documents. See evidence."

A wrongful death suit is a civil lawsuit. People file them to get money damages from whoever is responsible for a death. I sipped my wine, savoring the smoky undertones. "I've never handled one."

"Mensa Sam can walk you through," Danielle said. "You'll owe him a big favor, but I bet he'll do it. And I did some of them with my first partner when I went out on my own. I can give you a little guidance. Unless it turns out there's a conflict with defending Santiago."

Sam was our office suite landlord, a personal injury attorney we both found annoying, including because of his obsession with his membership in the high I.Q. society Mensa. But he knew a lot about personal injury law. It was all he did.

"But what if I find things that point to Santiago? I'm sure Alexis doesn't want to sue him."

"That's the challenge. But she can drop the civil suit if it turns out Santiago did kill his wife. He needs to support her anyway, and he won't be able to inherit from Ivy if he caused her death."

"She has an older sister who would have to agree, too." I swirled another chip in the salsa. "I don't have to turn over what I find to the prosecution, do I?"

"No duty to do that. But keep to yourself everything you can so they don't follow your footsteps and find what you found."

5

Alexis hadn't told her aunt and uncle anything about me yet, so she didn't want me to come to their house. She took the train downtown from Geneva after school Tuesday afternoon, telling them she was spending the day with Eric at the skateboard park near Roosevelt Road and Michigan Avenue. They didn't ask too many questions because they liked Eric. I couldn't imagine who wouldn't.

And they did go to the skate park for a while, then met me around five at Café des Livres.

We all sat at one of the wrought iron tables outside.

"You understand if we do this, I'll be representing you, not your dad," I said.

Alexis' hair hung in chunky blocks. I guessed she hadn't styled it in days. The blue streak was fading to a dusty gray. Eric sat next to her, his chair an inch from hers, his right hand resting on her left knee.

She wore frayed blue jeans shorts that were ripped in just the right places to show they were bought that way, not worn out. It was a style I associated with people who never had to worry about money and so could wear torn clothes for fashion. In college, I had too often, with the help of costume designers in the small theaters where I got parts, sewn decorative beading over carefully shaped patches to cover holes in my jeans and get another few months' wear out of them.

All of which made me wonder about the uncle's claim that there was not enough money to cover both a bond and a lawyer.

I started explaining what I could and couldn't do if I acted as her lawyer.

Alexis clenched her hands into fists and bounced them on her thighs as she jiggled her feet. "But you said on the phone — "

I pushed my cup of Earl Grey tea to one side. "I said the lawsuit would give me a reason to ask questions and gather facts and documents. But your dad won't be the client, you will. And your sister. And your dad is Danielle's client, not mine."

Danielle had talked to Santiago Jimenez-Brown this morning by phone. He hired her. Santiago's sister had sent Danielle money for the retainer.

The metal chair legs wobbled as Alexis shifted position. "Okay."

"Also, because you're a minor, the suit will need to be in an adult's name on your behalf."

"My dad's?"

"Usually a parent would do that. But here there's a possible conflict, so the court won't let him."

"Because the police arrested him?" Eric's chin jutted forward. "The court just assumes he did it?"

"Not assumes. But he's a suspect. The judge will need to protect you, Alexis, because you're a minor. Which means being very careful to see that your chance to recover in this lawsuit is protected. The judge has no way to know if the police are right or wrong in arresting your dad. But if they're

27

right, he has a conflict because he won't want the truth to come out."

Alexis' lower lip puffed out and for a moment she looked more like four than fourteen. "It's not fair."

"It's not, and I'm sorry. But remember, the judge doesn't know you or your dad. It's not a judgment about him or the facts. It's a way for the courts to be very, very careful."

"Your aunt or uncle?" Eric said.

The corners of her mouth sagged. "They'll never do that."

That was all right with me. Anyone around Alexis who had been in town during the time her mom was killed was a suspect. And therefore not someone I wanted as a client.

"Why not?" Eric said.

"They think Dad did it."

Eric's hand fell away from Alexis' knee, but she clasped it with her own.

"I was thinking of your sister," I said. "You told me on the phone she's twenty-one. And she lives in Illinois."

"I don't know. She and Mom didn't get along at all, and she's really mad about everything." She stirred more sugar into her cappuccino. "What about my Aunt Perla?"

"Your dad's sister? She lives out of state, so she can't. Is there some reason you don't want your sister?"

Alexis studied her fingers. "It's stupid."

"How you feel isn't stupid," I said.

"It's just, she, like, only stayed a day after Mom's funeral. Then went right back to school. She doesn't care what happens to me."

I remembered feeling abandoned when my oldest sister went away to school. It wasn't easy to be left behind, especially in a family filled with grief.

"I don't know your sister, so I can't say what she cares about. I do know people grieve in very different ways. Could it be she rushed back to school because she felt so sad and upset and couldn't handle it?"

Alexis shrugged. "Maybe." She took out her phone. "I'll text you her number."

"Good. Let's all talk together at first, though," I said. "We'll pick a time."

Alexis picked at loose skin around her nail bed. Little beads of blood sprang up. "We can always drop it, right? If you find out anything that looks bad for my dad?"

"In the long run, I'm pretty sure the answer is yes. But you should know that because you're a minor, the court might want to weigh in on that first. To make sure your sister and I are protecting your interests."

I'd spent much of Sunday afternoon after the singing job researching issues about minors bringing lawsuits. The next morning I quizzed Mensa Sam, the personal injury lawyer, to be sure I understood what I learned. It meant working late last night so I could keep up with my paying clients' cases, but it was worth it. Because now I felt confident answering all Alexis' and Eric's questions.

"But if the court thought he did it, wouldn't it be protecting Alexis' interests to go ahead?" Eric asked.

"If her dad has money he's not using to support her and her sister, and the lawsuit is the only way to get those funds, then yes. The court might not let us drop the suit." I inched my chair closer to the table. "In that case, I could withdraw as your attorney but the court would look for someone else to handle it. But from everything you've told me, and your uncle told you, your dad doesn't have money stashed away to get. So there'd be no reason for the court to do that."

"And you're not going to look for bad things about him? Like the police are doing?"

For someone convinced of her dad's innocence, she expressed a lot of concern. Like me at that age, she knew to look around the corners of life for what might be coming next.

"I'll look for the truth. And any information that shows who's responsible for your mom's death."

In a perfect world I'd discover some weird chemical reaction that poisoned Ivy but was the fault of a manufacturer, not anyone Alexis knew and trusted.

No, that was wrong. In a perfect world, parents wouldn't die and leave their children.

Eric folded his arms over his chest. "But if something points to her dad, then what?"

Alexis looked at me, hands still for once, her eyes narrowed. She wanted a real answer, not stock reassurances.

"I won't tell you to sue your dad, and I won't do anything the law doesn't require me to do to bring that evidence to light. But I'm not going to manufacture evidence against anyone else or pretend that someone else is responsible. You understand that?"

"Yeah." She started picking at her nail bed again.

"You're sure?"

"I'm sure." Blood ran down the side of her finger.

"Okay." I took a clean tissue from my shoulder bag and handed it to her. "We'll talk to your sister, and if she agrees I'll put something in writing."

"How's my dad going to support us if he's in jail?" Alexis said.

I sighed. "It's a problem a lot of defendants have. If they have a job before being arrested and can't afford to bond themselves out, they usually lose their jobs."

"But they get them back, right, once they're released?" Alexis said.

"Lots of them do."

I decided not to add that if they got out after pleading guilty to any crime, the employer might not take them back.

And it wasn't easy looking for work with a criminal record. That was an issue for down the road.

"Don't worry," Eric said. "Truck drivers are in big demand now. I just read an article about it."

I wanted to hug him right there, he was such a good kid. He wasn't wrong about truck drivers. I had a client who ran a trucking company and lamented finding qualified people. If Santiago pled to any sort of felony, though, I doubted he'd still be employable.

Eric offered to go in and get another cappuccino for Alexis and hot water for me. We both said yes. Then I took out my legal pad and started asking Alexis questions.

6

Alexis rubbed her hands together. "I didn't see my mom the day she died. I don't know what happened."

"That's okay. Why don't you tell me about your mom. What she was like?"

I wanted to start with something Alexis might feel more comfortable with than the facts surrounding her mom's death. Also, in law I learned early on that open-ended questions are almost always best when you're trying to get information. It lets the witness tell the story in their own way, which usually means the person relaxes and talks more.

"My mom had more money," Alexis said. "When they met."

"What do you mean?" I wrote a dollar sign and a plus next to Ivy's name. That the topic of money came to mind first when I asked about her parents' relationship told me a lot.

Alexis twirled one of her rings, a thick metal one. "I don't know why I said that. My uncle always says it."

"Why does he say it do you think?"

"He never got over Mommy – Mom – marrying a truck driver."

Eric returned and set fresh, hot drinks on the table.

"Did your mom have her store when they met?"

I was pretty sure she hadn't. Though I hadn't had much chance to research Ivy, I had found her bio as the owner of a vegan cosmetics store. The store was inside a block-wide building near the Chicago Board of Trade. Its anchor tenants were Starbucks and the Wintrust Bank. I had cut through that building pretty often during winters when I worked at my old firm and had never seen the store.

"No. She only started it, like, a year or two ago. She and dad had to work out a bunch of things. Something about marital property?"

I made a note to look for anything about the store when I pulled the domestic relations court file. It was already on my To Do list.

A driver near the intersection of Dearborn and Harrison laid on the horn, blasting our ear drums. I waited until the noise stopped and asked, "So what did your mom do for a living when she met your dad?"

After the question was out I realized it contained an assumption that Ivy's money had come from work rather than being family money.

"Something in banking. Or finance? Money or investments. But she quit a long time ago."

"Before you were born?"

That was the measuring stick for most kids. Maybe most adults, too. For my Gram, who is in her late seventies, anything from 1980 on still feels recent.

"Between when my sister was born and I was born, I think. They moved here from Boston. And lived with my aunt and uncle for a while until Mom got a job somewhere."

"Also in finance?"

"Um, yeah, I think so. But she said she was unhappy not being home with us, so she decided to stay home full time."

"And did your dad work during that time?"

"Yeah. He always says moving to Chicago didn't really change work for him. He still drove over-the-road and was just based out of a different office. And he got a lot of time off, like six weeks in summer."

"But you said he only drives in the Chicago area now."

"Right. He switched two or three years ago. Said he got tired of being on the road so much. He wanted to feel like he lived somewhere, not out of his truck."

I circled the timeframe in my notes. And wondered if his decision to be home more contributed to his marriage ending. Maybe Ivy and Santiago had gotten along better in smaller doses.

"So when your uncle said your mom had more money – does that mean she saved a lot when she was in the financial world? Or she inherited money?"

"Not inherited."

Alexis told me she had never met her grandparents on her Mom's side. Ivy hadn't talked much about them, other than that they were both dead by the time she reached college and she had to make her own way.

"Do you know how your parents met?" I said.

"Bowling? I know Dad was in, like, a league. Mom and her friends hung out at the bar. I think her friend's boyfriend did standup comedy. Something like that. Mom saw Dad bowling and thought he was cute and went over to talk to him."

"Did they date very long before they got married?"

"Like two years? Maybe less. I'm not sure."

After a few more questions about her family, I asked about the house. Her mom, she said, lived in a three-flat in Andersonville, a Chicago neighborhood about seven miles north of downtown. She and Santiago bought it with another couple. The Jimenez-Browns lived on the second and third floor, and the other couple on the first. They all shared the basement.

Alexis added that she thought maybe only her mom owned it, which I found interesting. In Illinois, any property you get or income you earn while married is marital property, meaning it's legally owned by both of you. If you want to keep assets owned before marriage separate, they need to stay totally split. The other spouse can't contribute to them.

I don't do divorce law, but I guessed keeping a house separate would be a challenge. If Santiago made part of the mortgage payments or paid for remodeling, it could easily become marital property. Another point to check out in the court file. Plus I moved the owner of the first floor near the top of my interview list.

"Any idea why your uncle believes your dad is guilty?" I said.

"Just that my dad was at the apartment alone to take care of the dog the Friday before Mom died."

Alexis sat straight in her chair, her hands wrapped around her cappuccino.

"We can stop talking any time," I said.

"No, you know, let's keep going. I want you to get started."

"Okay. If it gets too upsetting, though, let me know. Do you know who found your mom?"

"Her friend from downstairs. Ellison. She lives alone there now. She and her husband got divorced. She called the police because Ralph – that's Mom's dog – kept barking and barking. Mom didn't answer her phone or the door. So Ellison called the police and they broke in."

I wondered why Ellison didn't have a key if they were such good friends. My friend Lauren and I own condos in the same building – a converted printing factory in Chicago's Printers Row neighborhood. We have each other's keys in case of emergencies.

"Do you know if the police figured out what type of poison was used?"

"Antifreeze? I think that's what they told my uncle. But I don't know if it was in her food or a drink or what."

"Did they find the antifreeze in her home?"

"Not sure."

"Eric said your dad still had a key to your mom's place?"

"Yeah. He was there every other week or so. He fixed things for her. Like if a cabinet door broke or something."

So it wasn't unusual for Santiago to be there, which to me made his visit the day before she died less suspicious.

"Did he work on her car?" I said.

"She doesn't have a car anymore. He took it with him."

Less reason for antifreeze to be at Ivy's home at all, then.

"How long ago did he move out?"

She fiddled with the cup, spinning it in the saucer. "Uh, about two years ago."

"And you said before they get along?"

"I—not as good as when they were together. But Dad still got along better with Mom than most people." She pulled at the edges of the Kleenex wrapped around her finger.

"People didn't get along with your mom?"

Alexis' shoulders drew together. "You had to do things Mom's way. You know, she wanted help loading the dishwasher, but the forks had to be turned tines down and not fall against each other. She called it nesting. Don't let the silverware nest. And food had to be passed left to right at the table and if you were putting an egg in a cake mix, this is before she was vegan, you had to break the egg first in a separate bowl and sniff it to make sure it hadn't gone bad. If you missed a step, she got really mad."

"OCD?" I said. "Obsessive –"

"I know. My sister always accused her of that, but she never, like, kept all the corners square or washed her hands

36

all the time or those things. She just wanted things her way. It drove Amber crazy." She looked down and cleared her throat. "She and Mom couldn't stop arguing. About stupid things. Like, Amber would say why not have the forks stems down? That way the little tines don't get stuck in the holes at the bottom of the silverware holder. And Mom would talk about spots on the silverware and then they'd be all into Amber not liking our house and just everything."

"How about you? Did you get along with your mom?"

Alexis swallowed hard. "Yeah. I just did things her way. You know, what's the big deal? I watched Amber, and it never got her anywhere to argue. So I put the forks in tines down or whatever. It's not the end of the world. And that way Mom wasn't always checking on me the way she did on Amber. She trusted me. Even though I broke the rules more than Amber."

"Any particular rules?"

"Oh, do all my homework before playing any online games. Don't hang out with any friends she hasn't met. Which was sometimes hard because she didn't consider it meeting them if it was online. It had to be in person, but she didn't like to go to school events or anything. And not everyone could come to my house before we could hang out."

I looked up from my legal pad. "So you ignored that rule sometimes?"

Her forehead creased. "You're not going to tell my uncle and aunt are you? That I don't always follow the rules?"

"I don't think anyone always follows the rules. But no. As your attorney, I can't tell anyone anything you say to me in confidence."

Technically with Eric sitting there this wasn't a confidential conversation. But I had no intention of telling her secrets. Not unless keeping quiet posed a risk to her safety.

I sipped my tea. Despite the sticky August weather, I

found its warmth soothing. "Back to your dad. You said they argued a lot recently. Just during the divorce process?"

"A little before that. But they hardly ever argued until I was, like, eleven? Dad doesn't argue with anyone. He's like me. You know, he goes along with you. If you want to see a movie, he'll go to the movies and see what you want to see. He says the point is to be with who you want to be with, not what you're doing."

"What did they argue about?"

She shrugged. "Everything kind of."

Part of me was surprised she didn't know more. I wondered if I'd been as unaware of my parents' lives as a teenager. Probably, given how surprised I was by their sudden move "home" to Edwardsville when I was sixteen.

"Did anything else change in your family around that time? Something that might have sparked arguments?"

"Well, Dad started driving locally. So he was around more. Mom was starting the store. So she wasn't home as much. And my sister went away to school."

"Did your mom and dad fight about anything in particular around the time of your mom's death?"

She shook her head. "If they did, I didn't hear about it."

"Would you? Did your mom or dad confide in you?"

Almost whenever my mom talked to me as I was growing up, other than when she gave me voice lessons, she spilled out whatever she felt anxious or upset about. She did the same to my sister. My dad sometimes talked to us, too, about what concerned him. He said he didn't want to talk to my mom and add to her anxiety. It was part of why a tiny part of me – no, a pretty large part of me – felt relieved after they moved away. I didn't need to be a sounding board anymore.

But from my other friends and therapy, I knew that wasn't exactly normal behavior for parents. Or at least it wasn't ideal behavior.

"No, they didn't talk to us about each other much. They always made everything sound like they decided together," Alexis said.

"Even after they separated?"

"Yeah, pretty much. We could never, like, play them off one another. I think my mom read some parenting book about how bad that was or something."

That could show a couple handling their parenting and their divorce in a healthy way. Or it could show one making all the decisions and the other agreeing on a united front. Or probably any of a number of other parenting approaches. But it did suggest they both cared a great deal about their kids.

Which seemed to me not consistent with Santiago killing his wife and leaving his children without a mother.

I flipped down the pages on my legal pad and slid it into my accordion folder. It was after two, and Eric's mom was picking the two of them up from the skate park at three-thirty. I wanted Alexis to have time for some fun if she could manage it.

"That's enough to get me started, assuming your sister agrees when we talk to her tonight. Any questions that you have?"

"All I can think about is my dad being locked up, how wrong it is. Not about my mom. Like, at her funeral I cried. But I keep only thinking about my dad. Do you think that makes me a bad person?"

I reached across the table and touched the back of her hand. "People grieve in lots of different ways. When Eric's dad died, it took me a long time to let myself really feel it. Now sometimes I still cry at odd times, but I didn't at all at first. However you're feeling, it's okay."

I watched as the two of them walked south on Dearborn Street, hands linked, toting their skateboards. And wished I could do more for her.

7

My friend Lauren and I had been planning to have drinks together that night after she finished an open house at a condo down the street. But Alexis texted that she and her sister could talk with me at eight. I asked Lauren to come over a little later with a bottle of wine, and for dinner I microwaved Stouffer's lasagna. It's not nearly as good as my Gram's, but it reminded me a little of home.

Then I sat at the patio table in the outdoor deck area just off my condo's back door. It's shared with only a few other neighbors, so it's pretty private. Especially tonight, when it was still nearly eighty-five degrees out and humid. Everyone was barricaded inside in the air conditioning. But I felt too restless and cooped up inside.

I poured a tall glass of ice water and put the phone on speaker.

Alexis barely finished introducing me when Amber interrupted. "What's the point of a lawsuit?"

Her photos on social media showed an older version of Alexis with sleek dark hair, clearer skin, and a tattoo of a flying raven across her bare shoulder. Her voice was pitched much lower than Alexis', making me imagine she would appear taller and a bit larger if she stood next to Alexis, though pitch doesn't always correlate to size. In the background I heard voices rising and falling, tinny crowd sounds from what was probably a sports game on TV, and the clink of glasses and dishes.

"It may not become a lawsuit," I said. "But you and your sister retaining me can give me a reason to ask people questions and for them to want to answer to help you both. And down the road it could help me get documents and information from people who don't want to share with us."

"And you really think you can find something that proves my dad didn't do this?" Her emphasis on "really" suggested she doubted it.

"That's the goal. I can't promise I'll succeed. But I'll try. If you both want me to."

Something knocked against Amber's phone. Amber's muffled voice told someone to give her a few minutes.

Behind me, my glass door slid open and Lauren stepped out onto my deck. She wore khaki shorts and a black tank top and had pulled her short, shiny blond hair into a ponytail, a nod to the heat. She held a bottle of chilled Riesling, its sides wet with condensation, in one hand and a bag of chips in the other. I had told her to just come in since I'd be on the phone.

The conversation should be confidential, so I clicked off speaker and held the phone to my ear.

"Amber?" I said.

Lauren set everything on the table and disappeared inside again.

"I just don't know if it's a good idea," Amber said. "Maybe we ought to stay out of it."

"Sure, fine for you," Alexis said. "So who cares about me?"

More clattering in the background from Amber's side. "What's that supposed to mean?"

"All you care about is all your friends and parties at school. You're glad to be away. While I'm squeezed into Aunt Sylvania's and Uncle Hank's. I'm the one who helped Dad box up all mom's stuff. I'm the one who doesn't get to go back home."

"I don't either," Amber said.

The age difference between Alexis and her sister was similar to mine with my sister Kendra. She was the oldest. Then there was the original Q.C. Davis, who died before I was born, then me. I felt lost and angry when Kendra went away to school. We hadn't spent that much time together as kids because of the age difference. Still, she had taught me to tie my shoes and to count and to imagine places I wanted to go on vacation when I woke up scared from bad dreams.

I missed her when she left, and maybe she missed me, but she couldn't wait to go.

"But you live at school," Alexis said. "That's home for you."

Lauren returned with two wine glasses and a corkscrew to open the Riesling. Usually I don't like white wine. But the dessert wine would be sweet and cool, and I could use that.

"Fine, whatever. But what's in this for Quille? Why's she doing this?" Amber said.

"She's not charging us," Alexis said.

"Only costs," I said. "If there's some recovery. Unless we have to go to trial, and then a ten percent fee, which goes to the personal injury lawyer who's helping me."

Trying a case with Mensa Sam didn't appeal to me, but I needed his expertise. And he had surprised me by not asking for a third of any amount we recovered, which is the typical amount a personal injury lawyer would take.

"Why the charity?" Amber said.

"She's a really good friend of Eric's," Alexis said.

"Oh." Her voice warmed a bit. "That little boyfriend of yours. The one I met at the wake?"

"Yes."

I noticed Alexis didn't deny the term the way Eric had. Which seemed like a good thing for him.

"Well, I guess if you want to donate your time, Quille," Amber said. "Just don't make any promises you can't keep. This is hard enough on Alexis."

"I'm fine," Alexis said. "It's Dad we should worry about."

"Dad can take care of himself."

"Yeah, that's why he's in jail," Alexis said.

"Alexis. Amber," I said. "This is a hard time. A terrible time. For both of you, for your dad, for everyone who cared about your mom. Amber's right, I can't promise anything. And it will be hard for both of you. You may need to talk to people to get them to open up to me. I might have questions for you. Lawsuits can put a strain on people emotionally – more than you're already feeling, which I imagine is hard to believe. But I'll do my best for you, and Danielle will do her best for your dad. And I hope, with all of that, we can get your dad out of jail."

A lawsuit makes it harder to let go of pain or anger. It focuses people on their suffering or what they've lost as they try to get someone else to pay for it. It might be that the other party bears responsibility for the injury and should pay, but the process makes it hard to let go and move forward. Clients expect it to make them feel better, and mostly it doesn't. At least not until quite a while after it's over.

"Okay," Amber said. "It's – you're probably both right. I just don't want Alexis to be disappointed."

After answering a few more questions about how the

process worked I promised to send a contract to both Alexis and Amber, though only Amber needed to sign.

After I ended the call, I reached for the wine glass Lauren had filled for me. "After all this, I hope I can find answers. Otherwise all I'll do is create more discord between the sisters on top of everything else they're going through."

8

"I guarantee that discord was already there," Lauren said after I told her about the parts of the call that weren't confidential.

She spoke with certainty despite being an only child. Lauren usually had a pretty good read on people, though. And I valued her insights partly because her childhood, and her whole life, had been so different from mine. She saw things I didn't, and vice versa.

The wine tasted sweet with a faint hint of apple. I studied the sun dropping behind the buildings to the west. "Probably. But I still don't want to make it worse."

"You're sure you're okay with doing this? It's got to hit close to home."

"You sound like Ty. It's nothing like my family."

Lauren pulled apart the bag of chips with a pop. "Seriously? Controlling mom? Tragic death? Try-to-get-along-with-everyone dad? And big sis is off at college, happily away from it all."

"My mom's too depressed and anxious to be controlling."

"Quille, that's exactly how she is controlling. Everything

revolves around her. Maybe she's not doing it on purpose, and Ivy it sounds like was, but the result's the same. Kudos to you and Kendra for breaking away."

"No, we –" I stopped, drank a little more wine, and reached for a handful of chips. Sour cream and onion flavored. My favorite. "Okay, maybe. But it's different."

"Maybe. But you're not just a little angry at Amber on Alexis' behalf? For leaving her here to deal?"

I sighed and drank the wine. "A little. But school's important. She shouldn't have to derail her education after losing her mom, too."

"No. But it sounds like she could take a stab at being a little more supportive. It has to suck to be Alexis right now."

"It's not easy for either of them," I said.

Once she made up her mind, Amber wasn't slow to act. I sent her a contract in the morning and she returned a signed and scanned PDF by four that afternoon.

After getting a root beer – the only beverage Mensa Sam stocked for tenants in the shared kitchen – I made a list of people close to Ivy. I sent it to Amber and Alexis and asked them to add anyone else they thought I ought to talk to or know about. Also, for some people, I asked one or the other of the girls to call or text and specifically ask them to talk with me. Then I reviewed my list of legal deadlines. Two new cases had come in late the week before. That meant income I badly needed, but also too many projects due by the end of the week. Meaning it would be another late night.

I called Ty to say I'd need to skip dinner but could meet him for drinks, then spent the next two hours revising a memo to a client who had been sued for sending unsolicited faxes. Something I hadn't realized anybody did anymore.

I printed it to make it more likely I'd spot any typos when I reread it in the morning and looked over the Ivy list.

It seemed to me the first person to talk to was Santiago Jimenez-Brown himself.

~

Danielle spends almost every morning in one courtroom or another, and sometimes part of the afternoon as well. But most days she pops into our shared office by three-thirty or four. This time it was five before she arrived and then it was to pick up some photos she had forgotten and needed for a half-day trial the next morning.

I asked her what I needed to do to visit Santiago in jail.

She clicked her mouse to scroll through email. "You don't. Not yet and not without me. I need to see him on my own first. We've only talked on the phone."

"You don't trust me to visit alone?"

"It's not that. Hold on." She typed a few words, hit Enter, then spun her chair to face me. "I don't want you to go alone because what if he says something that hurts his defense? Or what if you do? None of your conversations with him are privileged."

"Oh. Right."

An attorney's communications with a client are privileged, meaning no one else is allowed to find out about them except in very unusual circumstances. But I wasn't Santiago's attorney.

"Look, I get it," she said. "For Alexis and her sister, the most important thing is to know someone else did this. Someone else killed their mom. But whether Santiago did it or not, if your work for them makes it more likely he gets convicted, I'm thinking they won't want that."

I couldn't argue with that. I sat back in my chair. It wasn't that I had a great desire to see the inside of the Cook County jail. But not being able to talk to Santiago made it a lot harder to put together the pieces.

"A phone call?" I said. "With you on the line?"

"They're monitored. And recorded. Remember how mad I got at Louis See-You-In-The-Next-Life Lyzinski?"

"The whole office suite remembers that."

Danielle had come back from court fuming and cursing. More than I had ever heard her do before.

"That's what he did. Middle of a double-murder trial. One night after court he called his buddy from jail. Told him what to say on the witness stand the next day. I told him a hundred times it's a recorded line." She pushed together loose papers on her desk and shoved them into a file, creasing the top ones. "Plus there's a message that tells you it's recorded when you start the call. He claimed he didn't think anyone ever listened to the recordings. Guess what – they do. I got to court the next day and my witness was barred." She banged the file folder on the edge of the desk.

"And it still gets to you."

"You bet. Worked my ass off to get him out of jail and he does a thing like that. How someone who runs a multi-level drug ring as large as his could be that stupid."

"Can I at least take Alexis to visit if I don't ask Santiago anything?" That would give me a chance to observe Santiago with his daughter. More important, Alexis could see her dad. So far her uncle refused to take her.

Danielle took a breath, straightened the papers, and shook her head. "Only a parent or guardian can take a minor to visit someone."

"That seems harsh."

"You really want random adults to be able to bring minors into jails to see prisoners?"

I sighed. "I can imagine only about a hundred ways that can go wrong."

"Give it some time. Her aunt or uncle may relax a bit on it. It's a depressing place to see someone, though. All underground. No windows. That might be the real reason they don't want to take her there."

"I want to talk to the aunt and uncle, Hank and Sylvania Brown," I said. "Any issue with that?"

"That's Santiago's family?"

"No, Ivy's brother and his wife. Brown was her last name."

It's never made sense to me that women are expected to abandon their own names when they marry and men aren't. I had a few women friends in both theater and law that defied convention and kept their own names. But so many women dropped their last names entirely in favor of their husband's, or used theirs only in the middle, that I'd been surprised when I realized Brown had been Ivy's last name and Jimenez had been Santiago's.

It made me like Ivy a little though I hadn't met her.

"Go for it," Danielle said. "No recordings, though. No transcripts. Those the prosecutor could subpoena from you."

"Just notes," I said. "I promise."

9
———

Alexis' aunt owned a yoga studio in St. Charles, a suburb not far from Geneva, where she and her husband lived. I figured around three in the afternoon might be slow there. It was too late to be lunch hour, when some people might attend classes, and too early for the after-work crowd.

Before I called, I printed out a series of labels that said: "Privileged. Attorney-Client Work Product. These notes contain thoughts and mental impressions."

I did that to make it completely clear that I wasn't transcribing anyone's exact words but instead writing my own thoughts. That meant that, under the law, the notes were considered my personal work product, part of preparing a case or defense, and no one else was entitled to see them. Including any prosecutor or any other attorney who might take over the case from me.

This way, if anyone said anything negative about Santiago, I wasn't obligated to share it.

I got voicemail, but Sylvania Brown called me back twenty minutes later.

"So you're that attorney Alexis has been talking to,"

Sylvania said. Her voice sounded a bit husky, as if she'd either been crying recently or smoked a lot, but it had warm undertones.

"Yes. Did she explain why?"

"She says you might bring a civil lawsuit if someone other than Santiago did this. But my husband says it's a waste of time. That you're giving her false hope."

"I can't make any promises," I said. "But Alexis really does believe her dad is innocent."

"What girl doesn't think her dad is wonderful?"

"You may be right about that," I said, which I've found is always a better response than disagreeing when you're hoping for someone's cooperation. "Are you willing to help out, though? I was hoping I could meet with you and your husband."

A shuffling sound came through the phone, as if she might have shifted it from one hand to the other. "Hank says there are costs. For a lawsuit. Medical records and transcripts and things like that."

It sounded like Hank was familiar with litigation. I wrote a note to run searches for lawsuits by or against him.

"There are," I said. "But I'll be careful how much I spend and pay those costs as I go. I don't plan to ask for reimbursement unless there's a recovery."

Absorbing the costs was reckless for me financially, especially when I was already working for free. My business clients paid costs, if there were any, on a monthly basis along with my bill. But I couldn't imagine asking Alexis or her sister to do that.

"Well, I suppose there's no downside to that for the girls. But it's hard for me to get away from the studio if you want to meet in person."

"I can come to you."

I wanted to see where Alexis was living now, and I didn't

mind driving. While I don't own a car, Lauren does. She parks in my parking space, and I use her car. It's a good deal for both of us.

The challenge was that it took forty-five minutes on a good day to get to Geneva, and few good days happen when it comes to traffic in the Chicago area.

Between my court dates and client conferences and the class schedule Sylvania had, we struggled to find a time to meet. As we talked, I scrolled through her yoga studio website to see if Sylvania was as busy as she said. Her schedule showed classes on everything from gentle stretching to essential oils to something called emotional tuning. I couldn't tell which ones she personally taught.

"I'd like to talk to your husband, too," I said.

I had debated talking to them separately, but sometimes you learn more about people when you see them interact with someone they care about.

"Then mornings are better. He's at the store afternoons and evenings."

"Ivy's store?"

That struck me as odd. That morning while at court for one of my cases, I had pulled a copy of Ivy's will. It named Santiago as the executor. The court records showed Hank filed a petition to substitute himself because Santiago was in prison, but the court hadn't heard that petition yet. So he didn't have any power to handle Ivy's affairs.

"It's not Ivy's store." Sylvania's voice took on a slight edge. It must be a mistake people made often. "It's Ivy's and Hank's. Was. He and Ivy were partners."

"Oh. I didn't realize. Alexis told me it was her mom's store."

The Secretary of State website also didn't list Hank Brown as an officer or manager of Ivy's Vegan Cosmetics, only Ivy as president.

"She probably never saw him there. Hank's more of a back-office type. He handles the bookkeeping, runs the computer system, updates inventory. Ivy managed the people and the marketing. If you let Hank do it, he'd let everyone walk all over him."

Sylvania spoke quickly. I wondered if she felt nervous talking to me. Or simply overwhelmed at the thought of Hank adding Ivy's responsibilities to his own.

"So Ivy was more the face of the store?" I said.

"Yes. And Hank was fine with that. He didn't like to be center stage. She did."

Hank not spending time in the front of the store might be the reason Alexis never mentioned him. But it also suggested Ivy never talked about Hank's role to her daughter. Then again, teenagers aren't known for paying attention to what the adults in their lives do or say. I had been an odd child, hyper-aware of my parents' moods and actions. Especially my mother's.

"With her investment background I'm surprised Ivy didn't handle the money," I said.

Finance and accounting aren't one and the same, but there's a lot of crossover. Also, Alexis had mentioned her uncle taught English Literature. My research turned up a listing for him as an adjunct faculty member at Loyola University, which meant he taught part-time and was low paid. It made sense he had other professional work. But nothing in his profile hinted that he ran a vegan cosmetics store.

"Ivy discovered she hated finance. She left at first to stay home with Amber. When the girls both reached school age, she tried going back, and she was not happy."

I wondered how deep Ivy's dislike ran. Whether it might be enough that she left all the store's financial issues to her brother. Plenty of cases I worked on in my eight years as a lawyer involved family businesses gone wrong, often with one family member taking advantage of another or outright cheating another or being accused of it. I doubted it was as common as it seemed to me, though. No one goes to see a litigation lawyer because everything's going great, so I see a skewed version of the world.

But it definitely wasn't uncommon.

Sylvania and I finally agreed to an early morning meeting the following week on the only day she felt sure Hank could be there and that I had free.

I felt tempted to ask her before we hung up if she thought Santiago was guilty. But I wanted to see her in person when we got to that topic. With most people, their expressions and body language tell you a lot about how they feel.

And whether they're being honest.

10

Danielle had an appointment to visit Santiago alone Sunday morning at the jail. I hoped after that she'd agree to take me to see him. In the meantime, I had multiple social media sites to review that included Ivy's blog posts and videos going back over a decade. And Amber had called her Aunt Perla, Santiago's sister, to ask her to talk to me. Perla answered my follow-up email right away and we planned to talk at six. She agreed to video, which made me happy. I wanted to see her.

At five-thirty I got a sandwich from the café downstairs to stave off hunger if the call ran long. The last thing I needed was for a migraine to knock me flat for hours, and hunger was a trigger. At ten minutes to six I took the doubled-over sticky note I use to block the camera on my laptop and opened FaceTime. The view of my office showed brown accordion files and manilla folders teetering in stacks on the credenza. When I sat in my chair it blocked some of that view, but it still looked messy.

Not a good image for trying to get a stranger to trust me.

Also not the way I liked to keep my office, but lately I finished work so late that I didn't take the time to neaten everything before I left. I spent the next five minutes putting the papers in the right file folders and storing them in the credenza drawers. Danielle's files lined the long wall inside our office door, so they didn't show.

I combed my hair, smoothed on a little extra foundation to lighten the dark spots under my eyes and the stubborn yellowish bruise that remained on my jawline, and refreshed my lipstick.

My research told me Perla was a mid-level manager at a paper company in Ohio. With so much of business, publishing, and news online, I couldn't imagine times were good.

I called right at six, and she answered immediately. She had the same rounded face I'd seen in photos of Santiago and wore a yellow long-sleeved collared shirt and red-framed reading glasses on a serpentine chain around her neck. Like me, Perla wore lipstick, but hers was bright red and brightened her skin, which was a half-shade darker than mine. It made me think I ought to try that color rather than my usual neutral lipliners. Also like me, her fingernails, when they came into the frame, were rounded but not polished.

Gray cubicle walls surrounded her, dotted with colorful sticky notes between pages of what looked like columns of figures.

I said I was sorry about Santiago and asked how she was doing.

She twisted the cap off a pen she was holding. "In shock. I'm in shock. It was enough, Ivy's death. Then Santiago's arrested, my nieces are basically without parents...Amber broke down when she called to ask me to talk to you."

I was glad Amber felt free to share her feelings with someone. Maybe her shortness with Alexis came from not wanting to show her little sister how upset she was.

"You're close with them?" I said.

She nodded. "Always. I'd be there now if I could. But since

last Spring I've been doing the work of three people. Layoffs. My boss has sympathy, but she's overloaded herself. We got way behind when I took time for the funeral. And I can't lose my job. I'm splitting Santiago's legal fees."

"That has to be hard." I glanced at the row of Danielle's files on the floor. Most of her clients struggled to pay her fees. It was her least favorite part of her job – having to collect. But attorneys who didn't learn to do it didn't last long.

Perla took off her glasses. "It's terrible. But he feels good about your friend, the attorney. Thinks he'll be better off than with a public defender."

"Can I ask – I'm assuming you don't think he did it?"

"Of course I don't. I'd pay his bills regardless, but he didn't. Not Santiago."

"Is there something particular that makes you sure? I ask because –"

"No one's going to say her brother would commit murder?"

"Right," I said. A few of Danielle's clients did not think it was a big deal to kill someone else. I figured even their siblings, though, would hesitate to outright say it.

"I'm sure that's true. But Santiago, you could ask anyone, it's not possible. He's that guy, the one who catches spiders or mice and takes them outside instead of killing them. He stepped on a wasp once when we were kids. He was barefoot. Howled like he was dying. And still got mad at me for killing it after I pulled it out of his foot."

"How a person treats animals isn't always the same as humans," I said.

I thought of my neighbor, who cradles his Pomeranian in his arms in the elevator if another dog comes in, cooing to soothe him. But he lets the dog stay on the floor lunging and snapping at kids when they pass in the lobby. He says it's their problem if they're afraid of dogs, not his.

"But Santiago was the same with people." Perla's hands, closed into fists, moved down and out of the camera frame. I heard a thunk that was probably them hitting her desk. "It's why it's all so insane. No one had more patience with Ivy than Santiago."

"Did he need patience to deal with her?"

"Everybody needed patience to deal with Ivy."

Off-camera, I wrote the word Patience on my legal pad and circled it so I'd remember to go back to it. Then I went on to a key question. "How did Santiago feel about the divorce?"

Perla's head and shoulders filled the screen as she leaned into the camera. "Relieved."

"Right away?"

That struck me as unlikely. Most people I knew who divorced, no matter how bad the marriage, felt some personal sense of failure and loss. But I didn't want to suggest answers to her.

Her lips pursed. "Maybe not right away. Maybe I felt relieved for him. The marriage had been bad for a long time, but I don't think he saw it. So when they decided on the separation, that was hard for Santiago. But once he actually moved out, I saw a difference in him. He was much more relaxed. Happier."

Out in the reception area, the bell on the door jangled. Someone from the building's cleaning service called out, "Housekeeping." I excused myself to doublecheck. A thief broke into my office when I was looking into Marco's death, and I wasn't taking any chances.

But the usual cleaning woman waved to me, and I returned to the screen.

"When you say the marriage was bad, what do you mean?" I said.

"They were so different. I think it's that thing – was that thing – where opposites attract, and then they drive each other crazy." She waved her hand. "Not crazy. I don't mean that. Not like he became super angry or anything. God, I'm so afraid of saying the wrong thing."

"Please don't worry how you say things. I'm not the police," I said. "Or the prosecutor. My only goal is to help the girls, and they want to show Santiago didn't do this."

She closed her eyes, squeezed them tight for a moment. "Okay. Yes. Santiago, he felt frustrated for years with how rigid Ivy was. And he probably drove her cr – got on her nerves, too. But they stuck it out, both of them, for the girls. But once Alexis was nearly in high school, and Amber off to college, Santiago started feeling it wasn't worth it anymore."

"He told you that?"

"I read between the lines if you know what I mean. Santiago, he didn't talk about his feelings a lot."

That was true about a lot of people, including me. But it could easily feed into a narrative where Santiago repressed his feelings for years and finally decided to take out all his anger at one time.

I turned a page on my legal pad. "And you saw a change when he moved out. He was more relaxed?"

"Oh, yes. He didn't need to watch every word he said and everything he did anymore."

Despite my closed office door, the bubble-gum smell of the disinfectant the cleaning service used filtered into my office.

"He had to do that with Ivy?" I said.

"Yes, yes. She was always quick to tell him – to tell anyone – he didn't do something right, or didn't say the right thing. Meaning in line with how Ivy saw things or did things."

One of the cleaning crew knocked on my door to get the garbage can. I motioned them in and pushed the can out from under my desk with my feet as I asked Perla for examples.

"So let's say he wanted to get hot dogs at the ballpark she'd go on about all the awful ways factory farming affects the environment. Or if you used a paper towel, you got a lecture on waste. The longer I knew her, the more topics she acted like an expert on. And she didn't care how you might feel, she just kept giving her opinions."

I suspected Perla's comments related to more than how Ivy treated Santiago. "Is that what you meant about needing patience to deal with Ivy?"

Perla glanced to one side, then at the camera again and nodded. "I'm sorry to speak ill of the dead. But Ivy was horrid. Just horrid."

"In what way?"

"When she and Santiago met, I had just divorced. Very painful, very difficult. Ivy, I swear she made a point to say how well matched she and Santiago were. How they did all these classes with the church to prepare, and their marriage would last because of all the effort they made."

"She said this to you?"

"To me, in front of me. Too many times to count. Mama told me at first I was being too sensitive. That Ivy was just excited and talking generally. But when I finally told Santiago how upsetting it was, he got it. Ivy stopped doing it after that. I think he talked to her."

It didn't seem like a good sign if you had to start out apologizing for the person you were with.

I skimmed my notes. "You said your mother thought you were oversensitive at first. Did she change her mind about that?"

"A couple years later. My husband – the second one, we're still together – and I had trouble conceiving. We tried for years. Right before Thanksgiving, the year Alexis was born, I started fertility treatments. And Ivy must have said ten times at dinner and after how it was a good thing she and Santiago had kids since I obviously wasn't going to. And I just lost it. Lost it." Perla rubbed her forehead. "I don't know why it hit me so hard that time. Maybe the hormones affecting me. Because Ivy said that kind of thing all the time. But I had just had it. Had it. I told my mother we were staying away on Christmas if she planned to include Ivy. Broke my heart because I wouldn't see Santiago or the girls, but I could not handle it. Could not."

Perla's rounded cheeks flushed despite that the incident happened fourteen years before. If she hadn't been at home in Ohio the week before Ivy's death I might have subscribed to the theory of revenge being best served cold.

"Did she know you were trying?"

Perla shook her head. "No. I didn't want people asking me all the time how it was going. But it shouldn't matter. Why would you say that to anyone? Ever?"

"I agree with you." At thirty-four, I heard my share of "what are you waiting for" comments about whether and when I had kids, sometimes from people I barely knew.

"Did Santiago say anything about all this?"

"He apologized separately. Told me Ivy's family life had been very hard. Her dad was a big drinker when she was a kid. He got worse and worse until he barely functioned. The mom worked two jobs to keep the lights on, so Ivy cooked and cleaned and raised her brother. She learned to shut out everything else, and he said it made her blind to other people's feelings at times."

It sounded like Ivy hadn't had much of a childhood. I wasn't sure that was a good excuse for trampling other people's feelings, though.

"He never told you that before?"

"A little. But not in depth. Ivy was a very private person when she wasn't telling everyone else what to do. She didn't like people to know about her family."

"And her brother is Hank?" I said. The uncle who was so certain of Santiago's guilt.

"Right, Hank. There's a middle brother, too, but he was estranged from the family. Lives in the U.K. Didn't even come for Ivy's funeral."

Alexis had told me she'd never met that uncle. I planned to check the prosecution's file to see if the police followed up on him.

"And her parents are deceased?"

"Yes, yes. Ivy's dad died in a car crash – hit a tree – when she was fourteen. As I understand it, her mother was a teetotaler until then. But she started drinking. Died of a heart attack five years later. Santiago said it turned Ivy into a control freak. He said she had a softer side she didn't show to many people."

"That had to be very hard for her and her brothers," I said.

"I'm sure. Yet there were times I thought, but you're an adult now. Get some counseling, deal with your issues. Or at least learn to treat other people better."

"Do you know that she didn't? Get counseling, that is?"

"According to Santiago, she didn't. He tried to get her to go to marriage counseling a few times and she wouldn't. She felt no one could change the past, so what was the point?"

"Sounds like something my mother would say." I ran my pen down the page. "Do you think the prosecution would be able to argue a divorce would have made Santiago worse off financially?"

I figured that was a better way to frame the question than to ask outright about Santiago's finances. A lot of people feel uncomfortable talking about money.

"Maybe?" Perla grimaced. "Money always seemed to be tight after they split up. For him, not her. I got the impression

Ivy had a lot set aside before she and Santiago married. And she handled all the money for both of them."

Interesting, given that Sylvania said Ivy didn't like finance. But perhaps Santiago just wasn't a money person.

Fortunately for my law practice, a lot of people aren't, including lawyers. Liking numbers and having an undergraduate accounting major helps me get work. I'm not sure why math and tracking money makes people uncomfortable. Numbers are clear and predictable. They add up or they don't. Unlike people.

"I'm going to start going through her social media tonight," I said. "But is there anything else you can tell me about Ivy that might help me understand her?"

"She had this way of reading people. Then she said or did things in just such a way to either goad them or charm them. The way she charmed my parents at first. But even then, people went along with her, but at some point they were done. I got the impression she always had to look for new friends. To start over. I sometimes thought she must be very lonely."

If Perla had said that to the police, she might have unwittingly helped build the case against her brother. The idea that people went along with Ivy and then suddenly were done with her could make it sound like whether Santiago wanted the divorce or not, at some point Ivy pushed too many buttons and he was "done."

We talked a little longer, but Perla's eyes kept flicking toward the bottom right corner of her screen and I guessed she was looking at the time. For all the negative things she said about Ivy, though, when I asked at the end, Perla couldn't think of anyone who would want to kill her.

"No question she annoyed people. But you don't kill someone because she asks you for a favor once too often. You just start saying no."

Perla gave me a minute to look over my notes while she answered a few emails. I finished by asking who she thought knew Ivy the best other than Santiago.

"Probably that couple that shared the house with them. The woman especially, Ellison. She and Ivy were good friends."

11

Ty had this crazy idea he might want to see me during the week rather than just get texts saying why I needed to cancel dinner. He came over to my place around seven. He was thinking of selling his boat, which used up most of his available cash and time, so he could travel more during summers.

The heavy humidity gave way to rain just as he arrived. The drops splattered the deck in a steady rhythm. We heard them despite the closed sliding doors and blasting air conditioning. Ty sat on my sofa and researched sale prices and travel destinations on his iPad. I had brought home my work laptop. At my small dining table near the glass doors I scrolled through Ivy's social media.

At some point, Ty set a glass on the table near my mouse.

I took out my earbuds and sipped the drink, loving the light lime taste mixed with a strong ginger flavor. "Thanks. What is it?"

"Irish mule. Ginger beer, fresh lime, and a hint of bourbon."

"I might like this as much as a whiskey sour."

"And it's easier to make. You didn't have any eggs. I checked."

"So quiet. I didn't hear you rooting around the fridge."

"You were so absorbed. But it's been over an hour."

"Really?" I glanced through the doors. The rain had turned to drizzle, and a damp, fresh smell filtered in through the closed doors. With the clouded sky, it looked more like midnight than a little after eight.

Ty peered over my shoulder. "All those are Ivy?"

"You wouldn't think so, would you? But yeah."

My screen showed three different paused videos. In the one from the mid-2000s Ivy sat at a small square mahogany conference table in a book-lined office, an old-fashioned set of accounting journals in front of her. She wore glasses with heavy frames. Her hair was similar to mine in color – nearly black with dark brown lowlights. But hers was straight and silky and swung in a bob around her triangular face. In the frozen video frame her brown eyes gazed steadily at the camera, and she held a heavy brass pen angled toward it.

The next video showed Ivy near a kitchen island. No glasses, her hair long and loose, though still straight, around her shoulders. She wore a fitted white T-shirt and faded blue jeans ripped at the knees. Much like Alexis' the day I met her. She bent over a sleek black laptop. Small bowls of herbs lined the counter, with a sprig of prairie flowers at the end. The laptop screen showed the word Ivy's Choice in swirling letters.

The third, and the most recent, featured Ivy in front of a display of hair and skin care items. Her hair now sported two streaks of pure white that contrasted the rest, which was now an inky black. No more lowlights. It was pulled into a bun but with perfectly matching curling tendrils on either side. Her crisp, sleeveless lime green dress and ballet flats gave her a professional yet slightly artsy look. It must be her store. It had shining hardwood floors and interior brick walls.

In theater I had learned the importance of dressing the part in a literal sense. But it took me a few years in the world of business to understand that it applied to real life as well. Once I grasped that, I felt much less uncomfortable in new situations and places, especially ones where I suspected everyone else grew up in homes where my parents' entire annual income would barely feed the family pets. If I could dress the part, though, I could act the part.

Ivy had clearly mastered that early in life.

Ty pointed to the one with the mahogany table. "I'm guessing that's from her time in finance. She give any good advice?"

"Some sound basics, like take advantage of your employer's 401(k) matching. Mixed with sales pitches for products that aren't great investments, like whole life insurance and mutual funds with big fees. But if her sister-in-law is right and Ivy didn't like it, I couldn't tell. She seemed really enthusiastic."

Ivy had also explained things well when it came to the basics, which had probably helped her sell. As to the high fees and the dubious investment value of life insurance she was less than forthright. But that was the nature of that type of adviser and the reason I avoided them. Joe particularly disliked that commissioned salespeople were allowed to market themselves as advisers. He said it made advisers like him, whose responsibility was to their clients and not their commissions, look bad.

"Maybe she was enthusiastic about the commissions." Ty pointed to video featuring a blue jeaned Ivy. "Some kind of home business?"

"Haven't watched that much from this time period yet. But it seems like her start with veganism. She talks about the environment and clean eating and sustainable farming all under the umbrella Ivy's Choice. Looks like the website, when it still existed, included products she recommended. I'm assuming she got some sort of commission on that too."

"All those bowls. Did she make something, too?" Ty said.

"My best guess? Those are for show. At least, she doesn't use them in that video. But there are over a hundred videos, so maybe I haven't gotten to the right ones yet."

Ty sat next to me, setting his iPad on the table. "Tell me you're not going to watch all of them."

"I can't. That's more than a hundred just from that time period, plus thousands of blog posts. Ivy definitely made use of social media and content marketing. I'm trying to figure out the best way to narrow it down."

I watched some early videos aimed at people with significant funds to invest. They linked to a now-defunct webpage for a finance firm in Chicago. Gradually the topics shifted to money management for new moms. Ivy's look softened. Rather than a suit, she wore a blazer over dressy tank tops with jeans, much like my own current office uniform. Her hair shifted to a sleek ponytail. She occasionally covered ways to invest, but more often gave tips on things like saving money by cooking at home, selling a second car and using car-sharing instead, and keeping clothes and toys in good shape to pass on to the next sibling.

The shift to vegan themes struck me as more abrupt, but I might have missed the in between videos. And as someone who'd changed careers more than once myself, I admired Ivy's transition skills.

Ivy's online presence for the most part excluded Santiago and the children. In the handful of videos I watched she talked about her husband and daughters now and then, but never by name.

A few recent videos featured a large dog. I spun the laptop to show Ty.

"Doberman?" I'm not a dog person, but there are some breeds I recognize.

He peered at it. He's a little more of a fan of dogs than I am, having had two of them as a kid. "Not purebred I don't think. But maybe. What happened to it?"

"What do you mean?"

"No one's living there. Who's taking care of the dog?" he said.

"I didn't think about that."

I texted Alexis. She responded a few minutes later and told me the shelter where Ivy had gotten the dog had taken him back, promising to find a home for him.

After bookmarking several of Ivy's various sites and pages, I slid my chair next to Ty's. His iPad showed photos of small boats similar to his. "So, are you selling yours? Did you decide?"

Selfishly, I wished he'd keep it. I liked riding on it on the lake. And loved when he dropped the anchor and we simply floated.

"Ah, probably not now. Too many people sell toward the end of the season. Plus new models are coming out, so manufacturers are giving deals on this year's new ones that haven't sold."

"But you'll have to store it all year."

"Yeah, I know. Gives me the year to be sure I want to sell, though." He moved behind me and rubbed my shoulders, his thumbs digging into the spots on both sides where my muscles always ache after too long at the laptop. "Any chance I can persuade you to do something more fun with the rest of the night than watch videos?"

"Just one email to send. But don't stop. That feels great." I emailed Ellison, Ivy's downstairs neighbor, copying Alexis and Amber and asking if we could meet. Then I shut my eyes and enjoyed the feel of Ty's hands. "So. What else do you have in mind?"

My loft condo has an open floor plan. The king-sized bed is just beyond the living room area under a sleeping loft.

Ty took my hand and pulled me to my feet. "You like to solve puzzles. See if you can figure it out."

I shut the laptop.

12

Ellison Irving answered my email around midnight, but I saw it when I checked first thing in the morning. Her email signature included a link to her website. I scrolled through it while Ty showered.

A licensed certified social worker, Ellison offered therapy to individuals. Her website promised reasonable rates and telehealth visits for anyone who lived too far to visit in person or wanted to save fossil fuels by using the Internet rather than any sort of transportation. She started her career working for DCFS, the Department of Children and Family Services for the State of Illinois.

She was willing to meet that evening at the house in Andersonville. I said yes though it meant shifting plans with Ty once again. He understood how eager I was to see where Ivy had lived.

∽

Some lawyers swear by scheduling and calendar apps. I tried three or four of them but found I spent more time entering things into them, leaving less time to do things. So I keep my calendar online but I cross tasks and projects off a simple list on my smartphone. It's much easier.

At eight a.m. I scrolled through my To Do list. Each item for today, and there were far too many of them, was highlighted. I set the phone face down and took a long drink from a travel mug of Earl Grey tea I'd brought from home. While I had showered and dressed, Ty had made a pot for me using loose leaf tea he got me at a shop near where he lives in the West Loop.

First on my list were discovery requests, which are written requests to send to the other side, in a breach of contract case. But I also had a voicemail from another lawyer, also a former actor, who sometimes referred cases to me. I decided to get some other work done before calling back. I didn't know how long he might want to talk, and I already had a ten a.m. conference call on a case with a brother trying to force his sister out of the family carpet cleaning business. I wished I hadn't taken it. The more I got to know my client the less sympathy I felt for him. I hoped to settle it soon despite that it meant less money coming in each month.

At nearly eleven, the sister's lawyer called back and said she might consider the settlement offer if my client wrote an apology. I doubted that would happen, but I could always hope.

After returning the referring attorney's call, I grabbed a couple power bars in place of lunch and opened the Circuit Court of Cook County's website.

The Domestic Relations division of the Circuit Court oversees Cook County divorce cases. I started by searching under Ivy's name. Anyone can access the lists of divorce filings and see all the documents filed in the court case.

I learned Ivy Jimenez-Brown and R. Santiago Jimenez-Brown had been referred for marriage and family counseling.

It also looked like one of them had been sent to parenting classes, but I couldn't tell which. The case went on for nearly two years with both sides exchanging written documents. The attorneys took quite a few depositions, which is where witnesses answer questions outside of court but under oath. I doubted the transcripts of those depositions were public, but I added checking into that to my To Do list.

The docket listing confirmed that a court date to finally dissolve the marriage had been set for three days after Ivy died. I also saw an order awarding custody to Santiago. That came after a motion that referred to neglect of a child. The motion itself wasn't available online. I wasn't sure why, but I ought to be able to view it at the courthouse unless the court had blocked access to it for some reason.

The last court entry referred to spreading the death of record, a legal term for the filing to tell the court a party died.

I finished about half of what I needed to before I hopped on the Brown Line to Lincoln Square. A week ago, not knowing how busy my work life would get, I had set up a meeting with a new client at her bakery. She'd been sued over an ad where she said her brownies were made with Chicago's chocolatiest chips.

The meeting made the day hectic, but I wasn't sorry I needed to go to it. If I avoided L breakdowns and ate a sandwich at the bakery, I had time for an important stop before I went to visit Ivy's downstairs neighbor, Ellison.

13

I'm not much of one for going to graves. That's my mother's obsession. But every now and then I wanted a quiet moment to think of Marco.

The L, Chicago's subway and elevated train system, is color coded. The Brown Line, a mostly elevated train that runs around downtown and then shoots north, took me within a block of the bakery. After my meeting, I walked five blocks south to a vintage apartment complex practically right on the Brown Line's Damen Avenue stop.

I had no desire to go inside the building, though I suspected the entry code from two years ago still worked. I had found Marco's body inside his apartment and was afraid the smell of the aging carpet and wood might take me right back to that night.

Outside in the courtyard, though, was a place where he and I had sat more than once. I shut my eyes and breathed deep. The courtyard had a rich, late August smell of green leaves, mud, and car exhaust from the street. I'd met Marco in late Fall and he'd died in early Spring the following year. We never spent a summer together, though I had imagined it a thousand times. The blue waves of Lake Michigan, the hot sun on Taste of Chicago and Blues Fest. I pressed my hand flat on the bench, feeling the rough stone under my fingers.

One thing my mother always said resonated with me. Why couldn't we go back in time to see people the way we can return to a place we love? Why could I touch the bench but not Marco?

My phone rang. I sighed and checked the display, expecting a sales call. It was Joe.

"You've got finance questions?" he said. In the background I heard voices, probably people with offices down the hall from him.

"Sort of."

I asked him a bit about the type of work Ivy had done when she lived in Boston. Joe's approach and client base were different from Ivy's, but he knew about many areas of finance. Plus, it was the one thing I'd felt sure he would call me back about.

He answered my questions, then said, "Where are you? I hear traffic. And birds."

Until that moment I hadn't noticed them, but he was right. A row of swallows chirped away above me along a wide tree branch.

"Outside Marco's apartment building. I was nearby for a meeting and decided to stop for a few minutes."

"I won't keep you then."

"No, wait. I need to ask you something. Are you upset with me? I've been waiting until I saw you to ask but you've been a bit –"

"Elusive?"

"I was going to say absent, but sure." I drew my knees up to my chest, wrapped my free arm around them, and rested my chin on my knees. There was silence on the other end. The birds sounded louder in my ears. "Joe?"

"Yeah, I'm here." A door creaked. The voices in the background cut off.

"So?" I said.

"So – I'm sorry. I was kind of a jerk when you started seeing Ty."

"You were. Lauren thought that maybe –" I hesitated. It would be better to talk in person, but who knew when that would happen. As Danielle said, better to clear the air.

"What?" Joe said.

"She thought you might have feelings for me, and that's why you reacted that way to Ty."

"Lauren thought that? No. I mean – you know you mean the world to me, but no. It was more – I wanted to be happy for you. And Ty. But seeing you made me feel worse after Heather and I broke up."

I chewed my lower lip. In high school I did a self-study project on depression. My college therapist said it was an attempt to understand my mother. From it, I knew there were studies showing that most people who see a photo of someone happy feel happier themselves. Except if you're depressed, and then it can make you feel worse.

So what Joe said ought to ring true. Yet it didn't feel quite right.

"Is there something more than the break up?"

"About you? No. But yes, in a way. About Heather. I proposed."

"Seriously?"

So far as I knew, Joe had never proposed to anyone. Or considered doing it. I always thought of him as someone who preferred to go his own way, much as I did a lot of the time.

"Yeah, can you believe it? I ran all over the city trying to find the right ring. Which I decidedly did not find. And she said no."

"Not because of the ring?"

"In a way. She felt it showed I didn't really know her, didn't know what she wanted."

"You couldn't just exchange it?"

Brakes squealed and a truck shuddered to a halt on Damen behind me. I glanced over and saw pedestrians crossing.

"I'm sure it wasn't just the ring. That's only what set it off."

"I'm sorry to hear that."

"Yeah, I've been in a bad place about it. I knew if you and I talked I'd need to tell you about it and I didn't want to. Talk about it, think about it, anything. You know the feeling."

"I have no idea what you're talking about."

We both laughed. Though I'd been ten when we met and he'd been eighteen, I saw early on that, like me, part of what he loved about acting was the chance to feel and show emotions we otherwise kept to ourselves. And sometimes from ourselves, as my therapist in college had also pointed out. I thought I had gotten better at it over the last decade. It never occurred to me to wonder if Joe had or not. We didn't talk a lot about relationships.

According to the CTA Trip Planner webpage, it should take me only fifteen minutes to get to Ivy's house from here. But bus schedules in Chicago are aspirational at best, so I wasn't counting on that. I checked the time on my phone, stood, and started walking toward the bus stop.

I still felt unsettled about Joe. "So can we hang out sometime soon?"

"Yeah, definitely. I'll buy you a drink at that wine bar where we met that time," he said.

"You really must not be going out much. It closed. In July." I fished my CTA card out of my purse as I approached the stop.

"Huh. Really."

I reached the bus stop and peered down the street. To my

surprise, the Number 50 Ashland/Clark bus was only half a block away. "Palmer House lobby?"

"Yep, text me some dates when five is good."

I rarely finish work before five, but Joe's schedule is more like the one the traders keep. Which means he leaves his office early.

"Okay."

"You can tell me more about this murder," Joe said. "Be careful, though, okay?"

I promised I would as I boarded the bus. And wondered if he'd answer when I sent him some dates.

14

The house where Ivy once lived stood on a tree-lined street in Andersonville. The neighborhood includes single-family homes on tree-lined streets, long blocks with a mix of apartment buildings and businesses, and a main street lined with restaurants, furniture stores, antique stores, and one of Chicago's oldest independent bookstores.

Ellison Irving met me on her front porch. She wore brown sandals with thick soles, a green T-shirt dress that reached to mid-thigh and stretched a bit tight at her rounded middle, and no makeup or jewelry. Her pale skin looked a bit reddish at the tip of her chin but otherwise her complexion was smooth and clear. She led me through the first floor, a vintage apartment with worn hardwood floors, original moldings, and a tiny bathroom, to an enclosed back porch. Its door led to five outdoor steps down to the back yard. There, a chicken sat atop a coop that ran along the back fence. Another hen pecked away in the grass and a third fluttered its wings on the bottom step.

"Something to drink?" Ellison said. "Whiskey? Coffee? Beer?"

I said water was fine, and she disappeared into the kitchen.

The chickens started squawking, spooked by something I couldn't see. All three skittered into the coop. A moment later a black cat emerged from under the bushes.

"There are snakes out there, too," Ellison said from behind me.

"Sorry?" I turned.

She set a turquoise-colored glass pitcher on the bamboo coffee table and filled two glasses of water. "Snakes. Freaked me out when I moved in. Not poisonous but I was definitely not used to them. The occasional rat, sure. Keeping my purse strapped over my body while sitting in a Starbucks – second nature. But a garden snake? Not something I'm equipped for."

I sat across from her and sipped the water. It tasted cool and had a faint cucumber flavor from the slices floating in the pitcher.

"I didn't know you could keep chickens in Chicago," I said.

"Oh, yeah. The eggs are fantastic. You just can't sell them. The eggs, not the chickens. So I trade my neighbor on that side –" she waved east "– eggs for her green beans and a neighbor across the street gives me tomatoes. Which is awesome because I hate gardening, but I love fresh produce."

"And chickens?"

"My ex-husband's idea. Now we're split up and I'm left to take care of them. But at least I get the eggs." She folded her hands together and rested them on her knee. "So what's the deal with this lawsuit Alexis told me about? The police arrested Santiago, so, what, you're suing him? Why?"

"We're not suing anyone right now."

"Because he has to support those girls anyway, and I

doubt he has much in the way of assets. I'm assuming insurance wouldn't cover him for a deliberate killing."

"It wouldn't. It's bad public policy for insurers to cover criminal acts. But there's no plan to sue Santiago. Alexis is convinced he didn't kill Ivy. That someone else did."

"Huh." She rocked forward and back in her wicker chair. "I've got to say, I can't really see it myself. Santiago as the culprit, I mean. I was shocked when he was arrested. But a marriage, you never know what's really going on inside it, and it usually is the husband isn't it, when a woman's dead? Or the boyfriend."

"Are you speaking based on your professional experience?"

Ellison tucked her dark hair behind her ear. "Well, I don't do family counseling. Just individual. But sure, it's something I learned in school and I saw more than once when I was at DCFS. But also, I can't think of anyone who'd kill Ivy."

"But you think Santiago could?"

She spread her hands wide. "I really don't. I just don't know what else to think."

"How did it happen that you bought this house together?"

"About a year after I met Ivy, I mentioned how my husband at the time and I wished we could afford a house with a yard. In a neighborhood that felt residential, but we wanted to be in the city. The price anywhere was way more than we could afford. Ivy said she and Santiago felt the same. They had Amber already and she was pregnant with Alexis and hoping to quit her job and stay home with the girls."

"It's a big commitment to get on a mortgage with someone," I said.

As much as I knew about business deals that went wrong and ended in court, I'd never do it. Plus, I saw my sister struggling to deal with the fallout after her husband nearly bankrupted them without her knowledge. As hard as I worked all my life, if I ever got married I'd find it tricky to tie my credit or assets to anyone else. And to another couple's – I didn't think so.

"It is, but it had pluses for everyone. My husband and I, we chose not to have kids, but not because we don't like them. For personal and environmental reasons. This way we got to live with people who had kids. It expanded our family. We had holidays together, and the girls spent a lot of time at our apartment. Santiago was an over-the-road trucker at the time, so he was gone a lot. It gave Ivy other adults to talk to when he was gone, too, and childcare. I know it probably sounds strange."

"Not to me," I said. "I grew up in an apartment across the hall from my Gram's. I more or less lived in both places until I was sixteen, then moved in with her. She's the one who raised me."

"A lot of people think it's weird if you're not related by blood, though."

"I don't think it's weird. But I'm guessing complicated legally."

The lawyer and accountant part of my brain could imagine far too many ways that type of arrangement could go wrong.

"It required a lot of trust on all sides during the purchase process. Whose credit got the mortgage, who came up with the cash for the down payment. Balancing it all out."

"Who did?" I said. "Come up with the down payment. Have the credit."

Ellison's posture stiffened. "Does that matter?"

"Maybe not," I said. "But whatever you're comfortable telling me might help. Money can always be a motive for a crime."

If we filed a lawsuit, I could subpoena those types of records. But you need a defendant you truly believe is responsible for the death to file a suit. And so far the only one on deck was Santiago.

Ellison tilted her head to one side. "Okay. Here's what I can tell you. My ex and I had good credit, but not a ton of cash. Ivy and Santiago chipped in more than their share for the down payment, and she had good credit. Santiago didn't."

"Debt problems?" I said.

Ellison shook her head and sipped her water. "The opposite. He preferred paying cash for things, so he didn't build a credit history. He was so mad. Felt like the mortgage companies were holding it against him that he'd been so responsible. So Ivy was the one on the mortgage, and the deed, because she's the one who had the credit to be able to borrow the bulk of their share. Though he put in more cash toward the down payment."

"It seems a little unfair to not include him on the deed."

"We created a contract to balance it out over time. It got complicated with the divorces. With my divorce, legally the house got split apart into two separate condos. My ex bought me out on ours, and Ivy and Santiago got their two-flat. I think Santiago still wasn't on the deed, but I'm not sure. I was preoccupied with my own issues."

"Do you know what the plan was for splitting up the house with their divorce?"

"No idea. Ivy and I weren't speaking by then."

If Santiago lost the house it might give him a motive, at least in the eyes of the police, for killing Ivy. Her will not only named him as executor but left everything to him. Surprising given their imminent divorce, but a family law attorney I knew once told me many of his clients put off changing their wills for far too long. He said it was a form of denial. About the divorce, or the idea of death, or both.

If convicted of Ivy's murder, though, Illinois law barred

LISA M. LILLY

Santiago from inheriting. In that case, his share went to the girls.

"Is that why you didn't have a key? I heard that the police had to break in."

Ellison glanced out at the yard. The chickens, apparently feeling confident the cat had found other creatures to plague, had emerged again from their coop. "Yep. Ivy was mad at me. So mad she changed the locks."

"Why was she mad?"

Ellison sighed. "It has to do with Santiago getting custody of Alexis."

"Alexis told me she chose to live with her dad. Because she didn't like vegan eating. And she worried her dad would be lonely, while Ivy had you and your husband here."

Alexis had confided that in me via text as I rode the L to Ellison's.

"Yeah, that's not even remotely what happened," Ellison said. "There was a hearing, and then a court order. Santiago didn't want Alexis to think badly of her mom, so he somehow convinced Alexis to choose to live with him, when really she would have been required to."

"Because Ivy was a vegan?"

While wanting cheeseburgers sounded like an unlikely reason to award custody, the vegan eating might go against a judge's views on what a teenager needed in her diet.

"It wasn't that. Ivy wasn't taking care of Alexis. Worse, she was harming her. And I testified to that in court. Ivy never forgave me."

15

My glass, wet with condensation, almost slipped from my hand. I maneuvered it onto the table. "She abused Alexis?"

"Not the way you probably mean." Ellison crossed her arms over her chest. "You noticed Alexis is skinny?"

"Thin."

"Thin, skinny. My point is, she weighs twenty-five pounds more now than she did when the judge ordered that she go live with Santiago."

"Twenty-five pounds?"

I shut my eyes for a moment and pictured Alexis. She was an inch or so shorter than me, so somewhere around 5'5". I'd been thin as a teenager, too, especially the year that I grew to my final height, but I had weighed more than a hundred pounds. Alexis couldn't be more than one ten now.

"Yep. She was eighty pounds when she moved to Santiago's. And it wasn't just the weight that worried me. Alexis was throwing up all the time. Santiago thought she might be bulimic. Happily – no, none of it's happy – but it wasn't something Alexis was doing on purpose. The vomiting stopped once she lived with Santiago."

I wondered if Alexis' comment about her mom having a weak stomach was related to this information.

"You think Ivy was – what? Poisoning her own daughter?"

Nothing either daughter said suggested such a dark relationship. But if Ivy had been poisoning Alexis, she might also have accidentally poisoned herself. Though surely Ellison had told all of this to the police, too.

"No, no. Not the way Ivy was poisoned. But she was, in a way. It started when she got into veganism."

"A vegan diet made Alexis vomit?" I said.

My personal experience was limited, as I'd never tried any particular eating plan. My Gram was a fan of everything in moderation, and I mostly agreed. A fair number of my friends from my acting days, though, ate vegan or vegetarian. They had various challenges with it, like finding restaurants with better options than a plate of broccoli and pasta. A few lost weight. One gained weight. But I hadn't heard of any of them getting sick.

"No, no. A plant-based diet on its own won't make you sick. But Ivy, like a lot of crunchy people—"

"Crunchy?"

Ellison shrugged and gave a half-laugh. "Sorry. Picked it up from my dad. It's a little outdated. What his generation called people who touted all-natural foods and ate a lot of granola. Not that Ivy ate granola – unless she made it herself so it had no honey."

"So Ivy wasn't just vegan, everything had to be natural?"

"And organic, whatever that means. There's no real standard for organic, did you know that? But if it was labeled organic or natural Ivy was all for it, no questions asked."

"Very black and white about it."

"Yep. Natural: good. Artificial: bad. Never mind that synthetic insulin saves lives, and all kinds of natural things can kill you."

A wicker stem poked into the back of my thigh, and I shifted in the chair. "But I'm assuming Ivy wasn't feeding Alexis hemlock or poisoned mushrooms."

"No, but she had all these – I'll use the word again – crunchy beliefs that defy reality. Like if produce was labeled organic you didn't need to wash it."

"Not true?" I said. My Gram had taught me to wash all produce wherever it came from, so I'd never really thought about it.

"It might not have pesticide," Ellison said. "But it still can have e coli, salmonella, listeria. Any of the bacteria that make people ill. Which is why you shouldn't eat the unwashed sample fruits they try to give you at the Farmers' Markets."

There's a market in my neighborhood every Saturday in spring and summer. I made a mental note to stop sampling the strawberries.

"But isn't meat more of an issue? Like raw chicken?" I said.

"As many people get food poisoning from fruits and vegetables as meat. But I could never convince Ivy of that. Sorry." Ellison waved her hand. "All the things I saw at DCFS and later in the school system. People not taking care of their kids, especially when they have the means to do it, drives me crazy."

"And you put Ivy in that category?"

It didn't seem strong enough as a motive for murder, but it did make me wonder why Ellison wasn't on the suspect list. She claimed Ivy changed the locks, but Ellison did live in the same building. Who was to say she hadn't managed to get her hands on a new key or found another way in.

"In the last few years? Yes. She and Alexis ate everything unwashed –cucumbers, apples, lettuce. Even after that recall of romaine lettuce. And I can't tell you how many times I saw her take unwashed berries straight from a container and put them on Alexis' whole grain cereal."

"I've eaten unwashed strawberries and didn't get sick."

"Ever had a twenty-four-hour stomach flu? That's not flu. It's bacteria you ingested. Also, sure, you're not going to get sick every time. Our digestive systems are pretty good at protecting us. But if you eat contaminated food over and over and over your odds are not good."

"Alexis said her mom had a weak stomach."

"Actually, her stomach was probably pretty strong with all the bacteria she ate. But she did have a lot of digestive issues, and she never believed me that she could avoid them if she took a little care with her food. Here's another example. She left cooked rice sitting on the stove for days and ate it each day. That's a breeding ground for spores that grow into bacteria."

"You pointed that out?"

"She shrugged and said it was whole grain rice. As if that gave it some sort of magic ability to withstand bacteria."

"I'm surprised the judge didn't just order Ivy to take some sort of food safety class."

"He did. Ivy refused to go. Said those classes were all run by Big Agra or something. But it went beyond food safety. Ivy started making Alexis this breakfast shake each day. She put hydrangea powder in it, more than two grams. It's supposed to help with hay fever, but if you take it in that dose or for more than a few days, it can cause dizziness, nausea. Vomiting."

"And the FDA allows it to be sold?"

"Oh, sure. It's a supplement, not a drug. The FDA doesn't regulate supplements other than to say they can't make specific health claims. If you want to sell someone something with no oversight, call it a supplement. The evidence is clear, but Ivy refused to stop taking it herself or giving it to Alexis. That's what tipped the judge over."

I poured myself another glass of water. It seemed to me that Ivy must have grasped that she'd lose her daughter with that attitude. "Is there any chance Ivy didn't want custody?"

"On some level? Maybe. But as soon as I told her I planned to testify she stopped talking to me. And she stuck with it. So by the time the judge entered the custody order, I had no idea where her head was at."

"What about Amber? When she was home from school visiting, did she have similar problems?"

"None. Amber's not big on listening to her mom. Wasn't big on it. After Ivy went all vegan, organic, yada yada, Amber ate only packaged items at home or came downstairs to eat with me."

That also had probably made Ivy resent Ellison. Though my mom rarely spent time with me when I was a kid beyond giving me singing lessons, she often made snippy comments about me hanging around Gram's apartment or at the lighting store where Gram worked.

Ellison's concern for Alexis and Amber struck me as genuine. Still, I couldn't ignore that she seemed as likely as Santiago to have access to Ivy's home. Also, someone who knew so much about what made people sick might know how to poison them.

And, given their conflicts, Ellison might see poisoning Ivy as a sort of poetic justice.

16

I asked if Ivy seemed concerned when Ellison pointed out the connection between hydrangea and Alexis vomiting.

"She didn't believe it."

"But why did she think Alexis was getting sick? And that her weight was low?"

"She said like mother, like daughter. That Alexis inherited her so-called weak stomach. And that their systems hadn't adjusted to a total plant-based diet yet."

Through the side window I saw a heavyset woman with a cane make her way onto the side of her wrapround porch and perch in a rocker. The chickens hopped toward her, and she tossed something to them, setting off a feeding frenzy.

It was nearly seven-thirty, and I wanted to catch the bus home before it got too much later. I feel safer riding buses in the evening than the L because I can sit near the driver. But for the most part I try not to be on public transportation after eight-thirty or nine at night.

I asked Ellison how she and Ivy had met. She told me at an animal rights rally over a decade before. Ellison, though, wasn't vegetarian or vegan.

"For me, it's more about what animals' lives are like, how they're treated when they're raised, than about not eating them," Ellison said. "Like our chickens. They roam the yard, we make sure the coop is clean and warm enough in winter. In these agribusiness places the chickens are so close to one another they can't move. There are dead chickens everywhere that haven't been taken away yet, and they basically live in their own droppings. That's why they have to feed them all those antibiotics."

That might put me off chicken parmesan for a while.

Ellison jiggled her knee. "I feel the same about experimenting on them."

"You're in favor of animal rights but okay with experimenting on them?"

We were getting far afield from Ivy but I'm always curious about why people believe what they do. Both my professions – law and acting – involve stepping into other people's shoes, really trying to understand them. It makes it hard for me to draw bright lines on most issues. Life is more complex than that.

"Again, it's about how you treat them. And why the experiments are done. I'm not okay with rabbits going blind so some cosmetic company can make a longer lasting mascara. But if lab rat research could eliminate, say, Lou Gehrig's disease, I'm okay with that."

It was a pretty specific reference. "Did someone you know have it?"

"My mom. It's a terrible way to die. You basically suffocate to death."

"I'm so sorry."

I had wondered if part of her position was that bunnies were cute and rats creepy, but given her mom, that didn't sound like the reason.

"It gave me let's say a certain lack of patience with Ivy's

pseudoscience. She kept trying to convince me that turning vegan would have stopped my mom's disease which is just – there's no basis for that. It's ridiculous."

"It sounds like things weren't great between the two of you even before you clashed over Alexis?"

Ellison drank more water and set her glass on the side table. "That's accurate. From when she really dug into the vegan thing on it got tough. She also harangued me about how no one but her cared about the environment because people kept eating meat and dairy. Which she knew I did, obviously." She gestured toward the chicken coop.

"A passive-aggressive way to goad you into change?"

"Oh, she was aggressive-aggressive too. Told me all the time I should change my eating. I finally pointed out that overpopulation and automobile exhaust are huge contributors to climate change, and that she conveniently didn't focus on those. She and Santiago had two kids and two Ford Explorers, at least they did when the kids were small."

"I thought Santiago took a car with him? Or SUV I guess?"

"He did. While he lived here, though, he drove one SUV and Ivy drove the other. They sold hers a few years before the separation."

She couldn't show me Ivy's part of the house without a key. But she did walk me up two flights of outdoor back steps that sagged under our weight. We stopped on the third-floor landing. Through the door's small, square window I saw an enclosed porch with the same footprint as Ellison's. But Ivy's had a wide pass through window to her kitchen.

A high-top square butcher block table dominated the space. The cabinets beyond it were painted light gray.

"You couldn't see Ivy when you came up here yourself? The night you called the police?"

"No. They found her farther back in the apartment. In the

hall between her bedroom and the living room, I think. Maybe she was heading for the bathroom."

I followed her down the stairs. "Did you see Santiago here the day before?"

"No. I was out running errands most of the day."

"Before you and Ivy had a falling out, did you ever walk the dog for her?"

"Not a chance. That dog is mean." We paused on the second-floor landing. It, too, had a heavy wooden door, and the window in it showed an unfinished porch filled with boxes. No pass through window, so no way to see other parts of the apartment.

"Mean how?" I said.

"Well, the first day she brought him home he killed one of our chickens. From then on, I insisted she keep Ralph on a chain, a short one, if he was out in the yard."

"What happens to Ivy's apartments now?" I said.

"Not sure. I guess the estate, whenever it's sorted out, could rent them to people separately. Or sell both. They're classified as separate units legally."

"So now you'll be living below strangers," I said.

"Yep. I don't have the money, or enough credit, to buy them myself or I might as an investment."

Ellison didn't seem to benefit from Ivy's death in any obvious way. But I'd learned in previous investigations, including into Marco's death, that things are always more complicated than they appear on first look.

Before I left, I asked Ellison who might be able to tell me the most about Ivy. She gave me a name that was already on my list, but pretty far down. She'd been the maid of honor at Ivy's wedding.

What Ellison told me, though, put her on the top of the list. Mei Leonhard had been the last person to see Ivy alive.

17

The drive to Miller Beach, where Mei Leonhard lived, took less time than I expected. But it was Sunday, and traffic was light. After driving less than forty-five minutes, I exited the expressway. Not far from the Indiana Dunes, I passed a shuttered grade school. All around it weeds grew through cracks in the asphalt. A rusty gray metal swing set, minus the swings, stood as the last remembrance of playgrounds past.

I felt conscious of the shininess of Lauren's Volvo, which I'd borrowed for the drive. It was five years old, but probably worth more than most of the cars and SUVs parked in driveways and along the roadsides. There were no sidewalks here, just lawns extending to the street.

Until Mei sent me her address, I had never heard of Miller Beach. It's a neighborhood of Gary, Indiana, on the edge of the dunes. Once a separate town, it has a thriving arts community and a more solid tax base than the rest of Gary. That became clear when the neighborhood shifted as I turned onto a residential street near the Miller railroad stop. As I got deeper into the area, crumbling brick buildings gave way to brightly-painted wooden frame houses, split-level ranch homes, and, eventually, large brick and multi-level houses that looked newly refurbished. Leafy old trees lined the streets.

Some of the homes fronted Lake Michigan, with views that in Chicago would put them in the million-dollar-plus price range. Here, I guessed they cost about half that. According to its website, a lot of Chicagoans made Miller Beach a second home. Somewhere to get away from the rush of the city, or to retire when they finished working.

I pulled into the driveway of what my map app told me was Mei Leonhard's home. While it wasn't on the lake it was close enough that I felt its dampness in the air as I stepped out of the car and onto the gravel drive. I wore a light gray blazer over jeans and a tank top. My aim was to look lawyer-like but not too formal. For that reason and the heat, I had pulled my long, wavy hair into a loose ponytail.

In her email Mei had said to come to the side door. It was painted glossy white and had a leaded glass window shaped like a half moon in the top. But no one answered.

I checked my phone. Five minutes early. A tiny sharp stone from the gravel drive got into my right sandal as I walked around the back of the house. I paused and wriggled my foot to shake it out.

The air smelled of cut grass, floral scents, and mud. A slight, short woman with skin a shade darker than mine knelt in the grass pulling weeds from a bed of multicolored flowers. I felt like I ought to be able to identify them. But I grew up in an apartment. A couple of my friends in grade school lived in houses with yards, but no one's parents had a great love of gardening.

"Mei?" I said.

She wore long loose-fitting khaki shorts, canvas gloves, and an oversized white T-shirt. She twisted her head in my direction but didn't stand or stop yanking at the weeds. "Quille?"

I stood on the edge of the driveway a few feet from her. "Yes. Thanks so much for being willing to talk with me."

The sun beat down, and sweat beaded on my neck under my hair. It's one of the many downsides of keeping it long. But short, it balloons all around my face. Not a good look.

"I don't know how it will help. Already talked to the police." She yanked on a particularly stubborn weed.

"They're not sharing any information with me, so I appreciate your time."

"Fire away."

"You saw Ivy the night before she died. Did she seem upset about anything?" I said.

"No more than usual for Ivy. Less, really."

I shifted my leather shoulder bag to my left side and pulled out a pocket-sized yellow legal pad and pen. Awkward as it felt to write while standing in the driveway, I made three quick notes in a column on the first page. "Did she mention her divorce? It was supposed to be final on Tuesday."

Mei kept pulling weeds. "Oh, yes. She said she felt relieved about that."

Relieved. The same word Perla had used for Santiago's feelings. Maybe the divorce had been amicable once the custody dispute ended.

"You said no more than usual. Was Ivy usually upset about things?"

"I shouldn't have said that. Before last month I hadn't seen her in a decade or more." Mei wiped her forehead without taking her gloves off. It left a smear of dirt across her skin. "I suggested Skyping a couple times but she never had time."

Another note for the left column. "So did you have a falling out, or you just lost touch?"

"No."

I struggled out of my blazer, which was way too hot for an August afternoon, feeling irritated with myself. One of the first things I learned about questioning witnesses was to not ask a compound question: one that included two parts so you didn't know which part the witness answered.

"No, you didn't have a falling out?" I said.

A weed Mei had been fighting with gave way. The momentum set her back on her heels. "We did and we didn't."

A small stone bench with an ornate back sat under a tree behind Mei. I walked over and sat. I would have rather stayed where I could see her face, but it was easier to take notes while sitting. Plus I might think better if I felt more comfortable.

"Can you tell me more about that?"

Mei dropped a handful of what looked to be as many healthy stalks as weeds into a pile. "Long story."

"I'd like to hear it. I'm trying to get a better sense of Ivy's life right now."

I wanted to delve further into the last time she'd seen Ivy, too. But given that Mei was so closed off, getting her talking about Ivy as a person seemed like a better approach.

"Hard for me to say much about that," Mei sighed and stood. "My knees are shot. And I forgot to wear a hat."

I scribbled an asterisk next to the words Falling Out in my notes and followed her into the house.

The kitchen had a linoleum floor that was cracked and discolored in spots. But the living and dining area sported glossy dark hardwood.

She took a clear glass pitcher from an aging refrigerator. "Iced tea?"

The liquid inside had a reddish tinge. "Flavored?" I said.

"With cherries from my tree. Plus I usually add some frozen ones to keep it chilled when it's hot like this."

"Thank you. That sounds fantastic."

She took a baggie of frozen cherries from the freezer and dropped a handful in each glass.

We sat on wicker chairs in her screened-in three-season porch. Outside, the cherry tree's heavy branches hung over a shallow pond Mei told me was filled with koi.

"You were going to tell me about why you hadn't seen Ivy in so long," I said, though my impression was she was avoiding telling me.

Mei uncrossed and recrossed her legs. Most people look heavier in baggy clothes, but her legs were so slim they looked almost sticklike. "It was my fault, I guess. Or my choice. Hard to say. I was thinking about that last night. We used to be so close."

"Alexis told me you were her mom's maid of honor."

"I was. It's part of why I was so shocked when Ivy told me about this whole vegan thing. It was a big deal to her to have filet mignon at the reception."

"So not a vegan wedding."

"Oh no. If you didn't want red meat, you could have fish. Shrimp cocktail appetizers, oysters, filet mignon, multiple sides. I guess there were vegetables there. Somewhere. A giant dessert table. A dozen kinds of cheese, custom-made ice cream bars nestled in this ice sculpture, cake, cupcakes with whipped frosting."

"All things she later stopped eating."

"Right."

"She became vegan a few years ago, right? Any idea why?"

"I feel like I should know that. I'm sure she had it all over social media, but that's just not something I do much of. Too much else to do."

"I understand that," I said.

Now and then I posted on my law firm pages about recent wins or tax law developments, but that was it. As an actor, my mother and my Gram had been insistent about my crafting my image and doing publicity. It was one of the few things they agreed on. But it made me feel like a product rather than a person, and that had been before social media. I had little interest in doing any more of that than I had to as an adult.

"You said the wedding was a challenge. What did you mean?"

Mei shook her head and glanced out at her garden again. Sun shone across it, reflecting off spinning artificial sunflowers along the border between her yard and the next one.

Usually silence makes people talk. They want to fill it. But not Mei.

I tasted my tea. The cherries made it tart against the black tea flavor. I liked the combination.

Finally, I said, "It can be really hard when you had differences with someone who died."

"Differences. I suppose that's a way to put it. The wedding was...how old are you?"

"Thirty-four," I said.

Mei glanced at my left hand. I used to wear a ring Marco gave me there, but I switched it to my right about a year after he died. Around when I started seeing Ty.

"And single?" she said.

"Yes," I said.

"Then maybe you'll understand. Though it's different now. I hope. I was about thirty-two and single, and Ivy a couple years older, when we met at a financial services conference in Boston. And discovered we lived in the same neighborhood. Four blocks apart."

Mei's bio had told me she was a financial adviser and an adjunct professor at the University of Chicago. She taught a series of business and finance courses. She was new at the last part, having only moved to this area in January. Before starting her own advising firm she worked in the private client group for one of the largest banks in the country.

"And you were both single," I said.

"Right. A lot of people married by their late twenties then. We both got a lot of questions about when we were going to find someone, were we too picky. Didn't we want children. We kind of bonded over that and being young women in finance. At least young looking. We both got mistaken for being just out of college a lot."

"Sounds like you had a lot in common," I said.

"We did. Plus we worked too many hours, ate at our offices most nights unless we went to some sort of networking event. So once a week we tried to get together and make dinner. Have one home-cooked meal we ate at a relaxed pace, even if it was at nine at night.

"And we talked on the phone. Which was a thing then. No texting yet. But then she met Santiago."

18

I unlocked my phone and opened the spreadsheet where I'd started a timeline of what I'd learned so far. "And all of this was around 2000, right?"

"Yes. In March or April. And I understood. You meet someone you truly like, you start seeing each other, of course you have less time to spend with other people. But some of my friendships at that point had lasted longer than any romantic relationship I'd had. Which is still true. My marriage lasted six years. I've got friends from my first year of college."

"I've known my friend Joe since I was ten."

I mentioned him because it's always good to find an area of agreement with someone you're hoping will open up to you. Plus he was on my mind, as we hadn't been able to settle on an evening to meet. It had as much to do with my schedule as his, but it nagged at me.

Outside, a bird trilled.

"Even when I got married, I always made time for my friends. Maybe not quite as much, but I did."

"Ivy wasn't like that?" I said.

"She was the opposite of that. Weekends were 'couples time.' All right. A lot of people feel that way. But she also couldn't get together weekday evenings if Santiago was around."

"But he was gone a lot, wasn't he? Because he drove over-the-road?"

"Not when they first started seeing each other. That started right before the move to Chicago. Plus I wasn't seeing anyone, so I didn't get to meet him until I invited a coworker who was a man into coming with me to dinner. Ivy wanted it to feel like a double date."

It was lucky my friends didn't feel that way. Before Marco, it had been years since I'd dated anyone seriously. It reminded me of things my Gram had told me about when her friends had gotten married.

"1950s mentality."

"Yes. I was so surprised. I knew Ivy wanted to meet someone, but she'd dated people before and didn't disappear. It felt like all the other things in her life, including me, were more or less placeholders until she found someone she thought was Mr. Right."

"Was this coming from Santiago? He was controlling?"

If so, that didn't bode well for Alexis's hopes that I'd exonerate her dad. Just because someone was controlling in a relationship didn't make him a murderer. But it hardly ruled him out.

"I wondered about that at first. But once they moved in together, she got out more. Because he told her he didn't need her 'underfoot' all the time. Which angered her. She said she made all this effort to nurture the relationship and now he wanted her around less."

Mei sipped her tea. She didn't seem inclined to say anything more.

"When you met Santiago, what did you think of him?"

"Very laid back. In a group, he faded into the background. Ivy did the talking for them both."

I wondered if that led to resentment. Add to it that Ivy always handled the money and her general controlling nature and Santiago had a lot to resent. At least, if I were the prosecutor, that would be the story I'd tell.

"Was Ivy jealous or possessive?" I said. "Not wanting you to meet him unless you were attached?"

"I don't think that was it. When I asked, she said she thought it would be awkward. That I'd be a third wheel. Maybe she wasn't that odd, maybe I was the strange one. I hear young people now go out in groups all the time, but that didn't happen much when I was younger."

I wasn't quite sure what to think. None of my life experience is typical, so I never quite know where I fit with others my age. Also, if Ivy felt that way about the importance of couples, I wondered if some small part of her jettisoning Ellison related to Ellison no longer being married. And if she worried that now whatever couples friends she had would drop her after her divorce.

"Did you like Santiago?" I said.

"I found him hard to get to know. Ivy would rave about a movie they'd seen, and he'd just nod. I never knew if he liked it too or not. She said he talked a lot with her. That he was just someone who was better one-on-one. And he didn't like being the center of attention."

"So maybe he liked someone like Ivy who carried the ball for the two of them in a group," I said. "And it sounds like it worked for her."

"Oh, yes." Mei sighed. "I feel bad saying this because she's gone. But I did say it to her at the time, too. I think she liked having the upper hand. You see what I'm saying?"

I wasn't sure I did. "Socially?"

"Socially. Financially. Intellectually. My impression – I

only met Santiago a couple times – was that he's smart, but not book smart. No college. Didn't like high school. Liked to read but he didn't want to engage in deep conversations about books. Didn't like numbers."

"And Ivy – was she smart?"

In my view, intelligence is a complex mix of skills and factors, but Mei had used the word smart, so I was curious how she evaluated Ivy.

"She was –" Mei looked up, studying the ceiling, which was made of long boards painted white. "– savvy. Good at selling herself." Another pause. "She convinced people she was much smarter than them."

"Convinced? It sounds like you think she wasn't."

"No, no." Mei's shoulders drew together and her elbows pressed against her sides. "I – Ivy likely was smarter than most people."

"But?"

"I feel bad saying these things. I'm sure I'll sound awful, as if I walk around analyzing my friends' intellectual capacity."

"Not at all. I'm asking. I need a real sense of Ivy. If I wanted platitudes and accolades, I'd be satisfied reading her eulogy."

"All right. Ivy was head and shoulders beyond me when it came to networking. No question. But on substance – Ivy knew just enough to make the sales pitch. Beyond that – let's just say I wouldn't take her investment advice."

"Was that a problem in your friendship?"

"If we had stayed friends, it might have been. As I grew more professionally myself, grasped more, I saw her limits. And it got irritating because she acted like she was brilliant. Did a lot of bragging, disguised as an offer to help."

"How so?"

"Oh, she might call to point out a market trend I hadn't

mentioned. And she'd give this little apology, saying how she just had a knack for this sort of thing and not everyone does, and she was happy to help me out – all the time clearly enjoying the idea that she one-upped me. Except she hadn't. I just hadn't commented on the trend because it was obvious."

"Common sense?"

"If you knew the area, yes. Sometimes I worried for her that she'd do that with someone who didn't know her, someone she truly wanted to make an impression on. And that person would walk away amazed Ivy thought she'd uttered some deep insight. But I never said anything." Mei paused and studied the cherries sinking to the bottom of her glass. "Maybe it happened. Because after a while I noticed that, professionally, Ivy started spending most of her networking time with finance people who were, let's say, a little less sharp than average."

"So she could stand out? Feel smarter."

"That was my impression. I don't know if she did it consciously or not."

"So you think Ivy did something similar when she dated? Sought out men she felt she was smarter than?"

Mei grimaced. "Not smarter exactly. Less likely to challenge what she knew or thought she knew."

I checked my notes. She hadn't answered my original question. "And the wedding. You said it was a challenge?"

"The wedding." Mei held her glass in both hands and studied the reddish liquid inside it. "I had no idea what I was getting into when I said yes to being maid of honor."

"Getting into how?"

"Money-wise. And time-wise. Ivy and I probably made about the same amount for most of the years we knew each other. But she still worked for a firm with benefits and a retirement plan and all that. And I'd just gone out on my own. I never knew what I'd earn from month to month."

I nodded. "A roller coaster."

I budgeted pretty well, but I was familiar with the ups and downs of working for yourself.

"Exactly. I had no idea what all Ivy expected until the wedding machine started rolling. Instead of a bachelorette party she wanted, or I should say instructed us to organize, a full private spa day and a tour of Chicago nightclubs. Then dinner with a private chef in lieu of a shower. All with lots of alcohol. Which it sounds naïve, but I had no idea how much drinking costs. I'm not much of a drinker. Never was."

"Ivy was?"

"At the time, definitely," Mei said.

"Despite her parents' history?"

"She didn't see it as the same. She drank for fun, not to escape or because she couldn't cope with life, which is how she saw her parents. And I think that's right more or less. But she was always setting rules. She could only drink on weekends, other than a glass of wine at dinner. Or she'd switch to no more than three drinks on one night, unless it was a special occasion. Or she'd go a month without alcohol, then drink whatever she wanted for two months. It seemed like a lot of effort and thought about alcohol."

Which sounded a lot like her later approach to food.

"Ivy liked rules," I said.

Mei nodded.

"So for the wedding, who paid for all these events Ivy wanted?" I said.

"Her other bridesmaids and me. Thank God they chipped in. But I spent nearly three thousand dollars. A lot back then."

"A lot now," I said. Her tale made me suspect that if my friend Lauren, who came from money, ever got married I might need a small business loan. "Did you tell her you couldn't afford it?"

Mei twisted the hem of her overlong T-shirt. "The thing was, I could. It made me nervous, but I could. Though I never would have done so much discretionary spending my first year on my own otherwise."

I understood. Two and a half years ago, when I started my own law practice, I waited seven weeks before I so much as bought a chai latte. When I finally got one at the Starbucks in the Chase Bank building after depositing my first check from a client it was the best drink I ever tasted.

"Did you tell her how you felt?" I said.

"I did. And she said she was sorry, but if I hadn't wanted the financial obligation of being a maid of honor, I should've told her. And she sent me a couple links to articles about what's involved in being a maid of honor, and that's how they put it, a financial obligation you assumed. Of course, they were written by wedding planners. But I'm sure Ivy saw it as a way to show me she wasn't being unreasonable."

I shifted position on the couch. We'd been sitting a while, and between that, a few hits during training the day before, and the drive, my lower back twinged. "I'm not sure I could be as giving as you were about paying for so much for a friend who ditched me."

"I truly was grateful to her for the help with networking. Sometimes when I need to pitch new business or get a contract signed, I still channel Ivy. I think: What would Ivy say? And then I say it. And it works."

"How were things between the two of you after the wedding?"

"We had lunch a couple times and dinner once. Then she got pregnant and moved to Chicago to be near her brother and sister-in-law. I remember asking her when she was deciding on the move if she wouldn't miss her friends. And she just shrugged and said, 'Oh, I'll make new ones.'"

I raised my eyebrows. "Ouch."

I hoped I'd never find myself on the other end of a comment like that. My friends were like family to me.

"The next time I heard from her," Mei said, "other than a few emails, was to make sure I'd gotten her baby shower invitation. No one had ordered anything from the baby gift registry yet. She worried the invites had gotten lost."

Ivy sounded like an expensive friend to keep. "You didn't visit her in Chicago?"

"Once for that first baby shower. After that we mostly lost touch. I couldn't help feeling I wasn't any use to her anymore, so she didn't bother. Maybe that was unfair."

"But then you saw her last month? How did that come about?"

I tried to keep my tone neutral. But it seemed a bit coincidental that their friendship lapsed, then the first time Mei saw Ivy, Ivy was found dead a day later.

19

Mei folded her arms over her stomach. "It wasn't as if we weren't in touch at all. We emailed occasionally. When I decided to move here to Miller Beach I texted her. She was all excited to get together. Said she wanted to hear all about my new job and my move."

"Where did you meet her?"

"Starbucks in the Randolph Street Metra Electric train station."

"That's the underground one?" I said. I rarely took the train south, but I had a business mailbox near there and was pretty sure the underground Pedway connected to it.

"Right. I thought that was just the meeting place because Ivy said something about there being a couple places near Michigan Avenue that had vegan dinner options. But when I arrived, Ivy said she'd just started a cleanse, so she wasn't eating, and she was behind on inventory at her store and had to work that night, so she didn't have much time."

"Was she eating at all?"

A friend from my theater days did cleanses twice a year, so I knew there were a lot of different kinds.

"Not for a few days, I think. After that she planned to add certain foods a little at a time."

"Huh." I asked what foods and when, but Mei didn't know details.

"And she was doing inventory on a Friday night?" I said.

"She said weekends were the only evenings they closed, and she had something else planned for Saturday night."

I noted that on my phone. No one had said anything about Ivy having plans for that Saturday night. If she had, it seemed odd whoever she'd been meant to see hadn't raised an alarm when Ivy couldn't be reached.

"So did you spend much time with her at the Starbucks?"

Mei flipped her wrist as if flicking away a fly. "Maybe twenty minutes? She brought her own water in this fancy thermos. I got some herbal tea. She didn't ask a thing about my move or how I was settling in. Mostly she told me about her store. And gave me a sample lipstick – which was at least a match for my skin tone. Afterwards she sent me a link to sign up to her store's email list and her YouTube channel and some books the store sold on veganism."

"Are you a vegan? Or vegetarian?"

Mei waggled her hand back and forth. "I eat less meat than I used to. But I still eat it."

"You couldn't have gone with her to the store and talked as she did inventory?"

The store was about a mile and a half from the Metra train station Mei was talking about. Not super convenient, but Mei could've gotten off at an earlier stop on the same train line and been closer to it.

Mei shook her glass back and forth, making the few ice cubes left in it swirl around. "I suggested that. But she said she would be so focused on what she was doing that she wouldn't really be able to pay attention."

"Did Ivy at least apologize for dragging you downtown for a short visit?"

"Not really. It was like she'd become Ivy by a factor of ten," Mei said. "Even the wedding, I believe she genuinely didn't see that she was expecting an awful lot. There were all those articles suggesting that if you get married, people owe it to you to help pay for your wedding and your honeymoon, too. But this time, it felt so clear it was all about Ivy. I was someone new she could hand a sample and give a sales pitch to, and then she was done."

I didn't feel sure Ivy had changed. It sounded more like Mei, with the perspective of years away, at last saw Ivy's behavior for what it was.

Mei had little else to tell me. She confirmed what Perla had said about Ivy's parents. And, like Perla, Mei said Ivy's challenging childhood was why she cut her a bit more slack for her need to control situations and run things.

Mei walked me out to the car. I thanked her again and got in the car. Inside, it felt like an oven on broil. I left the driver's door open and cranked the air conditioning as I added a few more notes to my legal pad.

Mei's tale of Ivy dropping their friendship and treating friends cavalierly contrasted in some ways with Perla's view that it was Ivy's friends who hit a point where they'd had enough of her. But in other ways it fit. My impression was that if Mei had been willing to remain the giver, both literally in terms of gifts and as a sounding board and support system, Ivy might well have continued the friendship, such as it was.

I shut the driver door, scrolled through my calendar on my phone, and texted Joe some more dates. As I finished, a text came through from Danielle.

Visited Santiago this morning. Meet me if you're free tomorrow at preliminary hearing at 26th & Cal. You can watch & we can both talk to Santiago after.

The air conditioning at last blew blessedly cold air in my face. I lifted my hair off my neck and bent closer to the vent. I hadn't worked at all Saturday, reserving the day, night, and this morning for Ty. Tomorrow morning I had planned to work on the chocolate chip case and the new case referred by my actor friend. If the traffic gods favored me, though, I could be back downtown within the hour, put my notes from the conversation with Mei in order, and pop into the office to get a few things sorted out so I could fit in what I needed to this week.

I texted Danielle that I'd be there and put the car in gear.

20

I took the Blue Line to the stop nearest the courthouse at 26th Street and California Avenue. The neighborhood had a fairly high crime rate, and the five-block walk gave me plenty of time to practice more of what I'd learned in training. I scanned the buildings for stores I might run into if I needed help and made sure to stay aware of anyone heading toward me or walking too close behind me. But for the most part, few people were out on the hot, sunny morning, and no one looked twice at me.

Despite leaving half an hour earlier than I thought I needed to, I arrived just as the hearing began. The L train had stopped for no clear reason for twenty minutes, started again, then waited at a stop before mine to let other trains pass.

Danielle already sat at the counsel table near the judge's bench. Not being an attorney on the case, I sat on a wooden bench in an outer area for the public. Scratched glass enclosed the inner part of the courtroom, and those of us watching listened through a speaker. I guessed the morning's call included a lot of hearings because twelve or thirteen different clusters of people watched. Other than a couple young women in what looked like athletic attire, most people appeared to be Black or LatinX. It struck me because it's rarely the case when I go to court on civil cases for my clients.

Santiago sat next to Danielle wearing a gray prison uniform. I couldn't see his face clearly from my seat. But he sat with his shoulders square and his head steady, watching the attorneys and witnesses.

Or I should say witness. To my surprise, there was only one, the arresting officer. The whole hearing took less than ten minutes.

Santiago didn't testify. Danielle had explained to me ahead of time that she never put her client on the stand at this stage. She didn't want to give the prosecution any more information than she needed to or allow the prosecutor to question the client before she knew all the ins and outs of the case.

The officer testified based on what he did and what witnesses told him in their statements. What struck me as most incriminating was something Ivy's regular dog walker supposedly told police. He ran into Santiago at the house after a hearing in family court. Santiago was angry at Ivy and said, "She'll get what's coming to her."

That could mean a lot of things, but with Ivy dead a few weeks later, the prosecution obviously thought it meant a motive for murder.

The officer also said that store employees confirmed that inventory did take place over the weekend. No one else was in Friday night, but the store manager on Saturday morning found information Ivy left for her. I took some comfort for Mei that Ivy really had needed to work that evening, though it still seemed pretty thoughtless to drag Mei downtown for what turned out to be a sales pitch.

The last fact the officer testified to was that Santiago's fingerprints were found on the antifreeze bottle in the garage.

On cross-examination, Danielle asked him if the finger-prints could be from two years ago when Santiago lived there and if witnesses had told him Santiago still worked on his own car in the garage after the separation. The officer said yes to both.

He also agreed that no one had seen Santiago go out to the garage to get the antifreeze bottle, take it upstairs three floors to poison Ivy's food, then bring it back down the stairs and out to the garage. Including a next-door neighbor who told police that she sat on her side porch that afternoon and had a clear view of the yard.

The judge then cut off Danielle's questioning and found probable cause.

Danielle came out to talk to me while the next hearing went forward. We stepped out into the hall.

"Any questions for me before we visit Santiago?" she said. "Because, remember, this is Hello–Good-bye for you. I don't want to risk him making any statements that don't fall under attorney-client privilege.

"I couldn't hear everything," I said. "What food did the cop say the antifreeze was in?"

"There was vegetable puree in a nearly-empty bowl near the sink. Looks like green slop in the photos."

I tapped my fingers against my leg. "Are the police certain the antifreeze was only in the vegetable puree? And nothing else?"

"Hard to be absolute on that. The other contents of the refrigerator were tested and came up negative. But if Ivy drank or ate all of something else and washed her dishes, there'd be no way to tell. Why?"

"Mei Leonhard told me yesterday that Ivy was on a cleanse."

Nothing had been said about that during the hearing. The officer only shared that Mei was the last person known to have seen Ivy alive and the time and date, but nothing more.

Danielle peered through the glass door to see if the next hearing had finished. She turned back to me. "A cleanse. That's a weight loss thing? Ivy was pretty thin."

"You could do it for weight loss. But some people believe it cleans toxins out of your system."

I'd done a little research the night before after I finished as much as I could of my legal work. It had been after ten when I left my office.

"Like what the liver and kidney already do for free?"

I shrugged. "I didn't say it made sense. It's also to isolate problem foods. So you might not eat for a day or two, then add grains only, then vegetables and fruit, then dairy. Or you might do nothing but drink water and then juice for a week."

"And Ivy was doing this?" Danielle said.

"That's what Mei said. The night before she died she was only drinking water."

"It fits a witness statement from a Starbucks barista. She remembered Ivy because it irritates her when people bring in their own drinks and don't buy anything. And Ivy sat there the whole time holding her own drink and sipping it."

"Could Mei have slipped something into it? The barista couldn't have watched every minute."

Mei seemed like a nice person, but from experience I knew people could put on a show.

But Danielle shook her head. "If she had, Ivy would've died a lot sooner."

Danielle didn't want me to ask Santiago about the cleanse until she had a chance to talk to him alone, and I promised I wouldn't.

"Here's something else," I said. "The State's Attorney's questions emphasized that no one else was reported to be in

Ivy's home for the last five days. But Ivy could have made the puree earlier than that."

Danielle raised her eyebrows. "Would you eat something you made more than a week ago? Oh – wait. You said her downstairs neighbor –"

"Right, Ellison. She said Ivy ate old food all the time. Ellison testified to that in domestic relations court."

"I'll get that transcript. It's good to expand the time window."

Danielle's comment made me wonder if Santiago hadn't told her about Alexis's vomiting or the reason for the custody decision. Which could mean Santiago was still being kind about his wife. Or that Ellison hadn't told the truth. Or, most likely, Santiago had a lot more on his mind and didn't connect the issues.

The two young women I had noticed earlier exited the courtroom.

"If the timeframe expands, that could put the dog walker back in the mix," I said.

"Except according to that same neighbor, Ellison, the dog walker only has a key to the second floor where the dog lives." Danielle's phone buzzed. She clicked it off and tucked it into her suit jacket pocket. "Not to the third floor where the main kitchen is and where the puree was found."

"The dog has its own floor?"

"Ivy apparently liked things clean. She cooked only on the third floor, which is also where her bedroom and dining room were. And a spare room. She kept the dog on the second floor where she used the family room and had spare bedrooms for her daughters."

"It can't be that hard to get from one floor to the other from inside," I said. "I don't see how the police ruled out the dog walker."

"No sign of forced entry, he was out of town, also no motive."

"But they don't need motive," I said.

Motive isn't an element of first-degree murder in Illinois. I had also reviewed the Illinois criminal code sections the night before, confirming what I remembered from law school.

"No, but it can drive investigations," Danielle said. "And it helps persuade a jury."

Danielle promised to send me the dog walker's name and contact information. But she warned me again to be careful what we discussed and what I wrote down.

Then she glanced through the courtroom door. "They're done. Time for you to meet Santiago."

21

The public seating area was empty now, as was the inner courtroom except for the bailiff. Danielle headed for the door beyond the judge's bench.

The bailiff stopped me. "Can't take your purse in."

"Oh." I slipped it off my shoulder, unsure what to do with it.

He held out his hand. "I'll take it."

One of the first rules of living and working in Chicago is don't let go of your purse or put your wallet where anyone else can easily reach it. But I didn't have any choice, so I handed it over.

I noticed Danielle's shoulder bag, which must have her purse in it, sat on the counsel table. I hadn't noticed her set it down, but she was obviously used to leaving it.

As the bailiff unlocked the heavy wooden door, Danielle glanced over her shoulder at me. "Don't get too close to the bars. And let me take the lead. Lots of people listening."

The courtroom itself had left me feeling claustrophobic with its lack of windows and low ceiling. The inner room felt far more so. It had a musty smell that reminded me of old, wet gym clothes. Bars on three sides locked in all the male defendants who had hearings that morning. I stepped to one side to check out the far end of the room. Just past the last cell a hallway led to corridors behind the courtroom. Danielle had told me those led to elevators that took the inmates back underground where they were led through tunnels into the Cook County jail next door.

The jail itself was almost entirely underground. Prisoners brought in for their court hearings literally never saw the light of day.

One of them grabbed the bars and looked at me. "Hey, baby, you got a card?"

His tone held no menace, but I kept in mind the advice Danielle had given me the night before. Don't look scared, but don't forget some of the men are violent offenders, and I wouldn't know which ones by sight.

I smiled but kept my distance and looked him right in the eyes. "Sorry, they don't trust me with them."

He laughed. "Let me know – maybe that changes."

Santiago approached the bars. He held himself as he had in court, very straight, shoulders square, but up close I saw the white hairs in his eyebrows and along his part and his sagging jaw line.

Danielle introduced us. Despite the surroundings, I almost held out my hand to shake, then remembered no contact was allowed. I pulled back at the last second and nodded.

"What does losing now mean for my chances at trial?" Santiago said.

"Nothing," Danielle said. "At trial, the prosecution has to prove guilt beyond a reasonable doubt. For this hearing, the prosecution only needed to prove probable cause by a preponderance of the evidence."

Santiago's brow furrowed.

"It means more likely than not," Danielle said. "Sometimes attorneys describe it as 50.01%. And the question wasn't your guilt. It was whether the police had a reasonable basis to arrest you. A whole different question. So don't be discouraged. I told you on the phone. I lose 90% of these hearings."

He rocked forward and back on his heels. "You said that. But I don't understand. Then why do them?"

"Not all defense attorneys do. But it helps us. Locks the arresting officer into his testimony. Now he's on paper – meaning under oath, and there's a record of it. It's a lot harder for him to claim later that there's something a witness said, or something he did, that somehow didn't get into the police report. If he does do that, the jury will be suspicious. So I learn more about the prosecution's case, but we reveal nothing about ours because you didn't take the stand."

Santiago rubbed the creases over his eyes. "I wish I could have. The officer made it sound so – Ivy and I weren't angry at each other. A while back –"

Danielle raised her hand, motioning him to stop. "Save it for when you and I are in private."

"I was only going to say every couple gets angry in a divorce. But we were past that." His arms dropped to his sides. "But I've thought and thought about who could have done this. Ivy – no one would want to kill her. Whoever did it, it had to be some sort of terrible mistake."

I didn't know what to say to that. No matter how unusual Ivy's eating habits might have been, no one was going to believe antifreeze got in her food by mistake. Especially when the only antifreeze bottle on the premises was in the garage.

Danielle answered a few more of Santiago's questions about what was likely to happen over the next few weeks.

"I appreciate what you're trying to do for my girls," he said to me just before we left.

"I'll do whatever I can," I said.

"All I want is for them to be taken care of," Santiago said. "When Amber left for school, she and her mom were fighting. Amber was so mad. She pretends on the phone to me she's fine now, but I hear it in her voice. Trying to be grown up. But she's lost. And Alexis told me if she'd been there, still living at Ivy's, this never would've happened."

I bit my lip. It ought to have occurred to me Alexis and Amber might feel guilty. Kids are always willing to blame themselves for what their parents do.

"I need to be there for them," Santiago said. "That's all that matters."

Back at the office, Danielle returned one call after another from other clients. She's at court so much she always has a backlog when she gets to her desk.

I worked until around four, then changed out of my suit, which I hung in a garment bag on my office door, and into skinny jeans and a light gray tank top. I put on a Marc Jacobs charcoal blazer and switched to a pair of designer, but not leather, low-heeled sandals, then added my Kate Spade pendant and gold bangle bracelets. I wanted to look like I had money to spend at a vegan cosmetics store.

For me, though, looking well off or, for that matter, solidly middle class, feels like a costume of sorts. Something I learned to look like as I moved into the business world. I carefully constructed my image the same way as when I played roles on stage, though there I had help from costume designers and props masters. From them I learned to haunt secondhand stores and outlet stores, plowing through end-of-season and clearance sales in upscale stores to buy on a budget. My blazer had come from Neiman Marcus' outlet Last Call before it closed, and nearly all my designer purses and shoulder bags came from Nordstrom Rack on State Street.

As a result, a tiny part of me watches to see if anyone will spot the college kid whose lunch money lasted only through Thursday under the polished, successful-looking lawyer. Normally it didn't matter. I simply faked it until I felt better and no one was the wiser.

But this was about Alexis and Amber, so I wanted back up. The real thing, or as close as I could get.

Which is why I had called Lauren.

22

The Wintrust building spans an entire block on the south edge of downtown Chicago. The long sides are on Jackson across from the Chicago Stock Exchange and Quincy, a narrow street that looks more like an alley because it's only a block long at that spot. That's where the businesses' dock doors and loading areas are. Trucks pull in to load and unload. There's little automobile traffic and most pedestrians walk right past without noticing the street at all.

You can enter the building on Clark Street and walk straight through across shiny marble floors to exit on LaSalle Street. Businesses line either side of the building with entrances facing onto the wide center corridor. That corridor also features seating islands with upholstered couches and armchairs, and a jewelry store with glass walls all around. Starbucks is an anchor tenant on Clark and Jackson. It has both an entrance to the street and one to the building's interior.

Ivy's store was one that only had a customer entrance from inside the building. But I waited for Lauren outside the Starbucks. She was running late, so I returned client emails on my phone, glancing around every few minutes to be sure no one hurrying past took advantage of my inattention and tried to grab the phone from my hand or my purse from my shoulders. I'd left my shoulder bag at the office. It was leather, as were the other two I had, because I often carried heavy files. In a vegan store, it would give me away.

Lauren hurried around the corner ten minutes later. Her blond hair shone in the sun and her Manolo Blahnik shoes clacked on the sidewalk. Unlike me, on an average day everything Lauren wears from shoes to jeans to jewelry screams that she has money and is willing to spend it on retail.

She hugged me. "Hey, sorry. Negotiations ran longer than I thought. But I finally have a closing date for that penthouse."

I met Lauren in law school, but she dropped out after a year and got her real estate license. She's never looked back.

"Congratulations," I said.

"To you too. Since you referred it. We totally need to celebrate. I'm thinking Oriole on me. Once it's signed. No sense counting chickens and all that."

Lauren focuses on residential, not commercial, real estate but she stays pretty aware of what's going on in both worlds. Which was the second reason I wanted her input today.

"So why would Ivy want a store in this building?" I said. "I already walked all around the outside. It's not visible from out there because it borders the dock side. On Quincy."

Quite a few large buildings in or near downtown are like that. It's as if there are interior streets inside the buildings. The establishments along them are hidden from anyone who doesn't need to cut through.

I figured it must be a difficult sell for a lot of retail businesses. Anyone looking for foot traffic couldn't be happy with no on-street window or storefront. For somewhere like Starbucks, the people who worked in the building might be enough of a clientele. But I didn't think enough people who wanted vegan cosmetics worked in this one building.

"She might not need the exposure," Lauren said. "Didn't you tell me this is the only vegan cosmetics store in or near downtown?"

"For miles," I said. "I found one other in Evanston and one in Orland Park, and that's it."

"Then people who care about vegan cosmetics will find it. And the lack of visibility means she probably got much better rent for a prime downtown location. Trendy vegan traders and lawyers and accountants can pop in here on their lunch hours or breaks, then she closes down on the weekends and has her free time unlike every other retailer."

We entered the gold revolving doors. The air conditioning sent a welcome blast of cold at my face.

"Huh. Could be," I said. "Based on the prices I saw when I looked online, people who aren't dedicated to veganism aren't likely to buy from here."

"Seriously," Lauren said. "I looked too. Those prices would embarrass Neiman Marcus. Before it went bankrupt, that is."

"I'll take your word for it."

Lauren rolled her eyes. "Well, right, I'm sure this is mega-higher than Walgreens or wherever you buy your cosmetics."

"I spend where I really need to. But I have it on good authority –"

"I know, I know. All your makeup artist friends told you what you can buy at Walgreens that matches department store quality. Seriously, Quille, you make good money as a lawyer. You don't need to scour every discount store for deals."

"This year's been a little lean."

"Not that lean. Let's check this place out."

Ivy's Vegan Cosmetics stood toward the middle of the

building next to a restaurant and bar with seating that extended into the corridor as if it were a real outdoor café. I made a mental note to check it out for winter time. It might be nice to have the illusion of outdoor dining.

The whole south side of the store was open to the interior of the building. The second we stepped in, the smell of the air changed. It had a clean scent, like a freshly mowed lawn right after it rains. A faint trickling sound came from every corner. At first I thought it was nature sounds playing over a loud speaker.

But as Lauren and I wandered the aisles I saw miniature stone fountains placed strategically so that at the very center of the store you almost felt like you were inside a waterfall. As with all retail in downtown Chicago, the aisles barely allowed two people to pass one another. All the same, the wide shelves and carefully aligned products with white space between them gave it a more relaxed and spacious feeling than seemed possible given the limited floor space.

I brought a two-ounce plant-based lotion that promised to lessen dark under eye circles to the counter.

Lauren joined me, holding an essential oil diffuser. She glanced around and waved a clerk over and showed her the diffuser. "This would make a totally lovely gift, don't you think? I knew Ivy's store would have something."

"You knew Ivy?" the clerk said.

"We're close with the family," I said. "It's so sad for Alexis and Amber."

The clerk nodded. "Awful." She looked at Lauren, likely sizing up her designer fashion from head to toe. "For a special occasion?"

"My mom's birthday. Next month."

"That one is beautiful. But if you want something really special –"

She led us to the back wall and took down a crystal-studded diffuser. It was pretty. And the priciest on the shelf. Lauren took it. The clerk waved to another aisle.

"If you have animal companions, we have some lovely items for them, too. Ivy picked them personally."

"We don't," I said. "But what a nice idea."

The clerk swiped Lauren's shiny black visa card at the checkout counter. She creased the wrapping paper for the diffuser and folded it over the box.

Lauren leaned in close, and said in a low voice, "So horrible about Ivy. And now her husband was arrested. I can't even imagine."

The clerk glanced around the store. It was empty other than us. All the same, she lowered her voice. "When she didn't come in that Monday, we all thought she was just out sick."

I kept what I hoped was a faint look of concern, and not irritation, on my face. It had been so easy to lead the clerk into talking about Ivy's death. I felt grateful for that because it might help me learn more. But disturbed because tragedy evokes this sort of morbid curiosity in people. On a gut level, I get it. It's human to feel that sort of fascination. It's a mix of wanting to believe something like it could never happen to you and wanting to know more so you can avoid that terrible fate. But that type of curiosity had followed my parents much of their lives.

Lauren nudged me, and I focused on the clerk again.

"I knew Ivy had a lot of digestive issues," I said. "But until Santiago was arrested, I wondered if that cleanse she was on made her sick."

I was curious whether Ivy's doing the cleanse was known to anyone else.

"Really? The cleanse?" The clerk's eyes opened wider. "She did them, like, three times a year. But if it killed her – oh, how bizarre that would be."

"I don't know if it was that," I said. "It just crossed my mind."

"Do you know where she bought it?" Lauren lowered her voice again, almost to a whisper. "It wasn't here, was it? That'd be so seriously ironic."

The clerk folded the ends of the wrapping paper together, cut off the excess, folded it again and taped it, making a perfect seal. "No, no. It was through someone in her women's networking group."

Lauren glanced around, as if concerned about people listening. "Do you think her husband really did it?"

The clerk's eyes lit up. "I don't know. But I met him once, and he barely looked at me. Like, he nodded hello, but when Ivy walked off to go in the back he just walked away and looked at the crystal display."

"Not a people person," I said.

"Not at all. But that doesn't mean he would kill someone, I guess."

"What happens to the store now? With Ivy gone?" Lauren said. "I hope you're staying open."

"We all hope so. No one knows if Hank will get a new partner or keep the store himself. Or close it. I hope he doesn't close it. It's really hard to find vegan cosmetics."

"It totally is." Lauren, who goes out for steak at least three times a month, spoke as if she'd scoured the city for such a store. "But why would he close it? I thought it was doing well?"

She handed Lauren her receipt. "All I know is the lease runs out in a couple months, and everyone's nervous."

"Hank always struck me as nicer than Ivy," Lauren said. "She's seriously intense. Was."

I had to admire how sincere and knowledgeable Lauren sounded. She knew nothing about Ivy or Hank, as I hadn't had a chance to fill her in much beyond Ivy being found dead and Santiago being arrested.

The clerk shrugged. "She yelled sometimes. But my supervisor told me you just needed to follow all her procedures – and she has them set for everything. That and tell her everything's under control. That was always her first question when she walked in after taking her dog for a walk. Is everything under control? You say yes, even if it's not. Then you scrambled to make sure you got it under control."

Another customer had come in while we were talking and asked about an all-natural plant-based shampoo. We slipped away before the clerk could wonder why we were asking so many questions.

Hot air and exhaust cascaded over us as we emerged onto Clark Street.

"Why would Ivy leave the store to walk the dog?" I said. "She lived all the way over in Andersonville. And she had a dog walker."

"He had the day off? Like the day she died?"

"Right, but then why not go home and walk the dog that day? Instead of asking Santiago?"

It might be just a matter of convenience. Santiago wasn't likely to have a day off work every time Ivy needed him.

Lauren shrugged. "The ways of dogs and dog owners are totally beyond me. And so they shall remain unless the Universe has some strange plan to torment me."

It occurred to me that other than Ty, almost none of my friends were dog lovers. Which was odd, given that every other person in my neighborhood seemed to have one. Maybe it said something about my character.

"I'm with you there," I said. "I'll have to ask Alexis when I see her tonight."

∼

The conversation with the clerk reminded me that I hadn't checked into Hank Brown's possible lawsuit experience. Lauren and I had a reservation for an early dinner down the block at Cochon Volant, a French restaurant with outdoor seating. My friend Carole had told me the name translated to Flying Pig. Which made sense, as the menu featured a lot of pork and ham-based dishes, though with fancier names and prices.

While Lauren quizzed the waiter about the wine, I searched on my iPad the various counties' electronic dockets.

But I didn't find any lawsuits in Cook County against Hank Brown. Nothing came up in DuPage or Kane counties either. After we ordered, I switched to PACER, an electronic database I subscribed to that allows me to search all federal filings for the entire United States. Unfortunately, it's set up so that you need to search each specific federal jurisdiction separately, and there are over fifty of them.

Lauren tapped the table. "Hey, there. If you planned to look at your iPad the whole time, why ask me to join you?"

"Sorry. One more thing."

Though I wasn't exactly rolling in extra cash, I emailed a paralegal who does freelance work for me and asked her to do some searching for me.

Luckily, she was free and looking for work. By the time Lauren and I finished our steak frites, she wrote me that Hank hadn't filed any lawsuits in the federal courts that sit in Illinois or in the neighboring states. The business databases I subscribe to didn't show any companies he owned other than the store with Ivy. And there didn't seem to be any litigation surrounding the store. Maybe Hank's knowledge of litigation had come from someone he knew rather than direct experience.

Lauren and I shared a plate of profiteroles – vanilla ice cream in between pastry puffs, smothered in chocolate sauce.

After that Lauren walked me to the Red Line station at State and Washington, then headed south to go home. I took the escalator underground to catch the train to Andersonville, texting Alexis that I was on the way. I was meeting her at Ivy's house. Tomorrow was a teacher's institute day at her high school, so she was staying overnight with a friend in the neighborhood.

As the train rumbled along I made a list of what to ask Alexis. Including where her mom got the cleanse. It might have nothing to do with her death. But it continued to bother me that someone poisoned Ivy when she might very well not have been eating that week.

23

My ride on the Red Line was long and hot. The train idled longer than usual at each stop with the doors open. Damp, urine-tinged air rushed in at the underground stops. Above ground it didn't smell as bad, but heat and humidity permeated the car. Plus I kept feeling like someone might be watching me. Yet whenever I looked around everyone else was staring at phones or books or looking dazedly into space with earbuds on.

Maybe the instructor was making me paranoid.

I forgot all of that when I arrived at the house. Alexis sat on the steps. Her hair still hung flat and heavy, and her undereye circles, if anything, had darkened. I sat next to her and told her about seeing Santiago, emphasizing that he looked healthy and was focused on getting out and being there for her and Amber.

She rubbed her hands over the ripped spots in her jeans. "I've heard awful things about jail. What happens there. You know, other convicts preying on prisoners."

"Danielle told me your dad's old enough, and looks strong enough, that they'll leave him alone."

Not much comfort for young men who spent time in prison, but right now what was important was the girl in front of me.

She nodded. Partly to distract her, I asked about the dog walker.

"I never met him," she said as she unlocked the front door closest to the stairs. It was one of two and led to an interior stairway.

"Do you know if your mom only gave him a key to the second floor, not the third?"

We stepped into the narrow stairwell and climbed. The stairs creaked but felt sturdy.

"Not sure. Sounds like something she'd do. You'll see, the two floors are like different apartments. She and dad talked about renting out the second one after Amber went away to school."

I wanted to start where Ivy spent the most time, so we climbed to the third floor and Alexis unlocked an interior door. Inside was a small entryway with one door to a closet and an open archway to the living room. The long, narrow room flowed into the dining room. The floors were light-colored wood.

"It's bamboo," Alexis said. "Mom had it put in a couple years ago when the original hardwood got too worn. She wanted renewable wood."

The faux-leather couch and recliner looked a bit worn, but sturdy. Alexis told me her uncle, once he became executor of Ivy's will, wanted to sell everything. He had already called an estate sale company to see if they could handle all of it.

"So when you all lived here, you needed your keys to get from this floor to the second floor?" I said.

We peered into Ivy's bedroom. It was along the east side of the house and had two square windows. A queen-sized bed nearly filled the room.

"In the front, yeah. Everything stayed locked. But in the back we left all the doors open. Ellison, too. We could all go between floors any time. Until she and Mom had some kind of argument. Then Mom changed all the locks and started keeping all the doors locked all the time."

"Your mom changed the locks to both floors?"

"Yeah. She gave me and Dad keys to each."

"Not Amber?"

"I don't think Amber. She was away at school. And this summer she only came a couple times to Mom's and didn't stay over. I still had Ellison's key, so I went down there a lot if Mom wasn't around and I was here."

She pointed me down the hall to her room. A twin bed sat under a slanting ceiling. A dresser stood against the opposite wall, only a few feet away.

"When we all lived here Amber and I had bedrooms downstairs. But since we only visited sometimes, she moved everybody up here. That's when the second floor kind of became the dog's floor. And her home office."

"How often did you stay here?"

"Like, every other weekend. Sometimes every. Dad insisted on sending food with me, though. I think he thought I was anorexic or something."

"Did you feel caught in the middle?"

"Because Mom wanted me to eat vegan and Dad said no? Kind of. But she and Dad agreed her diet might not be right for me and I should choose when I was eighteen."

My best guess was that Ivy only "agreed" to that after the court ordered her to. But at least she hadn't said anything to make Alexis angry at her dad.

The kitchen featured a butcher block table and a farmhouse sink.

"See, that door we kept open when I was a kid." Alexis

gestured to the heavy door to the back porch. "Oh, and you should see something."

She spun and hurried toward the front of the house, gesturing me to follow. Her steps had a bounce I hadn't seen before. It gave me a glimpse of what she might have been like as a child. Or maybe as a teenager before life yanked the rug out from under her.

She opened the door to Ivy's bedroom closet and moved aside a wide shoe rack with sparkling white tennis shoes, multiple faux-leather brown and black pumps, and hiking boots. Underneath in the center of the worn hardwood closet floor was a square trap door with a black metal handle. The door was nailed shut. I shone my phone's flashlight on it. The nail heads looked scratched and worn.

"Amber told me she loved this when she was a kid," she said. "There's a ladder inside. Or just rungs, really, along the side of a sort of tunnel going down."

"Like a ship's ladder," I said.

"Yeah, I guess. She loved to climb down to the second floor, but Mom wouldn't let her go down all the way to Ellison's. She said it would be rude to pop in like that."

"But it goes to Ellison's?"

"It did. But Mom's had it nailed shut since I learned to crawl. That's, like, the first thing Amber got mad at me about. That's what everyone says."

"I would have loved this, too, when I was a kid," I said. "I used to go between my parents' apartment and my Gram's. Across the hall. But a hidden passageway would have made me so happy."

It made me happy here, too. Though the nails showed this one had been nailed shut for a long time, where there was one hidden passageway there might be another. Confirming my view that it couldn't be that hard to get into Ivy's home without a key.

"Yeah, that's exactly what Amber pretended. That it was a secret passageway. Everyone knew about it, though."

"But why a trap door in a closet?"

"Mom told us the guy who owned the house before was kind of crazy. After we moved in, she and Dad found all sorts of weird things. Like windows drywalled over. Mom said there was a tangle of electrical cords between the basement and the first floor that looked like two octopi mating."

We walked out and down the back outside stairs to the second floor. Alexis opened the door with a separate key. I tried her other keys to be sure, but none worked. The kitchen there was arranged the same as the one above, but the appliances were older. The counters were bare of small appliances or canisters and there was no dish rack in the sink. Rather than a butcher block table with counter height stools, a rectangular table stretched across the center of the floor with one chair.

"My mom used this as a home office, especially when she ran her business online only." Alexis pointed to updated electrical outlets. "She was always thinking she'd fix up the back porch to have a view of the yard. But that was one time my dad put his foot down. Said it was crazy to spend money rehabbing the back porch when we had so much other unused space."

Alexis told me when she'd been growing up the next room served as a family room. Now it stood empty. The floor, darker than the one upstairs, showed scratches that Alexis said came from the dog's claws. One of the smaller bedrooms served as a closet. A queen-sized bed and a row of bookshelves that held office supplies furnished a guest room.

Amber's old bedroom was long and narrow to leave room

for the stairway. It was below Ivy's third-floor bedroom and had a trap door in an interior closet wall that had been nailed shut.

"That's where you could get out from the ladder," Alexis said. "This was my nursery when I was born."

Now that I had a sense of the two floors as a whole, I wanted to look again at the third-floor kitchen where someone poisoned Ivy's food. That kitchen had limited cabinet space filled with dishes, glasses, pots, and pans, and the pantry was well stocked with staples, including the organic rice Ellison had mentioned. Also more rows of dishes, glasses, bowls and cookware.

The mugs on a middle shelf all had their handles facing the same way.

I pointed to a row of dog food bags on the floor with different colored wrappers. Each angled exactly the same way, showing the same section of the brand name.

"Vegan dog food? Never knew there was such a thing."

Alexis made a face and stuck out her tongue for a second. "Yeah, yuck. My dad says it's crazy. That dogs' stomachs need meat."

That seemed logical to me. "Do you miss Ralph?"

She rubbed her hands over her arms. "Mom only got him a few months before I moved to Dad's. I wasn't that close to him. He was a Doberman. A rescue dog, and he was skittish. That's what Mom called it."

All I knew about Dobermans was that they supposedly could snap your neck with their jaws. The allure of a dog that can do that is lost on me, but it couldn't be easy for Alexis to have one more major change.

"Meaning what?"

"Easy to upset. She always said don't make sudden moves around him and you'll be fine. Oh, and don't be afraid because he could sense fear."

Sure, that would set my mind at ease about someone's giant dog.

"Did he ever bite you?"

"Uh-uh. Mostly he just stared at me. At everyone. Like he might lunge any minute, but he didn't."

We headed down the outside back stairs. I asked about the cleanses her mom did.

"Oh, she was big on those. Did one every season except winter because of something about your body needing more nourishment for winter. But every spring, summer, and fall."

"How did she first find out about them?"

She paused on the second-floor landing. "Uh, through her women's group? It was for, you know, business. My aunt's in it. They meet here once a month. Every third Sunday."

"Do you know the person's name who sold the cleanse?"

"Tammy something. She's nice." Alexis' hand flew to her mouth. "Do you think anyone told her?"

"I'll find out," I said. "If I can find her."

Alexis said the contact information would be in her mom's phone, but I didn't have access to that. I felt a sudden longing for the days of paper address books. My Gram still kept a spiral one on a white and metal utility cart in the kitchen corner. It had once held an old-fashioned dial phone, too. Even she, though, kept her newer contacts only in her phone.

"You don't think Tammy did something to the cleanse, do you?" Alexis said.

"I don't have any reason to think so."

We'd reached the yard. Something Alexis said nagged at

me. I opened my calendar app. "Third Sunday you said? Then the last one was the week before she died."

"Yeah. The group met here. Sometimes I join them but I didn't that time. I had a paper due, like, Monday and I put it off to the last minute."

No one had mentioned the women's group before, though it quite possibly was the networking group the clerk talked about. I made a mental note to see if Danielle knew about it.

"Do you know how many women are in the group?"

"Like seven or eight I think. But it rained Sunday, so Mom said hardly anyone came."

Alexis showed me the basement, which we reached by going down concrete steps along the side of the house. It was the only entrance. Tiny windows near the ceiling faced east and very little light came in. Alexis turned on an overhead light, which was nothing more than a bare bulb on a chain. The laundry room near the door had a washer and dryer, and near it was a small half-bath. The floor throughout was concrete painted light gray, and the walls were concrete block. Another bare bulb hung at the far end.

I shone the beam of my flashlight app on a square door in the ceiling. "Is that the same passageway?"

"Yeah. Amber never climbed all the way down here, though. The basement creeps her out. Me too."

Thick paint, now coated with dust, covered the creases between the door and the ceiling, making it clear no one had opened it recently. Probably not for decades.

I took some photos, but didn't see anything interesting.

As we locked the basement door and walked around to the front of the house I felt as if I were missing something. Or that I'd seen something that might be helpful but I couldn't quite grasp what it was. But I'd taken photos of the house, too, inside and outside throughout my visit. Maybe something would come to me when I looked them over again.

Alexis locked the door and we walked next door to talk to the neighbor who had a view of the yard. And who was so sure no one entered the house the day before Ivy's death other than Santiago.

24

When I was in grade school I often sat and read after school while my mom lay on the couch in front of the TV watching old sitcoms on one of the cable channels. During the worst of her depression, she found it hard to do anything else, but she liked some company in the room. The three to five p.m. slot featured back-to-back reruns of Bewitched, the old black and white show about a witch married to a human.

The main characters had a neighbor, Mrs. Kravitz, who spied on them through her front window. Ivy's next-door neighbor clearly came from that mode. Not in personality or looks, as she was kind and a bit on the heavy side, with a full face and wide hips. But, like Mrs. Kravitz, she knew all the neighborhood comings and goings.

"I'm sort of a self-appointed one-woman neighborhood watch," Mary said.

"It's true," Alexis said. "She stopped a break in across the street a couple years ago when she shouted out that she was calling police."

Mary had a bad hip that made it hard for her to get

around. So she spent nice days in a rocker on her wrap-around front porch, getting up as needed to ease her hip pain.

She told me that when the weather got worse, she shifted inside to a recliner that faced her picture window and watched the street. But in nice weather, she preferred the side porch because she liked the pretty view of people's yards and gardens. Sometimes she tossed feed to Ellison's chickens, as I'd seen her do when I was interviewing Ellison.

Alexis took a seat in one of two wide, empty rockers to Mary's left. She apparently kept them for visitors. A wide wooden swing hung from the porch ceiling where the porch curved from side to front.

"I'm so sorry, dear, about everything that's happened." She squeezed Alexis' hand. "I wish I had seen someone else go into the place. Breaks my heart to think of your dad in jail."

I walked behind Mary's rocker and studied Ivy's yard and house next door. The stairs to the basement weren't visible from here, as they were on the other side of Ivy's house. Also, there were low bushes on either side of the narrow sidewalk from the garage to the side of the house. The same side where the basement stairs were.

"If someone came out of the garage and crawled along the sidewalk to the basement stairs, you couldn't see it?"

"No, I can't see that. I told the police that. But cars need to enter the alley there." She waved toward the end of the cul-de-sac. "And I can see that. But someone might be able to sneak in on foot."

"You told the police that, too?"

"I did, I did. And that Santiago's a kind man. Cleaned out my gutters for me early this summer, wouldn't let me pay him."

Alexis put her feet flat on the porch and paused her rocker. "Did you tell the police Dad didn't do it?"

"I told them that and wrote it in my statement I signed, sweetheart. But it would have helped a lot more if I had seen someone else go into the house."

It was nearly dark, and after we left, I walked Alexis to her friend's house a few blocks away. She was excited to see her friend. And staying overnight there meant she didn't need to tell her aunt and uncle she was meeting me.

I didn't like encouraging her to keep things from them. But I hadn't met them yet. Our meeting was later in the week, on Thursday. And I'd learned the hard way that it pays not to trust anyone when you're looking into a murder.

Clark Street was only five blocks from Alexis's friend's house, and the No. 22 Clark bus took me within a few blocks of my condo. On the hour-long ride I forced myself to research and review case law on my iPad for my chocolate chip brownie case. I thought I had a better-than-average chance of getting the case knocked out of court early on. Which meant not much more than a less-than-zero chance, as most judges like to give plaintiffs the opportunity to try their case in front of a jury rather than having it dismissed by a judge. So I needed to focus.

In the back of my mind, though, I kept turning over the dog walker's statement to the police. I couldn't think of any reason that Santiago, after winning custody of Alexis, would tell Ivy she would get what was coming to her. It seemed more likely to me he might've said she got what was coming to her for mistreating Alexis.

And since Roy, the dog walker, hadn't appeared in court, Danielle hadn't been able to cross-examine him and get context or poke holes in what he said. She also hadn't been able to ask more about his alibi. The police had verified that he'd been out of town Thursday and Friday. But he'd been in the Chicago area Saturday. He claimed to have spent the entire weekend with his girlfriend, and she backed him up.

But Danielle told me juries didn't find alibis from family members or girlfriends nearly as persuasive as from strangers. So that might not get him off the hook.

Though it was late, I stopped at Lauren's condo before going to mine. Over a glass of wine, she volunteered to pretend to be a dog owner and try to set up a meeting with Roy. But if he had something useful to say, I didn't think tricking him into a meeting would make him very likely to want to help.

Instead, despite that I had a ton of emails from my latest family business case to read through, I called him first thing in the morning. I thought he might not answer a call from an unfamiliar number. But he picked up on the second ring.

25

I spun my chair away from my computer screen so I wouldn't be distracted by the emails. "Hi, Roy. My name is Quille Davis. I'm a friend of Alexis Jimenez-Brown."

"Great. I have a little room in my schedule —"

His words sounded rushed, but his voice had warm tones with a tiny hint of vibrato that made me want to keep listening to it.

"It's not about dog walking. It's about Ivy."

"Oh. Ivy. Of course." His voice became muted. "Who are you again?"

"A friend of Alexis's, and her and Amber's lawyer."

"Why do they need a lawyer?"

I walked over to look out the wide window next to Danielle's desk. The bright sun made the trees and flowers in the flower boxes below look especially colorful.

"They don't think their dad did this. I'm trying to learn as much as I can to prove that. I'm hoping you're willing to help. Maybe meet somewhere to talk."

"I don't mind talking. But I want to make sure you're who you say. I'll text Alexis. If she confirms, I'll call you back."

Before turning to other work, I texted Alexis to tell her about the call and ask if she had known Roy had her number. She said she hadn't, but maybe her mom had given it to him in case of an emergency with the dog.

I kept checking my phone to be sure I hadn't missed a call. After an hour, I went downstairs and sat outside at Café des Livres with an iced chai tea and my iPad. Being outside helped me feel less restless.

Roy called nearly an hour and a half after our first conversation. "Sorry, had to pick up a couple dogs. Is this about what I told the police? About what Santiago said?"

I wanted to see his face and body language, and I offered to meet him somewhere near his home or one of his dog walks. But his walks were nowhere near downtown. He mostly worked in neighborhoods near where Ivy had lived. There was no way I could get there within the next week.

Still, it was useful information. I noted the different locations he offered. I might want to see if I could catch him by surprise one day. Or at least observe him from a distance. For now, I had to be satisfied with quizzing him by phone.

"Can you tell me exactly what you told the police?"

"That Santiago said Ivy would get what was coming to her someday."

I heard dogs barking in the background as he spoke, some deep-throated, some high and yippy.

"And when was this?"

Roy told me Santiago said it when he was at the house loading boxes into his SUV. Things he hadn't taken when he first moved out. Ivy had asked Roy to come by and help because the dog might be upset by all the confusion.

"Wait, wait," I said. "I thought this statement was after the custody hearing."

"Right. That's what Ivy told me."

"Specifically that there had just been a custody hearing?"

"Uh...I think so. Or at least that Santiago was mad at her and it had something to do with custody of Alexis and the hearing."

"Hold on."

Four guys wearing baseball caps burst out of the café as I opened the docket sheet from the family law case on my iPad. The outdoor seating area was crowded. They squeezed around a table across from me. Scrolling through the online docket, I saw two hearings had taken place. One early on, when Ellison testified. The judge awarded Santiago custody soon after. Then at another hearing a few months ago, the judge entered an order changing visitation but not custody.

"Did this happen within the last few months?" I said.

"More like a year or so. Right after I started walking Ralph."

The State's Attorney had made it sound like Santiago said what he did after the recent hearing. I wondered whether the police officer who testified knew that the statement was made two years before or whether he had thought the timing was more recent.

"Did you tell the police that?"

"Maybe? I might have just said after the custody hearing. Or that it was about custody. I was pretty flipped out by it all."

"Did Santiago seem threatening to you? When he said something about Ivy getting what was coming to her?"

"Not really threatening. Mad. Like what you say to blow off steam? I told the police Ivy didn't seem like she was afraid of him."

I asked for his general impressions of Santiago. Roy said he'd only met him a couple times. And that Santiago didn't talk much with new people.

"Ivy said it made it hard for him to get to know people on his own," Roy said.

I shifted my iced chai to the part of the table that was in

the shade. The ice had nearly all melted. "How did that come up in conversation?"

"Huh. Not sure. Probably she was explaining why he seemed not very friendly."

"Did you walk Ralph every day for Ivy?"

"Every weekday or Saturday that she was at the store. She took Mondays off."

My fingers, wet with condensation from my glass, slipped on the iPad keys. I backspaced and typed another note. "And Santiago sometimes filled in for you?"

"A few times. But I'm almost always available except Sundays."

"A friend of Ivy's told me she used to leave the store to go home and walk the dog. Would that be when you were busy?"

"Oh. Sure, yeah, or if I was sick. She might've done that once in a while."

It didn't seem strange that Roy might need a day off now and then. But Ivy walking the dog herself on weekdays "once in a while" didn't quite fit with him being "almost always available."

Still, people aren't always as precise with words as lawyers push them to be. Or suggest to juries they would be if they weren't hiding something. So the word choices alone didn't concern me. But his voice pitched higher when he answered, and he paused before speaking. As if he had to think through his answers.

"How well did you know Ivy?"

"Mostly I don't see my clients. They're at work when I come to take the dogs out. I guess I got to know Ivy a little bit more than some others because Ralph was a lot to manage. Sometimes she asked me to come by when she was home. Like if she had a major project going or a lot of people over so that I could keep Ralph busy."

Roy confirmed what he had told the police about being out of town and then spending the weekend with his girl-friend. He seemed sincere when he told me to call anytime if I had any more questions.

After we hung up, I took a few more notes. I sent another text to Joe – we were still trying to find a time to meet.

Then I reviewed everything I had learned so far about Hank and Sylvania Brown. Tomorrow I was booked back-to-back with client calls and other legal work, but the following day I was driving to their house in Geneva.

26

Sylvania and Hank Brown's home was one of the smallest in its neighborhood and it sat between Geneva's Main Street and the Fox River. Three-story houses on either side of it featured turrets, wide wraparound porches, and wide expanses of lawn.

The side door, where Sylvania had told me to knock, led directly into a narrow kitchen. Appliances lined one long wall and a small four-seat table sat under a square window against the other. Gold and red tassels hung on either side of the doorway to the living room.

The small living room windows behind the overstuffed couch gave a view of the brick wall of the candle shop next door. The front picture window should have let in natural light. But the five-foot tall hedges all along the front walk blocked most of it.

A bulky armchair and ottoman that looked like they had been purchased for a much larger house sat in front of the front door. A person could squeeze behind it to get out, but it looked like a tight fit.

A heavy antique coffee table sat awkwardly beyond the

ottoman and in front of the sofa. A stairway led to the second floor, which Alexis had told me had only two bedrooms. I guessed the door in a corner of the living room led to the basement family room where Alexis slept on a pull out couch.

The air smelled of sage and vanilla, but the five pillar candles on the coffee table stood unlit. Eight or nine tinted crystals hung on thin chains from the ceiling in front of the picture window.

The oversized furnishings, small rooms, and low ceilings made me feel hemmed in the moment I entered the house. In the best of circumstances, I had to think Alexis would feel trapped here. I felt sure she'd be concerned for her dad no matter where she was living. But being in this cramped space with an aunt and uncle she felt didn't like her father must feel like torture.

I told Hank and Sylvania that I had stopped by the store and it seemed like a wonderful place.

Sylvania smiled and nodded. Her whole body, not only her head, drifted up and down. "We spent a lot building out the space."

"A big investment," I said.

Hank sat next to her, arms crossed and resting on his rounded belly. The two were a study in contrasts. His body language was stilted and his gestures small, almost as if he were inside an invisible box. He wore a red short-sleeved golf shirt loose over khaki pants. Ash-gray frosted his sideburns, thick mustache, and mousy brown hair. If I met him sepa-rately, I doubted I'd think him particularly overweight. More like stout. But next to his wife, who was lean and muscular, he appeared soft and stuffed into his clothes.

Sylvania's brown hair had coppery highlights and fell in waves around her shoulders. She wore a knee-length sleeve-less dress made of an almost felt-like material that moved fluidly with her body. When she talked, she gestured or swayed her whole body in ways that sometimes emphasized and sometimes contradicted her words.

It made me think of actors who work in large auditorium-type theaters. Unlike television or movies or the kinds of small theaters I had mostly worked in as a child actress, in a large theater the audience usually can't see the actors' faces, at least not very well. So instead you need to use your entire body to convey emotion.

Sylvania's bio on her yoga center site nowhere mentioned acting. Or dancing, which her body movements also suggested. She had mainly done yoga, energy healing, and chakra work.

"Oh, yes," she said. "To get the store rolling, Ivy dipped into her retirement and investment accounts from before she met Santiago. But we needed to borrow." Sylvania frowned and swept her right arm around, encompassing the whole room with one whip-like gesture. "And downsize."

Hank kept his arms clamped together over his stomach. "Worth it, though."

The downsizing explained the too-big furnishings in the crowded space. In addition to the frown, Sylvania's words suggested she wasn't sure it was worth it. Most people don't blurt out their finances to a stranger. I wondered if Sylvania and Hank had gained financially through Ivy's death.

"Sylvania, you seem —" I sorted through ways to say what I wanted to say without sounding insensitive. "– a little disturbed about that."

She tilted her head to one side. "I am, I am. It pales in comparison to Ivy's death, but it's still an issue."

Hank glanced sideways at her. "Honey."

"I don't mind who knows. When they formed the partnership, Ivy promised to make Hank a beneficiary of her IRA. He did the same for her. That way, if one of them outlived the other the remaining partner could buy out the estate. Keep the store running."

"Instead of buying life insurance on one another?" I said.

While I didn't help businesses get started, I was familiar with a lot of partnership contracts. I saw what happened afterwards when people didn't make solid agreements or plan for the future.

"Exactly. But what she didn't tell us is that there was next to nothing left in that IRA." Sylvania mimed turning over a container and shaking it. "She took it all out to finance her share."

Hank huffed. "I'm sure she thought the store would make money faster and she'd refill her IRA."

"Maybe." Sylvania waggled her hand back and forth. "But she ought to have told us that was her plan. Then we could have done the same. It wasn't fair."

I agreed with Sylvania. And withdrawing from an IRA struck me as an odd move for a finance person to make. With the tax penalties applied to money taken out early, I couldn't imagine why Ivy hadn't borrowed. Interest rates were low, so borrowing was far cheaper. Unless she had bad credit, something I planned to check.

I waited to see if Sylvania or Hank might volunteer anything else.

"It leaves us in difficult circumstances," she said.

"Not that difficult," Hank said.

Sylvania turned to stare at him. "We need to come up with cash or credit to buy out Ivy's share if you want to keep running the store. I call that difficult."

If true, it answered my question about whether they gained from Ivy's death. And suggested there was some reason for the store clerk's concern about the store closing.

I looked at Hank. "And do you? Want to?"

"It's always been my dream to run a business," Hank said.

"I worked in retail all through college. A lot of people don't enjoy it, but I did."

"My Gram works in a lighting store," I said. "Has for as long as I can remember. She really likes it."

"Hank and I need to talk more before doing anything." Sylvania's right hand opened and closed as if it were a puppet talking.

"Were you and Ivy close?" I asked her.

"Oh, yes." Her head didn't shake, but her neck swayed rhythmically from side-to-side. A movement much closer to a No than a Yes.

"But?"

"What do you mean, but?"

"You sort of shook your head no when I asked if you were close."

"Did I? I suppose – well – yes, we were. When my mother died, Ivy was there for me in a hundred ways that no one else thought of. Selling the car, tracking down the insurance – my mother must have had a dozen small life insurance policies, a thousand dollars each that she took out at different times. But there were times when Ivy – I don't like to criticize –"

Her head swiveled toward Hank. He patted her arm and said, "Ivy was a bit challenging."

Sylvania rolled her eyes.

When neither elaborated, I said, "I've heard she liked things her own way."

"Insisted on it," Hank said.

"And it worked." Sylvania's left index finger and middle finger tapped the air on each word. As if there were an invisible blackboard in front of her. "People gave her what she wanted. They might resent it but they did."

I looked at Hank. "Was that true at the store?"

Sylvania answered before her husband could. "I thought so. Hank didn't."

Hank shrugged, and his red shirt rode up for a second, threatening to expose his pale belly. "I was used to Ivy. How she did things."

I asked what he meant.

Hank said when they got press coverage, Ivy presented herself as "the owner." Also that Ivy tended to tell everyone she owned the store without mentioning Hank. I guessed that might be another reason Amber and Alexis also referred to it as their mother's store, never mentioning their uncle's involvement.

"Did you mind that?" I said.

Hank shook his head. "I don't love the spotlight. Ivy does – did. She did a lot of social media. Checked how many Likes she had. Got upset if there weren't enough. Reminded me of a teenager that way sometimes."

Sylvania pushed a lock of shiny hair behind her ear. "Well, it is important for a business to have a social media presence."

"Hank, are you older or younger than Ivy?" I said.

"Younger," Hank said. "By ten years."

I took a long drink of tea, a blend with too much peppermint for my taste. It also had gone cold, but it gave me a moment to consider all they'd told me. "Sylvania, you said people gave Ivy what she wanted. Like what?"

"Say you went to dinner with her." Sylvania mimed eating with the fork. "You never got to sit until she had been shown at least three different tables. Then once you sat down, Ivy always needed something special. If the waiter brought olive oil, she wanted olive oil with herbs in it. If it had herbs, she wanted lemon zest or fresh garlic. And she mostly got it."

Hank smiled, the first time he had. He turned his head toward his wife and nodded. "You're a bit like that, too, sweetheart."

"Nowhere near how Ivy was."

"True?" I said to Hank.

I doubted he'd say No, but thought he might hesitate. But he didn't. "Ivy took it to an extreme. It could be worrisome."

An interesting word choice.

"Worrisome how?"

Hank raised one finger halfway. "Now and then I worried if the waiters might be spitting in the food."

"Really?" I said.

"Not literally, I hope," Hank said. "But I bet they wanted to. She made their jobs harder. In my view, it's better to go with the flow a bit than make everyone do what you want them to do."

As he spoke, Sylvania made a wrapping motion with her hand, as if binding someone tightly.

I asked about the Sunday women's networking meeting. Sylvania gave me the names of the other three women there, glancing at the miniature grandfather clock on the wall as she did. It hung over a potted plant with stalks so tall and vines so unwieldly they almost blocked the clockface.

She also texted me their contact information, including that of the woman she thought might have sold Ivy the cleanse. Then she asked, "Is there much more you need?"

"Just quickly, the dog. Ralph. Alexis didn't want to keep him after Ivy's death?"

"She's not really close with Ralph," Sylvania said. "And I worried for our cat. Hank said it killed someone's pet rabbit."

I noticed the use of the pronoun "it" for Ralph and wondered if Sylvania disliked dogs.

"Could it have been a chicken?" I said.

"Hm." Her hands outlined the shape of a chicken. "Maybe."

"Her friend Ellison's?" I said.

Hank's chin bobbed almost imperceptibly. "That's probably right. I knew there was some incident when Ivy first got the dog, and that sounds right."

"But that's what dogs do, isn't it?" Sylvania said. "Kill rabbits and birds and such."

Not out-and-out against dogs then. Maybe just this one.

"Alexis also mentioned Ralph growled at people."

"Oh, yes," Sylvania said. "He growled. Especially at men. And whatever people tell you about their dog really being friendly, if a dog growls, it's warning you it'll attack soon if you don't back off. Still, I might have tried to take it in, but I don't see how we could keep a large dog here." She made a boxing gesture, as if squeezing Ralph into a tiny space. "We're too crammed in. My son's room barely fits his twin bed and his computer table, and poor Alexis is sleeping on a pullout in the basement family room."

She wasn't wrong about the space. If the other rooms were furnished this way, it wasn't a place for a large dog. The yard out back wasn't much more than a few feet of grass between the house and the vinyl-sided two-car garage.

Hank's eyes flicked toward the grandfather clock.

"One last question," I said. "Do you believe Santiago is the one who poisoned Ivy? Either of you?"

"Well, the police arrested him," Sylvania said.

"They wouldn't have done that without evidence," Hank said.

Two interesting non-answers. "Not everyone arrested is guilty."

"True." But Sylvania's shoulders raised in the faintest shrug.

And Hank said, "Most of them are."

"If Santiago did kill Ivy, any thoughts on why?"

Sylvania answered first. "We've talked about this, and it doesn't make sense if it's supposed to be a personal motive. Santiago's the one who wanted the divorce."

"But could be financially it was harder than he expected," Hank said. "Ivy was worth much more before the marriage, and my sister didn't like to share. She told me she kept her assets separate. And she handled all the money for the two of them, so could be he didn't know how bad off he'd be once they split."

"I thought Ivy didn't like handling money," I said.

"She didn't. That's why I did it for the store," Hank said. "But between the two of them, she knew more about it. So she managed the family finances."

I glanced at Sylvania. "And you're sure Santiago wanted the divorce, not Ivy?"

"She didn't want it. But after a while, she wasn't unhappy about it." Sylvania drew her fingers down the corners of her mouth as if making a sad face. "They were fighting a lot."

Hank stared at his wife. "Were they?"

"Oh, yes." She shifted her gaze back to me. "Ivy and I talked more than she and Hank did."

I glanced at Hank, and he nodded. "I'm not much of a talker, especially at work. I like to get things done, not talk about them."

I wasn't sure the two needed to be mutually exclusive, but apparently Hank thought so.

After thanking them again, I gathered my things and left. As I drove east toward the city, I deliberately turned my thoughts to the new case I had about chocolate chip brownies, hoping that if I let everything Hank and Sylvania told me percolate that later I'd spot something I had missed. Overall, I wasn't sure any of it helped Santiago's case.

When I got home, I called the woman who ran the cleanse. She didn't answer, but she texted me back late that evening and said she could talk by phone at ten the next morning. I had a pretty full schedule already, especially since

Ty and I were driving to Edwardsville Saturday to visit my parents, but I agreed.

I set my alarm for five-thirty a.m. and crawled into bed. I'm more of a morning than a late-night person, but that was early for me. But it was the only way I was likely to get everything done that I needed to do and still call Tammy at ten a.m.

27

An attorney I knew from law school had sent me the chocolate chip case in July. The plaintiff claimed she was deceived
by my client's ad about brownies made with "the chocolatiest
chips in Chicago," which she said was fraudulent. Supposedly, the plaintiff spent nearly a hundred dollars on brownies
before discovering that another bakery had chocolate chip
brownies that tasted more chocolaty. No one would sue for a
hundred dollars, but the consumer fraud law in Illinois
allows extra damages. I was working on a motion to dismiss
the entire case based on pretty strong Illinois Supreme Court
opinions that showed that this type of language was just
typical advertising language.

The motion was due by the end of the day. I shut off the
phone, ignored email, and worked on it for three hours
straight. Then I took a break to pick up tea and a chocolate
chip scone from the café downstairs, which tasted pretty
chocolaty, proofread the motion, and made my last changes
just before ten a.m.

After saving it in a separate folder where I kept only the
documents to upload to the court, I found a Linked In profile

for Tammy Solomon, the woman who might have sold Ivy the cleanse. In her profile photo she wore a navy blazer with padded shoulders almost, but not quite, as pronounced as the fashion had been for women in the eighties, and a striking garnet pendant around her neck. She made me think of the woman who ran the Tupperware parties my Gram brought me to as a kid.

"I was so sorry to hear about Ivy's death," Tammy said. Her voice was a low alto and sounded warm and caring. The type of voice that made you want to agree with her and listen to her.

"The police talked to you about it?" I said.

"Oh, yes. They wanted to know all about our meeting that Sunday."

I asked her to tell me about it. Especially about anyone who had left the family room that afternoon. But she didn't think anyone had, other than for less than five minutes to use the restroom.

"Would you notice if anyone left or for how long?" I said. "If everyone was just talking?"

Tammy laughed. "You've never been to one of Ivy's meetings. Each person had ten minutes to highlight a particular month's actions toward our goals. Then we went around and gave ten-minute sales pitches."

"To sell one another things?" That seemed like a business model that would wear out quickly.

"Well, that was nice if it happened. But no, mostly to practice. Because each person got feedback on the pitches. Then we discussed whatever sales or marketing book we were reading together."

I wrote notes on the meeting structure. "And you're sure no one left for more than five minutes because...?"

"I don't remember anyone leaving at all. But it couldn't have been for more than a few minutes if anyone did. Ivy insisted everyone be there for every part of the meeting. It was only fair. Otherwise maybe I'd give my pitch, then disappear while the next two people gave theirs."

"Was that a problem?" I said.

"It happened with a new member here and there. I'm making it sound very rigid, but really, it did help keep things friendly and fair. Everyone agreed to the rules when they joined. So if someone interrupted or tried to duck out on giving feedback, you could just remind them of the rules they agreed to.

"So if someone left to use the restroom, everything stopped?"

"Right. It made it very noticeable if you were gone."

I tapped my fingers on my notepad. The meeting had seemed like such a good possibility to show other people had access to Ivy's kitchen. Yet it seemed unlikely anyone could go upstairs, go through Ivy's refrigerator and poison her food, and get downstairs again, let alone trek to the garage for antifreeze, without a noticeable absence. And without anyone hearing doors slamming. Especially with a Doberman around.

It was possible if a person brought antifreeze in a hidden container, knew in advance which food to poison, and was very, very good at moving silently. But that was a lot of Ifs.

I asked Tammy if she had sold a cleanse to Ivy.

"I did. Though it's been a few years."

My shoulders sagged. It didn't seem likely that Tammy had sold Ivy the cleanse she was doing after all. But when I asked, Tammy said she was sure it was.

"I took this intentional eating course and got certified about five years ago. I want to say I met Ivy two years later, right after I started doing classes on intentional eating at Sylvania's studio."

I swiveled my chair away from my laptop screen. "And Ivy

bought a cleanse from you? Or participated in one? I don't know how it works."

"Bought and participated. You get recipes when you take part, plus a launch day video chat with me and everyone else who participates. Then there's an online forum and I send daily emails to encourage people. Plus we have check ins, especially if someone does a two-week cleanse to see how it's going. I run three of them a year. Spring, summer, and fall. I don't do winter because I feel like it's a tough season in the Chicago area and people are better off just eating their regular diets."

"Do the cleanses change every year?"

"They change every season and there's a significant update every couple years. I have customers who buy every new one that comes out. But you can just keep using that first set of recipes on your own if you want."

"And that's what you think Ivy did?"

"Most likely. We had a bit of an issue over it."

"What sort of issue?" I flipped over a new page on my legal pad. It seemed everyone I met had some sort of problem with Ivy. Making it stranger that the police honed in on Santiago.

"I don't mind telling you. I'm kind of wondering why you're asking though." A note of wariness had crept into Tammy's voice. I was used to that, and I understood it. People are rarely excited about talking with attorneys, especially ones who handle lawsuits.

"I'm not thinking there's anything wrong with the cleanse," I said. "Or suspecting you of something. I'm not sure the cleanse matters. But I'm finding it odd that the police think Santiago poisoned Ivy's food when she was on a cleanse that might very well be about not eating. It might be a way to poke holes in the theory that he had this grand plan to poison her."

"Well, if she did the cleanse she bought from me, there is eating at a certain point. All of the ones I sell start with two days of fasting. Liquids only. Then you move toward certain kinds of juices. After that it varies, but there is solid food after about five days."

"Is there anything that looks like a bright green vegetable, or fruit I guess it could be, puree?"

"I don't think so. Hold on." I heard a clicking key in the background. While I waited, I proofread a paragraph of my motion.

Tammy spoke a few moments later. "Okay, I found the ones from the year Ivy bought hers. There's sweet potato soup, but that wouldn't be green. Also, the recommendation is to have all the fruits and vegetables whole past the juice phase. That way you get all the fiber which helps fill you up."

"And the issue?"

"I suppose there's no harm in telling you. I feel sort of bad with her dead. It doesn't paint her in a great light and she can't respond. Though it also wasn't terrible."

"If it makes you feel better, a lot of people seem to have had conflicts with Ivy."

"All right." I heard an intake of breath on the other end of the line. "She bought the first cleanse from me. Then she proposed that she could modify it so it was better suited to a vegan diet. The ones I sell add dairy and animal products back in at the very end. So when vegans sign up, or vegetarians, I tell them to leave off those days."

"And Ivy had a better idea?"

"A different one. She wanted to modify it so it was all vegan, then sell it through her website and later her store. I jumped through a lot of hoops to get that okayed. I buy the cleanses through a vendor. Whatever I sell has to comply with its rules and branding. But I thought I could work with Ivy and open a whole new market."

"I take it teaming with Ivy didn't work out?"

"Hardly. A month later, Ivy said she couldn't figure out how to make the cleanse vegan and be true to its goals. About six months after that, though, one of my customers saw a video Ivy did about a vegan cleanse. She modified everything so it wasn't quite copying. But it was close enough that my customer recognized it. Which put me in some hot water with my vendor."

"Was there legal action?"

"In the end, they let it go. It's a pretty small company. I talked with the owner and we both agreed better to focus on our business instead of some lawsuit that might go nowhere."

"As a litigator I'll tell you that was probably a wise choice. Though it's good for me that not everyone thinks that way."

Tammy laughed. It was a deep, relaxed sort of laugh that made me smile as well. "I'm sure. And if everyone just ate sensibly, I'd probably be out my side hustle. So was anything I told you helpful?"

"Maybe," I said. "Except it's creating more work for me. I think I need to watch more of Ivy's food videos."

"Better you than me. Even two years ago there were a lot of them."

I thanked her, hung up, and went back to my legal work. My motion got filed within the hour, but I had work on three other cases to finish today and I still needed to pack for the visit to my parents. I had meant to do it earlier in the week but just hadn't gotten to it.

At ten p.m., my small travel bag packed, I sat at my kitchen counter and watched Ivy's online videos, zeroing in on those that related to diet or eating. First, I watched the ones from the year she'd bought the cleanse and found nothing that seemed particularly enlightening. I switched to three months before her death.

At midnight, I finally had something that might help Santiago.

~

Fortunately, Danielle usually came to the office Saturday mornings to catch up on all the work she didn't get to when she ran – or drove – from courtroom to courtroom and courthouse to courthouse during the week. Around nine-thirty a.m. she met me at the café. I got a dark hot chocolate despite the hot weather. After so little sleep and so much work, and because I anticipated a day and a half of catering to my mother while dodging her criticisms, I needed a treat.

We settled at a wrought iron table near the planters that separated the seating area from Dearborn Street's bicycle lane. A kid on a racing bike sped by as I shifted my chair so its back legs weren't on a grate.

Danielle set her café au lait on the table and dropped into the chair across from me. "Okay. Got my coffee. What's your news?"

I inhaled the rich, dark chocolate scent from my bone china mug. "What if the killer wasn't trying to poison Ivy, but the dog?"

"Come again?"

"One of Ivy's videos, a couple of them actually, show her making this vegan food for dogs. It looks like what you described. Kind of a bright green slop of mixed vegetables plus some vitamins and protein powder specifically made for dogs. She says it's something to drizzle on top of vegan dog food."

"Huh." Danielle rested her elbows on the table, making it rock toward her. "So you're thinking someone broke into her home to poison the dog? Why?"

"No one I talked to feels comfortable around the dog. Her

neighbor, Ellison, doesn't want Ralph loose in the yard because he killed her chicken. Sylvania and Hank didn't even consider letting Alexis bring the dog with her. And Alexis didn't want to."

"So the girl doesn't like dogs, and her uncle and aunt don't see any reason to take it in if she doesn't."

"But think of all the loss Alexis suffered. Her mom's dead, her dad's in prison, she can't go live in either of the homes she knows. Her sister's away at school. And she doesn't even want to hang on to her mom's pet? That's got to be a pretty awful dog."

Danielle sipped her café au lait and wiped her mouth with a napkin. "I see your point."

"Plus, the dog supposedly growled at nearly everyone. What if it attacked somebody or hurt somebody and they're really angry?"

"Let's say the dog's the target. It doesn't help Santiago. He's still the only one the police know of who was in Ivy's home."

I twisted a thick section of my hair around my finger, a habit I've been trying to break, as I told her my theory that there was more than one passageway between floors.

"Maybe," she said.

"Also, if the dog's the target it expands who had a motive. You said motives can drive investigations. It could persuade the police to look a little harder at other suspects. Plus, wouldn't it be easier to convince the police or a jury that Ivy might have made that food well in advance for the dog? And be more careless about serving spoiled food to the dog than her child? So it further expands the amount of time someone could've come in and poisoned the food."

Danielle drummed her fingers on the table. "It's worth exploring. I'm not trying to discourage you. But keep in mind, the prosecution might just argue Santiago did it and aimed to kill the dog."

"That's not better?" Even as I said it, my criminal law professor's voice chided me in the back of my head. Under the law, it's the intent to do the act that matters.

Danielle picked up on my thought. "It's not a defense to first-degree murder if you meant to kill the dog, but you killed your wife instead. You still committed murder because you intentionally did something that could – and did – kill a human being."

My phone, sitting face down on the table, buzzed. "Would it at least help with sentencing? Not that we ever want it to get there."

"Depends on the judge. Like everything. Some of them, yeah, it wouldn't seem as bad to try to kill a dog. But you get a judge who's a dog lover or feels strongly about cruelty to animals, could have the opposite effect."

"Amber and Alexis might feel better if their dad tried to kill the dog and not Ivy, though," I said.

But probably not much better, as he would still have done it.

I glanced at the phone. The buzzing had been a text from Ty saying he could be ready to leave for Edwardsville by eleven. He'd been out of town on business the last two days and had flown home late last night. I told him eleven was perfect. After Danielle left, I drank more of my hot cocoa, studied the blooming flowers in the boxes around the seating area, and told myself a weekend away might help me get a new perspective on Santiago's case.

Plus with Ty there to take my mom's attention, I might get to visit with my dad more than I usually did.

28

I poured my mother some more water and sat in the wide wooden chair next to her. Bright white, yellow, and pink flowers piled on the covered fire pit.

"So I got this new case," I said. "It's about chocolate chip brownies. Like those giant ones you like from the bakery."

The sound of a fiddle and my dad's flatpicking wove in between the thumping of a stand-up acoustic bass and steady rhythm guitar chords. Dad and three of his friends played old-time country and folk music at local venues and parties. Today they were entertaining us in the yard despite the heat and humidity, making the weekend feel a bit festive.

My mother sipped the water and handed it back. "This is warm. I hate warm water. You know that."

The glass felt cool to my touch, and icy condensation coated the sides. But I took it back to the long folding table along the garage where plastic tumblers, plates, and picnic food was spread out. Dealing with my mother became easier for me when, a few years back, I decided to think of her the same way I handled difficult, demanding clients. Do what I could to respond to their demands because it's my job, but don't take it personally and don't expect a thank you. Or any response other than more demands.

Of course, with clients I get paid. And now that I work for myself, I can refuse to represent them if it becomes intolerable.

As I returned with fresh ice water, the musicians segued from the Wabash Cannonball to another instrumental. Not my type of music, but my mother was tapping her feet, something I rarely saw.

Ty must have noticed my mother's tapping, too. He stood and held out his hand to her.

"Can I persuade you to dance, Mrs. Davis?" Ty said.

"You barn dance?" I said to Ty.

"I have many skills you've yet to learn about." Ty's hand hung in the air as my mother studied him.

"Nothing surprises me," I said.

But at that moment, my mother did. She took Ty's hand.

They danced across the side yard below the clothesline and around the metal swing set with its lone tire swing. It took my mom a few minutes to get into the swing of things. But soon her blond hair flew out, shiny and long, in the sun, and she spun and hopped. It was the liveliest I'd ever seen her.

My dad stepped away from the other three musicians, leaving them to carry the tune. He made us two whiskey sours just the way I like them with fresh-squeezed lemon juice, rye whiskey, and egg white, and joined me near the firepit.

I leaned close so he could hear over the music. "I didn't know Mom liked to dance."

"We used to go to barn dances all the time. Before – before you were born."

I nodded. Before meant before the original Q.C. Davis had been kidnapped and later killed. For all that memories of her were everywhere when I was growing up, the words kidnapped, died, and killed were almost never spoken.

"It's nice to see her enjoy something," I said.

"The new medication is perking her up."

"I hope it lasts," I said.

Over the years, my mother tried a lot of anti-depressant and anti-anxiety medications. It was hard to get the right mix. Some helped for a while, then didn't. Others seemed to do nothing. This was the most animated I'd seen her, so maybe the doctors had found a good combination.

After two more dances, my mom said she needed a rest. She sat again. The ice had melted in her water, but as I stood to get her more, Ty took my hand.

"Can your band play a waltz, Mr. Davis?" Ty said. "So I can dance with Quille, too? I hear she's not a barn dance fan."

Dad laughed and stood. "First my wife, then my daughter. You're quite a hit in this family." He picked up his guitar and glanced at my mother. "Tennessee Waltz?"

She shocked me again by standing to one side of the musicians. After the introduction, she started singing. She had a low, throaty alto, completely different from my own light soprano. I hadn't heard it in years.

Ty held me close as we moved one, two-three, one, two-three barefoot in the grass. I couldn't help myself. I sang the harmony on the chorus.

"You sound great together," Ty said when we sat down again.

"We should. Lots of practice."

My mother and I had sung this song over and over when I was a kid learning harmony singing.

My mother smiled. "Years of voice coaching. Q.C. – Quille was quick at it. Almost as good as my Q.C. It's a shame she doesn't sing anymore."

Ty's eyebrows rose. "She sings all the time. Haven't you heard her trio?"

My mother brushed wisps of bangs out of her eyes. "They never take any jobs around here."

"It's hard for all three of us to get away at once," I said. "We mostly stick to the Chicago area."

My mother leaned toward Ty and lowered her voice. "And Quille refuses to do musicals anymore. That's where you should have heard her." She tilted her head toward me, her chin pointing. "I don't know why you stopped."

"We've talked about this, Mom."

She waved her hand. "Oh, therapy talk. What good has it ever done anyone? Dwelling on the past."

I refrained from pointing out that given the sheer number of photos of the original Q.C. framed throughout the house, including a three foot by four foot blow up over the television, she was no one to complain about anyone else dwelling on the past. It was one of many points my therapist had helped me let go of.

At dinner, we ate outside on the wide patio in front of Foundry Public House on Main Street. As Ty and Dad dug into the smoked chicken thighs for an appetizer, Dad asked more about Ty's childhood. My mother picked at a mini grilled cheese sandwich and actually listened to Ty's stories about his first years in Minneapolis. Like me, though for different reasons, he felt he didn't belong as a kid. The other middle school students made fun of his accent and quite a few had never seen anyone Black before in person. But unlike me, Ty had a grand time winning everyone over. Or at least he made it sound that way.

"Then there was the first time it snowed," he said. "My youngest sister and I stared out the front picture window at these white flakes coming down. She ran through the house to the back door, opened it and said, 'It's happening back here too!'"

My mother laughed. In the late evening sunlight, her face looked full and her fair skin more like the peaches and cream complexion I saw in old photos of her and the original Q.C.

That alone told me how much the medication was helping. When she went through periods of depression, which happened often when I was little, she looked gaunt and chalky, her hair lanky and oily. I hoped this new phase would last.

We were finishing shared flatbreads when my phone rang. It was Alexis. I stepped out of the seating area and stood near the curb. Unlike main streets in Chicago, the air here smelled of freshly mowed grass from the lawn of the courthouse across the street. And despite it being Saturday night, parking spots still stood open, and I had no trouble hearing Alexis on the phone. No rush of traffic and honking horns as there would have been at home.

"What did you do?" Alexis said, her voice choked. "What did you say?"

"Alexis? What happened?"

"My dad's pleading guilty. Because of what you found. He's pleading guilty."

29

"Alexis, I didn't find anything that pointed to your dad." I crossed the street and sat on a bench in front of the courthouse. A three-story rectangular marble building, it gives the entire area a stately look. "Is this something your aunt or uncle told you? Maybe they misunderstood."

"I talked to my dad himself. How could you do this to us? You said you were going to help."

"I'll talk to Danielle. We'll figure this out. I promise," I said.

"What's to figure out?"

I did my best to calm her down. As soon as we hung up, I called Danielle, then texted, then stood and walked to the end of the block, hoping for an answer. I stopped in the middle of the sidewalk when it came.

Sorry. With Viv. Didn't know S had decided anything. But will go over what I can with you tomorrow. It'll be ok.

"Okay for who?" I said to the phone, then jammed it into my purse. At least it explained why Danielle hadn't given me or Alexis a heads up.

"Hey." Ty wrapped his arms around me from behind.

With my focus on the phone, I hadn't heard or seen him approach. Something my instructor would chide me for. I leaned into him.

He rested his chin on the top of my head. "What's going on?"

I told him, and we walked together toward the other end of the block, hands linked.

"And Danielle's not calling you back?"

"Saturday nights with her daughter are sacred when she can get them. I'm surprised she even had the phone on. I just don't understand how this could have happened."

"How can I help?" Ty said.

We crossed the street and paused in front of a closed flower shop a half block from the restaurant. "I'm not sure you can. Other than what you're already doing. My mom loves you. It gives me a chance to breathe."

He smiled. "I'm glad. On both counts. I sort of like you breathing."

He kissed my forehead, and we rejoined my parents. The dinner plates had been cleared, and brightly colored, laminated dessert menus sat in their place.

My mother looked up from sipping her drink. "It's about time. I want to order dessert."

"Everything okay?" my dad said as Ty and I took our seats again.

"It's this case I'm working on. My client's mom died, and her dad's accused of murder. He's planning to plead guilty."

"You're representing a killer?" My mother turned toward me, her elbow knocking into her glass of cranberry-apple juice and seltzer.

I grabbed the glass before it tipped over. "I don't represent him. Also, I don't believe he's a killer."

My dad wiped the splash of fizzy red liquid that had gotten onto the table. "But he confessed?"

"He's thinking about a plea bargain. It's not the same thing."

"Does he have to confess as part of it?" Ty asked.

"I'm not sure. I'll need to ask Danielle."

"Why would he confess if he didn't do it?" my mother said.

"Lots of reasons. To get out of prison for one."

Alexis hadn't had many details, but I'd gathered that Santiago could be out of jail in a few months. Which told me whatever charge he was pleading to, it wasn't first-degree murder. That has a minimum sentence of twenty years in Illinois.

"And you're in favor of that? For a murderer?" My mother glared at me, her jaw clenched.

"I'm not in favor of any of it."

My mother ought to be the last person to assume anyone was guilty. Gram had told me the police focused on her and my dad for months after Q.C.'s disappearance. It was part of why they moved away from Edwardsville after I was born. Because no one ever believed they hadn't been involved in her death.

My mother sucked down what was left of her drink, as if it were alcohol and she needed it. "You should be concerned about his victim, not him."

"I'm doing this for the victims," I said. "For Ivy and her daughters. They've already lost their mother. They can't lose their dad too."

Dad moved his dessert menu aside. "You said he could get out of jail soon. If that's true, they won't lose their dad. He'll be there for them. Isn't that better? Whether his daughters think so or not?"

"Maybe," I said. "But I can't imagine they're letting him plead to a misdemeanor. Which means he'll be a felon. It won't be easy to support his daughters."

Most employers won't hire felons. It's part of the cycle of crime leading to more crime that Danielle sees all the time. It also leaves some of her clients homeless, as felons can't live in public housing or get housing assistance and private landlords aren't lining up to rent to them. And anyone convicted of any drug offense, felony or misdemeanor, can't get federal student grants or loans.

I checked my phone again, on the off chance Danielle might have texted a little more information. But there was nothing.

"How much are these girls paying you?" My mother's blue eyes, lighter and larger than mine, bored into me.

"I'm not charging them. If there's a recovery the other attorney will get some fees if he ends up helping out. But I'm doing it as a favor."

Mensa Sam had surprised me and agreed to only take a fee if he did significant trial work or preparation for trial.

She held her head and body still, as if poised for flight or attack. "Charity begins at home."

The waiter approached but, hearing my mother's tone of voice, veered to another table.

It was good my mother had more energy these days. But she was easier to deal with in some ways when she was feeling blue. At least then I knew what to say to her. Now I had no idea what was setting her off. I couldn't remember the last time she asked anything about my work. Or about me, for that matter.

"What's this about?" I said.

My mother shrugged and sucked her cranberry drink through a straw. I was sure she was waiting for me to wheedle out of her what had upset her. But after spending decades twisting myself in all directions to try to make her happy, I no longer wanted to take the bait.

I waved to the waiter and told him we wanted to order dessert.

Ty, though, didn't grow up with my mother. He also came from a healthier family that faced their feelings. After the waiter took down our orders and walked away, he asked my mother if there was something she wanted to talk about.

"Yes," my mother said. "Quille investigates all these crimes for strangers. But she's never investigated her own sister's death. I want to know why that is."

30

My mouth dropped open. It took me a second to recover. "You want me to investigate the real – the original – Q.C.'s death?"

"She's your family. It's like you've forgotten her."

"I can hardly forget her, Mom. You gave me her name."

"A name you don't use." She pointed her straw toward me. "All I hear from you is Quille Quille Quille Quille."

Ty gave me an apologetic look.

"I prefer Quille. Which is still her name, by the way."

It wasn't a new conversation for us, despite my mother acting like it was. But her wanting me to investigate was new. And curious. I'd grown up hearing tales of the amazing and fabulously talented Q.C. Davis, but what little I knew about the kidnapping and her death came from my Gram.

The waiter set our desserts down. A brownie a la mode for Ty and me, cheesecake for my dad, and a scoop of vanilla ice cream with caramel sauce for my mother.

My mother dipped her spoon into the caramel sauce, skimming it off the top of the ice cream. "All I want is for you to show a little concern for your sister. Maybe look into her death, rather than doing these investigations for other people."

"Investigate – really?"

I'm not a gambler. I work too hard for my money to find losing it fun. But before this conversation, given the chance, I would have bet my monthly mortgage payment that my mother had no idea I helped uncover the truth behind Marco's death, found a missing college student last year, or caught the perpetrator of a vehicular homicide.

Dad placed his hand over my mother's. "It's too dangerous. We've talked about this."

Now my dad had shocked me. I stared at him. "You have?"

"I don't want you looking for a killer," he said.

"He's probably dead," my mother said. "All I want is answers. Peace. No one ever looked into anyone but us. How could they find the truth?"

The ice cream on my brownie had melted all over the plate, and I hadn't touched it. "But the FBI took the focus off you, didn't they?"

"And got nowhere," my mother said.

"It was too late." My dad rubbed his forehead. "At least I think so. They only broadened the investigation after that other poor girl was found and they couldn't link it to us. That's when they stopped seeing us as the main suspects. But not before."

"I'm so sorry," Ty said. "That had to be awful."

My mother's fingers twirled a section of her long, straight hair. "So why haven't you ever tried to find the truth?"

"It never crossed my mind you wanted me to," I said.

"We don't," Dad said.

"You could try," my mother said.

31

"Are you thinking about it?" Ty said. We were in my parents' yard again. Dusk had fallen and cicadas up in the trees started singing.

Ty turned the long serving table from our backyard lunch earlier in the day on its side. When we got home from the restaurant, we'd volunteered to clean up the yard. My parents were inside getting ready for bed.

I folded down the metal table legs. "No. The crimes I've looked into, they've been recent. And personal. My acting skills, my lawyer skills, helped me ask questions. Get people to talk to me. But this -- whoever killed Q.C. could be someone none of us knows. And it's been so long. It's not like I know forensics. Or statistics or crime patterns. Whatever experts use on cold cases. It's almost impossible I could learn anything the FBI didn't thirty-four years ago."

Cricket chirps had joined the cicadas. Ty gathered the plastic tumblers and we headed toward the house. "You never thought before about looking at your sister's case? Not that I want you to, whatever your mother says."

I opened the back door for him. "I did a paper on it in

college. Sort of. It was about kidnapping cases in general. But I used my family story as a window into it. That's when I learned more about the real – the original Q.C. Davis. And started therapy."

My parents wash and reuse plastic plates, cups, and utensils. In the kitchen, Ty turned on the hot water and let it run. My parents' house has old pipes that groan. And take a while to warm up.

I set the plates under the cold spray.

"Well, I'm sorry for your parents," Ty squeezed the liquid detergent. A soapy, lemony scent filled the air. "But whoever did that to your sister and that other little girl is a serial killer. It's selfish, but I'm happy you want to stay far away from it."

"I'm good with you being selfish."

"So what was Q.C. the first really like? Did you ever find out?" Ty said. "Other than the perfect child who never disobeyed and won every contest she entered?"

"Saw the photos up and down the hallway, huh?"

"It's hard to miss them. Were those everywhere when you were growing up?"

"Oh, yeah." I dried one of the plates he'd rinsed. "On the hall right outside my room. It was part of why I liked Gram's apartment better. She had photos of all of us, not just bouncy, cute, blond Q.C. Mom was so disappointed I didn't look anything like her."

"You're not exactly not cute, Quille."

"No, but no one's going to call me blond and bouncy. Or blue-eyed and chubby cheeked."

In the few baby photos of me that existed I stared at the camera with a serious expression. Skinny, dark-haired, and with an olive complexion, even as a toddler I looked much more like my dad than my mom. My hair, like his, sprayed out all over in messy curls until I grew it long and learned which products could ease it into waves.

But, like Q.C., I could sing. If I hadn't been able to, I wasn't sure my mother would have made it out of bed to spend any time with me at all.

I glanced at my phone. Still nothing from Danielle.

Ty handed me another plastic plate to dry. "Not much chance for you to be a regular kid. Is that why you don't want children?"

I set the plate in the stack on the counter. "I never said I actively don't want them."

"But you don't actively want them."

"You said you were okay with that. Are you rethinking?"

He shut off the water and turned toward me. "Nope. Life can be amazing in a hundred different ways. Only one of them is having kids."

"But if it were just up to you?"

"It never would be. It takes two to have kids."

"But if it were?"

He kissed my forehead. "Okay, counselor. If it were up to me and only me, I think I'm a little on the other side of you. I can be happy either way but probably lean toward kids. But I told you. Not a deal breaker."

I leaned into him. He smelled of the outdoors – trees and flowers and a little bug spray. Like camping or hiking or running through the woods.

"Good."

A little after nine the next morning, as I sat at the white wood table in my parents' enclosed sun porch, I got a text from Danielle. She apologized for not answering sooner. Her ex had stayed over – they had a very friendly divorce – but she said she could call me later in the morning.

My dad had insisted on making chocolate chip pancakes,

a favorite of mine. It made the whole first floor smell of maple syrup and dark chocolate. Unfortunately, it also reminded me of the work left to do on my chocolate chip case.

I drank some orange juice and asked my mom if she had been serious about wanting me to investigate Q.C.'s death.

She shook her head. "I was in a bad mood. Hearing about that woman killed, it brought too much back. I don't need to reopen old wounds. And it's ridiculous to think you could find anything. You're not a real detective."

"I'm not," I said.

Ty and I left around ten. Ty drove so I could talk on the phone. I stared at the miles of cornfields as we rolled past. I love Chicago with its beautiful buildings and the energy I feel when I walk the streets. But I also find the expanse of flat ground, blue sky, and golden corn fields on the drive back soothing.

Danielle called around eleven.

"Why didn't you tell me Santiago's planning to plea bargain?" I said. "Alexis is devastated."

"First, hello, good morning. Second, remember the conversation we had? Santiago's my client. Not his daughters."

"But –"

"And my conversations with him are confidential."

"Alexis already told me about this, so it's not anymore." The car jolted as we went over a pothole. "And I'm sorry. Good morning."

"Look, there are a few things I can tell you. The first is nothing is set in stone. The State's Attorney made an offer. Which I conveyed, as I'm required to do. But it's not a great offer. Not yet anyway."

"Alexis seemed to think Santiago's all ready to plead." I

buzzed the window down to get some fresh air. Warm wind washed over me along with the smell of fertilizer.

"He's ready to get out of jail. I'm hoping we'll get to a deal that's acceptable."

"How can it be acceptable that he pleads guilty to something he didn't do?"

I probably sounded as unreasonable to her as my mother did to me. But I felt tired and worried.

"If I can get it down to reckless homicide, it might be. That's up to Santiago. Not to me or you or his daughters. I feel for them, and I know how much you want to help them. But it's his decision."

"Reckless homicide is still a felony, isn't it?"

"But it's not murder."

"I'm not sure Alexis and Amber will appreciate the distinction."

"I bet they'll appreciate the distinction between probation plus time served and their dad being in prison for the next twenty years or more."

I rested my head back against the headrest. Danielle wasn't wrong. But I couldn't stop hearing Alexis' anguished voice. I didn't know if she could handle her dad admitting to killing her mom no matter what the prosecutor called the crime.

"What's the justification for reckless homicide?" I said.

"The theory is that he was trying to poison the dog and had no idea his wife ever ate the same food."

I squeezed my eyes shut. "So what I found triggered this."

In the video that I forwarded to Danielle, Ivy demonstrated blending five different vegetables and protein powder and vitamins. She made it into a paste that she layered with pretty swirls on top of the vegan dog food. It was meant to be a treat for the dog. But she showed how humans could eat it too. She filled a bowl of it for herself and ate it on camera. The video was titled Share a Meal with Your Beloved Friend.

"Quille, this is a good thing. First-degree murder has a twenty-year minimum sentence. Minimum. Santiago would have to serve 100% of that. And he could be sentenced to far longer. To life."

"But what about the expanded time window for the poison? And that more people with motives to kill the dog than Ivy means more suspects. Doesn't all of that create reasonable doubt?"

"Sure, it all means a bigger chance a jury will find reasonable doubt. The Assistant State's Attorney recognized that. That's why there's an offer. Which right now is second degree and seven years at eighty-five percent."

I did quick math in my head. "He'd serve almost six years. You're not considering that?"

"Minus time served. But I doubt Santiago would accept that. Like I said, we're negotiating."

"But it's a good chance of a Not Guilty. Don't you think? You only need to convince one juror," I said.

Juries in Illinois have to be unanimous.

"Sounds good in theory," Danielle said. "But let's say I get it down to reckless homicide. And there's, say, a one in one thousand chance of spending twenty, thirty, or forty years behind bars versus getting out in three months for certain. What would you do?"

I knew she was right. As I said, I'm not a gambler.

32

My face felt hot and sweaty. I hit the button to close the window and leaned toward the air conditioning vent. "I'd take the deal."

"Almost anyone would," Danielle said. "That's what you need to explain to Alexis if it comes to that. And Amber."

"As a felon, will he get his job back?"

"It's tough with a violent felony. But given his employment history, he might. Or he might get hired elsewhere. Depends on the company policy."

That made me feel better about Santiago's prospects. And worse about stopping at truck stops when taking long drives.

"Also, he's for sure got a better chance of supporting his girls out of prison than in. You did a good thing, Quille. Your work was key."

"But not so key the State's Attorney will drop the charges."

"No, but I never expected that."

I pulled the phone from my ear and stared at it for a second. "You didn't? I did."

Her sigh came clearly through the phone. "Because you want to find truth. Crusade for justice. I get that. But my job is to defend my client and help him figure out what makes the most sense. I'd go to trial in a heartbeat on these facts, and who knows what else we might find with a little more time. It's a very triable case, and I told Santiago that. But I'm not the one who spends life behind bars if we lose. And neither are you."

I chewed my lower lip. "What if I find something more after he pleads guilty? Something that makes it clear he didn't do it? Can you get the plea set aside? Or expunged?"

"Possible but not likely. Once there's a plea of guilty you need to prove actual innocence, not just raise a reasonable doubt. Doesn't happen too often."

"But there was that guy in the news last week –"

"I'm going to stop you right there. Unless Santiago's best buddies with the president and hasn't thought to mention it, forget it. When you plead guilty you state in open court, for the record, that you understand the charges, you've been advised by your attorney, and you've chosen to plead guilty while understanding all the consequences. There're no do overs. Not for regular people."

Ty tapped my arm and motioned toward square blue signs showing gas stations and food. I nodded. I wasn't hungry, but stretching my legs might help clear my head.

"You said you're negotiating," I said to Danielle. "How long will that take?"

"Hard to say. I haven't dealt with this particular ASA before. My best guess – in three or four weeks we could be in court."

"So I need to find something before then."

"If the girls want you to try, I can't stop you. But be careful, Quille. Until a plea is entered and the court accepts it, the State's Attorney can still back out. Don't do anything that will make him change his mind."

33

Monday the temperature skyrocketed to ninety-five degrees, with the humidity at eighty-five percent. Inside the Daley Center courtroom, the air conditioning struggled to keep pace. A few strands of hair stuck to the side of my face and I brushed them away and kept talking.

"In short, your honor, this type of claim is exactly what the Illinois Supreme Court ruled in *Barbara's Sales* doesn't rise to the level of fraud," I said. "There, the defendant said its computer chip was the best and fastest. The court found that's not a specific factual claim. It's like saying you serve the best cheesecake ever. Or, as here, that my client bakes the chocolatiest chocolate chip brownies in Chicago. It's not the kind of statement that the Illinois Consumer Fraud Act prohibits."

The judge glanced at my opposing counsel, a young guy in a gray suit and narrow tie whose pants legs were a little too short.

"Any further response, counsel?"

"No, Judge. Just what I already argued. That chocolatiest

is specific. It's something that can be determined. In a contest, for example."

The judge glanced at me. I shook my head. I had already covered that argument and, unlike the lawyer on the other side, I didn't think the judge needed repetition to get it.

The judge gathered the pages in front of him into a stack and squared them against the side of the bench, making a clunking sound that echoed over the microphone. "All right. I read the briefs. I've heard your arguments. Ms. Davis, I'm inclined to agree that chocolatiest chip is not enough."

I suppressed a sigh. This judge always started by naming the good points made by the side he planned to rule against in the end.

"But at this stage of the case, if the plaintiff can allege any set of facts that might entitle him to relief, I have to let the case go forward," the judge said. "He hasn't done so yet, but I'll give him a chance to fix that. The complaint is dismissed without prejudice. Plaintiff has thirty days to file a second amended complaint. Twenty-one days to respond."

I let out my breath. Given how the judge had started, this was better than I expected. The judge agreed with me that the lawsuit as is wasn't enough. So now the plaintiff could try to add new facts, if he had any, that showed my client said something fraudulent. It wasn't an outright win for me, but it was better than a loss.

After how much I'd disappointed Alexis, I'd take whatever win I could get on any front.

"Do you have any other facts?" I asked the other lawyer as we exited the courtroom. He had graduated law school last year. I suspected his boss had given him the case because he knew it was a loser. But he'd been lucky in that it had been assigned to a judge who almost never dismissed a case early on.

"Maybe," he said. "At least I didn't lose my first argument. Not entirely."

"Not entirely." I hit the elevator button. "No offense, but here's hoping you do next time."

He stepped into the elevator after me. "Don't you want me to win? I win, you have more work. You make more money. My boss says that's what all defense attorneys want."

"Not this one. I want to do my best for my client." I leaned back against the elevator wall. "Also, I have more work than I need right now."

Unfortunately, between Santiago's case and a couple clients who owed me money, a lot of it was work no one was paying me for. Back at my office, I sent the chocolate chip client an email with the news and put the date from the judge's order in my calendar. Then I sent out reminders to the clients whose bills were past due. One was four months overdue, so I had to add that I couldn't do further work on the case and would withdraw if I weren't paid within twenty days.

That unpleasant task done, I shut my door and stood at my window and stared down at Dearborn Street below.

Both Amber and Alexis had told me they wanted me to continue my investigation. Alexis calmed down a bit when I explained what Danielle had said. But she and Amber were subdued throughout. Their questions showed their fear that their dad would spend his life under a shadow of guilt. They desperately wanted him home. And they wanted just as much for the world to know he hadn't done this.

I grabbed my Santiago file and fished out the legal pads, now filled with notes. Between the visit to my parents and the news about the possible plea bargain I felt like I had lost the thread. In a low voice so I didn't disturb anyone in the rest of the suite, I talked through the evidence as if I were presenting it to the judge.

Finally, I decided to focus on the dog poisoning idea. It

obviously seemed plausible to the prosecutor because it trig-gered the plea discussions. Only I didn't buy that Santiago had done it. Danielle hadn't shared any motive Santiago had, if there was one, for wanting the dog dead. No one and nothing suggested he disliked the dog. Just the opposite – he was one of only two people other than Ivy who took care of Ralph.

It was time to talk again to the other one, Roy.

I spent the evening catching up on more of my law work.

The next morning I prepared to do some multi-tasking. I dressed in workout clothes, my hair tucked under a baseball cap I borrowed from Mensa Sam. I got to my office by six a.m. I had to take off the cap so the building security guard recog-nized me and let me in, despite that I had my entry fob with me.

After an hour and a half of revising a brief for one of my cases, I saved it to reread on my phone on the L. Then I walked to the Harold Washington Library L stop, hopped on the Brown Line, and took it north. The temperature had dropped to eighty overnight, but still I sweated plenty as I jogged around Ravenswood, a neighborhood a short train ride north of where I lived. It included more than one of the possible meeting places Roy suggested the first time we spoke. I'd made a careful note of his schedule. I planned to intercept him but figured it was worth doing a little research first.

After about half an hour I spotted someone I thought was him. Luckily for me, he was staring at his phone and typing as a large poodle explored a small patch of grass between the street and the sidewalk. He had a digital camera slung over his shoulder on a thick, black strap. I was able to pause on the corner and get a close enough view to confirm that this guy matched Roy's social media photos.

After that I jogged across the street and around the block, spotting him again as he and the poodle walked north. I followed at a safe distance until he returned the poodle to an aging Victorian house. Then he walked three blocks and disappeared into a brick apartment building for about ten minutes.

I took advantage of the time to step behind a giant metal clothing drop off bin for charity. I stripped off my sweat-soaked black T-shirt and wrapped it around my waist, revealing a bright pink tank top, one of Lauren's, I had on underneath. I took off the cap, folded it and tucked it into my fanny pack, and put my hair into a ponytail. It would be harder for Roy to notice someone following him if I looked different.

At least my endurance training was paying off. Much as I abhorred running in any form, I had no trouble jogging around multiple blocks to keep an eye on Roy as he walked three more dogs, two large and one mid-sized. A few months ago, more than a quarter mile would have worn me out, no question.

In addition to getting my exercise in, now I knew that professionally Roy was what he claimed to be. A photographer who helped pay the bills by dog walking. His next stop suggested he also had been honest about his personal life. A young woman who looked to be about his age met him at a dog park. The kiss hello and hand holding made me think this was the girlfriend he mentioned to me and to the police.

Though Roy simply having a girlfriend didn't mean he hadn't killed Ivy.

I headed for the nearest Starbucks. Basking in the air conditioning, I unwound the ponytail and finger combed my long hair so it fell around my face. Then I called Roy.

"Ah, Jesus," he said when I told him that Santiago planned to plead guilty. "That's awful."

I sat at a tall counter along the front window directly under an air conditioning vent. The air smelled of dark roast coffee and cinnamon. "I think so. But you knew he'd been arrested, so why is this more upsetting?"

So far I hadn't told him Santiago would probably be out of prison soon if he pled guilty. Or any other details. I wanted to get Roy's reaction to the guilty plea first.

"I kept thinking they'd find the real killer and let Santiago out."

"That could still happen. If you really want to help, you can."

"How? I don't know who killed Ivy."

"But you might have some ideas about who wanted to kill the dog."

∾

Roy must've felt guilty about relaying Santiago's statement to the police. When I told him I was in Ravenswood, he came right over to meet me.

After he got a cup of iced coffee, he settled onto a metal stool next to me. "Okay, I've been thinking about it. Who might want to poison Ralph. Obviously, there's Ellison, but I think –"

"Ellison?"

"Ralph put her dad in the hospital."

"What? When was this?" I had just reviewed my notes yesterday. Ellison hadn't mentioned her dad. She'd told me her mom had ALS, but she'd said nothing about her father.

"Six months ago? After the chicken incident. You knew about that?" Roy said.

I nodded.

Roy turned his iced coffee around a couple times in his hands. "Ivy promised to keep Ralph on a chain any time he was in the yard. And never let him loose in any of the house's common areas. But one day she forgot to lock the back door. Ralph pushed it open, went down the stairs, and fell asleep in front of Ellison's door. Her dad was visiting. He opened the door without looking outside first and it banged into Ralph."

"The back stairway or the front?"

"Back."

I shut my eyes and pictured that part of the house. "So Ralph was on the landing, and then there's about seven wooden steps down into the yard from there."

"Never counted them, but that seems right."

"And was this before or after Ivy and Ellison had their falling out?" I said.

"After, I'm pretty sure. Because Alexis wasn't living there anymore."

If Ivy forgot and left the door unlocked that day, she might have left it unlocked another time as well. Between that and knowing there was at least one secret passageway, it seemed to me Ellison was the most likely person to be able to get into Ivy's kitchen.

"So what happened when the door banged into Ralph?"

"Ellison's dad loves animals, and I guess she didn't warn him about Ralph. Or maybe he interacted with Ralph before and it went fine, I don't know. He lives out of state, and he doesn't visit much."

I nodded, making a mental note about how much Roy knew about Ivy's neighbor.

"Anyway, Ralph I guess stood. I don't know if he growled or anything. But Ellison's dad stepped out onto the landing and must have moved wrong or something and Ralph lunged for him. The man's seventy or eighty or something, probably not super limber. He stumbled and fell down the stairs. Broke his hip and his arm. Needed a bunch of pins around his wrist."

"That's awful."

Also, dog lover or not, I found it shocking Roy seemed to pinpoint the problem being a seventy-something man's lack of flexibility, not a lunging dog. I hated to think of my Gram in a similar situation.

"Yeah, pretty bad. Ivy and Ellison already weren't talking, and this didn't make it better." Roy frowned and folded his arms over his chest. "Especially after Ellison's dad made an insurance claim."

"Well, sure," I said. "It makes sense her insurance should cover his bills."

"He's old. I'm sure he's on Medicare."

"People on Medicare still end up with bills. Also, Medicare's a government program. Why should it pay bills when Ivy letting her dog out caused the injury?"

Uncovered medical bills were another thing that hung over my childhood. My dad had good insurance for a lot of the time, but it had capped mental health benefits. Which meant my mother's medications, plus some alternative treatments she tried, all had to come out of pocket.

"But it was an accident. The guy startled the dog. It's not the dog's fault."

"Is that how Ivy felt?"

"Of course. It's not like she did it on purpose. She made a mistake with the door, that's all."

"But that's what liability insurance is for – when you make a mistake and it injures someone."

Not to mention it had been a serious mistake. Ivy knew the dog needed to be on a leash and shouldn't be in the common area. Given Ellison's dad's age, I guessed a full recovery would be challenging. He might well still be in rehab.

Roy shrugged. "I'm just saying Ivy was mad. She didn't expect her friend to make an insurance claim against her."

"Her friend who she had stopped talking to."

"Well, yeah. That's true."

I wound a section of my hair around my finger. There was so much here. Ellison might have held a grudge over her dad. Also, she hadn't mentioned it when we talked, which seemed pretty strange. It made me wonder if she had a reason for covering up. The story also confirmed my idea that the dog might have hurt someone.

"Do you know if there was a lawsuit?"

Despite that Ivy was a difficult person, it seemed extreme to be upset about an insurance claim. That's what home-owners insurance is for. But people tend to take being named in a lawsuit very personally.

"No idea."

"You were about to say something else when I asked about Ellison. Were there other incidents with Ralph?" I said.

"I don't know about anything specific."

That wasn't a denial.

"Something general, then? That made you think there might have been an earlier incident."

"No incident." He glanced at the street. A CTA bus lumbered past and shuddered to a halt at a bus stop half a block down. "But maybe two, three months before Ellison's dad, Ivy started asking me to come by when she had people over."

"Come by?"

"Yeah, to help with the dog. Watch him so he didn't wander over to anyone."

"Did she say why?"

He shook his head. "She said something about people saying he was dangerous."

"Dangerous? That's the word she used?"

In between my other work the night before I had run a few searches for laws and rules about dogs. And learned about a City of Chicago ordinance that requires people who own dogs the city found to be dangerous to keep them confined. If a dog labeled dangerous attacks someone, the City could fine the owner. Also, the City might put the dog to sleep.

"Pretty sure," Roy said. "She was pretty mad about it."

"Did she say what people? Could it have been the City of Chicago?"

"Maybe. She didn't say."

"And this was before the incident with Ellison's dad?"

"Yeah. Because Ivy said if she knew Ellison would be so vindictive, she would've had me move in to watch Ralph the whole time Ellison's dad visited. It was sort of a joke but not really."

Interesting joke to make with your dog walker. I wondered if the humor hinted at anything else.

"Then were you there the Sunday before Ivy died? When Ivy's networking group met?"

The main reason I doubted anyone at the Sunday meeting poisoned Ivy's food was that according to what Tammy had told me, which all the police witness statements confirmed, no one had been out of the family room. But also I had thought that the dog would probably bark at anyone who tried to go up to the other floor. Now it seemed the dog might not have been there.

But Roy shook his head again. "I do a lot of weddings on weekends, so I don't take dog walking work on Sundays in spring or summer."

"So you think Ralph was there?"

"Unless she found someone else to take him, and I don't know who that would be besides Santiago. She might have shut him in a spare bedroom, but she didn't like doing that. She felt it was mean."

I thought about Roy's defense of Ivy's actions, him being there when Santiago moved his things out, and his awkwardness when we talked on the phone and I asked why Ivy would leave the store during the day to walk her dog.

"It seems like Ivy told you a lot about herself. Not just the dog but Ellison's family, Santiago, the girls."

He shifted in his chair and took a swig of coffee. "She liked to talk to me. She had a lot of acquaintances, and a lot of social media followers I guess. But not a lot of friends."

"Did you follow her on social media?"

"Nah. It's all so negative these days, you know? I post for my dog-walking business and for my photography under my studio name. But I keep my personal life off of it."

He hadn't learned about Ivy online, then. And my question about Ivy prompted him to think about his personal life.

I pushed aside my phone and looked him in the face. "I get the sense you and Ivy might've been more than friends."

He studied me for a moment. "Why do you say that?"

"When we first talked you said you only saw her occasionally. Now you told me she talked to you a lot. She gave you Alexis's number. You were there when Santiago picked up things. You know a lot about her. She relied on you."

"So, what, you assume we were hooking up?"

I almost didn't want to push him on it. If he'd been sleeping with Ivy it made him another suspect. But that cut both ways. If I were a prosecutor, I might argue that Santiago was jealous of Ivy's new relationship. Or try to show she got involved with Roy before the separation.

"I'm not assuming, I'm asking. You don't have to tell me. But the more I know about Ivy the more likely I can help her daughters."

He twisted the paper from his straw. "There's nothing wrong with it. The age difference didn't bother me."

"Did it bother Ivy?"

"Not really."

"But you talked about it," I said.

"It's why she didn't want to tell anyone else. I guess she felt odd about it."

I found it interesting the first defensive thing he said about the relationship was about age. He didn't seem concerned about the murder investigation. Which might mean he had nothing to do with it. Or he was great at lying. My very first boyfriend, an actor, took falsehood to the level of art.

"Do the police know about your relationship?"

"Never came up. I wasn't hiding it. But we weren't still seeing each other, and I didn't see how it had anything to do with her death."

Whatever Roy thought, maybe the police did know. I hadn't seen it in the witness statements, but between Ellison downstairs and Mary next door, it seemed like someone must have noticed.

"Was it ever serious between you and Ivy?"

"Define serious."

"Were you in love? Did you have plans for the future?"

"Not in love. And she wasn't looking for anything with a future. She said she had been married a long time. Now she wanted to see what not being married was like."

"Did that upset you?"

An L train had come in at the nearest station and two groups of commuters surged into the main door, pushing past us toward the baristas. I scooched my stool closer to the counter to give them more room.

Roy shifted his stool as well. "For, like, a second. But I saw pretty fast she was right. The more time we spent together, the more I could see we didn't have much in common except loving dogs. Which is a cool thing. I always seem to hook up with cat people. It's a problem."

"Did Santiago know about you and Ivy?"

Santiago's witness statement hadn't said anything about Roy, but he might have kept that to himself.

"Doubt it. Sometimes I hung out at her place if she got home when I was bringing the dog back or if she was working at home and needed help with the dog. But everyone knew Ralph was a handful. Plus she missed Ralph when she had long days at the store. So I loaded him in my car and brought him downtown so we could walk along the lakefront."

That explained why Ivy left the store to walk the dog.

Roy claimed they stopped seeing each other about two months before Ivy's death. At first he said it was mutual. When I pushed, as I knew hardly anyone who split up in a mutual way, he said Ivy broke it off. But he met his girlfriend soon after and hadn't been too upset.

If he really was into the girlfriend, Roy probably hadn't killed Ivy out of jealousy. On the other hand, I personally think anyone who kills a person must be so warped emotionally or mentally that they're not operating on the same set of principles as the rest of us. So who knew.

"Any idea what Ivy was planning to do the Saturday night that she died? Her friend Mei said she had plans that night but no one knows what they were."

"If she did, she didn't tell me. But there's no reason she would."

Roy didn't know whether or not Ivy had been seeing anyone else. I asked him more about Ivy's relationships, but nothing he told me stood out as any different from what other people had said or helped pinpoint other possible suspects.

After he left, I texted Ellison to see if she would talk to me again. Then I headed to the L.

Thirty minutes later I was in my office again. I still hadn't heard back from Ellison. But I meant to track her down one way or another.

34

"Welcome to my world," Detective Sergeant Beckwell said. He's a supervisor in the Violent Crimes unit of the Chicago Police Department and led the investigation into Marco's death when his division was shorthanded. We had become friends, after a fashion, having both done one another favors. For once, I hadn't called him for help, though. He had called me to ask how my training was going and if the instructor he connected me to was helpful.

After I told him yes and thanked him again, I shared my frustration that someone I interviewed failed to tell me something important. I was thinking both of Roy not mentioning the affair to the police but also of Ellison and her dad. Though Beckwell's division wasn't handling this investigation, I didn't tell him any specifics.

"Happens all the time," Beckwell said. "People think if they're not guilty and they decided something's not relevant there's no reason to mention it to the investigating officer or the detective."

"It's not that different in litigation," I said. "But at least there I have a ton of documents to review before I interview people and it helps give me ideas what else to ask. Here, I'm flying blind."

"Again, welcome to my world."

DePaul, the law school I attended, offers both full-time and part-time programs. Though I attended full time, I often took evening classes because I worked four days a week at the accounting firm where I had gotten a job after college. My schedule meant a lot of the people I knew best in law school were part-time students. I loved the classes with them because they brought great life experiences. Danielle had gone to law school at night while working as a police officer. I imagined being in class with her and talking about probable cause would've been fascinating.

My classmates had included more than one nurse, a medical examiner for DuPage County, a Chicago public school high school teacher, and the CEO of the midsized company that sent him to law school solely so that he could better understand his company's legal issues and communicate with the outside lawyers.

Right now, though, the person who interested me was Ursie Hartlip. I hadn't known her well, but during law school she worked for the City of Chicago at O'Hare. From mutual friends I knew she'd cycled through several different Chicago legal departments since we graduated. I crossed my fingers that in true Chicago fashion she knew someone who knew someone who could find the information I needed.

And that she would be willing to help despite that I hadn't seen her for years.

It was a good bet she would. One reason I chose to go to DePaul was its alumni. Most lawyers I met who came from there were hard-working and friendly. Plus, people tended to stay in the Chicago area. So it was likely you would run into whoever you did a favor for again and might be able to get one in return.

I emailed Ursie and she said she could talk to me around five. I said that worked, though Joe and I had finally been planning on drinks this evening. And Ellison had surprised me by returning my call and saying she could meet me at seven tonight after an appointment she had downtown.

It was the only time she had free for weeks. I texted to see if Joe could meet at six rather than five, which would still give us an hour and half before Ellison was free. He couldn't, but said he'd check and send me dates for later in the month.

We still hadn't met in person. But at least he answered all my texts right away like he had in the pre-Heather days.

"Quille, it's great to hear from you," Ursie said. "I've only got ten minutes or so before I need to leave for a meeting, but tell me quick what you need."

I had included some background in the email, but not too much, keeping in mind that the prosecutor might end up seeing anything I sent to Ursie. As quickly as I could I told her what I needed.

"Huh. With the budget cuts, animal complaints might still be paper. But if you're lucky there's a database with findings. It's not really my area. I'm assuming you searched online?"

My laptop beeped with an email from a client. I muted the sound so I could concentrate on the phone conversation. "I spent an hour doing that before I emailed you. Nothing came up. Zero."

"And this could be important to a murder case? I didn't know you did criminal."

"I don't, exactly. It's a long story. But it seems like someone might've had a grudge against a murder victim because of her dog, which at least one person called dangerous. It made me think of the ordinance."

"Well, everyone else in the city loves Fido these days, so the dog must have done something pretty extreme. I have a friend in Animal Control who might be able to help. Though mostly she deals with people claiming they have emotional support animals and other people getting mad at them for it. Last month someone wanted to bring an emotional support python on a plane."

"Real life snakes on a plane? In a cage I hope," I said.

One of the assistants from the other end of the suite waved good-bye to me on her way out and I waved back.

"Nope," Ursie said. "She claimed she had to have it wrapped around her shoulders. So glad I'm not at O'Hare anymore. Anyway, I'll check with my friend and see if it's okay to share her info. She can probably tell you where to search or who to call. Fair warning, though. Don't ask about the python. You'll be on the phone for an hour."

"Because it's none of your business, that's why." Ellison sprawled in the metal chair, her left leg crossed so that her ankle rested on her right knee. She wore leggings that went to just above the knee and a loose sleeveless top that ballooned over them.

We sat in the paved outdoor seating area near Buckingham Fountain. It's one of my favorite spots, so when Ellison said she had a meeting on Michigan Avenue and could meet me after, I suggested it. Metal chairs and tables are scattered around the fountain. Tonight, a three-person band with a wooden flute, a mandolin, and a guitar played upbeat New Age music and a tall guy beyond them was selling bright pink and green neon glow sticks. The lake breeze felt cool, and I had a vanilla ice cream cone from a vendor.

"Maybe not, but I thought you wanted to help Amber and Alexis," I said.

A young woman wheeled a popcorn cart past. The smell of caramel and salt filled the air.

"I do want to help them. Which is why I'm here right now with you. But I didn't kill Ivy, and neither did my dad. He only got out of the nursing home where he rehabbed a month ago. He can't walk down the stairs from his house without help thanks to Ralph. And his fall, that was two weeks after my mom died. That's why he came to visit. So, no, I wasn't going to send you in his direction to hound him with questions while he's still recovering. Or tell the police anything about him."

"I wouldn't have hounded him. Or talked to him if you asked me not to. I'm not the police."

She gripped her paper coffee cup, squeezing it at the center. "Yeah, well, I don't know you. Alexis might trust you because her little friend does. And maybe you're a great person. But this is my dad. I don't owe you anything."

I licked the vanilla drips off the sugar cone, but a little still got on my fingers, making them sticky.

"I know you don't. I'm just worried about Santiago and what happens to Alexis and Amber if he pleads guilty. You're a licensed social worker. You know the effect that being a felon has on a person's life."

Her grip on the cup loosened a bit. "I do. I do. This is just – it's been a really hard time."

"I can't even imagine," I said, though in some ways I could. Between growing up in my sister's shadow and helping care for a mother with serious mental health issues, then grieving Marco's death, I felt like I understood grief. But it was different for everyone.

Ellison brushed her bangs away from her forehead. "So now you know about my dad. What difference does it make?"

I wasn't sure how much to tell Ellison about my strategy. But if she killed Ivy, she already knew all the important facts. And if she didn't, she might cooperate more if I told her more.

"I'm wondering if your dad filed a lawsuit against Ivy."

"I don't know. We don't talk about it. Does it matter?"

I found it hard to believe her dad never talked about the claim. Most of my business clients aren't eager to share that they've been sued or that they're suing someone. It doesn't inspire a lot of confidence in customers. And Mensa Sam always tells his clients not to talk about their personal injury cases. Partly because if they recover money, everyone they ever met comes out of the woodwork hoping for a loan or for help buying a car or something else. But he says ninety-nine percent of the clients don't listen to him. Some feel worried about the lawsuit and need to talk, others are angry at the defendant and want to vent to their family and friends. Hardly anyone is neutral enough about a lawsuit to never mention it.

"I'm wondering if his lawyer got information from Ivy about any other times the dog attacked anyone. To show the dog had a pattern."

"Wouldn't the dog killing my chicken be enough?"

"It could be more significant if it attacked another person. There could be higher penalties for Ivy, so your dad's lawyer might want to know that."

Her head drew back, bringing her chin toward her chest. "I guess I could ask him. I'll let you know."

"Did you ever hear anything about Ralph attacking anyone else?"

Ellison shook her head. "But remember, Ivy hadn't been talking to me for almost two years."

"How well do you know Roy?"

"The dog walker? I chatted with him every now and then when he came over."

"Every now and then meaning once a month? Twice a week?"

"Probably once a week. Why?"

Despite Roy having been out of town the weekend of Ivy's death, more and more I was thinking he couldn't be ruled out. He certainly would've known, as Ellison did, how long Ivy kept food. And given his affair with her, I found it hard to believe that he never had access to the kitchen.

"What do you think of him?" I asked.

Ellison shrugged. "Seems nice enough. And he's a great photographer. I recommended him for a friend's wedding. Most people take their own shots now but some people like to have a professional."

"You ever wonder if he and Ivy were involved?"

She tilted her head to one side. "It crossed my mind. He was around a lot starting maybe a year ago. If Ivy and I had still been talking, I definitely would have asked her."

I finished my cone and tossed my napkin in a nearby blue plastic garbage bin. Chicago puts out a lot of recycling and trash bins, part of why it's cleaner than most large cities.

"Anything other than the amount of time he spent that made you think there was something going on?"

"Hm." Ellison's lips pressed together. "Not really. Their body language when they were together didn't look any different to me. I admit I kind of watched a bit. I was curious. But Ivy wasn't really a demonstrative person. She rarely hugged her girls or held hands with Santiago or anything. So I don't know if that meant anything."

"Do you think Roy is the type of guy Ivy might become serious about?"

"Long-term? I don't know. I got the impression Ivy was sort of liking having her place to herself."

"But you said she got so angry with you about your role in losing custody of Alexis."

"She was. But I really think that was because my testimony clashed with her image of herself as the perfect parent. As Mom-in-Chief. I never got the impression Ivy loved parenting, though. I kind of think it drove her crazy. The messiness of it. Once Alexis was gone, she could line up everything on the shelves just the way she wanted it. Make whatever food she wanted."

"Didn't she do all those things anyway? I thought Alexis pretty much did things her way?"

"When it came down to it, sure. But now she could do it without any ripples from living with someone else."

If Ellison was right, I hoped Alexis had never sensed that from Ivy. There was nothing like knowing your mother found life easier without you around.

Ellison didn't have any other thoughts about Roy and Ivy. Or any reason to think Roy had been angry at Ivy. But the fact that he reported to the police the statement Santiago supposedly made while hiding that he himself had been involved with Ivy still gave me pause.

It was a beautiful night. Ty was taking clients out on his boat. I'd been invited, but hadn't wanted to miss the chance to talk with Ellison. I texted Lauren to see if she wanted to join me at the fountain. Dusk was falling, and every Wednesday the city sets off fireworks at Navy Pier once it gets dark. You can see them from the concrete steps on the east side of the fountain. Whenever it's nice out, residents gather there to watch.

Lauren texted back right away and said she'd hop in a cab and meet me in ten minutes. While I waited, I stared at the sparkling chain of traffic lights curving along Lake Shore Drive. And thought about who else might know about any times Ralph attacked or bit anyone. Alexis and Amber had already told me they didn't know of any incidents with Ralph, including the one with Ellison's father.

Amber said it could have happened and she would never have known because she didn't talk with her mom that often once she went away to school. And Alexis thought her mom might not have told her because Alexis already wasn't that comfortable around Ralph.

I wondered if Ivy hadn't wanted to admit to anyone that her perfect pet misbehaved.

Next to Ellison and Roy, Hank and Sylvania seemed most likely to know the dog's history. They were also most likely, as family members, to have spare keys. And Sylvania had been there the Sunday before Ivy's death.

But if Sylvania had tried to poison the dog, I doubted she'd be jumping to tell me why.

It took Lauren nearly twenty minutes, but the wait was worth it. She had a container of three kinds of cheese, a box of gourmet sesame seed crackers, and two small thermoses filled with Pinot Noir. Ty had told me that in Paris residents and tourists gathered on the city's bridges and in the park to watch the Eiffel Tower light show every night at ten. They openly drank wine. It was almost unFrench not to.

Chicago's a bit less laid back. Alcohol isn't allowed in city parks. But if everyone seems sober and no one is waving around bottles or cans, you can usually discreetly drink a little.

Lauren also brought a blanket to spread across the steps. We sat side by side.

I started to tell her about Ellison, but she handed me a cheese slice on a cracker and interrupted. "First I want to know how the weekend with Ty and your parents went."

When I filled her in, she was nowhere near as surprised as I had been that my mom raised my investigating the original Q.C.'s kidnapping and death.

"I totally see it." Lauren drank from her thermos.

"You do?" I shifted closer to her as a couple with three kids squeezed onto the stairs next to us.

Behind us, colored lights flashed over different parts of the fountain, highlighting the sculptures in it and blinking in time with orchestral music piped over loudspeakers. Another part of Chicago's nightly displays.

"Definitely. With your mom everything has to be about her. So you found this thing that you're good at, that people come to you for. And instead of saying she's proud of you or asking you about it, she has to find a way to make it all about her. Figuring you'll fail and feel awful about it."

"I don't think she hopes I'll fail," I said. "I think she wants answers. Thinks that will help her get closure."

I hadn't spent any time focusing on my mom with so much else on my mind. But the words came out before I processed them. It had been on the back burner.

A huge pop sounded as the first crimson and blue fireworks burst across the night sky.

"Seriously?" Lauren said. "It's one thing for you to look into cases where the police are understaffed and don't have the same personal interests you do. But the FBI? They've got, like, databases and serial killer taskforces and all kinds of resources you don't have."

"No, I know. But I was talking to Danielle about it." Later during the car ride home I had called her back to ask her advice in case my mom asked me again about Q.C.'s murder. "She said the only way she could see me getting anywhere is if there's someone close to the family who tells me something they held back from the FBI. And it's something key, but they didn't feel comfortable talking about it. Or didn't think it was important. Like Roy not telling the police he was sleeping with Ivy."

"A pretty major data point to leave out," Lauren said. "Are you sure he didn't do it?"

Above the lake a series of fireworks that formed into the shapes of tiny hearts popped and sizzled. Someone had gotten creative. I waited until they faded to answer.

"My gut says no, but I could be wrong. Anyway, Danielle said that the police, the FBI, everyone feels nervous talking to them whether they have something to hide or not. So it also sometimes makes it hard for people to think things through. Sometimes they say things that don't make sense and get the investigation off on the wrong track. Other times they leave things out."

"You are not seriously thinking of doing this Q.C. investigation, are you?" Lauren asked.

I shifted on the step. The concrete was digging into the backs of my thighs. "No. I have enough on my plate."

Lauren took out more crackers. "Good. So back to Ty. What did they think of him?"

"Loved him. Mom especially. She actually danced with him. And he was great with her."

The air smelled of sulfur. Smoky remnants of the hearts drifted south on the breeze as the show continued. I told Lauren about the conversation Ty and I had in my parents' kitchen about having children. Or not.

"Uh-oh. He's a fence sitter."

"A what?"

"Fence sitter. Someone who claims to not be sure if they want kids. Then half the time they get serious about someone and suddenly decide they want kids and break up with the person who doesn't want them. Like that homeopathic doctor I was seeing last year."

"I thought he didn't care if he had kids."

"Exactly. He swore that up and down in the beginning. Then after three months suddenly he was like he couldn't see himself with anyone who didn't absolutely want children."

Lauren disliked kids, at least until they got old enough to have in-depth conversations. From five years old on she knew she didn't want to have them. She refused to play with baby dolls in kindergarten. I've never felt a strong need to have my own children, but I like most kids, and love my niece and nephew and Eric.

"You were wavering on him, anyway," I said.

"Sure – all that woo-woo magical thinking annoyed me. But it's a real thing, the fence-sitting."

"Marco and I both felt like we'd be okay either way. Doesn't that make me a fence sitter?"

Marco had told me early on he felt he could be quite happy not having more children, as he already had Eric. But he also liked the idea, if I wanted to have kids, of being a better dad than he had been before. When Eric was born, Marco was a busy surgeon gradually getting addicted to alcohol. He repaired his relationship with Eric after he got sober and changed professions, but it took a lot of effort.

Which is when it hit me that while through my teens and twenties I had more or less assumed I would have kids because that's what everyone I knew did, I didn't feel a strong need to do it.

Marco and I hadn't decided anything for sure. After Marco died, though, I resisted my sister's attempts to get me to date so I could meet someone soon and have children. It didn't seem like a good way to go about life or finding someone I could be happy with.

Lauren knew all of that.

She sipped her wine. "Not really. Whether someone wanted kids was never something you felt like you needed to know. Not with Marco, not with Ty, not with the meager handful of guys you dated before that. If you definitely wanted kids, it would have been."

Lauren might not want kids, but she firmly believed being part of a couple was better than being single. Though unlike a lot of people I'd met who felt that way, she was willing to stay single if she didn't meet someone she felt was right for her.

"So Ty and I are in the same place," I said.

Her blond hair swung as she shook her head. "It's different for guys. He has forever to decide. He could see you for five years and then decide he has this overwhelming need to add to the gene pool."

"I don't think that's going to happen."

"I'm just saying. If you want a future with him, you need to know for sure where he stands."

"I don't think that's going to be an issue."

"Then what is? Something's bothering you after the weekend."

I thought about Ty whirling my mom and then me around the yard. "Maybe that I won't be enough fun for him. That I work too much."

"You're not seriously worried about that? I see you two as a good balance for each other."

My phone dinged, and I fished it out of my cross-body purse. Ursie had sent me contact information for a colleague who worked for the City of Chicago Animal Care and Control

Agency. It was too late to call now, but I could try her first thing in the morning.

"Speaking of work, we should head back." I took a last swallow of my wine, enjoying the dark cherry aftertaste. "I need to get in early tomorrow."

Most people had drifted off at the end of the fireworks, and the lights around the fountain blinked off. On weeknights, downtown Chicago becomes pretty quiet by ten p.m. Usually I try to get home long before then.

Lauren closed the cracker box and screwed her thermos top tight. "Unlike all the other mornings."

I laughed and stood. "Yeah, this month's been like that."

We walked along Columbus Drive, keeping nearer the wide street with its strings of cars rather than walking along the shadowy trees and bushes that lined each side of the sidewalk. As we turned on Balbo and headed toward the city, as always the vista of buildings, their windows lit like stars, their names in different colored light across their tops, struck me. Whatever its problems, Chicago was beautiful. Especially at night.

I called Ursie's colleague around seven-thirty a.m., as soon as I got into my office, and left a message. Then, before I started on my legal work, I ran some searches of the Cook County electronic docket. No lawsuits against Ivy Jimenez-Brown, Ivy Brown, or Ivy Jimenez in any of the divisions. Since Ivy lived in Chicago, most likely any suit against her would be in Cook County. And one by Ellison's father would almost have to be. Lawsuits need to be filed either where the defendant lived or where the incident occurred, and both were in Cook County.

Ursie's colleague returned my call around nine. She apologized and explained she could offer only limited help. "A few years ago I could've given you what you need easily. But there's big emphasis on transparency with the new mayor. Makes it hard to get people information."

"A paradoxical result of more transparency," I said.

She laughed. "Like everything, right? I should have said more emphasis on the public as a whole knowing how to get information. And a sort of moratorium on people getting information through favors."

Like a lot of cities, Chicago runs on favors and political clout. Things had improved since my Gram's time for sure, but I had my doubts about how much. When trying to find out the facts about Marco's death I'd met a man whose job was literally called a permit facilitator. Which meant someone who knew the right people to get building permits issued more quickly. And the right people didn't mean people who understood the law or did construction.

Unfortunately, I wasn't one of the right people. I suspected those who were skated through the system like always and the rest of us lived in a tangle of growing red tape.

"So as a member of the public how would I get the information I'm looking for?"

"Complaints about an animal owned by Ivy Jimenez, also known as Ivy Jimenez-Brown or Ivy Brown?"

"Yes," I said. I hadn't said the name, so Ursie must have passed it on. "FOIA request?"

Illinois has a statute, the Freedom of Information Act, that allows citizens to access public records. You have to request the records you want from the specific agency.

"Yes. From my agency. The address to use is on the website."

"Are you the contact person?"

I leaned toward the speaker phone, as if it would help me get what I needed. Given that she knew Ivy's name, maybe she planned to ship the information right out to me.

"No, sorry, I'm not."

I settled back in my chair again. "And I'm assuming it's no speedier getting a response than it's ever been?"

"Worse. Budget cuts."

No surprise there. Despite ever-increasing property tax bills, and the extra taxes Chicagoans pay on everything from dining out to shopping at Target, the city is broke. Worse than broke. It's deep in debt.

I stared at the interior brick wall over my laptop monitor. There must be something Ursie's friend could do or she wouldn't have bothered calling back.

"Any chance you could at least tell me if there's anything there to get?"

"So, I can't really tell you that. But being as you're a good friend of Ursie's, if there were nothing at all I'd certainly let you know so you wouldn't waste time. I'm guessing if there was nothing, or even only one minor complaint, it probably wouldn't be worth it to you."

Even one would interest me, but I understood what she was saying. "I appreciate that. You're right, I wouldn't want to waste time."

"I didn't think so. But I encourage you to file the request. You just never know what you'll learn."

"Thanks," I said. "Thanks very much."

I made a note to send Ursie a bottle of wine as a thank you.

In my Santiago file I noted: *More than one animal complaint in Chicago against Ivy.*

I filled out the form and printed it, as the website required mailing paper rather than emailing. I wasn't likely to get my FOIA response until many months after Santiago entered his plea if he did it. But at least now I knew I was on to something.

I just needed to find a different way to learn about the previous incidents.

~

Late that afternoon I knocked on Ivy's next-door neighbor's front door. I'd called ahead, and Mary called to me from her side porch to come around.

"Thanks so much for taking time for me," I said.

"Oh, well, it is a big favor." Mary held up a crossword puzzle book. Her cane lay on the porch floor next to her. "I've got so much to do."

For just a second, before I remembered how much pain she must be in, I envied her. I couldn't remember any time in my life when I sat for more than twenty minutes alone and read or worked a crossword puzzle or rocked in a rocking chair.

I sat on the second rocker next to her and asked about incidents with Ralph.

"Oh, of course, there was Ellison's father. But you probably know about that. It's why you're asking."

I nodded. "I'd like to hear what you know about it."

"That poor man. Had to be in the hospital here for weeks before they transferred him to a facility near his home. By helicopter. It was too far to drive him with his injuries."

"Ivy told you that?"

Nothing I knew about Ivy suggested she wandered across the yard to chat with neighbors.

"No, Ellison did once when she picked up groceries for me. She does that now and again if my son can't. Very nice of her. I have big orders delivered, but in between I like to get fresh produce."

I asked about other incidents where Ralph attacked anyone.

"Never heard about any. But it would explain why Roy started coming around more. You've met Roy?"

"The dog walker." I flipped a page on my legal pad. "When was it that he started coming around more?"

"Five, six months ago?"

"He started walking the dog two years ago, though?"

"Yes, once a day, Monday through Saturday. But about six months ago I noticed when Ivy was home and other people came to see her, he'd be there out in the front or side yard, playing with the dog."

"Was he here for any of the Sunday meetings Ivy had? You know the ones I mean?"

"Oh, yes. Every third Sunday or so she had some sort of women's networking meeting."

"She told you what the meetings were for?"

"Santiago did."

"And you tracked which Sundays?"

She smiled. "I know what you're thinking. I'm not that nosy. Or that bored. But my son often visits on Sunday, and if it was Ivy's Sunday parking was a lot more challenging. So we tried to avoid those days."

I nodded. The reality of living in most parts of Chicago is parking considerations drive a lot of decisions if you plan to take a car anywhere. One of many reasons I didn't own one. Most people I knew who did paid to park at home, then again wherever they worked, then again if they went out after work. That's why I let Lauren use my parking space, and she lets me use her car.

"So was Roy, the dog walker, there for the meetings?"

Roy had already told me no, but I believe in double checking.

"I don't remember seeing him on meeting days."

"Was he there the Sunday before Ivy died?"

"Pretty sure he wasn't. The police asked me about people

going in and out that whole week. I only remember Roy weekdays, and only early in the week. Then Santiago at least twice. Including Friday." Her hands dropped into her lap. "I still feel awful that my saying that might have gotten Santiago arrested."

"He told the police that, too. I saw his witness statement, so don't feel bad," I said. "Did Roy ever stop by when Ivy was home alone?"

Her shoulders drew back. "Why?"

"Say Ivy was working at home and wanted Ralph out of the – entertained."

Mary's posture softened. "He did sometimes come by while she worked."

"And when did that start?"

"Sometime early in the year. Not sure when – but I noticed more often he might be in the yard playing with Ralph and then Ivy came out. The first time it surprised me."

"Did you ever think they might be involved? If you did, it's okay. He admitted to me they were."

I wasn't quite sure I ought to share that, but Mary's body language suggested she knew already and didn't want to say anything.

She sighed. "That's a relief. I didn't want to gossip. Roy told me."

That was interesting. Everyone seemed to like to talk to Mary. Everyone except Ivy. "Really? When?"

"A few months after he started stopping by Ivy's more. He used to chain the dog outside sometimes and watch from my porch for a change of scene when Ivy had company. As for why, I think he wanted to talk to someone who knew Ivy. He only told me after they split. Apparently, it was somewhat mutual. He found a new girlfriend. But Ivy had more or less pushed him away, saying over and over that there was no future for them."

"Do you think Santiago might have been jealous if he knew?"

Ivy pushing Roy away suggested a motive for him. On the other hand, if Roy told Mary, he wasn't exactly being discreet. Which made me think Santiago might have known. Another possible motive for him for murder.

It seemed the more I learned, the better job I did tossing out bread crumbs for the prosecution of Santiago.

"No? Probably no. I'm sure no one really wants to think of their wife, soon-to-be-ex or not, with someone else. But I saw Santiago with Ivy enough over the years. By the time he moved out, it looked to me like it had been over for a long time."

"What do you mean?"

"Ivy always seemed impatient, and he seemed removed. She always had her hands at her hips, shifting her weight from one side to the other." Mary rocked her chair and stared at the peeling boards of the porch's ceiling. "Though that wasn't new I suppose. That was Ivy. But Santiago – he struck me as more and more detached. He literally stood far from her when they talked. Or walked. Or sat out in the yard."

"Like he was angry?"

I was asking her to read a lot into body language. But years of questioning witnesses and, before that, acting taught me how much our body language conveys. And how much other people read that body language whether they know that's what they're doing or not.

Her eyes turned toward the ceiling again for a few seconds. "No. Not angry. More like he was tired. Arms limp at his sides. His steps slow. After he moved out, when he came by, he had a bounce in his step again. Energy. He ran up the steps like he used to do when his kids were younger. If you ask me, divorcing her was the best thing in his life."

"But he still might not have liked her seeing someone else?"

"I'm just saying anyone might not like that. But I never pegged him for a jealous man."

"Did you tell the police about Roy and Ivy?"

"If they'd asked, I would have, I suppose. But I got the sense it was a short affair. A month or two, over for a while before she died. So I didn't bring it up."

That fit with what Roy had said.

"And the police didn't ask?"

She shook her head, setting her silvery hair swaying. "It wouldn't make him or Santiago look good, would it?"

It shocked me that whoever questioned Mary hadn't asked. But the Chicago Police Department has been struggling to reorganize for quite a while. A report a few years back highlighted problems with murder investigations. For one, there was no dedicated department that covered murders. It was part of why the Detective Sergeant I'd become friends with, after a fashion, sometimes helped me out once I proved he could trust me and I had skills he could use.

Also, sometimes even good questioners don't phrase a question just the right way. And people who don't trust the police aren't going to fill in the blanks for them.

"I asked you before, but now that you've thought about it more, any idea who might have wanted to kill Ivy?"

"I have thought and thought. And I just don't know. No doubt Ivy rubbed plenty of people the wrong way. But murder? I can't imagine."

"How about Ralph?"

She studied me. "You're thinking he was the real target?"

"Maybe," I said. "It seems easier to believe someone might poison a dog than a human."

"I'm not sure you're right about that. A lot of people feel more strongly about their pets than their families."

"Maybe generally. But how about Ralph versus Ivy?"

"Hm. I suppose you're thinking of Ellison, but I can't see her doing that. Encourage her dad to sue Ivy? Sure. But Ellison as a killer? The woman handfeeds her chickens and we had to talk her into traps for the rats that attack the coop. She didn't even want to kill them."

"No other ideas for me?"

"No, I'm sorry. I hope you find whoever did this. I hate to see those girls orphaned. And that's what they'll be if Santiago spends his life in prison."

I sighed inwardly. She made a good argument for Santiago pleading guilty. Getting out in a few months versus a lifetime. Who wouldn't take that deal?

35

Having spent so much time on Santiago's issues, I needed to work late that night. Around seven p.m. that night I settled at a table outside at Café des Livres, printouts of Illinois appellate court opinions about an issue for one of my contract cases spread out around me. When it's late, I focus better by reading on paper. And when I get out of my office.

After an hour of reading about the ins and outs of hospital billing, Carole, the owner, joined me. Despite the heat she looked cool and elegant in a full skirt with swirls of color and a tailored black top.

She brought me a raspberry tart on the house. Ever since I helped her look for a missing friend during a blizzard – an incident that led to both Lauren and me getting injured – if Carole's at the café she won't let me or my friends pay for anything. She tells her counter clerks to comp me when she's not around, too, but I insist on paying. Otherwise, I'd start feeling bad about frequenting the café so often.

"How's the new place?" I said.

We hadn't had much chance to talk since she and her husband had moved to a new condo. They'd been forced to move out of River City, a complex on the edge of the Printer's Row neighborhood that converted from condos back to apartments. It also had been where we'd all been trapped by a blizzard the year before, so personally I thought it was just as well to steer clear of it.

The new condo was about two miles farther south, in an area with less traffic, more trees, and new buildings.

Carole waved her hand. "The condo, *c'est beau*. But I miss walking to work. *Je deteste l'autobus*. So jerky, those drivers. Stop, go, slam on the brakes. No one knows how to drive here."

From what I'd heard from Ty, Paris wasn't known for its smooth or careful drivers, but I had no firsthand experience. I decided to focus on the positive.

"But you're happy with the redecorating you did?"

"*Ah, oui*. Always I love to decorate."

My phone buzzed with a text from an unfamiliar number. All it said was *2 incidents*. Confirmation that there had been another complaint about Ralph filed with the City, assuming Ellison's accounted for one of them.

I texted a thank you.

It would be dark soon, and I headed back to my office. I turned on my laptop to make a few last changes to a motion I'd written earlier in the week. It took a long time for the computer to recognize my log in. And when it did, gibberish flew across the screen.

Afraid to reboot for fear that I might have a virus and make it worse, I dialed my IT consultant. Luckily, he was working late, too. Unluckily, there was no way for him to remote access in given what I was seeing. I sent him a photo of the screen.

"Uh, yeah, don't reboot," he said. "And don't shut it off. In fact, don't do anything."

"That bad?"

"Wish I could be there now but I'm dealing with another emergency. How's six a.m. tomorrow morning?"

That wasn't reassuring.

~

The next morning by six-thirty Shawn was clicking away at my laptop keys. "You get someone really mad at you?"

I swigged my tea, desperate for caffeine. Fortunately, a lot of traders go to the café, so Carole opens at four every weekday morning. "Besides my mother?"

"I'm serious. This type of attack, not random. This individual knows what they're doing. But it's a lot of trouble to go through for a one-person law firm."

"Don't hackers sometimes just mess with people?"

The attack coincided with me asking questions about the dog, and that made me wonder. But every law firm I know worries about Internet security and computer problems. I couldn't assume this related to Santiago's case.

I also didn't want to suggest conclusions to Shawn. In law, I learned quickly that many people will follow you to wherever your question points them. That can be useful to make a point, but it can also keep you from learning the truth.

"Sure, RCCs - random chaos causers – are out there. But as a rule they target big companies. Where you can cause the most chaos. This, there's no major ripple effect."

"It'll ripple through my life."

"Yeah, it'll give you a headache. Sorry, I don't mean literally." He paused his typing and glanced at me. He knows about my migraines. One hit hard during our first get-to-know-you meeting.

"I know. So you think the purpose of this is what?"

"Not certain what we're dealing with yet, so don't hold me to this. But it looks twofold. Make it hard for you to do your

228

work. And show the hacker what you're working on. A lawyer on the other side maybe?"

I sank into the padded chair at Danielle's desk and shook my head. Both his points fit better with someone trying to interfere with my investigation about Santiago.

"If this were a legal thriller, sure," I said. "But there aren't a whole lot of secrets or surprises in my cases. I argue the law based on what the other side alleges in a lawsuit. Or what the parties say in deposition or on the language of the contract."

"You don't go to trial?"

"Rarely. And even then, we exchange all our evidence ahead of time. It's called discovery. Once in a great while some attorneys might try to hide bad evidence for their clients – or their clients hide it from them – but it's against the court rules and the rules for attorneys. And not my style anyway. I tell my clients to tell the truth about the facts and let me worry about the consequences."

"But your opponents might not know that."

I mentally ran through all my cases and the lawyers who represented the other side. Nothing so dramatic made sense for any of them. And in tax matters, I represented clients against the IRS, the City, and the State of Illinois. All of them were underfunded. No way were they spending time or money going after me.

"How long will this take to fix?" I said.

"Hard to say just yet. But you might want to break out that spare laptop."

I waved toward the credenza where a three-year-old rose gold laptop sat. "Already here. See? I do listen to you."

Based on Shawn's instructions after a break in a couple years ago, I backed up all my files every Friday to a spare laptop I kept at home. But that meant these were six days out of date.

"Is it safe to go into my online backup?" I said.

"I wouldn't. Those files are probably corrupted."

Perfect. That was at least twenty hours of work I needed to re-create, none of which could be billed to clients.

Fortunately, I keep my calendar entirely online and it syncs to my phone. I spent the next half hour figuring out what had to be done immediately and what could wait. I worked in the office suite's kitchen at the long table along an interior brick wall. Within three hours I had finished the documents I needed to file tomorrow. Shawn still stared at the screen, clicking keys, when I walked in and grabbed my paper files about Santiago's case. I left a cold root beer on the desk for him.

In the kitchen I studied my notes. Alexis and Amber had said they didn't know of any dog attacks. But something triggered the second City of Chicago complaint. Another attack, or....

It took a few minutes to find the ordinance again. I scrolled to its definitions and confirmed that a dog didn't need to attack for a victim to file a complaint. A dangerous animal included one that chased or approached someone in "an apparent attitude of attack" more than once without provocation.

I slumped in my chair. With all the work I had to re-create, the last thing I wanted to do was spend hours contacting all the people Ivy knew to see if there had been an incident. I skimmed the witness statements the prosecution had turned over. No one had mentioned an incident with Ralph. But if the investigating officer didn't ask, why would they?

My stomach growled. I was playing with fire putting off lunch. Hunger is a migraine trigger. But I felt as if I were missing something obvious.

Though I had done it twice before, I searched the Cook County electronic docket again for any lawsuits against Ivy. It was always worth checking more than once because the search function on the site was never perfect. If the name was misspelled or you typed the name in the Defendant rather than the Plaintiff search box you would miss a lawsuit. I also checked for any suit against Santiago in case it had been filed under his name.

As before, I found nothing. I paused and did shoulder rolls to loosen my muscles.

I felt doubly frustrated because I knew there was an easy way to get that information. Whoever handled Ellison's father's insurance claim almost certainly checked into previous complaints. Both Ellison's and the neighbor's comments about the long hospital stay, rehab, and a medical helicopter ride made me think it was more likely he had filed a lawsuit, not just an insurance claim. That type of injury is so large that it's rare for an insurer to simply pay. Or for a lawyer to advise an injured plaintiff to accept a payment before he was back to full strength or as close as it was possible to get.

Downstairs I got a scone and cup of *chocolat chaud noir* at the café to go. The air felt balmy and the sun had shifted enough west that the building blocked it, so the five outdoor tables were filled. I headed for Printers Row Park, which is really more of a brick and concrete plaza. But there's a stone fountain in the center, a circular mound of grass edged with more concrete, and a couple wrought iron benches. Plus curved blocks of concrete with backwards letters on them meant to look like type from the old printing presses.

None of it makes for comfortable seating, so I had no trouble snagging a block to sit on. I cared less about comfort and more about change of scene.

As I savored the rich, dark chocolate, I paged through my handwritten notes on what Mary had said about Ellison's father. The helicopter. They had to fly him to the other hospital because it was too far to drive. I balanced the cup of cocoa on the rock and rifled through the pages from my second visit with Ellison. Her dad was from Michigan.

Of course. On my phone I opened PACER, a database for federal lawsuits, and searched in the Northern District of Illinois. When two parties in a lawsuit are from different states, the plaintiff can file in federal court. The idea is that the home state court might be unfair to someone from out of state. As a resident of Michigan, Ellison's dad could have filed against Ivy in federal court.

I didn't know why he'd want to. The common wisdom is that Cook County jurors will award more than those in federal court. But perhaps his lawyer didn't believe that. Or liked federal court for some other reason.

I typed in the names. And was rewarded.

Ellison's dad, through an attorney in Traverse City, Michigan, filed suit against Ivy three months after the incident. As I read a list of all the documents and court orders, I finished the scone. Then I paused to swallow three Advil from the compact bottle in my purse. I was afraid I had waited too long. I could feel a throbbing in the back of my head. But maybe it'd stay at that level. In which case I could still think, if not clearly.

All the lawsuit document titles listed looked fairly routine. None seemed likely to tell me about any previous incidents. The trial date was set for February, so I guessed both sides exchanged quite a lot of information already. But those types of documents don't usually get into the public record.

Disappointed not to find an easy answer I pressed my forehead into my hands. I ought to have gotten something more substantial to eat. Now I felt queasy and wasn't sure what I could keep down.

As I headed back toward the café, thinking some sort of

thick soup might work, it occurred to me that Sylvania and Hank might know about the lawsuit. If Ivy confided in anyone, it would likely be them. Hank was not only her brother but her business partner.

But if one of them had something to do with her death, my questions would raise their suspicions.

Darts of pain shot through my forehead and bored into the back of my skull. Not blinding pain. Yet.

So food and darkness first. Think more later.

I took beef barley soup home, shut my blinds, ate, then lay on my bed, an ice pack on the back of my neck, imagining the ice absorbing the white-hot arrows of pain. Gradually the Advil and ice eased the pounding in my head. I drifted into a light sleep where I dreamed about being on stage again with a stabbing pain at my temples. When I awoke, though, the pain lessened.

After rolling onto my side, I levered upright, palms flat on the bed. No pain. I got to my feet, inched to my kitchen area and got a glass of water. Something I ought to have been drinking more of all morning.

I left the blinds shut as insurance and opened the federal court's website on my phone. After enlarging the screen so my eyes didn't strain, I scanned the titles of the documents the parties filed, which was all I could look at for free. Sometimes court documents are mislabeled. It was a long shot, and the court would charge me per page read, but I started opening each motion. And finally found something.

The court listed it as a different kind of motion, but it was what's called a motion for partial summary judgment as to liability. In it, the plaintiff's attorney asked the judge to decide Ivy had acted unreasonably – had been negligent – based on the testimony and evidence filed with the motion. The attorney argued the City of Chicago Ordinance required Ivy to keep her dog confined because the City had declared

Ralph a dangerous dog. Since everyone agreed the dog had been loose, Ivy ought to be liable.

What was key for me was the reason the City found Ralph to be dangerous. There were two previous incidents. First, Ralph killed Ellison's chicken. The second incident involved a little girl.

The plaintiff's attorney had questioned Corine Killion, the girl's mother, in a deposition.

I opened the PDF of exhibits and scrolled to her testimony.

Q. So you and your daughter left the dog park around 3:15 that day?

A. Right. We had our Dachshund, Sonny, with us. He ran ahead, pulling Annie along behind him. She was so happy that day – laughing, smiling.

Q. Annie was happy?

A. Yes, Annie. Sonny, too. Poor Sonny.

Q. So Sonny runs ahead, Annie runs after him. Then what happened?

A. From nowhere – it seemed like from nowhere – this huge Doberman ran around from behind me. It must have come from the dog park. It lunged at Sonny. Grabbed him in its jaws, right around Sonny's middle, and just shook its head back and forth.

Q. Just so the record is clear – this dog that lunged, this was a Doberman you later learned was named Ralph?

A. Yes. Ralph. What a name for a dog.

Q. And Ralph used his jaws to grab Sonny – your Dachshund – around Sonny's middle and Ralph shook Sonny?

A. Exactly. It was – I can't tell you. It only hit me

later how awful that was for Sonny. Because when it happened, all I could see was Annie. She ran after Sonny, she wanted to save him –

Mr. Prall: Objection. Lack of foundation. Speculation. The witness has no idea what her daughter wanted to do.

A. Of course I do. I –

Ms. Spellman: Mrs. Killion, please don't worry about the objections. I'll respond to them. (to Mr. Prall) And, please, no speaking objections. I don't need you coaching the witness.

Mr. Prall: I'm not –

Ms. Spellman: Let's move forward so we can get Mrs. Killion out of here. This has been hard enough for her. Mrs. Killion, putting aside just for the moment what your daughter might have felt or been thinking, please tell me what you saw happen.

A. Annie ran for the two dogs. Made a beeline for them. And I screamed at her, God help me just screamed at her to stop. I love Sonny, too, and it was awful seeing all that blood, but I couldn't...I couldn't....if Annie...

Q. Do you need a break? Let's take a break.

A break was taken. The deposition resumed at 3:43 p.m. The same parties and counsel were present.

Ms. Spellman: So please tell me what happened after you screamed at your daughter to stop.

A. I kept yelling, and I ran after her and grabbed her by the elbow. I wrenched her arm, God help me. It was sprained. But she sort of skidded to a stop. But she was so close to the dogs – it was just – it was –

Q. How close?

A. Very. Too close. Right on top of them.

Q. Less than an arm's length away?

A. Less. Much less. Sonny was howling, the poor dog, and Annie reached her hand toward him with her free hand, and she was tiny – she was four at the time and the smallest girl in her pre-K class.

Q. What happened when she reached for Sonny?

A. The Doberman swung his head toward her. I don't know exactly what happened. I was running toward them. But the next thing I know her hand's bleeding and she's howling. But I made it to her by then and I scooped her up, just scooped her up in my arms and backpedaled as fast as I could to get her away.

Q. Did anyone else try to intervene?

A. No. This woman came strolling out of the dog park after the Doberman.

Q. Did you later find out who she was?

A. Yes. Ivy Jimenez-Brown. She strolled out after him. Just strolled. Like she had all the time in the world.

Q. Was she looking toward the dogs?

A. You know, I don't know. I spun around with Annie and caught sight of this woman as she meandered out. She picked up speed a moment after I saw her, so maybe she couldn't see what was happening before that.

Mr. Prall: Objection –

Mrs. Killion: Or she saw me look at her and decided she had to pretend to care.

Mr. Prall: – to the witness's speculation.

Ms. Spellman: You can ignore him. Was there anything blocking her view so far as you could tell?

A. Well, that dog park, there are hedges, pretty tall hedges around the fence. It helps keep the dogs inside from being distracted by people or other dogs outside the park. So from inside, you don't see that much of the parking lot until you walk out.

Q. And where was Ivy – Ms. Jimenez-Brown – when you first saw her?

A. She was just passing through the gate. Between the hedges.

Q. And you said then she picked up speed. Did she run?

A. She moved faster. Maybe a jog? I was so focused on Annie. She was sobbing.

Q. When Ms. Jimenez-Brown started moving faster, where did she go?

A. She went past me. I was calling 911, and she went toward the dogs. I yelled at her to do something.

Q. Did you know the big Doberman belonged to her?

A. I saw them in the dog park together. It was chilly that day, and there weren't that many people there. I noticed her and the Doberman.

Q. What did she do when she reached the dogs?

A. Nothing. Just watched my Sonny flailing his little legs and her dog shaking its head around. Blood was spraying. I screamed at her – probably scared Annie half to death and –

Mr. Prall: Objection, speculation.

Ms. Spellman: Would you stop? She's entitled to testify to what she thought about the effect on her daughter.

Mr. Prall: Do you want to call the judge? We can call the judge.

Ms. Spellman: We don't need to call the judge. Let's move on. Mrs. Killion, what did you scream at Ivy?

A. I don't remember the words. But to do something. Get her dog. And she yelled at me –

actually yelled at me – and said you don't reach into a dog fight. That even a child should know that.

Q. What happened –

A. Even a child knows – what kind of person says a thing like that?

Q. What happened after she said that?

A. It's kind of jumbled. In my mind. Someone in a uniform came up. Maybe a park attendant? Or a police officer? But the Doberman let go and Sonny just flopped on the pavement.

Q. Flopped?

A. Yes. He was, he was – he was dead. His body flopped. An ambulance came and the paramedics bandaged Annie's hand and got her in the ambulance. She was crying so hard, saying we had to save Sonny. But you could see – there was blood everywhere. I gave my cell phone number to the uniformed guy and got in the ambulance.

Q. Where did it take you?

A. St. Joseph's Hospital. The emergency room. They put a splint on the arm that I yanked on. And Annie had to have surgery to clean the wound in her hand. And stitches. They said it was lucky the teeth missed any major arteries –

Mr. Prall: Objection. Lack of foundation, the witness is not a doctor.

A. – and she still can't close her fist all the way.

That was it for the testimony attached to the motion. The motion filled in the rest of the story. The girl needed multiple stitches and a month of physical therapy. I guessed Ivy's insurance covered the bills and perhaps paid some additional amount because there was no mention of Mrs. Killion filing a lawsuit. Also, as best I could tell from the attached pages, no attorney appeared for Mrs. Killion at the deposition.

I wondered about the logistics of Ralph biting or scratching the little girl. If he still held the smaller dog in his mouth, I wasn't sure he could also bite the girl. Sonny might have dropped to the pavement before Ivy exited the dog park. But it didn't matter. Dogs, labeled dangerous or not, are required to be leashed in Chicago. So no question from a legal perspective that Ivy was at fault for Annie's injuries and trauma.

I texted Shawn and learned he still labored over my computer. So no reason to go back to the office. I found the brief Ivy's attorney filed.

In it, he argued Ivy did keep her dog confined to her own property after the dog park altercation. She co-owned the house with Ellison, and the back stairs where Ralph attacked Ellison's father were part of the house. Also, if the City truly believed Ralph was dangerous, it would have required the dog to be put to sleep and it didn't.

The motion didn't quote any of Ivy's exact words or attach pages from her testimony. I wondered if Ivy had come across as too unsympathetic for that. The gist of her testimony was that the Dachshund provoked Ralph by snapping at his legs – something Mrs. Killion denied. Also that Ellison's chicken had provoked Ralph by pecking him, which Ellison denied.

I twisted my hair around my fingers. Nothing in the motion suggested Corine Killion knew Ivy before the incident or ever contacted her outside of the lawsuit. I felt like I'd run into a blind alley in terms of finding other suspects.

On the other hand, this case might provide an even greater motive for Ellison. To know for sure, I needed to talk to her dad's attorney.

36

"What's your interest in this again? Are you suing the estate?"

Ms. Spellman, Ellison's dad's attorney, practiced in Traverse City, Michigan, where he was from. She had called me back from her boat. I heard seagulls in the background. She told me she often worked from it when the weather was nice enough for boating.

I explained as briefly as I could how I was trying to help Alexis and Amber.

"So do you represent the estate? If so, I can't talk to you," the attorney said.

I shifted another couch cushion behind my back to help keep my spine and neck straight. Post-migraine, good posture helps me feel stronger. "My first question doesn't involve anything confidential. I just want to know if there were any previous incidents with Ivy's dog. I already requested public records about dog complaints, but it's a slow, slow process."

"I suppose I can tell you that. It's in the court record. There was the one where the dog killed a kitten, I think. And the other involved a child near a dog park. I deposed her mother."

"I read part of the deposition," I said. "Could it have been a chicken? The first incident?"

"Oh, yes. A chicken. Not kitten. I keep mixing that up. Do a lot of people keep chickens in Chicago?"

"Not in my neighborhood. No one has yards," I said. "But no other incidents?"

"That was it."

I ran my pen down my legal pad, skimming what I had written. My writing looked squiggly, another post-migraine effect. "You were worried about whether I represent the estate. Is there not enough insurance to cover this?"

Normally, Ivy's homeowner's policy ought to pay for any verdict or settlement. But if she didn't have enough insurance, she would personally owe whatever the insurance didn't pay. Or, in this case, her estate would.

"Bingo."

"But the incident with the girl – was there insurance for that?"

"I don't know. Whether she had insurance for that isn't relevant to my case. But the current policy, the one that covers the attack on my client, is with a substandard carrier."

She told me the name. It was notorious for selling policies with very little coverage and for taking forever to pay.

"So the estate's assets are at risk?" I said.

"Most definitely."

"Whether they tender the policy or not?"

An insurer can agree to offer the entire amount of a policy on the condition that the other side agrees to accept that and not sue the homeowner. A lot of times the plaintiff accepts because until you have a verdict, you're not entitled to learn about whether the defendant has any assets anyway.

But if a policy is very low, and the damages are very high, it's worth it to take the chance and try to collect.

There was a pause. I held myself still, waiting.

"I really can't answer that."

Which meant it was an issue. I thanked her and hung up.

Research on social media told me that Ellison's dad was sixty-three. So, contrary to what the dog walker thought, his bills weren't covered by Medicare. Also, he was a self-employed contractor. Which meant that if he had health insurance at all, it was most likely a policy like mine, with a deductible upwards of $7,000. Add to that the need for treatment away from home and so probably outside his network, he was likely looking at a pile of medical bills.

Depending how low Ivy's insurance policy limit was, it might leave him owing quite a bit. And with no compensation for pain he suffered and however long he'd been out of work.

I didn't know if the money issues added up to enough to motivate Ellison to kill Ivy. But she might very well have wanted to kill the dog.

37

Sylvania claimed she was too busy to meet with me unless I could come out to Geneva again. Much as I wanted to, with all the work I had to catch up on and re-creating access to my law firm computer files, there was no way I could do it until late in the following week. So instead, on Friday afternoon I went to the store and asked for Hank.

He was in but on the phone in his office. The clerk who went looking for him told me I could wait in the break area, which was in the warehouse.

It looked like a miniature version of the warehouse at the lighting store where my Gram worked and where I spent many hours as a kid doing homework. The floors were exposed concrete. Different sized cardboard boxes of merchandise lined metal shelves. Like his sister, Hank kept everything well organized and neat. Keys with different colored keychains hung on a small rack right outside his small, square office. The employee lockers that lined one wall sported color-coded nametags.

Hank waved me in after about ten minutes, and I sank into a green vinyl chair. A heavy glass candy dish on his desk held individually wrapped pink and yellow lifesavers. If I counted them, I bet I would have found an equal number of each color. And if I came back during the winter, the colors would switch to red and green.

"I was hoping to ask you more about Ivy's Doberman. Ralph. And why you think Santiago tried to poison him. If you think that."

I'd decided if Hank and Sylvania had anything to do with Ivy's death, my best chance of getting information was to make them feel safe. Which meant acting as if I were leaning toward believing in Santiago's guilt and persuading his daughters to let all of this go.

Hank straightened the papers in his wire mesh tray, though they already lay flat, their edges aligned. "I don't know what else to think. I'm going by Santiago saying he's guilty."

"Does it ring true to you?"

"Why does that matter?" he said.

"It might help Alexis and Amber come to terms with it. You know them so much better than I do, but they both seem to be struggling. If you could shed some light on why their dad might have done this, maybe they could accept it."

His shoulders rounded as he rested his arms on his desk in front of him. "I'm happy to talk with them anytime."

I uncrossed my legs and let my hands rest on my knees. "I'm not sure they're able to talk about it. But I need to report to them about what I've done and haven't done, learned and haven't learned. They're willing to hear that. They want an update. So if I could include something that could help them understand, it might make the process easier."

He rocked his chair back. It was black faux-leather, shiny and smooth. Its chrome legs had none of the scratches and smudges common to office chairs. Either new or he took pains to keep it in good condition.

"But what can I say that would help? I don't know what was in my brother-in-law's mind."

"Well, the theory is that Santiago was trying to poison Ralph. Did the dog ever try to bite Santiago? Snarl at him? Things like that."

"Ralph didn't love anyone other than Ivy. But he seemed fine with Santiago."

"So why would Santiago try to kill him?"

Hank's eyes turned toward the ceiling. "Jealousy?"

"Of the dog?"

"It's all I can think. Ivy loved that dog. It's the only creature I ever saw her dote on."

"Dote meaning?"

"Put little bows on its head." He pointed to the back of his own head with one finger. "She didn't do that for her girls. Oh, and she never yelled at Ralph. Ever."

"She yelled at Santiago?"

He pursed his lips. "Not yell exactly. That's the wrong word. But she had this way of speaking. She raised her voice, and her words became very – precise. That's the word. And you knew she was angry."

"And she used that tone with Santiago?"

"With everyone. Everyone but Ralph."

Something in his tone made me wonder if Hank might have been jealous of Ralph.

"Including people here? At the store?"

"Especially here. Ivy runs – ran – a tight ship. But I didn't mind. Saved me from being the bad guy. I like the numbers."

"And are the numbers good?" I said.

"Amazingly good. I wondered a little if there would be enough demand when we started this. But Ivy – she was right."

I wanted to ask to see his books to confirm that. But that would make it clear I didn't think Santiago was guilty. Also, no right-minded business person hands over their books to a stranger, so I wouldn't accomplish anything other than putting him on edge.

"Going back to Ralph – you knew he killed her friend Ellison's chicken –"

He waved his hand as if swatting a fly. "As my wife said, that's just a dog being a dog."

"But did you know about Ellison's dad? And the little girl?"

Two lines appeared between his eyebrows. "Little girl? Dad? What are you talking about?"

He didn't seem all that surprised. Maybe he had guessed where I was going. Or maybe he already knew.

I told him about both incidents.

He pressed his hands to his rounded cheeks. "Oh, no. No, that's awful. That poor little girl."

"Not Ellison's father?" I said.

"Well, that's not good. But I wasn't there. I don't know what happened."

"I've seen the medical bills. He was very seriously injured."

"But you said he fell. People trip. If he didn't watch where he was going –" Hank said. "And I never thought Ivy ought to have to keep the dog on a leash on her own property. Sylvania disagreed, but that woman, Ellison, she seemed to have a grudge against Ivy."

Apparently defending dogs was a bit of a genetic thing.

"Was there a reason your wife thought Ralph needed to be leashed?" I said.

"She's – no, no particular reason. She just thought Dobermans are so powerful. And he wasn't very friendly. Better to keep him on a leash."

"Is she afraid of dogs?"

"Sylvania? No. We had dogs for years. We're planning to

get one again, but we're both gone so much that it doesn't make sense right now."

"But the incident with the little girl, do you think Ivy ought to have had Ralph on a leash?"

"That, yes." He sighed, his whole body heaving. "Really she ought to have controlled the dog overall. Taken it to obedience school. Something. It wasn't the dog's fault."

"And the attorney for the estate never told you all this? If you're becoming the executor, you'll need to be informed about possible claims."

"I'm still waiting on papers to appoint me. Santiago objected, so there had to be notice and a hearing. It hasn't happened yet."

That sounded right from what I knew about the process. I couldn't imagine the judge not granting the motion, though.

"Do you think Ralph is dangerous?" I said.

Hank glanced to his left at a giant whiteboard with what looked like sales figures on it. "I don't think he's warm and fuzzy. But Ivy had such a blind spot about that dog."

"Why do you think that was?"

He shook his head. "Ivy — people were a challenge for her. She demanded a lot, and she almost always felt disappointed. Had to be hard for Santiago to live with. But she drove herself, too. Expected herself to be perfect. As if the whole world would fall apart if she weren't."

The sympathy for Santiago in the middle of all the words struck me. If Hank really thought Santiago killed his sister, I expected him to be angry, not sympathetic. Grief takes so many different forms, though. And sometimes people process it years later.

Or stay stuck in it, like my mom.

"Did Santiago ever tell you it was hard to live with Ivy?"

Hank's eyes cut to the right. "No, no. He never said anything bad about her to me. But I grew up with Ivy. And watched her with those girls – so intense. She drove Amber away. I figure she drove Santiago away, too, then drove him over the edge."

"Are you angry at him then?"

His chair thunked forward. "Of course I'm angry at him. What kind of question is that? He killed my sister."

As a former child actress and a lawyer, I have lots of experience being yelled at, usually by men. Theater directors, judges, clients, other lawyers. I don't like it. But I've learned to consider the words, not the tone, make adjustments only if I think I need to, then put it aside and keep doing my job.

Which, here, included wondering why Hank decided to suddenly act angry.

"I didn't mean to suggest you weren't," I said. "It must be terrible to lose your sister and not know what happened."

He cleared his throat. "It is. I don't talk about it much, but it is. I didn't mean to shout at you."

"It's okay. It sounds like you're saying Ivy felt freer to relax with Ralph. To let go of expectations?"

He shifted his chair backwards and it bumped against the wall behind him. "Yes, that's it. Dogs don't evaluate you. If you feed them and take care of them, they love you. So much simpler than people."

"Is that why she didn't want to train him? Or leash him?"

"She believed in giving him freedom. It was the one place in life where she let herself stop controlling everything."

I had to think Ivy hadn't picked the best place to let go of control.

"Did you ever talk to Ivy about Ralph? That he might be a danger?"

Hank sidestepped the question. "I didn't have a reason to, did I? I didn't know about these incidents."

"But you knew the dog was difficult."

He crossed his arms and rested them on his stomach. "I

didn't know it was that bad. And I don't see what it has to do with anything."

I couldn't think of anything else to ask for now. After asking about Alexis and hearing, without much surprise, that she and her little cousin argued a little but mostly got along, I left.

In the store itself, I noticed again how neat everything looked. Someone had aligned all the items an exact half inch from the front edge of each shelf. I had seen something similar recently, but I couldn't think where.

As I walked back to my office it hit me. It was in the photos I'd taken at Ivy's.

38

Shawn was still working on my main firm laptop, and Mensa Sam was talking with one of the other tenants in the kitchen. So I sat at Danielle's desk and scrolled through the photographs of Ivy's home on my phone. I put a few from the basement into a separate folder. Then I came to the ones I took in the pantry. One of them showed shelves of dishes. I enlarged it.

And there it was. A middle pantry shelf held drinking glasses. All of them were arranged upside down so that when you took one you needed to flip it over to fill it. Only one item on the shelf was different. A thermos. It was beautiful, with crystals around the center. And it sat right side up.

Maybe Ivy placed it that way because, unlike the glasses, it had a top. But it also stood out because it wasn't aligned with the front of the other glasses. Instead, it sat back a few centimeters. Plus it seemed unlikely she would place it with the glasses. The other larger containers were on a higher shelf.

I was sure I'd seen a thermos like it before. Maybe in the investigative photos from Ivy's kitchen. Unfortunately, the

Assistant State's Attorney had sent all the photos electronically, so they had been saved on my work laptop. They came in after my last backup, so they wouldn't be on my spare laptop. And I didn't know Danielle's password.

But I did have my email on my phone, and Danielle had forwarded some of the evidence via email. After opening an email from her with an attachment, I found the file with photographs from Ivy's kitchen. One showed a thermos sitting on the butcher block counter next to the sink. It matched the one in the pantry except it had a faint reddish stain around the rim, possibly from lipstick. It looked like there was a design on the lower part of it, but I couldn't see what it was.

I tapped my fingers on my desk. So Ivy had two thermoses. It felt like it mattered for some reason – but why? I shut my eyes and pictured the different people I had talked to about Ivy. Someone had mentioned a thermos. I also felt like I'd seen one before, and not only in the police photograph.

In my head, I heard the voices and words of people I'd talked to. It was a skill I developed as an actor practicing lines, and it helped me remember what witnesses and clients said in interviews and when they testified.

I saw the screened-in porch and the cherry tree outside it. Mei. I rifled through my paper notes and found it.

Mei had said Ivy was carrying a fancy thermos the night they met for coffee.

I texted Mei and asked if she could describe the thermos that Ivy had been carrying.

While I waited for Mei's response, I contacted the lawyer representing the plaintiff in one of my family business cases and asked for some extra time to file a response to his motion given my computer problems. He agreed to an extra fourteen days. I prepared an agreed order and a short motion to go with it, grateful he was unlike Prall, the attorney who made all the objections in the deposition I'd read.

By the time I finished, Shawn had some marginally good news. He thought he would have me up and running by Monday.

With that, he packed his briefcase to leave for the night. He had set some diagnostics to run overnight and promised to return tomorrow, despite that it was Saturday. I refused to think about how much his firm's weekend rate was going to cost me.

As he left the office suite, Mei's answering text came.

Silver or white. Pretty colored crystals around the center. Had her store logo on it.

The store logo. That might be the design I could almost see in the photos.

Any idea if she had more than one?

She told me it was custom from her store. So maybe.

If I had seen the thermos somewhere, the most logical place would have been at Ivy's store. But I felt sure it was in Ivy's online photos or videos.

I texted both Amber and Alexis the photo from the pantry. Both thought it looked familiar, but neither remembered anything particular about it or whether their mom had more than one that looked like it.

It was after six. I took a break to walk to the Potbellies down the street to get a meatball sandwich. I ate in my office as I watched Ivy's YouTube channel. After checking numerous videos about animals, I searched for cleanses. I found the one Tammy had told me about where she talked about the vegan cleanse.

At least I thought that was it. It matched the time frame. Ivy went through all the ingredients and recommendations, never mentioning that she had gotten the recipes from anyone else.

In the next video I fast forwarded through I saw her holding what looked like the thermos. I hit pause, then advanced a frame at a time. On screen, Ivy turned the thermos so her viewers could see the inside. At the bottom, underneath a screen of clear Lucite, were black rocks. Ivy said they were lava rocks and would provide good energy. She recommended that to stay hydrated during the cleanse you always carry water in this type of thermos. The rocks would purify it.

It wasn't clear how the rocks could do that through Lucite, or at all, but that didn't stop Ivy from pointing viewers to the link below the video where they could purchase a thermos from her store.

I followed the link. The price for the thermos struck me as shockingly high — over two hundred dollars. Yes, it had lava rocks, a jeweled exterior, and could be used for hot or cold. But I grew up in a home where my Gram washed plasticware to reuse at the next party out of concern for her budget, not the environment.

Ivy, though, would only have paid the wholesale price, so perhaps she had bought more than one.

I texted the video to Roy and asked if he remembered Ivy having this thermos.

Sure. She liked drinking water from it. Something about the rocks filtering the water

She have more than one?

Don't think so only saw one. She reused it a lot

Why do you remember that?

I used to tell her she should wash it more

That didn't prove anything. But it did suggest the thermos on the counter belonged to Ivy and the one in the pantry might have been put there by someone else. Someone who filled it with antifreeze ahead of time, poured it into Ivy's food, and had to stash it in the pantry too fast to align it perfectly with the other items.

After texting Ty to tell him I'd be at his place in half an hour, I texted Alexis and asked if she could let me into the house again tomorrow. Then I called Lauren and asked her to do a little more shopping. That way I didn't have to risk running into Hank if I returned there myself.

39

At eleven the next morning, Lauren plopped a paper bag on the office kitchen table and took out a thermos. It looked exactly like the ones in the photos except it didn't have any sort of logo on it.

"The clerk told me I could have it customized with a logo here or here." She pointed to two different spots on the thermos. "That's included in the purchase price if you want it. And it has the rocks in the Lucite that are supposed to bring good energy or whatever. And a vacuum sealed top. Supposedly you can turn it upside down and shake it and no spills, no leaks."

We filled it with water, sealed it, and tested it out. It lived up to the claims. Which meant someone could carry a thermos of antifreeze in a purse or backpack without worry about it leaking and needing to explain the smell or stain from it.

I ran my fingers over the jeweled exterior. The small rose, violet, and aquamarine crystals weren't real gemstones, but looked stunning in the sunlight streaming in through the windows. "How many thermoses were on the shelf?"

"Well, that's a totally interesting thing. This was the only one. I asked the clerk if they were ordering more and she said that it doesn't sell that often. It is one of the pricier things in the store. And they have about five other thermoses that are also pretty and cost half as much."

"None of which means Ivy might not have had more than one," I said. "I'm guessing the mark up on this might be over a hundred percent. Gram told me at the lighting store the most expensive lamps also have the highest markup percentage."

"Oh, definitely," Lauren said. "That's why all the new construction here is luxury condos. Throwing in granite countertops and high-end appliances doubles the cost to the builder but it triples the price for the consumer. People like luxury, and the more it costs, the more they think it's worth. And the more they feel they're worth."

It was an interesting comment from someone who loved designer brands as much as Lauren did. I'm a fan, too, if I can find a deal on them. I like them for the effect dressing well and carrying a designer shoulder bag has on potential clients, who assume it indicates success.

"You think Ivy had a thermos from her own store as a status symbol?"

Lauren waggled her hand. "Possible. From what you told me about her, though, and with a logo on it, I'm guessing it was more for advertising."

I met Alexis at the house in the late afternoon. She was staying overnight at her friend's house again so that she wouldn't have to tell her aunt and uncle she was meeting me. I felt bad about asking her to keep lying by omission, but I still didn't want them to know any more than necessary about what I was doing.

"It's okay," Alexis said as we walked up to the third floor. "A lot of times I didn't tell Mom what I was doing. So it's nothing new for me."

We walked through all the third-floor rooms. Despite honing in on the thermos in the photos, it was possible there was something else I'd missed on a previous visit.

Nothing came to mind, though, and the neatness of the closet in Ivy's bedroom reinforced my view that the misplaced thermos was completely out of character for her. In the pantry, I pulled on latex gloves and took the thermos off the shelf. The logo of Ivy's store was emblazoned on the front. The inside looked clean. I sniffed. I couldn't smell anything unusual. But I dropped the glass into a plastic baggie, added the top, which had been sitting on the shelf behind it, and sealed the bag.

"You're sure you don't know if your mom had more than one of these?"

Alexis studied it. "Now that I see it up close, I kinda remember these crystals. But I never really noticed what she drank out of."

"Did you ever see anyone else with a thermos like this? Like Ellison or Roy? Maybe your mom gave them out as gifts?"

Alexis shook her head. "She wasn't a huge gift giver."

"How about your Aunt Sylvania? Or your Uncle Hank? I thought they might have ones like this one, with the store logos."

"I haven't seen one at the house. Maybe at Aunt Sylvania's yoga studio."

That's when it clicked. Where I'd seen the thermos before.

40

On my phone I navigated to the website for Sylvania's yoga studio. I flipped through photographs of different classes and finally found the one I was looking for. In the background, when I enlarged the photo, a pretty jeweled thermos sat on the counter behind Sylvania as she led the class. It sat at a bad angle for me to see the full logo, but otherwise it was a perfect match.

It seemed odd that she hadn't had it customized with her own studio's logo rather than that of Ivy's store. Though it was Hank's store as well, so maybe it was a way of cross-promoting.

I didn't feel sure what the thermos in the photo proved. But if the one in Ivy's pantry had residue from antifreeze, maybe it would be enough to get Santiago off the hook. Or at least convince him not to plead guilty.

"I want to look in the basement, too," I told Alexis.

We walked down the stairs. The only lighting were open bulbs on chains. One hung over the washer and dryer. Another at the center of the dry-walled room. I walked in. It smelled of mildew and faintly of sewer gas. I shone the flashlight from my phone up into the top right corner.

"Here," I said. "You told me that connects with the passageway to your mom's closets that she nailed shut. But do you know that for sure? Because I don't think it lines up."

My years of theater work left me with a good sense of spatial relations. Or maybe I had that naturally and it helped me with blocking – the process of learning and remembering where to stand and move on stage – when I started acting. As a kid, it helped me get jobs because I always remembered right where I was supposed to be and when.

"I'm pretty sure. But I'll check with Amber."

Alexis texted while I checked the utility closet. There was a metal ladder inside, but no tools. Ellison must keep her own in her apartment.

"Amber thinks it's the same one," Alexis said. "But she's not sure. Neither of us climbed up there. We were more tree climbers."

If this was a different passageway, it might also connect Ellison's and Ivy's homes. A long shot, but I needed to check everything with Santiago on the verge of pleading guilty.

"Do you mind if I come back tomorrow or the next day with a ladder and a friend and check it out?" I said.

"Can I watch?"

"I wouldn't mind, but it might be when you're in school. Can I borrow your key?"

She worked her key off the key ring and handed it to me. "Promise you'll tell me what you find."

"I promise," I said.

I stopped at the office before I went home so I could lock the thermos, sealed in a plastic bag, in the office safe Danielle and I shared. On the bus ride home I'd texted her about it, but she was on her way to pick up her daughter, so she answered only that we'd talk on Monday.

When I returned to the house late Sunday afternoon, expecting to meet Lauren on the front porch, Joe was there, too. He and I had last texted a few days ago, still trying to find a time to meet for drinks at the Palmer House.

He gave me a quick hug, more of a squeeze of my shoulders. "Hey, Q., sorry – I owe you a call. Things've been a little hectic."

Joe's the only one I let get away with calling me Q. He knew me first as Q.C., and it still comes to his mind now and then.

"For me, too," I said. "Work on a Sunday?"

He wore charcoal gray pants, a collared shirt, and a lightweight sport jacket.

"I gave a continuing education seminar."

Lauren had told me she had a few condo showings today, but she had clearly changed after. Her short blond hair was pinned out of her face, and she wore jeans, designer running shoes, and a tank top. Even after a summer of swimming and biking her shoulders and bare arms didn't look tan, though maybe a shade less ghostly white than usual. My skin had deepened to a bronze shade I loved, though the rest of the year I'd rather have Lauren's peaches and cream complexion.

She gestured at Joe. "Figured we should have reinforcements. Especially if you're planning to crawl around between floors or something. No way am I going to be in the basement alone trying to figure out whether to call for help if you don't come back."

I started to say that was ridiculous, but my exploits had gotten both Lauren and me injured before. I didn't blame her for wanting someone else around.

"Good idea," I said. "Let's look around, see if you agree with me."

We took a quick walk through the basement, then a slower pass through the third floor. I showed them the trap door under Ivy's shoe rack. Both agreed it might be a little off from the trap door in the basement ceiling. But they weren't sure if they would have noticed if I hadn't.

We took the back stairs down to the second floor, locking and unlocking each door. The locks must have been oiled recently, as they moved easily and noiselessly.

Lauren clicked the timer on her phone as we entered the second-floor kitchen area. "Fifteen seconds."

"Probably a little longer to go up," I said. "But not too much if a person has keys."

They agreed the side door in the second-floor closet lined up with the trap door above. We didn't see anywhere else a second hidden passageway might lead to.

"So the basement opening leads up to this or it's a separate way to get to Ellison's," Lauren said.

"One way to find out," I said.

In the basement again, I opened my powder blue toolset. My mom had gotten it for me for Christmas one year when I bought my first condo.

Lauren held the ladder as I climbed. The trap door had been painted with thick, off-white paint. When I pried it open it with a flathead screwdriver it nearly banged my head, and I swayed on the ladder. Lauren let out a yelp of fear, but she held the ladder steady and I kept my balance.

I shone my flashlight from my phone up into the opening. It was a dark, narrow passageway with unfinished wood all around and climbing rungs along one side.

"You are not seriously climbing up there," Lauren said.

41

"It's safer than climbing down," I said. "If a rung feels squishy when I grab it I won't climb up any farther. I'll come back."

"What if you get stuck? I'm not coming up after you."

Lauren's usually the first to dive into an adventure, so her hesitancy made me pause. I glanced at Joe. "Will you?"

He peered up into the narrow passageway. "Why does it matter? We didn't see any place it connected to in Ivy's."

"Just because we didn't see it doesn't mean it's not there. Remember Flytrap?" I said, naming a mystery play we'd been in together.

"Totally not fair using obscure theater references," Lauren said. "Also, this is life, not a play."

"How else can I find out where this goes?" I said. "Alexis said there were all kinds of odd things in the house. Remember the bonus room I told you both about at Caleb's dad's? Maybe something like that."

My childhood friend Caleb's father owned a townhouse that had a bonus room off the master bedroom's walk-in closet, one no one who didn't live there would ever notice. It might very well have saved my life the previous spring.

Lauren crossed her arms over her chest. "Sure, but that had a door. You had to pry this open. It's obvious nobody's gone up there in years."

Lauren wasn't wrong, but I couldn't shake the feeling that something in Ivy's home meshed with this door.

"Look, I'll climb the first few rungs inside and see what it looks like. Then I promise I'll come down and we'll decide the next step together. And I came prepared."

I reached into the pocket of my cargo pants and took out a headlamp Mensa Sam used when he biked at night. Its lightweight strap fastened with Velcro in the back with the beam at the front so I wouldn't need to use my hands to hold my phone or a real flashlight.

"Let me look first," Joe said.

I rolled my eyes. "Because you're the man?"

He clicked on the flashlight on his phone. "Because I'm taller."

"And I have seriously more confidence he won't just keep climbing if it looks dangerous," Lauren said.

At a little over six feet, Joe was at least four inches taller than I am and half a foot taller than Lauren. Though I didn't see what that had to do with anything. I also was dressed more appropriately. My cargo pants were long out of style but practical, and my black T-shirt had seen enough days that I had no problem tossing it if it got ripped.

But he was already gripping the sides of the ladder.

I handed him the headlamp. "Fine, if you want to ruin your business clothes."

Joe tucked his phone in his shirt pocket, lit the headlamp, and started climbing toward the trap door in the ceiling. "They need to be cleaned anyway."

I held the ladder on one side, and Lauren grabbed the other. It trembled a bit with each step but for the most part held steady. Dust rained down, some into my eyes. I blinked it away, but my eyes still felt gritty.

As Joe neared the top, he gripped the first rung of the ship's ladder inside the passageway. He climbed until we saw only his feet on the second from the top ladder rung, then kept going, disappearing into the passageway above us.

Lauren cupped her hands around her mouth and shouted. "How high are you?"

"Near the first floor maybe." Joe's voice sounded muffled and tinny.

"Come back," I said.

"Hang on – eee."

I might have laughed at Joe's shriek – so unlike him, but black things rained down around us. Lauren jumped away. I hung onto the ladder but squeezed my eyes shut again.

"Don't move," Lauren said. She batted at my hair from behind while I tried not to think about what she was doing. "Okay, you can look. Though I definitely don't advise it."

I glanced down. Dead cockroaches lay at my feet, along with dirt and a couple dead flies.

"Nice." I shivered.

Joe climbed down, brushing dirt off himself. "The rungs I grabbed on felt solid enough. All I saw was more ladder and a lot of dust. And bugs."

"At least they're dead," I said. "Did it look like the passageway continued up?"

"Yep."

"Obviously no one's been up there in forever," Lauren said.

"But it goes somewhere," I said.

After some debate, Lauren agreed to head to the second floor to listen for me. I put on the headlamp. Joe stayed below to hold the ladder.

I started a three-way call and put it on speaker, then used a small bungee cord to hang the phone around my neck.

The rungs turned out to be about six inches apart – I measured them with a measuring tape I then tossed down to Joe. I counted rungs as I went, calling out when I hit five. It allowed Joe and Lauren to calculate how far I traveled, which I was also doing in my head, and to know they could still hear me.

The signal started to fade as I reached twenty feet, which ought to put me almost to the second floor. I tilted my head to shine the light directly above me.

"There's another trap door," I said.

"I can hardly hear you." Joe's voice sounded tinny and far away through the phone's speaker.

"Just a few more rungs," I said.

This door hadn't been painted shut. It also was above me, capping the passageway, not to one side. So it didn't match the trap door in Ivy's second-floor spare bedroom closet.

It had hinges and a handle. If I pulled down on it, the door ought to open. But I didn't know if anything might be on top of it. Or how heavy it was and whether that weight might throw me off balance. I didn't think the human body was meant to fall two stories.

"Lauren?"

"You're fading," she said. "Go back down."

"I'm going to knock."

"What?"

"Try to figure out where I am." I rapped my knuckles hard on the wall to my right.

"Quille?" she said.

I knocked four more times.

"Wow, seriously, you're...wall or....now it's.....floor...."

I inched up and kept knocking, though I couldn't hear Lauren anymore. I hoped she'd think to mark the spot on the floor or wall where she heard me. The door was within reach. I felt tempted to pull on it. But I remembered my instructor harping on avoiding hazards. And my promises to Eric and Alexis to be careful. I held on tight with one hand and used the other to take a photo of it.

After two more shots, I inched my way down. It felt like it took forever, but at last I heard Lauren and Joe saying my name through the phone. When I answered. Lauren said she thought she knew where I'd been.

Joe and I hurried to the second floor to join Lauren.

$\sim$

"I thought it was from there," Lauren said. "But there's nothing."

The guest bedroom's closet had no trap door in the floor, only the one in the side I already knew about. The family room also had nothing.

"This sitting area looks smaller than upstairs," I said.

"Don't furnished rooms look more inviting and bigger?" Joe said.

Lauren scanned the bare family room. "Depends on the furniture and the arrangement. But you're not wrong – a lot of empty spaces do look smaller. People have a hard time imagining what can fit in them. That's why I hate showing a place after the owners move out. Also, it shows all the scratches and marks."

She waved at the scratches Ralph had made in the hardwood floor.

"I don't think it's the lack of furniture," I said. "If there's a space, a room, between the guest bedroom and this area it would match with the trap door."

Lauren put her ear to the wall and knocked. Then she

shrugged. "Seriously no idea what that's supposed to tell me. I just always see people do it in movies."

"If there is a room," Joe said, "how likely is it anyone's been in there? That door was painted shut. And the bugs –"

"Yeah, I don't see Ivy climbing that ladder," I said. "Not with all the dirt and bugs."

Joe headed for the hallway. "There must be another way in."

The guest bedroom barely fit a bed and a tall wooden bookcase. The latter was filled with home office supplies, mostly pens and notecards that had curled and yellowed on the edges. It stood next to the closet we had already looked through, but might hide a door to a hidden room. With a lot of effort, Joe and I inched the bookcase away from the wall. And found nothing.

Joe stepped back and stared at the rectangle of paint, slightly darker than the sections around it that had been exposed to the sun. "Huh. I wanted it to be there. Or for the bookcase to swing open on its own."

"In any good play that would happen," I said.

The wall across from the bathroom had a linen closet. That closet, too, didn't seem to have any sort of false back. But I noticed what looked like a line next to it where the aging paint had cracked from the floor up toward the ceiling. I felt along the line.

"It's a seam." I pressed my fingers along it and felt some give. With a little effort, a narrow door swung open. Before stepping in, I clicked on my headlamp.

And saw a long, narrow room. Shallow bookshelves on one side ran from the floor to the ceiling. An old-fashioned sliding metal library ladder stood at the far end. A tall, narrow, four-drawer gray file cabinet stood at the end of the row of bookshelves. A weathered leather club chair with wide arms and an ottoman sat against the short wall opposite the door. When I flipped the light switch next to the hallway door, the desk lamp on the dark wood side table next to the club chair clicked on.

The wall that separated the hidden room from the living room was painted a bright apricot color that made the room feel warm and larger than it was. The other walls were off-white. All looked recently painted.

I took a few photos and texted them to Alexis and Amber, asking if either recognized the room.

"Ivy had a hideaway?" Lauren said from behind Joe. Neither had come into the room with me.

The books on the shelf at eye-level included a large number on veganism, herbal medicine, and animal rights. "I'm guessing yes."

"But she lived alone," Lauren said.

"Now," I said. "But not always."

If this was a place Ivy went to relax, it hadn't loosened her organizational skills. The books were grouped by topic but arranged largest to smallest within each category. Lower shelves included books on finance and business, many that I remembered Gram having on her shelves twenty years ago, and they'd been old then. That Ivy had basic finance books struck me as odd with her finance background. As if I had Law for Dummies on my shelves. But maybe these came from a time when she was deciding whether to go into finance or not.

I pulled on latex gloves just in case the police wanted to go over the room later.

"You're really thinking there's anything worth finding here?" Lauren said.

"Ivy kept this room private for some reason. Though I guess a sticky note saying Who Killed Me And Why is unlikely."

"You never know." Joe held out his hand, and I gave him a pair of gloves. Lauren sighed and took a pair as well.

"You don't think we should call the cops first?" Lauren said. "I mean, I totally wouldn't, but maybe we ought to think about it."

Given that the police hadn't done much for Santiago so far, I wanted a look before they got one.

"The reports say they searched the whole house the night of Ivy's death," I said. "And they released the crime scene. Let's try to leave it as we found it though."

Joe looked through the file cabinet and Lauren took books out, shook them to see if anything fell out, and put them back. All that dropped out were old receipts and a couple handwritten shopping lists.

I compared the books to the ones on shelves near the front entrance to the second floor.

Those books, the ones open to everyone, told a story of Ivy's life. There were college textbooks on the bottom, though only a small number, maybe from courses Ivy had liked. Two full shelves of books on sales techniques and networking. There were novels in hardback that looked like they'd come from some type of book of the month club in the 80s or 90s that focused on bestselling mainstream novels, then a row of science fiction paperbacks. Cookbooks and diet books. A row of books on starting your own business.

The hidden room included hardbacks and paperbacks on raising children. Two full rows. Most of those had titles that used what I guessed were euphemisms for kids that parents had trouble controlling. They referred to the children as spirited or independent or self-directed. If you thought those were good qualities, you probably didn't need books on how to deal with them. Most talked about things like providing structure, creating clear rules, and being the "pack leader."

In contrast, the books on dogs had softer titles. *Communi-*

cating With Your Animal Companion. Not Our Pets, Our Friends. Living In Harmony With A Canine. Freedom For All (Dogs). I wondered if Ivy's challenges with child raising led her to take the opposite tack with Ralph.

One book didn't quite fit with the others, at least to my eye as someone who knew little about canines. *Crate Training Your Aging Dog.* I looked at the copyright date. It was this year, so Ivy must have bought it recently.

In the center of the hidden bookshelf were books on relationships. Most of those dated from two years back, around when she and Santiago separated. They weren't about dealing with divorce – though there were a few of those in the finance section in the family room – but on getting past blocks in relationships, forging closer connections, and becoming less critical. Their pages weren't worn, but they had enough wrinkles and tiny folds in corners that I could tell they'd been read.

I ran my fingers over the titles. There were twenty-five of them, which was at least a book a month. Yet no one had mentioned seeing any positive changes in Ivy over the last two years. For the first time I felt a real sense of sadness for her as a person. As the mom, and wife, and friend, and sister I'd heard about. A woman who recognized her lack of skills and was trying to do better, but no one noticed.

"Could be that thing where people know you forever and just can't see that you've changed," Joe said.

"Or you can't reverse fifty-plus years of habits and choices in two years," Lauren said.

Amber answered my text saying that she didn't recognize the room.

"I guess she could have read the books and not put any of it into practice," I said. My Gram wasn't a fan of self-help books for that reason. She claimed most people read books instead of trying to make real progress in life. My mother had shelves of those types of books, which I think was Gram's point.

"This one's all old tax returns. From three decades ago." Joe closed the bottom file cabinet drawer. "From what you said about Ivy, though, she seems like someone who acted on what she learned. At least, in her career she did."

"It's totally scary to change," Lauren said. "She might have wanted to and just couldn't bring herself to do it."

I took photos of the front and back of the book on crating dogs. "You guys know anything about crate training?"

Unlike the finance and relationship books, the pages I thumbed through on this one remained crisp. The book's spine still felt stiff. Ivy might never have read it. Or she might have read it once, carefully, to keep it looking good.

Joe shrugged. "I've heard of it. The crate's like the dog's house."

"Like Snoopy's doghouse," Lauren said. "Kidding. Some of my clients crate their dogs. Sometimes so the dog stays in one spot at night. It's good for showings, too, though I prefer they leave and take their pets with them."

I did a quick search on my phone. "PETA doesn't like it. Says it increases hyperactivity and depression in dogs and is basically awful because dogs are social animals."

"But that's PETA," Lauren said. "Seriously, what else would they say?"

"Right, but it seems like Ivy would be on the PETA side, not the realtor side," I said.

I texted Alexis, who still hadn't answered about whether she had ever been inside the room, to also ask if Ralph had a crate. While I was taking a few more photos of the room, she answered No to both questions. She added that she wanted to see the room. I told her to call me tomorrow, but the police might want to see it first.

Joe retrieved the ladder from the basement and opened it

in the hidden room. I climbed to the top to inspect the ceiling. "Can't see any sort of trap door going up."

We checked the walls as best we could and didn't see any way to get from Ivy's sanctuary to the third floor. We went through the rest of the second floor room-by-room, studying all the surfaces and measuring room sizes. We didn't find any other trap doors or hidden rooms. We did the same on the third floor and in the basement. It took over two hours.

As satisfied as I could be, I emailed the room photos with an explanation to Danielle. She'd know if we needed to inform the police.

We sat at the butcher block counter in the third-floor kitchen. My face felt grimy from dust, and even Lauren, always pristine, had gray fuzz clinging to her clothes.

I pointed to smears of dirt across the arms of Joe's sport jacket. "Hope you were serious about the cleaners."

"No question. Or I would have stopped home to change first."

Lauren studied the photos on my phone. "So no super-secret way to get from Ellison's place to Ivy's."

After all the climbing and searching my head felt heavy. I propped my elbows on the table and rested my chin on my clasped hands. "That we could find. But I'm pretty satisfied there's none. And no other way from the second to third floor. So we're still looking for someone with a key."

"Other than Santiago," Joe said.

"Other than Santiago. I wish I knew him personally." Something tickled my upper arm. I slapped my hand over the itching skin, thinking of the cockroaches. But it was just my own hair. "Not that I can tell a killer from not-a-killer on sight. But if I had a feel for him, for who he is, it might be a little easier."

Social media had shown me nothing. Ivy didn't post about Santiago, and he didn't have his own accounts anywhere that I could find. Amber's and Alexis's pages included little about their parents.

Lauren shrugged. "I don't know if that would help. If he's someone who could kill his wife in cold blood, he could probably hide that side of himself."

"But if whoever did it was aiming for the dog – " Joe said.

"It's still a pretty cold thing to do," I said.

"And phenomenally dumb," Lauren said. "Who takes a chance like that?"

"Someone really angry at the dog," I said.

42

On Monday, Shawn still struggled to reboot my system. I worked on my old laptop outside at Café des Livres. After three hours recreating more lost work and drinking too much black tea, I scrolled through the photos of the crate training book on my phone. I wasn't sure if it bothered me because it was the only unusual thing we'd found or because it held a clue to Ivy's death. Or at least to a key part of her life. Though some of the other books surprised me, like the basic finance ones, none directly contradicted what people had told me were Ivy's core values.

I texted Roy, asking if we could meet. As I waited for an answer, I read through the PETA posts about crating again, then searched for and found more positive views of crating, including on a legal aid site that focused on animal rights. All the same, I couldn't see Ivy crating Ralph.

My phone buzzed.

Busy day but call me if you want to talk. Or if you can meet me in Ravenswood can talk in person.

We made plans to meet later in the day.

～

Before texting Roy, I had also texted Tammy Solomon. She called me early in the afternoon. I sat at my desk, my computer pushed to one side as it ran yet another diagnostic.

I told Tammy about the previous attacks Ralph made.

"Oh, that might explain something," she said.

I sat straighter and held my pen poised over my white legal pad. "What's that?"

"There was a point where Ivy started keeping the dog locked in the spare bedroom during our meetings."

I flipped pages until I found a timeline I had sketched out of the last two years of Ivy's life. "When was that?"

"Not sure exactly. I missed a lot of meetings last fall and through the winter. Traveling a lot for work. Then when I came back in spring, the dog was always locked up in the spare bedroom."

The timing made it at least six months before Ellison's dad had his encounter with Ralph in mid-March.

"Is there a reason you noticed that?" I said.

"Ivy never put the dog away before. She thought Ralph shouldn't be punished, as she put it, if humans felt uncomfortable with dogs."

I drew a giant star in my notes. That comment went a long way toward the idea that Ivy would never crate Ralph.

"Any other changes?"

"No, I don't – oh, wait. No one brought their kids anymore. And Ivy was kind of snappish when I asked where they were. She used to say it was good for kids to learn about networking early."

I circled the word Kids on the page so I'd come back to it. Right now I wanted to ask about snappish Ivy.

"Why do you think she snapped at you?"

"I got the impression someone asked her to lock the dog away. And she grudgingly did it but was mad about it."

"Someone in the group?"

"It must be or why else would she do it?" Tammy said.

"But no one told you they'd asked her to?"

"No. And now that you're asking, I'm not sure anyone did. Maybe it's just that I wished for so long she'd lock Ralph away that I just assumed someone finally convinced her to do it."

The bell on the suite door rang and loud men's voices filled the reception area. I rolled my chair backward and swung my door shut.

"Did Ivy say anything else about Ralph?"

"Something about trouble when I asked where he was. She said she didn't want to get Ralph in trouble. Then there was this sort of awkward silence and she started the meeting."

"Did Ivy say what kind of trouble?"

"No. The trouble part was more like one of those muttered comments people make. Which now that I think of it was odd for Ivy. Usually she came straight out with whatever she wanted to say."

"How did you feel about her locking up Ralph?" I said.

"Relieved. I think everyone was. I love dogs. I've got two. But that one made me nervous."

"Could the dog have attacked someone in the group?"

"No. If that happened, I'm sure someone would have told me."

I drank some more water and skimmed my notes. "You said people stopped bringing their kids. Who had kids?"

"At least four others and me, but I never brought mine. They're teenagers and into their own causes."

She gave me the names, which included Sylvania, two other women I'd spoken to, and a man who ran Farmers'

Markets in his town. According to Tammy, he stopped attending two months before Ivy's death.

Tammy didn't tell me about any specific incident herself with the dog. But she said Ralph always watched people and at times growled, which made her uncomfortable.

"So at that last meeting, the dog was locked in which bedroom?"

"The one right off the front entrance. He scratched and barked for probably the first half hour of the meeting and then must've gone to sleep."

I underlined that on my notepad. If he was penned in near the front door, Ralph might not have reacted if someone at the meeting slipped up the back stairs to the third floor. From everyone's memory, no one left the meeting long enough to go to the garage for antifreeze and back. But if someone brought antifreeze in a thermos or another container hidden inside a purse or backpack, that lessened the time needed to slip it into Ivy's food.

"Do you remember anyone at the meetings having a very pretty thermos? Gemstones around the center, a logo on it?"

"Oh, Ivy had something really pretty like that. Had filtered rocks in it. Or rocks that were supposed to filter water? Something like that. She tried to sell us all on them. But, really, two hundred dollars for a thermos?"

"Only Ivy?" I said.

"I'm pretty sure. But I suppose someone else could have had one and I didn't notice."

Tammy asked if I could hold for a moment while she answered an urgent email.

I stood and paced a circle around my office. Nothing Tammy said suggested anyone in the group wanted to poison the dog or Ivy. Just the opposite. Whatever prompted it, Ivy had kept the dog away from them.

The circled word Kids, though, gave me one idea.

I texted Alexis.

Is your cousin afraid of Ralph?

She answered right away, though she ought to be in class right now. I hoped her teacher would forgive me.

Percy's not afraid of anything.

I sighed. Not much there.

"One thing I don't understand," I said when Tammy got back on the line. "I've been told the dog had the run of the second floor. Why not just have the meetings on the third floor?"

"We used to. And the dog stayed on the second. But Ivy had this thing once Santiago and Amber were both gone. She said at least she could keep things the way she wanted. Clean. In order. So she just didn't let people on that third floor."

"Even if she had people over and made food?"

"She made the food in her upstairs kitchen and brought it down. Ivy really liked things a certain way."

"I'm getting that idea," I said.

43

"Not everyone sees crate training as cruel and unusual punishment," Roy said.

I walked next to him on a tree-lined side street in Ravenswood. The Metra railroad tracks ran next to us, and I could smell the creosote from the railroad ties in the hot sun. It took me back to my childhood.

"Did Ivy?"

He whistled and a little dog that looked like a mobile mop ambled back toward us. "I would have thought so."

"She never mentioned she was considering it? Or buying a book about it?"

The mop dog nosed around some scrubby looking plants, then lifted its leg over them.

"No."

"Would she have told you?" I said. "Since you weren't seeing each other anymore?"

"I still took care of Ralph. And we were still friends."

Interesting that he put it in that order.

"Also, she talked to me about finding an apartment that

allowed dogs. I'm sure she would have mentioned crating if she were thinking about that."

"Why was she looking at apartments?" I said.

"She planned to move out of the house eventually. Get a two-bedroom somewhere and rent out both floors of her place for the income. She still had a mortgage on the place, and I got the idea without Santiago's income it was going to be tricky."

The custody battle likely affected that. Illinois law requires a non-custodial parent to pay twenty percent of their income to the custodial parent for one child. Santiago having custody of Alexis meant Ivy owed him money rather than the other way around.

The more Roy and I talked about the pros and cons of crating the more convinced I became that Ivy would not have done it despite having the book about it.

"I found so much about crate training on the Internet. Are you surprised she bought a book about it?" I said.

Roy held out a treat to the little dog, who rolled over and waved his paws in the air. "Yeah, it's kind of weird. She's more apt to read books than I am, but most things she starts – started – by researching online. Hard to think she found anything that made her seriously consider crate training."

"And not talk to you about it."

"Yeah, that is surprising. I've been helping take care of Ralph since she got him."

"Do you miss him? Ralph?"

"What? No. Ivy's brother, Hank, passed on my info to Ralph's new guardians. So I still walk him five times a week. Don't get to play with him as much, but I see him. So it's all good."

During train ride back I scrolled through the photos of the hidden room and the books yet again. And finally saw something. As the automated voice called out "Ogilvie Transportation Center, last stop, all passengers must exit at Ogilvie," I zoomed in on the price tag on the bottom right corner of the back of the book.

It was from a store in Geneva, Illinois. Maybe Ivy hadn't bought the book after all.

44

The next morning, Danielle and I sat on one of the wide couches near the fireplace in Café des Livres. The fireplace was off, as it was still August and in the eighties outside. But rain drummed down onto the pavement, making inside the best option.

Danielle told me the Assistant State's Attorney was pushing Santiago to commit to the plea bargain by the end of next week.

"But what about the thermos?" I said.

Danielle stirred sugar into her black coffee. "I'll drop it off later today at the lab. I want to see what the analysis is before I tell the prosecution about it. But it might not make any difference at all."

"But if there's antifreeze –"

"If chemical tests show antifreeze was in that thermos, it only proves there were two possible ways Ivy ingested poison." Danielle held up two fingers. "From the bowl of veggie slop or after drinking from that thermos. Not that anyone other than Santiago poisoned her."

"But why would Ivy ever drink from a thermos and put it on her pantry shelf?"

"It's not the strangest thing a person can do."

"It is for Ivy. That must raise more of a doubt."

"To you, yes. Even to me. But with this prosecutor? I doubt it."

I gripped the edge of the sofa. "Why not?"

"It's where the State's Attorney's office is these days. Look, back when I was in the office, I would never have charged Santiago to begin with absent more evidence. It's not as anti any sort of deal as when Anita ran things. But it's not great."

Each county in Illinois elects the State's Attorney – in theory the lead prosecutor for any Illinois criminal case in that county. That person might or might not have a lot of experience as a criminal lawyer. What counted more was political connections and fundraising. Mayor Richard M. Daley was the State's Attorney for nine years before becoming mayor.

Assistant State's Attorneys try almost all the cases, but the State's Attorney's philosophy and campaign promises governs how the office runs. Danielle was referring to one of the State's Attorneys before the current one who had, at least based on what Danielle told me, prosecuted everything to the hilt. No flexibility, no recognition of weaknesses in the prosecution's case.

Under the ethics rules, prosecutors are different than other lawyers. All attorneys need to argue strongly for their clients' interests whether they agree with them or not. But prosecutors are also required to do justice. That means even if a victim is demanding an arrest or that charges be filed, the prosecutor isn't supposed to proceed if after investigating she sees no real basis for the charges.

"If there are fingerprints on the thermos," I said. "Wouldn't that make a difference?"

"If they belong to someone who has a motive, and who could've had access to Ivy's kitchen, that's our best shot. I might be able to persuade the state to drop the charges."

"And Santiago would be free," I said.

"Subject to being recharged if there was new and better evidence against him. But if a murderer put the thermos there," Danielle said, "it's probably been wiped clean."

"But you always tell me most criminals aren't geniuses. So maybe not."

"Except why leave it there at all? If someone smuggled it into Ivy's kitchen, why didn't that person smuggle it out again, empty this time?" Danielle said.

"Fear of being caught with it?" I said.

"Sure. But if that's the reason, whoever it was definitely wiped it clean," Danielle said. "See what I mean?"

"Wouldn't an extra thermos raise some doubt all on its own?"

Danielle drank some of her coffee. "If we could prove it's extra. But it's hard to prove someone didn't have something – in this case, more than one thermos. You can bring ten witnesses saying they never knew of her having more than one, but no one but Ivy knows for sure."

"What if I could find someone who says Ivy's sister-in-law Sylvania was really worried about the dog attacking her son?"

Danielle paused before sipping her coffee. "That's who you're focused on? Because you think she bought the crating book?"

"That and she had a thermos like Ivy's. It's in a photo on her website. If she was worried about Ralph, or if Ralph lunged at her child in the past, that would give her a motive to try to poison the dog."

"Send me a link to her site. I'll download the photo. But a lot of people worry, and they don't try to kill an animal. Or a person."

"But somebody did here. If it could be Santiago, why not Sylvania?"

"Or her husband Hank?"

I nodded. "Or Hank. Though I don't want to believe he'd kill his own sister's dog. Or risk killing his sister. But also, Sylvania's the one who was at the networking meeting, not Hank."

"Except Ivy agreed to pen the dog. And Sylvania stopped bringing her son. So the risk was contained. In fact, maybe Ivy penned the dog as an alternative to crating if you're right that Sylvania or Hank suggested it."

"Any suggestions on what else I should look into?"

Danielle studied the bookcases next to the fireplace for a few seconds. "Does Sylvania have the skills to hack into your computer system? Or does Hank?"

"Wouldn't you say that doesn't prove anything?"

"It doesn't. Not by itself. Which is all I'm saying about each of these different points you've made. But that doesn't mean none of it matters."

I took a long drink of dark hot cocoa. "Good. Because I was starting to wonder."

"I'm pushing you to do more to convince me because I'll need to convince the prosecutor. But think of all of it as building a house. Or, better, a wall." Danielle spread her arms wide. "A few random bricks don't mean much. But if you line up enough and keep stacking them, eventually it becomes a wall. And it could be enough to cause the Assistant State's Attorney to let this go."

I picked up my phone and found Sylvania's About page on her website. "Nothing in Sylvania's profile suggests she's got mad computer skills. But with a yoga studio...someone must handle her IT."

"That would mean paying someone to hack. Kind of

foolish if you don't want to leave a trail. Though you're right, my clients do foolish things all the time."

"Amber sometimes works for her aunt during the holidays. Maybe she'll know."

I sent off a text. I decided not to include Alexis. No reason to worry her about her aunt.

Danielle stacked her cup, saucer, and spoon to take it to the side counter. "Time for me to get to my other clients. Thank God I've got a day in the office."

I stood. "How long until you get a report from the lab?"

"I paid the fee for expediting. I'm hoping by next week."

"Before Santiago needs to plead."

"That's the plan. But the ASA keeps pushing. Unfortunately, moving cases faster was one of the new State's Attorney's key campaign promises."

45

"Aunt Sylvania's pretty good with computers," Amber said. "For someone her age."

It was just before sunset. I sat in Millennium Park near a giant sculpture of a head. Amber had returned my text while Ty and I had been watching an outdoor concert. He stayed to hear the last few pieces. The notes floated over to me on the warm breeze.

"Meaning?"

"She created the yoga studio's website herself, like, ten years ago. When it wasn't that easy to do like now. She knew coding, I guess, or learned it."

"Enough to know how to hack into someone else's computer system?" I said.

"Not sure. I'm just saying it wouldn't surprise me if she could."

"How about your uncle?"

Hank ran the store, which would require some amount of computer work.

"No idea. He never says much about the store. Or

anything. I usually see him with Aunt Sylvania and my mom around. So they do most of the talking. Or did."

It seemed pretty clear Ivy's marriage to Santiago followed a pattern she was used to from her relationship with her brother, and Hank married someone who held forth the way his sister had. But that didn't tell me anything about Ivy's death.

"Any idea who handled any computer issues for the store?"

"No clue. You know Mom and I didn't talk much the last few years. And Dad wasn't involved."

Sirens that had started in the distance grew louder. "Hold on a minute." I waited until two police cars sped past on Michigan Avenue heading toward Wacker Drive.

I asked Amber about the book, and Amber confirmed my view that it was unlikely her mom would have crated Ralph.

"Does it make sense to you that your aunt and uncle bought her the book?" I said.

"Since it's from that store in Geneva, I guess. But I don't know why they would."

"Because Sylvania wanted to bring your little cousin over with her?"

"Then wouldn't Mom put Ralph in the bedroom like you said?"

"What about at their house?" I said. "Did your mom bring him when she visited Hank or Sylvania?"

"Mom didn't go there a lot. She didn't like driving out of the city, and she didn't like taking the train because they didn't run often enough. They mostly came to see us."

"But you haven't been around very much for the last two years."

"True. Could be it was different. But I kind of doubt it."

"I want to ask Alexis," I said. "Since she's the one who knows more about your Mom's and Dad's day-to-day life. But she's living with your aunt and uncle, and I don't want to upset her. Or have her say anything that'll make them think I'm looking into them."

"Well, my view? Yeah, it'll upset her. But it'll upset her a lot more if my dad pleads guilty."

I hesitated to press my next point. Amber was an adult legally. But twenty isn't all that old, and I hated emphasizing that one of her relatives might be a killer. But she already knew that.

"And what about tipping them off?" I said. "If they did have something to do with it."

"Alexis somehow managed around my mom her whole life, God knows how, and it's not because she followed all the rules. No one could. She edited what she told my mom. So I think she can handle my aunt and uncle."

I felt reassured, but only to a point. Alexis might be good at navigating around Ivy, who wanted to feel in control of everything. But if Hank or Sylvania was a murderer, that was another thing altogether.

Eric wanted to show Alexis the café and have her meet Carole. Which provided a safe reason for Alexis to give her aunt and uncle for coming downtown the next evening.

Carole brought us heavy dark chocolate scones, an iced coffee for Alexis, a Pepsi for Eric, and an herbal tea for me.

Alexis picked a few crumbs off her scones. "Dad's trying to sound really calm like everything'll be okay. But he just never sounds like himself on the phone. It's got to be awful in there."

"For what it's worth," I said, "Danielle told me he seems to be keeping his spirits up."

"And at least one way or another he'll be home soon," Eric said.

Alexis sunk down in her chair. "But that's not, like, a good thing. Not if he has to lie and plead guilty."

Eric put his arm around her shoulder. "Right. Sorry. But maybe Quille has some good news."

Alexis tilted her head my way, her chin lifting a bit.

"No news, but I'm still hopeful," I said. I wanted to remind her that I hadn't promised anything, but I wasn't sure if that was to make myself feel better or her. "For now, I want to know about your mom's relationship with your aunt and uncle. You told me before they all got along pretty well?"

"Yeah. My mom and aunt talked on the phone a lot. And Mom seemed to get along with Uncle Hank. At least, she didn't criticize him much."

"You didn't mention when we first talked that he was her business partner. Is that because you didn't know?"

"I knew I guess. I just didn't really think about it. Like, Mom always said, 'I hired a new cashier today' or 'I need to order more lip balm.' Never 'we.' So I kind of got to thinking of it as just her store."

However much Hank claimed he was okay working behind the scenes, that would have to get irritating.

"Do you think her death relates to the store?" Eric said.

"It's something I'm exploring." I shifted my gaze back to Alexis. "Did your mom go out to your aunt and uncle's house very often?"

"Often? No. Maybe once or twice a year. For a holiday maybe, you know? But my Mom liked to host so she could cook what she wanted."

"Any other reason she didn't go there?"

"Well, she hated the suburbs."

"All suburbs? Or Geneva in particular?"

The suburbs of Chicago are vastly different from one

another in so many ways, including the architecture, the demographics, income levels, and types of streets. I knew people who just preferred city life, but it was hard to hate the suburbs as a group. What you hated about one might be fantastic in another.

"I guess Geneva. She said it was fakey and kitschy. Like my aunt and uncle's house is. But I've kind of gotten used to it."

I broke off a section of scone. It still felt hot from the oven. "The house struck me as crowded but not really kitschy." I associated that term with gingham chickens and salt shakers shaped like cows.

"Yeah, but fakey. Like, she thought Aunt Sylvania went overboard on the whole crystal, feng shui, good energy thing." Alexis swigged her iced coffee. "She was dreading going to live there."

I set the scone down. "Going to live there? With your aunt and uncle? When?"

This was the first I'd heard about Ivy moving to Geneva. Roy said Ivy planned to get an apartment and rent out her home, but I had the impression that was down the road. Something I shouldn't have assumed, obviously.

"When her tenants moved in. It was supposed to be this month."

"She had tenants lined up?"

"Yeah, they were going to rent both floors. But they backed out after they heard Mom died there. Uncle Hank thinks really they got a better deal somewhere else, but it's kind of a mess because the estate still has no executor."

"And your mom was going to move this month?"

"Yeah. Like, three weeks after she died."

My tea, a lemon verbena, tasted strong enough, so I took the tea diffuser out of my teacup and set it in the saucer. "She wasn't looking for an apartment of her own?"

"Oh, yeah, she was. But it took her, like, a year and a half to find an apartment she liked when she and my dad first moved here. So she said she'd only stay a month or two in Geneva, but I knew it would be a lot longer."

"Did your dad know about this plan? Or Amber?"

Alexis twisted the silver ring on her pinky finger. "Uh, I don't think so. Mom said it wasn't Dad's business, and I tried not to talk to him about anything my mom did. And Amber, she never wants to hear about Mom."

"But Hank and Sylvania knew?"

Despite what I'd heard about Ivy, I doubted she planned to simply turn up at their door one day. But I wasn't about to assume anything else.

"Yeah. I heard Mom talking on the phone to Uncle Hank about it."

"And all of you stayed with Hank and Sylvania when you first moved from Chicago, right?"

"Well, not me. I wasn't born yet. But yeah."

"For a year and a half?"

"Yep. Amber said it was kind of fun. They had a really big house back then. And Uncle Hank especially loved having Amber around. He likes kids a lot and it took him and Aunt Sylvania a long time to have one."

"And this latest plan to move in with your aunt and uncle temporarily – your mom meant to bring Ralph with her?" I said.

"Oh, yeah. She would never have left Ralph with anyone else. Not that I can think who would take him. Dad's apartment doesn't allow pets."

All of which might explain either Sylvania or Hank buying a book for Ivy about crating her dog. I wondered how they felt about a Doberman coming to live with them.

A poodle chained to a bike lane sign near the outdoor

seating area strained at its leash, uttering little yips. Eric went over to pet it and it calmed down.

"Your cousin Percy, how old is he?" I said.

"Four."

The same age as the girl Ralph had nearly mauled. If I had a four-year-old, I wouldn't want him anywhere near Ralph. Hank and Sylvania both had a great reason to want to get rid of the dog. Hank claimed he and Sylvania hadn't known about the attack. But I had only his word for it.

"Any chance your aunt or uncle told your mom she couldn't move in?"

"Huh. Don't think so. Uncle Hank kind of owes Mom."

"Owes her how?"

"She, like, helped pay for his college. And loaned them money for their first house or something."

That was new information. I added it to the notes on my phone. "You said your cousin wasn't afraid of Ralph. How about your aunt and uncle?"

"What do you mean?"

"They didn't want you to bring Ralph with you when you moved there. Did they say why?"

"I didn't ask, not really. Ralph's Mom's dog, not mine. And everyone just assumed he couldn't go there. I think because the house is small."

"So they don't seem to like or not like Ralph?"

"Well, Uncle Hank overall likes dogs. Aunt Sylvania -- I'm not sure. Ralph made a lot of people uncomfortable. Maybe her, too."

After Alexis and Eric left, I hopped on the Pink Line at the Harold Washington Library stop to go to Ty's. I got off at Morgan and walked another five blocks. The whole trip took a little over twenty minutes. Through it I thought about Ivy letting her dog live on one entire floor so she could keep the other private. And neat.

And Sylvania, with her overcrowded home.

And Hank, with his coordinated workspace, so like Ivy in that way. Down to color coding. Including rows of keys.

I kept a spare set of keys for my condo in my office.

I paused outside the entrance to Ty's condo building and called Alexis, pressing my hand to my other ear to block out the traffic noise. "Did your mom keep spare keys to the house at work? In case she got locked out?"

"Oh, yeah. I didn't think of that. Yeah, she did. Because I was supposed to go there if I lost my keys."

"But was that just because she would probably be there?"

"No, there were keys. There's a rack there with keys for the business, and keys for Aunt Sylvania's and Uncle Hank's, and then our keys."

So, Hank and Sylvania could get into Ivy's. And might have had a pretty strong motive, not that either of them would probably admit it.

I knew who I needed information from next. If I could get her to talk to me.

46

Corine Killion wasn't hard to find. Though the federal court records didn't include her address or that of the dog park, the attorneys had taken her deposition at a court reporter's office in the Lincoln Park neighborhood of Chicago. The defendant's attorney's office was in downtown Chicago and the plaintiff's attorney's in Traverse City, Michigan. The combination made me think that the parties agreed to the Lincoln Park location to accommodate Ms. Killion, who wasn't a party to the lawsuit.

Also, she had mentioned the emergency room at St. Joseph's Hospital, and it was the closest Chicago hospital to Lincoln Park.

Francis and Corine Killion were listed at a street address right off the Armitage L stop in the heart of Lincoln Park. But the only phone number got me a Not In Service message. After searching a database I subscribed to and cross-referencing social media I was pretty sure the Corine Killion I found who owned an upscale women's designer clothing resale shop on Armitage was the same woman.

Finding her was one thing. Persuading her to talk to me was another.

I studied everything in my walk-in closet. My goal was to look like a potential customer of Corine's or someone who might be in her social circle. Because whether they're aware of it or not, almost everyone relaxes more around someone they perceive to be from the same background or social class as they are.

I shop designer brands at outlet stores, buying what appeals to me personally and gives me a professional look. But I don't shop designer resale, as I don't know all the brands well enough to know if I'm getting a good value. And there are many brands, the very ones the Lincoln Park store carried, that just will never be worth the price to me.

Fortunately, Lauren loves high-end fashion and follows trends.

I switched my workhorse-like worn leather Frye shoulder bag for Lauren's new Marc Jacobs cross-body bag. She assured me it was the latest style, something a woman who ran a designer resale shop would recognize. I wore my most expensive dark jeans, a black Valentino fringe tank top (also Lauren's), and my diamond chip earrings.

I took the L and arrived at seven-fifteen the next evening, just before closing. Lingering outside, I pretended to text on my phone and peered sideways through the store window. The woman behind the counter had a curvy figure and looked like the online photos I'd seen, if a few years older. She wore a tailored off-white blazer over a close-fitting top and jeans.

The boutique was quiet, other than a woman in a sundress looking over lacy shawls. After she left, I entered and approached the counter, smiling.

"Corine?" I opted for the first name, as the last would make this sound too formal or official.

She looked up from the shawl she was folding and smiled back. "Yes?"

"Hi, I'm Quille Davis. I'm hoping to talk to you about the Doberman attack on your daughter."

The Chicago Tribune covered the incident, so I hoped her mind wasn't immediately going to the lawsuit. Almost no one wants to talk to a lawyer they didn't contact first.

Her chin lifted a little. "What about it?"

"I'm not sure if you heard. The woman who owned the dog died recently. Ivy Jimenez-Brown."

"No, I didn't know." She set down the shawl and rested her hands on the display counter, palms flat on the glass. A small diamond on her left hand flashed in the light. "That's too bad. But why tell me?"

"Her husband was arrested for the murder. I'm working with her daughters. They're convinced he didn't do it. I'm a lawyer –" Her whole body stiffened, and I raised my hands in a surrender gesture. " – but this has nothing to do with any sort of claim against you."

"You work for that lawyer, Prall, Pratt?"

"No, no. Definitely not." He had been the argumentative lawyer in the deposition. "I don't usually handle personal injury at all. I'm a family friend who happens to be a lawyer. If we could talk for fifteen minutes or so, I'd appreciate it. Now while you're closing out, or if I could buy you a cup of coffee or a glass of wine after you finish."

She left the counter and replaced the folded shawl on an oval display table. "I do usually stop at Starbucks before heading home. But I don't know how I can help. And I really don't want anything more to do with that family."

"More?" My heart quickened. "Someone from the family talked to you? Other than Ivy?"

It was what I'd been hoping for. If Hank or Sylvania contacted Corine, I could prove they knew about the attack.

She paused to straighten the purses arranged on a shelf below a row of colorful scarves. "You don't know?"

"No."

"And how is it you think I can help again?"

"The prosecution now believes whoever killed Ivy may have meant to poison the dog –"

She snapped a clutch purse shut. "You think it was me?"

"No, no," I said. "I'm just trying to find out who else knew about the attack on your daughter. The more people who knew about it, the more people who might have seen the dog as a danger and tried to neutralize him."

I was taking a risk sharing my strategy. But if she'd done it, she wouldn't help me no matter what I said. And if she hadn't, the more open I was, the more likely she would help. At least that was my hope. I've found most people respond to honesty and kindness.

Plus there was no time to be cautious. Danielle was meeting with Santiago Monday, which was only four days away.

Corine fingered the gold trimmed edge of the purse. "I can believe someone wanted the dog out of the way. The instant that animal seized Sonny, if I had the means, I would've killed it myself. But once I calmed down, it was the owner who made me mad."

She turned and disappeared into the dressing rooms. I moved closer, careful not to block the door and make her feel hemmed in. "If I were you, I'd feel exactly the same way. Did your daughter heal all right?"

Corine emerged from the dressing room. "Fortunately, yes. Eventually. She regained full use of her hand. We found a game for her to play where she had to exercise those fingers. She's not even that frightened of dogs. It happened so fast. She was more devasted over losing Sonny than being hurt herself. I don't think she understood how close she came to that dog killing her. A blessing. But then I worry it won't make her be more careful."

"Did you get another dog?"

I didn't think that had anything to do with why I was here, but if she shared more about the event she might share more on other topics, too.

"Yes. Not another Dachshund. It made me too sad. But a little mutt. Annie loves him."

"So could we talk for a while at the Starbucks?"

Corine moved behind the counter again and hit a few buttons on the credit card reader. "I suppose it wouldn't hurt."

She told me it would take about fifteen minutes to finish. After a little pressing, she agreed to let me get a sandwich and a flat white for her, which she said was her usual quick dinner on Wednesday nights.

Across the street, I grabbed the last two turkey and dill Havarti sandwiches from the refrigerator case and ordered drinks. I sat in the shade outside, a boxed water for me and Corine's flat white in front of me. While I had never liked the taste of it, I loved the rich scent of coffee. I inhaled it, thrilled to have had some good luck at last. Contact with Corine could explain why Hank or Sylvania bought Ivy the crate your dog book. And could help show one or the other tried to eliminate the dog.

But when Corine joined me, it turned out the person who visited Corine, and when, was not what I expected.

47

"Santiago?" I dropped my pen, and it rolled onto the sidewalk. "I don't understand. He didn't even live with Ivy at the time."

Mind racing, I retrieved the pen and wiped it with my napkin, all the while wondering if I ought to just stop asking questions. I didn't see how Santiago knowing about the attack on Corine's daughter gave him a motive. And Corine might very well connect dots I didn't want to connect.

She took a long swallow of her flat white. "There was no insurance. To cover the claim. So he came to talk about settling it."

"Ivy had no homeowner's insurance?"

One of the most basic parts of a good finance plan is liability insurance. Otherwise an injured person can sue for any money you've managed to save, your home, and your future income. That Ivy, a former financial adviser, neglected to buy a policy seemed impossible.

Not to mention, she had a mortgage on her home. Lenders require borrowers to buy homeowners insurance.

"No, she had a policy. But there was some mistake when

she bought a new policy. That's what Santiago said. He did like you just did. Turned up at the store, asked to talk to me."

"Did he say what kind of mistake?"

It still boggled my mind.

"He said after he and Ivy separated, they switched insurance carriers to get better rates. By mistake there were two days between when the old policy lapsed and the new one started, and on the second of those days their dog attacked my dog. And my daughter."

I gripped my boxed water, feeling the cardboard sides give under my fingertips. What she was describing was the kind of error every conscientious lawyer I knew had nightmares about. An error recording a date, a missed piece of paperwork, when you thought you covered all the bases.

"Wasn't he fighting the insurance company? Or companies?" I didn't know a huge amount about that area of law, but it seemed like there might be some way to get one or the other to chip in.

"He didn't say."

"Did you see denial letters from either of the insurance companies?" I said.

It occurred to me Santiago and Ivy might simply have said they had no insurance and tried to negotiate themselves, playing on Corine's sympathies.

"Yes, yes. He gave me copies. I called one of the companies to check out his story."

I pushed aside my half-eaten sandwich. "So what happened when he came to see you?"

"He was so sorry. So apologetic. He said Ivy had been through so much stress with the separation, and that she'd just lost custody to him. And he knew that wasn't my problem, and it wasn't an excuse. But he said the dog was all Ivy had and it made her blind to how dangerous he was."

"He admitted the dog was dangerous?" I said. "He used

those words?"

Perhaps Santiago was the one who'd told Ivy she needed to put the dog in the bedroom during meetings so this didn't happen again. But it surprised me she had listened.

"Yes. He agreed with me about everything. And he seemed so genuinely sorry, though really he had nothing to do with it. My lawyer confirmed that he didn't buy Ralph for her. But he said he felt responsible because leaving Ivy was why she was struggling so. I felt like he meant it, and it helped me. To have him acknowledge that they were in the wrong. Or she was. I really don't see how it's his fault."

Most of the time I think the court system in the United States is a good one, or at least the best of all the ones out there. Allowing people to sue for injuries or resolve contract disputes in court keeps people from taking the law into their own hands.

But there are downsides. And one of them is that if a defendant apologizes, a plaintiff can use that statement in court. It leads lawyers to tell their clients never to apologize until the lawsuit is over. By that time, apologies don't mean much. And even then, if I settle a case, I don't have my clients admit they did anything wrong. It can come back to haunt them later.

But if people apologized early, I wondered how many lawsuits could be avoided.

"So you didn't sue Ivy," I said.

"No, I didn't."

"But I assume she must have paid something?"

She nodded. "Santiago and Ivy paid the medical bills plus some extra."

"Do you mind if I ask roughly how much? It might help me figure out some issues for the girls."

I read a study once that people are more apt to comply with a request if you give a reason. That includes a reason that is just restating the request, which was pretty close to what I'd just done.

Corine, though, wanted more. "How?"

"I don't have a clear reason to give you," I said. "I'm feeling my way along. But sometimes a fact makes a difference when you put it together with another fact that seems unrelated."

She looked doubtful. "I don't know. The settlement is confidential."

Ivy was dead and Santiago had more to worry about than settlement agreements. But I couldn't advise her to break the agreement.

"Probably that means not sharing the total amount paid. If you can give me a ballpark amount, it could help."

She took a few more bites of the sandwich. "Maybe if I look over the agreement again, I'll feel more comfortable."

I hated to let her leave it at that. Once I wasn't in front of her, it was too likely other things in her life would matter more than digging out a settlement document.

"Can you give me an idea how much treatment your daughter needed?"

"I guess I can tell you that. We posted on social media about it. Annie had outpatient surgery. And about six weeks of physical therapy. We're lucky, we have good health insurance through my husband's job. A lawyer friend I talked to thought we should ask for the whole amount of the bills anyway. But since Santiago was so kind, and he and Ivy had no insurance, I just wanted what we paid. And something for all that Annie went through. It seemed like that was fair."

"What about for you?" I said. I vaguely remembered from my tort law class that someone who witnessed something traumatic might be able to recover money as well. If their emotional distress was extreme.

"If it were against the insurance company, I would have

asked for that. For the horror of seeing that happen. But I wanted to get it all done. Get life back to normal."

"You settled before you were deposed in the other case?"

"A few months before."

I sat back. Santiago intervening on Ivy's behalf made sense. Though separated, their finances still would have been considered jointly owned. So if she got socked with a huge verdict and lost her home and investments, it would hurt him, too. And, in the long run, their daughters.

He might still resent the effort it took and however much he and Ivy paid. But trying to kill the dog, or Ivy, many months later seemed unlikely.

All the same, none of this helped me prove he didn't kill Ivy. Unless.... An idea started to take shape in my mind. Another way Hank or Sylvania might be involved.

"Could you tell me, not the total amount of the settlement, but if it was over a hundred thousand dollars?"

Corine played with the cardboard sleeve around her coffee. "It – I – I really can't say more."

"But it included what you owed for all the medical bills and something for Annie's pain and suffering?"

She nodded. "That's it."

Mensa Sam handled a lot of personal injury claims. He could likely tell me within ten or twenty thousand how much Santiago had paid.

"That helps. Thank you. Did you ever hear from Ivy or Santiago again?"

"We never heard from Ivy at all. But Santiago – he called once just to ask how Annie was doing. Which was very kind of him. I hope you can help him out."

Her comment said a lot about Santiago. In my experience, most people who tried to negotiate their own settlements did far worse than an attorney could do, and none of them left the plaintiff thinking they were kind. It added to my feeling that the girls were right about their dad.

But it was hardly proof he hadn't committed murder. If I were the prosecutor I'd argue he charmed Corine and turned around and took revenge on Ivy.

~

Mensa Sam was still in the office when I got back around eight p.m. In the summer he likes to bike in the morning, before it gets too hot out, so he often works late.

It's hard with Sam sometimes to get a word in edgewise, and he's not a great listener. He interrupted multiple times as I stood in his office doorway and told him about my meeting with Corine. The questions came faster when I asked for a range in which the case might have settled.

"Good health insurance? Meaning a group plan?" Sam said.

"She said her husband's employer, so I'm thinking yes. But I didn't ask."

"A good group plan, she might have only a thousand or two out of pocket on that. But she's a store owner, so if she's got her own individual plan –"

"It was through her husband's employer."

"– probably fifteen or twenty thousand max unless it's out of network. There's no –"

I dropped into a padded chair in front of his desk. "Right, I know, no out of pocket limit." As people who worked for ourselves, Sam and I both had the same limited options for buying health insurance. And felt lucky to have them. I was hoping to forestall a long explanation of what those plans were like, but it wasn't easy to stop Sam when he decided he needed to explain something. "But I'm guessing she wouldn't call that a good plan."

"One of those, she could owe thirty, forty, fifty thousand."

"Okay, so that's what you think the upper limit of the medical bills might be?" It seemed better to head him off before he launched into the Bronze, Silver, and Gold plans I reviewed myself every year.

"In a Gold plan, well, if she had Blue Cross she couldn't buy a Gold plan –"

I deliberately let my shoulders drop and my hands relax in my lap as Sam ran through all the permutations of university-affiliated hospital networks with the most advanced equipment and expert specialists, community hospitals with worse safety records, and the trade-off we all made balancing costs with covering potential worst-case scenarios.

When Sam finally wound down, I asked again, "So you're thinking thirty to fifty thousand is the upper limit of medical bills for those injuries?"

"No. Not upper limit. Twenty to thirty thousand total, possibly fifty thousand."

Which was the same as upper limit, but pointing that out would only waste more of my time. "And what would you think for pain and suffering?"

"How old's the girl?" Sam said.

"Four when it happened. But no permanent disability or after effects."

"Four. Okay. Any permanent disability?"

"None."

Suppressing a sigh, I glanced at my watch. Lauren had asked if I wanted to stop by for a glass of wine when I was done, but it was seeming less and less likely. But talking with Mensa Sam never went fast unless he was in a hurry. And he had been helpful so far with the case despite that there wasn't much chance he'd earn any money from it.

"I'd ask for another hundred thousand."

"And what do you think it might settle for if the Mom really wants it resolved quickly and feels a little sympathy for Santiago not having insurance?"

"That's a really personal decision. She didn't have a lawyer?"

I had told him that, too, already.

"No. Just informal advice from a friend who's a lawyer. And before you ask, no idea if the friend does personal injury law."

Sam rolled his eyes. "Does this lawyer friend even do personal injury?"

I often wondered how Sam ever got through a trial since he so rarely listened to the other side of any conversation. "I don't know."

He fell silent, staring at the row of diplomas, and his Mensa membership certificate, framed on his wall. "Quick settlement and all, my guess? With what you described? An extra forty or fifty thousand at least for pain and suffering and emotional distress."

I did some quick addition. Assuming Corine had group insurance, Santiago and Ivy had paid somewhere between forty-five thousand and sixty-five thousand dollars. Not an amount most people had lying around in cash.

They could have withdrawn from investment accounts, but Sylvania said Ivy tapped those to open the store. A loan against the house was possible if they had equity. But I was betting wherever Ivy got the money, she talked to her brother, as her business partner, about it. If nothing else, it would put her more in need of cash from the business. If the business relationship was a good one, most of my clients talked through money problems more often with their business partners than their spouses.

Which made the odds good that Hank, and possibly

Sylvania, knew about the child incident. I hoped Santiago knew for sure. And that Danielle wouldn't see any problem with him talking to me about it.

48

"He's sure Ivy spoke with Hank about it," Danielle said.

We stood near the floor-to-ceiling walls on the twentieth floor of the Daley Center. Danielle had been on the fourth floor for a DUI trial that finished early. I had a court call in the chocolate chip case in ten minutes.

As soon as I got home from talking with Corine, I'd called Danielle. She'd been interested enough to go see Santiago at the jail early in the morning.

"But we need to prove it," I said. "Did he say if there's a paper trail? If she withdrew a bulk sum from the store's accounts –"

Danielle shook her head. "She didn't. The money came from a mix of investment and bank accounts the two of them had together, plus a home equity credit line."

"So the transactions will show they withdrew money, but not who Ivy talked to about it."

The lawyer for the plaintiff emerged from the elevator banks and headed for the courtroom. "Hold on." I went over and asked him to stick his head out of the courtroom if the case was called while I was still talking to Danielle. He said he would.

I returned to Danielle, who sat on a long, polished wooden bench facing the windows. "So this doesn't help," I said. In fact, once again I suspected I'd made things worse. Santiago might well be angry at a dog that cost him nearly sixty thousand dollars. Or at his wife.

Danielle looked up from her phone. "Santiago said both Ivy and Hank took no salary for the bulk of the time the store was open. Part of why Ivy's child support payments were low. With the home equity loan payments, she needed to get paid monthly from the store."

I sat across from her, perching on the long radiators that ran along the base of the windows. "And that change suggests Hank knew what happened. He had to know because he did the books."

"Bingo."

I rested my elbows on my knees. "But we can't prove it. I'm not entitled to look at the store's books. Can you subpoena them?"

"If the criminal case continues. But Santiago doesn't want that. If you can get Hank to admit he knew –"

"How would I do that?"

"You got Corine Killion to talk."

"She's not a killer. I don't think. She had nothing to hide."

"Murder's an extreme behavior. But whoever did it is still human." Danielle pointed at me with her shiny brass pen. "You're good at getting humans to talk. If Hank admits Ivy told him about the incident, with everything else it might be enough to get the prosecution to back off. Or at least switch to something in the misdemeanor range. Which means Santiago gets out of prison and doesn't lose any of his options in life."

"And his girls will know their dad didn't murder their

mom." I gathered my briefcase and stood. "Except maybe their uncle did."

Danielle stood, too, and walked with me toward the courtroom. "It's not ideal."

∽

I wished I had a way to check out Hank's computer expertise. If he had the skills to hack my system and knew about Ralph attacking the little girl, that would make our case a lot stronger. But I didn't know anyone in Ivy's store. And, unlike with Sylvania's yoga studio, Amber had never worked there. By the time it opened, she and her mom were estranged enough that neither wanted that arrangement.

Alexis said computers frustrated Hank. But she had grown up using electronic devices. I wasn't sure I trusted her evaluation. Hank handled all the accounting and inventory for the store. That had to require computer knowledge, but I doubted my thoughts on that held the power to persuade the prosecutor of anything.

Which left me with trying to get him to admit that Ivy took the money and he knew why.

Unlike with Corine, I decided my best strategy was bluffing. I sent him an email from my law account, making it sound as legal-like and formal as possible. Despite that it said very little, I hoped it would convince him there was evidence behind my guesses.

Dear Hank:

As you are aware, I am pursuing a wrongful death claim on behalf of Amber and Alexis. I recently obtained evidence that Ivy paid over $50,000 (fifty thousand dollars) in total to a woman named Corine Killion. Given the timing, it appears to me such funds must relate to the incident where Ivy's dog attacked.

When we met last week, you stated you lacked knowledge of

that incident. Other evidence, however, indicates you did. In fact, Ivy began drawing additional funds from the store after she and Santiago paid Ms. Killion, and she explained to you the reason why.

While I am not required to do so, I would like to give you a chance to resolve this discrepancy before I take any further action. If you in fact did not know the reason Ivy needed to begin drawing funds, I need you to swear to that in writing in an affidavit, subject to penalties for perjury.

When is a good time for us to meet either at my office or your store? Early afternoons are best for me.

Quille C. Davis

Quille C. Davis LLC

The advantage of people holding stereotypes about lawyers is that sometimes I can play on them. I rarely use vague language and big words in my actual cases, but to the layperson it can sound intimidating.

Hank responded within the hour. He could meet me today at the store at six-thirty p.m. I checked the store's hours before answering. It was open until eight at night, so I wouldn't be alone with him. All the same, I followed my instructor's rules on having a backup. I asked Danielle first, since she was on the girls' case with me, and her presence would be most natural. But her daughter had a choir concert.

Fortunately, Ty was available. He planned to meet me there at 6:15. I planned to tell Hank we were on our way out to dinner. Ty could wait in the store or in the lunchroom area.

Just in case, I also told both Lauren and Joe where I'd be.

I arrived early and walked around the building, noting all the exits and guard stations. When I entered the store at ten after six, the clerk told me Hank had been out most of the day on other business but was on his way to the store now. He should be there in fifteen minutes. I was welcome to wait in the back.

After checking the door to Hank's office and finding it locked, I sat in the lunchroom. I texted Ty where to find me. I almost felt relieved the office was locked. Otherwise I would have been far too tempted to have a look at the computer, and I probably would have gotten caught.

Ty's text came in a few minutes later.

On L now, be there in 10

No one was in the warehouse, which seemed strange. But maybe it had been a slow day and the shelves were restocked throughout. Still, I walked toward the open door between the warehouse and the retail space.

The clerk met me at the door.

"Slow night?" I said.

"What? No. We just switched our hours. Thursdays are the only late night now."

I gripped my shoulder bag. "That wasn't on the website. Is it new?"

"Yeah. Ivy didn't believe in closing before eight, even on Fridays. But Hank says there's no point in staying open for the one or two stray customers that come in at night."

It made a certain amount of sense, but it still made me uneasy.

"So what's closing time?"

"Six-thirty." She went into Hank's office, opened the safe, and put a heavy leather pouch inside. "No one's here so I closed out a little early. You won't tell him, will you?"

My phone said it was only 6:20.

"What if a customer comes in?"

"They won't. No one hardly comes in after five-thirty or six. Everyone heads home or to neighborhoods with more bars and restaurants."

That didn't surprise me too much. The complex was on the south edge of the Loop. The only nearby restaurants were fast food that aimed more at the lunch crowd, and Ceres Table. Usually that had a huge crowd in its outdoor seating area, but it had flooded during mid-summer and the owners hadn't gotten it up and running again.

"I'll wait out front for him since you're locking up," I said.

"No need." The voice came from the mouth of the store, but it was a woman's voice, not Hank's.

Sylvania Brown glided into the warehouse. She wore the same type of clothes as when I'd met her. Yoga pants, a soft jersey, this one sleeveless, and ballet flats.

"Sylvania. How are you?"

She extended her hand to shake mine. Hers was warm but not sweaty. "Wonderful. I had a very peaceful day, but Hank got tied up at his meeting. He can talk with you tomorrow instead, or you and I can chat for a few minutes. I can probably answer your questions."

Nothing about her manner rang any bells, and I loved the thought of getting her alone to talk. But I was resolved to remain cautious. I glanced at my phone. Nothing from Ty suggesting he'd be late.

"Great. I saw a Starbucks on my way in. Can I buy you a cup of tea?"

"It closed at six. And I drink a custom blend anyway. Can I offer you some?" She mimed pouring a cup of tea. "I've got a stash in Hank's drawer."

"No, thank you. I'm good."

She headed into Hank's office. I stayed in the warehouse to avoid being in a small space with her. I sat at the long table where employees probably ate their lunches. A microwave and small refrigerator sat on a counter against the wall. Mugs and glasses soaked in soapy water in a plastic tub inside an industrial-sized sink.

I chose the seat nearest to the door to the store. That way I had a view of the exit to the building's interior corridor. Directly across from the store was the exit to Jackson Street. Across from there stood a large building that included the Stock Exchange and Ceres Table. Though the restaurant was closed, the building employed twenty-four-hour security guards because of the exchange.

"Water?" Sylvania crossed to the kitchen area and filled an electric kettle.

"No, thank you. Do you mind if I record?" I said.

"Of course not. Go right ahead."

I clicked the button on my iPhone. The recording might deter her from saying anything incriminating, but it felt like a good step for my own safety. Insurance, as the instructor would say.

She measured loose tea leaves that smelled of green grass and honey into a net diffuser.

"This is Quille C. Davis, recording a conversation with Sylvania Brown with her consent." I gave the address, date, and time. The time was after six-thirty. I was a little surprised Ty hadn't walked in the door yet.

The clerk called out goodnight, but she left the door between the warehouse and the store open.

"So formal." Sylvania sat across from me, scooting her chair away from the table. She curled one leg under her body and the other draped to the floor. Despite the casualness of the pose, I had the impression of a cat poised to spring.

"It's helpful if I listen down the road to know when and where," I said. "Did Hank share my email with you? About the money Ivy paid to Corine Killion?"

"He forwarded it to me." Sylvania made typing motions with her fingers. "You said she paid something like fifty thousand dollars, so she needed to make owner's draws after that."

"Yes. Did you know that before you read the email?"

"No, no." Her head – and body – swayed side-to-side. My internal imagery shifted from cat to serpent. "But it doesn't surprise me."

"It doesn't? Which part?"

"Any of it. That Ivy paid someone off, that the dog attacked a little girl, that she then needed to draw money from the store for something that wasn't Hank's fault."

The email hadn't said anything about a little girl. Only a dog attack.

"Are you surprised Hank didn't tell you?"

She pressed one fingertip to her chin. "A little. He doesn't tell me everything, though." Sylvania leaned forward and lowered her voice. "Especially about Ivy."

As Sylvania's body moved, it hit me what felt wrong to me. The heavy glass candy dish from Hank's office now sat on the table between Sylvania and me. A little closer to her. I wasn't sure if it had been there before or if she brought it out while I wasn't looking. If she threw it at me, it could do some serious damage.

I shifted my chair closer and rested my forearms on the table as if I were responding to her taking me into her confidence. "Why didn't he talk about Ivy in particular?"

"He knew the way Ivy devastated our finances upset me." Her hands cupped together and tilted, a wonderful interpretation of a ship about to capsize. I found it almost mesmerizing.

"Devastated – that's a strong word."

"Yet, that's what she did. And did she care? She did not," Sylvania said.

I glanced toward the open door between the warehouse and the darkened retail area. And it hit me that Ty wouldn't be able to get into the store from the building's interior walkway with the store closed and locked.

"Excuse me," I said. "My boyfriend's meeting me here. I

need to tell him to come to the Quincy entrance." That led directly from the street into the warehouse.

She smiled. "Oh, your boyfriend's meeting you. Of course. By all means." Her arm gestured in a rolling and-so-it-goes motion.

I felt sure she didn't believe me. She thought I was saying it to fake her out. Which in itself was disturbing because it suggested she was trying to make me feel uncomfortable. I quickly typed a message to Ty with instructions.

Sylvania's hand, when it dropped on the table, landed closer to the candy dish.

"How did she devastate your finances?" As I spoke, I reached for the candy, taking a few pieces and, as I did, drawing the dish closer to me. I unwrapped a piece of candy to make it seem more natural.

"Let me count the ways." Her fingers popped up one at a time as she started her list. "First and foremost, that wedding of hers. Ridiculous. Hank spent nearly as much on it as he chipped in for ours – though my parents paid most of that. But Ivy, no, Ivy had to have the most elaborate wedding. Then her children, always gifts to her children. By the time Percy finally came along, of course, she had two of her own. Hank said she couldn't be expected to give the same sort of gifts we did when childless. Really? Does that seem fair to you?"

"It doesn't," I said.

The candy tasted vaguely fruity. I wasn't quite sure what flavor it was supposed to be, but it didn't matter. In my haste to get the dish away from her I'd forgotten I might be dealing with a poisoner.

Every manners lesson my Gram drilled into me as a kid cried out against spitting out the candy. Not willing to be killed by politeness, though, I spit it into the wrapper. "Excuse me."

Sylvania's smile widened, nearly showing her wisdom teeth. "Everything all right?"

I nodded. "Sorry. I get migraines, and some flavors and smells set them off. I don't know what that one is, but it's not good for me."

She slid the dish closer. "Try the green."

"Thanks, I'll quit while I'm ahead." I felt a bit light-headed, but the room was hot and stuffy and I suspected it was fear, not poison, affecting me. All the same, I took a Styrofoam cup and filled it with water at the sink, then drank it down. "Are there other ways you felt Ivy cost you money?"

"The store, which I told you about. Downsizing, all just for poor Miss Ivy."

I sat down again, breathing more easily. The candy dish sat midway between us. "Is there a reason you say it that way – poor Miss Ivy?"

"It's what Hank always said. A variation. Poor Ivy. How devastated she was when her parents were killed. How disappointed she'd been to learn the extent of her father's philandering. His drinking. How hard life was for her." Sylvania mimed rubbing her eyes as if dashing away tears. "She was always boo-hooing."

That struck me as the first off note. It didn't fit with anyone else's description of Ivy as a tightly controlled woman who rarely shared her feelings. Though Sylvania did sound truly fed up.

"That's what Hank said about her? How hard her life was? Or did she say that to you?" I said.

"She said it to Hank and he told me. And do you know what I said?"

"What?"

She twirled one finger in a circle. "Boo-hoo. I had a hard life, too. Hank, Ivy, they acted like I skated through life. Everyone acted like that."

"But that wasn't true," I said.

"Of course it wasn't! Do you know when I was in college, I lived in this high rise, but in the smallest studio there. A six hundred fifty square foot studio, if you can imagine."

I could. I'd had a studio a third smaller than that during law school. But not in a high rise, in a vintage building. Vintage being a euphemism for a shower that took five minutes to get hot and then scalded, and a gas stove with only two working burners. But it had been cheap. Enough so that I could pay my bills without borrowing much.

"It was cramped, I bet."

"It was miniscule! All because my parents found it cheaper than the dorms to buy me a condo then sell it when I finished. They did it to *save* money. But my classmates thought I was rich. And I should buy drinks more often because my parents covered my tuition and the condo. It's not like it was my condo. Or that they gave me much in spending money."

Now who was boo-hooing.

"Did you resent that?" I felt less sweaty than before, and my breath came easily, so I felt reasonably sure I hadn't been poisoned.

"Of course I did."

"And Ivy took that same attitude toward you?"

"I didn't resent Ivy."

"If I were you, I would have."

"No, I just felt frustrated. Because Hank, whatever Ivy wanted from him, Ivy got."

"Like moving in with you and bringing Ralph with?" I said.

A clanging came from the direction of the Quincy Street exit, and for a second I thought it was Ty banging on the door. But it was just a truck rumbling by.

"Exactly. That vicious dog. No matter that it would probably kill our son." She snapped her hand shut like a dog's jaws.

I glanced at my phone – still nothing from Ty. And it was only six-fifty, too early for Lauren to raise an alarm.

"I wouldn't want it around children," I said, meaning it. "And I understand she refused to crate train it. Even after you bought her a book on it."

"Pff." She blew air out her mouth and up, stirring her bangs. "Hank's bright idea. As if a book would convince Ivy of anything. Or she'd learn anything from it. She was a terrible money manager, by the way, despite convincing people to let her handle their money. She knew it, too. That's why she quit."

"Excuse me, I need to send a text."

Where R U? Still in back with Sylvania who's talking way too much. It worries me.

Her willingness to say all this in a recording couldn't be a good sign. She didn't strike me as a throw-herself-on-the-grenade type. I had no thought that she was sharing in the hope of saving Santiago from prison.

"I suppose Santiago couldn't change her mind about Ralph," I said.

"Oh, no. He talked to her about that dog until he was blue in the face. She just never saw reason. Even Santiago said we needed to just say no. That Ivy would find an apartment of her own if she had to." Sylvania's head bobbed in agreement. "But Hank overruled that. He overruled me all the time. All. The. Time."

Her hand slapped the table on each of the last three words, moving closer to the candy dish. I shifted my shoulder bag, which sat on the chair next to me. I had a small nightstick inside, a gift from my instructor. Though we practiced with it the previous week, it didn't make me feel that much better. It's one thing to use a weapon in a practice fight with a teacher. It's another to react fast enough in a volatile situation. Studies show that most people freeze.

"And Santiago never overruled Ivy?" I said.

"Oh, no, he did not."

"Given all that you've told me, you must have wanted to get rid of Ralph."

"Oh, no," she said. "I'd never do that. I decided to get rid of Ivy."

49

As she spoke, Sylvania lunged. But not for the candy dish. Instead, she grabbed my phone, whirled, and flung it into the sink, straight into the tub of soapy water.

I ran for the Quincy exit, shoulder bag banging against my side. I might not have the recording, but I could testify to what she'd said.

But when I reached the large gray door and flung it open, a black iron grate had been drawn across it. A heavy padlock secured it shut. Sylvania must have done it before coming in. I saw the empty street outside but couldn't get to it. This late, no trucks were unloading, and no one was walking by.

Footsteps pounded behind me. I spun around. Sylvania bolted right at me, the candy dish in her hand. Shelves of boxes on either side of me hemmed me in. My mind reeled.

I heard my instructor's voice in my head telling me if I couldn't run, a surprise attack was my best bet.

A second before Sylvania reached me, I stepped toward her. Reflexively she slowed, giving me a moment to spin my body, drop to my knees, and duck my head. I hoped her momentum would make her tumble right over me and into the iron grate.

It almost worked. She skidded into me. Her toes sent shooting pains into my side, and the candy dish flew from her hand and skidded under the nearest shelf. She tripped forward, howling when she landed on the concrete floor. She was behind me, so I didn't see what part of her hit. I hoped her head.

I kicked hard to free myself and, I hoped, do more damage, and staggered to my feet. Somewhere in the scuffle I'd lost my grip on my shoulder bag, and I wasn't about to hunt for it. My gait lurched to one side as I ran back toward the lunch area. My hip and side throbbed. Having mapped several routes while waiting in the back, I veered sideways into the retail area, which was lit only by a few dim emergency lights.

But my mental map worked. It was the same way I'd learned blocking as an actress, and it didn't fail me now.

Clunking came from the warehouse. Possibly Sylvania shoving cartons out of her way, though I didn't remember any falling.

I forced myself to focus on escape. The exit to the building's main interior corridor was all the way across the store. As was the counter with the phone. Better to find some sort of weapon and ambush Sylvania than let her catch me. I veered down an aisle. I couldn't get my nightstick, but the store could supply the equivalent. The third aisle from the last held crystals large and small, including salt crystals people used for everything from outdoor seating to indoor nightlights. I grabbed one that felt about a foot and a half long and cylindrical, almost like a stake or a miniature fencepost. It had some heft to it. I eased around the corner and behind two stacks of dog food bags.

Vegan no doubt.

Deliberately slowing my breathing, I listened. Shuffling footsteps came from the warehouse and into the retail space. I hadn't seen how Sylvania fell. She might have twisted a knee or injured some other body part. Or she might be pretending.

My back against the rough brick interior wall, I shut my eyes. I couldn't see very well anyway, and I hoped it would help me focus on what I heard. My arms prickled from the cold. The air conditioning was off, but it had been going full blast earlier, making the retail area much colder than the warehouse.

The scent of cloves, honey, and green grass reached me first. Sylvania's strong tea, still on her breath. Or maybe it had spilled on her when she'd lunged. I opened my eyes and gripped the crystal. Its crevices made it feel secure in my grip despite my sweating fingers. I peered through a one-inch gap between the edges of the bags and the wall. A shadow passed over the nearest emergency light. Sylvania entering the pet aisle.

I shifted my weight onto my right foot, ready to spring when she passed the dog food bags. When she did, I leapt forward and swung hard at the back of her head, mindful of what my instructor told me – if you're going to fight, you have to fight with your all. Otherwise, you're better off running.

The crystal hit the back of her skull, and my hand jerked back in a recoil. I almost lost my grip, but hung on and swung again. Sylvania staggered forward and dropped to her knees, hands out in front of her. She held something in her hand. I stamped on her wrist. A crack shot through the empty store and a wave of nausea hit me. I staggered sideways, and what looked like my nightstick rolled away from her and down the aisle.

Sylvania was moaning and clutching her hand. Not sure how badly she was hurt, I ran for the heavy door that led to the corridor. I flipped one deadbolt after the other. After the third one I shoved the door. No grate. I ran out, blinded by bright corridor lights overhead and the glare off the white marble floor. My feet slid, but I righted myself and dashed for the nearest security guard desk, which was deserted. I darted past, shouting for help as loud as I could. Behind me I heard a heavy door slamming and footsteps.

Could be Sylvania, but I wasn't about to stop and look back.

I burst out of the building onto Jackson. The only traffic was blocks away. I ran across the street and plunged into the Board of Trade building.

A guard there pulled out her walkie talkie and started shouting into it as she ran toward me.

"Help. Being chased." I ran straight into her, unable to stop fast enough. She gripped me by the shoulders.

Now I did turn, twisting away from the guard, and saw Sylvania staggering across Jackson after me. I pointed. "Police, call the police."

A second guard appeared, and she grabbed Sylvania as she came through the revolving door. Sylvania flailed her arms and head as I backed away. The guard howled when she bit his hand, but he kept his grip on her.

In the distance, sirens wailed.

50

I sat in front of Detective Sergeant Beckwell's desk, a heavy sweater that smelled of pipe tobacco over my shoulders. I couldn't stop shivering. The paramedics said it was adrenalin overload and gave me hot tea as well.

"I'm most worried about Alexis," I said. "She's staying with Sylvania and Hank. If Hank was in on it."

"He's on his way here," Beckwell said. Luckily for me, he'd intervened when he saw my name. Since he knew me, he had let me tell the story my way, not rushing me or interrupting me.

"Was he really in meetings?" I said.

"Don't know. But he answered the cell phone number his wife gave us and he's coming to give a statement."

Because I was the attorney for Alexis, he said it was all right for me to arrange for somewhere for Alexis to stay for the night.

"She's friends with Eric Ruggirello," I said. "I'm hoping she can stay at his mom's. But I don't know her number by heart."

Marco's ex-wife could be difficult at times, but she was a good person.

"Mirabel?" Beckwell said. "I can call her for you."

"Thanks," I said. I expected him to pull information from the computer, as I assumed Mirabel's contact information was in there from when he investigated Marco's death.

But he hit a button on his cellphone, spoke a few words, and handed it to me.

Something to think about later.

When I explained the situation, Mirabel offered right away to drive to Geneva, pick up Alexis, and bring her back to stay in the guest room until something else could be figured out for her.

"I need to tell you something." I shifted, trying for a more comfortable position on the chair in the corner of the police station. Beckwell had allowed me to use a phone on an open desk. "It'll be a while before we know anything for sure. But it looks like your Aunt Sylvania may have had something to do with your mom's death."

"Aunt Sylvania? I – that's crazy. Why? How? Why would she do that?" Her voice squeaked at the end.

"She told me she wanted to harm your mother. Then she tried to break my phone to get rid of the recording of what she said. And she attacked me. Which makes me think she is guilty."

I purposely sidestepped the question of why Sylvania had done this. Overall, I wanted to tell Alexis the truth, at least as much of it as I'd learned. But I was too tired and sore and overwhelmed to decide if that was a wise thing to do.

"Does Uncle Hank – does he know? Is he, I mean, he's not, you know, part of this?"

"Your aunt didn't say. He might be as shocked as you are about all of this. He's on his way to the station now."

"Okay. I mean, not okay. But I guess it's good. That he's going to talk to the police."

"It's good," I said. "Where's Percy?"

"With Uncle Hank. They went shopping after school and to a movie. Oh, wait, does that mean he's bringing him to the station?"

That answered whether Hank had really been at meetings.

"He'll probably call someone to have him stay with. Eric's mom should be there soon. If she's not there within twenty minutes, call me back."

"This means dad will get out of prison, right?"

"I hope so. I'm calling Danielle later. She'll need to talk to the prosecutor."

I got Amber's number from Alexis, scribbling it on a pad of paper I found in the top desk drawer, and called her next. She sounded as shocked as Alexis, but then she said, "I never felt quite right about Aunt Sylvania. She just — I don't know – I felt like mom drove her crazy the way she did me. But Sylvania would never admit it. She was always saying how it was unhealthy for me to get so mad and how she learned to be calm and master her emotions. It bothered me because I thought she was criticizing me. But maybe the whole mastering emotions thing was her problem."

"Maybe. Are you feeling all right? This is a lot to take in."

In the background I heard laughing and talking.

"I'll be all right. I'll see if I can get a ride home this week-end. Be there for Alexis. I can't believe I thought – it sounds awful, but when Dad said he was going to plead guilty –"

"You were afraid he might've done it?"

"Great daughter, huh?"

My hip throbbed. I angled my chair differently and rested

my left side against the wall. "That does not make you a bad daughter. Or a bad person. No one expects someone they love to die suddenly, let alone be murdered. You can't help thinking about what might have happened. What you would do if it turns out someone you care about did it. That's not wrong."

"It feels pretty wrong."

"I'm sorry. It must feel that way. I don't know if it helps, since I only met your dad once. But everything I've heard about him, I'm sure he'll tell you he understands."

Ty walked through the police station door as I hung up.

$\sim$

"I am so sorry," Ty said.

"An L breakdown is not your fault." I took my foot out of the large bowl of ice water and dried it. The towel started to slip from my hands because they were shaking, but I pressed my knees together and grabbed it before it fell on the deck. I hoped Ty hadn't noticed. I was too tired to have an argument about whether I had taken too many chances. "Or where it broke down."

While I'd been talking to Sylvania in the warehouse, Ty had been stuck between two underground stations. Which meant his cell phone had no reception. When the train moved again, he got all my texts but couldn't reach me, as my phone was soaking with the mugs and glasses.

He'd been very relieved when he got my call from the police station.

Now he took the Ace bandage from my hand and rewrapped my foot and ankle as we talked. "I still think you should go to the emergency room."

We sat on the deck outside my condo. Ty had ordered pizza from Salerno's, my favorite place to get thin crust. The whole experience had made me hungry. Only two pieces of medium sausage pizza were left in the box on my patio table.

"I'm still paying off the bill from the last time. I didn't hit my head, my ankle hurts but I can walk. I'm mostly just bruised."

My ankle hadn't even started hurting until after the pain in my hip lessened.

He sat across from me and took my hands in his. "I meant to be there for you."

"On the upside, I tested out my training and it's really helping."

"This isn't a joke, Quille. You could have been killed. And where were Lauren and Joe? Why didn't they come looking for you?"

I rearranged a chair so I could rest my wrapped foot and ankle on it. "I was only at the store for about half an hour. I called Lauren right after you while I was waiting at the police station. She was at the store, asking questions, but no one could tell her what happened since the guard there wasn't around when I ran out."

"Right, but where was she before that?"

"She and Joe were together, with one of her clients who might want to work with Joe. He tried calling me separately and didn't get through. They went to the store, but I was already gone and at the police station. I told them not to come. I knew you were on the way."

I reached for his phone, which lay on the table. "You can make it all up to me by letting me use your phone. I need to call Danielle."

But I had trouble typing in Ty's passcode. He didn't comment on my shakiness, just opened the phone. Danielle answered the second time. Ty rubbed my ankle as I told her what happened.

I slept until eight the next morning, which is late for me. That still gave me plenty of time to meet Lauren at the café. She tends to be on a later schedule because a lot of her showings are in the evening during the week. She wanted to apologize in person for being MIA, buy me breakfast, and hear everything that had happened.

Carole brought me one of my favorites, a heavy chocolate chip scone almost as large as a plate, heated, and cut into quarters. I had four strips of crispy bacon on the side and a glass of orange juice. Lauren got there five minutes later.

She threw her arms around me. "I am so, so sorry."

"It's okay. It's not your job to be on call for me."

"I know, but I want to be. I'm so glad you're okay." She hugged me harder, then let go.

After she ordered a café au lait and the fruit plate, I filled her in on the events of the night before.

A server brought Lauren's order in the middle, but she waited until I finished to eat or drink anything.

"So Sylvania. Pretty seriously crazy town, huh?" Lauren sliced a strawberry into two perfect halves. "I would not have guessed that."

"Really? You never met her."

When I investigated crimes, Lauren often was at my side or helped question one witness or another. But she had been particularly busy over the last month or so. I wasn't sure why because the local real estate market was in a slump.

"All those yoga crystals you said she had in her home. Seems like she would be mellow and relaxed, not overflowing with rage," Lauren said.

"Maybe that's how she was trying to deal with it." I bit into my scone. The cake part was heavy and rich and the chocolate was dark. As always, the chocolate helped me feel calmer.

"Yeah, well, it obviously wasn't working. Will Santiago be released?"

"Danielle sounded pretty optimistic for a change. She's got a call with the ASA Monday morning," I said.

We talked a little longer about Santiago's prospects.

As I ate the last of my bacon Lauren said, "Listen, there's something else we need to talk about. Joe and I weren't with one of my clients last night."

I sipped more of my orange juice. The tart, citrus taste complemented the dark chocolate chips in the scone perfectly. "Okay. Where were you?"

"Oh, we were still out to dinner. My client couldn't make it at the last minute. And Joe and I got to talking. We've been hanging out a bit lately."

I set my glass down. "Meaning...?"

"Just spending time. We had lunch a few times last month and met for drinks. Neither of us was exactly saying it was any different than usual, but it has definitely been more often."

"It's not like you to take the long way around. What are you trying to tell me?"

Lauren twirled her fork, then set it on the edge of her fruit plate. "The thing is, I'm not exactly sure what it is. I'm just getting this feeling that Joe might be into me."

The breeze died down, and I shifted my chair to get under the shadow of the building. "Last spring you told me you thought he might be into me and that's why he was being kind of a jerk to Ty. You don't think that anymore?"

"Well, you said he told you he didn't feel that way, and I guess he would know."

"And what makes you think he's into you?"

"Partly how often he's asked if I want to have lunch."

"But you've always had lunch, right?"

She was right, though. It did say something. Especially considering he and I had still not matched our schedules to meet for drinks.

"Yeah, usually we have lunch or drinks once a month. I share info and real estate trends. He tells me about things in the economy that might affect my clients. We refer clients to each other so it's always a business write off. But, seriously, we've met for lunch or drinks almost once a week for the last six weeks."

"And he's the one initiating it?"

Joe always responded to my texts, but I couldn't recall many times in the last six weeks when he texted me first.

Lauren shrugged. "I probably texted him a few times."

"Have you asked him what's up?"

"I will. Depending how you feel about it."

"Isn't how you feel more important?"

"Sure, but I know how I feel. I always liked Joe and now that we've spent more time one-on-one and he's available, he's looking good. But he's been your friend forever. Would it be too weird?"

"It'd be weird." I took the largest crumb left on my plate and ate it. At least it had a giant chocolate chip in it. "For a while. But you're both my friends. I want you to be happy."

"You're sure you're not interested?"

"In Joe? No." I drank the last of my orange juice. "First, there's Ty. And second, Joe and I would be a terrible match romantically. Ty helps me lighten up and have fun. Joe and I might just sink into a black hole together."

"Too funny." Lauren relaxed, letting her body drop against the back of her chair. "He told me he likes me because I help him lighten up."

Joe had said that to me, too, over the years. But Lauren definitely had a more bubbly personality.

"Just one thing," I said.

"Anything."

"You are not allowed to have a bad breakup and stop being friends. Because no way am I choosing between you."

"Oh, seriously, have I ever had that kind of break up?"

"Um, yeah, that –"

"Law school does not count. No one is at their best in law school."

Danielle spent a week negotiating, and the Assistant State's Attorney agreed to drop all the charges against Santiago. Twelve hours later he was released from jail. He had lost his apartment, but he and Alexis moved into the second floor of Ivy's house. So the prospective tenant's decision not to move there turned out to be a good thing. Ellison was thrilled to have Alexis and Santiago back.

Ty and I joined Santiago, Ellison, and Alexis for a cookout in the yard. The chickens ran around for a while and then settled into their coop as dusk fell. When Ty and Ellison got into a conversation about how they both hoped to visit Sweden one day, and Alexis got absorbed in something on her phone, I drew my chair closer to Santiago's.

His hair was longer and wavier than when I saw him in the holding cell, but overall he looked the same. He held himself in a relaxed way. Nothing about him suggested the ordeal he'd been through.

"I didn't get a chance to say much to you when we first met," I said. "I am so sorry about Ivy. And for all you went through."

He touched the back of my hand. "What's important is my girls are all right and I can be there for them. I owe you for that. More than I can say."

"I was only doing my job."

"Danielle told me everything you did. She said she might have been able to beat the charges with all the questions there from the beginning, but I couldn't see myself gambling on a trial. It was you uncovering all the evidence that stopped me from having to make that choice."

"Will you be able to get your job back?"

"Looks like it. Truck drivers are still in big demand. And now that I don't have a record, there's nothing standing in the way."

"I'm relieved. Alexis seems much happier. Amber, too."

"In some ways I worry about her more. Dealing with her mother's death. It's harder to lose a parent when there are all these issues. Ivy's gone now, and Amber will never have a chance to have a good relationship with her."

"Do you think that might've happened if Ivy had lived?"

Santiago stared at his hands. "Hard to say. With age, Amber might have been able to be kinder to Ivy. To cut her some slack. It's a tough thing for most people to do when they're young."

"But you don't think Ivy might have changed her attitude toward Amber?"

He met my eyes. His were a shade of gray that matched the evening sky. "I doubt in any major way. The life she had, it was hard for her to be any different than she was. Fair or not, Amber was the one who probably would have needed to adjust. If she could."

We sat in silence for a few moments, listening to a dog barking from down the road and a neighbor's garage door opening.

"Can I ask you something?" I said. "Why you and Ivy decided to divorce. I'm sure it's not simple to explain."

"Not simple. But not complicated. We were always very different. In the beginning that balanced us off. But after a lot of years and two children it got harder. We had the same fights over and over. And mostly, we both started to feel unhappy all the time."

"But you were the one who left?"

"I'm the one who left. But Ivy was the first to suggest we separate."

That was something Danielle hadn't told me, if she'd known.

"Why?" I said.

"Some podcast guru she listened to said that if you're stuck in the same patterns sometimes it's worth separating. Taking a break from each other and then starting over. That was her plan. But once I left, I felt happier. More relaxed than I had ever been. Though I also felt like a failure. In my family, people don't divorce. But it was such a relief. I found I didn't want to try anymore."

"Ivy. Was she happier?"

"She wasn't less happy. If that makes any sense. So I thought if I was happier and she was about the same, with the girls almost grown up, it made more sense to split up. Not long after I told her that she started seeing Roy and she did seem a little happier."

I asked about the hidden room. He smiled. "Ivy's sanctuary. It was there when we moved in, trap door, ladder, and everything. Not hidden. But with Amber so little, we worried about her finding the trap door in the room and falling in. Or getting hurt trying to climb up from the basement. Ivy still wanted to use the room, so I wallpapered over the door and hid it. Not a perfect job, but enough to fool a toddler. And later Alexis too."

"Why did Ivy want it?"

"It's hard to believe now, but Amber was clingy when she was little. If Ivy was in her sight, she wanted to be right next to her. The room was Ivy's private place. Her escape. Amber didn't remember it was there, so if I was home or someone else was over, Ivy would disappear for a while. I'm not sure why she kept it once the girls grew up. And especially after Alexis moved out. She worked so hard to present an image of herself to everyone. Maybe she just liked the idea of a place no one else knew about."

51

Sylvania was charged with first-degree murder. Computer experts had retrieved the recording on my phone. While it wasn't a full confession, with the other evidence I put together Danielle told me she thought it was a strong case.

Detective Sergeant Beckwell filled me in on some of the investigation regarding Hank. He claimed to never have received an email from me and to not know why I had been at the warehouse. A forensic analysis of Hank and Sylvania's computers showed that she had likely intercepted my email and responded to set up the meeting, then finagled Hank into taking their son to the movies so both would be out of the way. She herself called the store clerk and told her Hank was running late. The clerk agreed that the message came from Sylvania. It just hadn't occurred to her to tell me that.

The thermos in Ivy's pantry showed trace amounts of antifreeze. It did not, though, show Sylvania's fingerprints on it. The store's records helped on that front. Only two thermoses had ever been ordered with the store's logo on them – one for Ivy and one for Hank. He admitted he never used it. Employees had seen Sylvania with it at the yoga center.

Not surprisingly, the police found antifreeze in Sylvania's and Hank's garage. That alone meant almost nothing. Chicago's winters are often frigid, and anyone with a car might keep a bottle or two of antifreeze. More damning was that one of the computers in the yoga center showed Internet search histories on poisoning with household chemicals. Someone had also searched for articles on famous poisoning cases and ways to avoid detecting poison. Other search histories involved vicious dogs, Dobermans, canine attacks on children under ten, and dog crating.

Nothing ever turned up regarding who Ivy had plans with for the Saturday night of her death. My best guess was that she invented the plans to avoid spending additional time with her old friend Mei, who didn't interest her beyond the chance for a quick sales pitch. Or more charitably, and given that Ivy felt the need for a hidden sanctuary, maybe she wanted an evening of downtime watching movies or reading.

Sylvania's home laptop showed traces of the hack into my computer system. She'd bought something called a virus construction kit online. The detective on the case told me that his expert advised that in terms of sophistication, it had been a relatively low-level job. In other words, my system wasn't that hard to penetrate. The virus had been hidden in a document "Hank" forwarded to me about an event at Alexis's school. It still had a doc extension, so I thought it safe to open.

All of which told me as much as I like Shawn, I needed to get a new IT guy. Mensa Sam had recommended Shawn, and Sam fancied himself knowledgeable about computers. This strongly suggested to me that Sam was not.

Hank was questioned several times, but never charged with anything. If he had helped Sylvania cover her crime, under the law he would be an accessory after the fact to murder. But the prosecutor said there wasn't sufficient evidence for her to feel confident that she could prove his involvement beyond a reasonable doubt.

In a civil lawsuit, the standard of proof is different. It's a preponderance of the evidence. Meaning instead of needing to prove the defendant guilty beyond a reasonable doubt, the plaintiff's attorney only needs to prove that it is more probable than not that the defendant is guilty.

Because of that difference, Mensa Sam and I told Santiago and the girls on a conference call that a civil lawsuit against both Hank and Sylvania for Ivy's death made sense. We could drop Hank if the evidence we collected showed he truly wasn't involved. The girls had mixed feelings about suing their uncle and aunt. This time, though, Amber was all for it and Alexis hesitated.

"I just want to forget it all. Never see or hear from them again." Alexis's voice came clearly through the speaker on Sam's landline.

My knees hit the front of Sam's desk when I scooted my chair forward to get closer to the phone. "Remember, your uncle might not have had anything to do with it."

I hated to think of Alexis losing touch with her uncle if he didn't know that Sylvania poisoned Ivy.

Amber, still at school, chimed in. "But he must've known that Aunt Sylvania did it. That's why we should go after him. How could he say he didn't? He lived with her."

"People don't necessarily know everything about their spouses. Or anyone they love. But I understand why you feel that way."

In the end, it was Santiago's decision. Since the divorce had never been finalized, he was entitled to collect as Ivy's spouse and heir, and the court had recently appointed him executor of her estate. He chose to go ahead with the lawsuit because it might help him pay for Amber's and Alexis's educations. More important, though, he felt that if Hank had been involved, he ought not to get away with it.

~

I saw Hank about three weeks after Sylvania was arrested. I went to the criminal court status hearing at the courthouse at 26th and California. The girls and Santiago wanted to know what happened, but none of them wanted to be there.

Hank sat on the other side of the courtroom. His formerly full cheeks sagged, and his temples, no longer salt and pepper, had gone white. His shoulders slumped.

I planned to keep my distance in case he didn't want to speak to me without his attorney there. But he approached me after we left the courtroom. His feet hit the floor heavily and slowly, a clomp clomp that echoed through the wide corridor door.

"Quille. How are the girls?"

"Happy to have their father back," I said.

He ran his hands over both sides of his face. "Santiago. I don't know how I'll ever face him. Though he'll probably never want to see me."

"It had to be very hard," I said. "I'm sure you were distraught over Ivy's death."

"I was so certain he did it. Alexis insisted I was wrong, and I wouldn't listen." He gripped my wrist. His fingers felt cool and clammy. "Will Amber and Alexis forgive me? I can't imagine never seeing my nieces again."

"I don't know," I said. "Do you think you were afraid to consider who might have done it if it wasn't Santiago?"

My question was a great example of why attorneys insist

on being there if their clients talk to the lawyer on the other side. Hank really shouldn't answer. I could use his words against him if he said something different on the witness stand. But he had approached me, and he had raised the subject. I owed it to the girls and Santiago to see if he would tell me anything.

And I was curious.

Hank looked up and down the hall as if expecting someone to appear and give him answers. "If I was, I didn't know it. I loved my sister. But God help me, I really thought living with her might have pushed Santiago over the edge."

My grip on the strap of my shoulder bag tightened. I'd been suggesting he didn't want to see the truth about his wife, but he talked as if Ivy were to blame. "So if Santiago had killed Ivy, it would've been her fault?"

He looked at the floor. "I'm sure it sounds terrible. But you had to know Ivy."

"It does sound terrible. And you're right, I didn't know Ivy. But murderers are responsible for their own actions. Ivy might have been a difficult person, but she was a human being doing her best to get through life. She didn't deserve what happened to her. No one deserves that."

His chin lifted but he still didn't meet my eyes. "You're right. Of course you're right. I suppose I'm still trying to justify not seeing what was right in front of me."

"Which was?"

He shuffled his feet. "Ivy and Sylvania were alike in one way. They were both used to getting what they wanted. Ivy because it was the only way she found to manage life. She had to take charge when we were kids, especially after our parents died but even before. She had to run things, take care of both of us, because no one else did."

"And Sylvania?"

"Her parents were so different. They gave Sylvania everything she ever needed or wanted. She was the center of their lives. Which at first I thought was wonderful. Parents who focused it all on their child. Who were there for her. It took a long time to realize that Sylvania expected everyone to do what her parents had done. To put her first."

"So each of the two women closest to you expected you to defer to her. Put her first. It couldn't have been easy when they disagreed."

He finally looked at me, eyes wide. "Not easy? Now there's an understatement. But for long stretches they got along. I thought they did. But I should've known better. I know Sylvania."

People passed by us, but I barely heard their voices or saw them, I was so focused on Hank. "What should you have known?" I asked.

"Ivy — if she was unhappy, she told you. You never had to wonder what she wanted or how she felt. But Sylvania did a slow burn. She demanded, she insisted, and almost always finally got what she wanted. But if she didn't, she pretended to be fine. And about six weeks or six months later she'd explode. I should've known. When she kept talking about the dog. I should've known."

My guess is Sylvania had deeper resentments than Ralph against Ivy. But it probably had been the catalyst. One that Hank ought to have recognized.

"I'm sorry for your loss," I said.

"Not as sorry as I am," he said.

I ducked into one of the side hallways that leads to the restrooms and answered a few emails on other cases. I wanted to give Hank some space with his own thoughts.

My walking pace is pretty fast, but I expected that he

would have left the parking garage across the street by the time I got there. As I pulled Lauren's car out of my spot, though, I saw him getting into his silver Lexus sedan. He moved so slowly that for second I thought he had frozen in place.

~

The next time Amber came home for a long weekend, Amber and Alexis decided to spend a Saturday afternoon at the park along the Fox River with their little cousin, Percy. The evidence and documents Mensa Sam and I had collected so far suggested that Hank likely had not known about Sylvania's actions, but the girls weren't quite ready to see their uncle yet. They picked Percy up and dropped him off with a neighbor.

Ty, Eric, and I met Amber and Alexis in Geneva. Ty and I bought dinner at Niche, the restaurant we'd gone to the night we met Alexis and Eric.

Amber told us she had to drop a class to keep up with everything, but she had good news, too. An internship over the summer would cover the missing credits and give her good experience. Santiago was back to work. Alexis looked better than when I first met her. She had gelled her hair, now with a purple streak rather than blue, into an artfully tousled short cut that set off her cheekbones. She sat straighter and laughed a little, though she fell silent often.

I asked how she was feeling.

"Still miss Mom," she said. "But it's better with Dad back. Not so hard to get through every day, you know?"

"Yes," I said. "I think you'll always miss her. And it'll be up and down for a long time. Maybe always. But there's a point when you'll remember the good things, the happy times, and not as much of the pain."

I didn't add that my parents never seemed to have reached that point. At least my mother hadn't. Alexis appeared to be on her way, and suggesting things would improve might help her get there. And she had closure. Knowing who killed Ivy didn't bring her back, but it saved Santiago, and it let all of them stop wondering.

Before dessert I excused myself to go to the restroom. Alexis walked with me. The chalkboard was still there with its question: *What do you want to do before you die?*

"Do you think my mom did the things she wanted?" Alexis said.

I ran a comb through my hair. "I hope so. It sounds like she was excited about the store." And Roy, at least for a while.

"She was. Like, she said she always wanted a business where people came in and she sold them things that made their life better right away. Not like the financial thing where it takes such a long time to see results."

"She talked to you about her business?"

"Sometimes, yeah. Why?"

"I'm glad she shared how she felt with you. That you had a good relationship."

"Yeah, mostly we did I guess." Alexis wrapped an arm around my waist. "I'm so glad you found who did it. Not just to get my dad back, but because Sylvania shouldn't get away with doing that to my mom. Thank you."

"You're welcome," I said.

When we got back to the table, Alexis told Eric about the chalkboard. Ty nodded. "There's one like it in the Men's Room, too. Quille and I saw them when we were here before."

We talked about the different answers people had listed.

"What would you guys write?" Eric said, glancing from me to Ty.

We answered at the same time.

Ty said, "Take a trip around the world."

I said, "Find my sister's killer."

Looking for more Q.C. Davis mysteries?

Visit LisaLilly.com to join Lisa M. Lilly's Readers Group and be first to find out about new releases and get bonus Q.C. Davis stories.

ABOUT THE AUTHOR

In addition to the Q.C. Davis Mystery series, which includes *The Worried Man*, *The Charming Man*, *The Fractured Man*, and *The Troubled Man*, Lisa M. Lilly is the author of the *Awakening* supernatural thriller series and the host of the podcast Buffy and the Art of Story.

Her stories and poems have appeared in numerous publications.

A resident of Chicago, Lilly is an attorney and a past Vice President of the Alliance Against Intoxicated Motorists. She joined AAIM after an intoxicated driver caused the deaths of her parents in 2007. Her book of essays, *Standing in Traffic*, is available on AAIM's website.

Join Lisa M. Lilly's email list to receive Q.C. Davis stories, a monthly e-newsletter, and updates on sales and new releases.

ALSO BY LISA M. LILLY

Q.C. Davis Mystery Series

The Worried Man (Q.C. Davis 1)

The Charming Man (Q.C. Davis 2)

The Fractured Man (Q.C. Davis 3)

The Troubled Man (Q.C. Davis 4)

Q.C. Davis Mysteries 1-3 Box Set/Omnibus

No Good Deeds (Short Story for e-newsletter subscribers)

No New Beginnings (Short Story for e-newsletter subscribers)

The Awakening Supernatural Thriller Series

The Awakening (Book 1)

The Unbelievers (Book 2)

The Conflagration (Book 3)

The Illumination (Book 4)

The Awakening Series Complete Supernatural Thriller Series Box Set/Omnibus

Other Fiction

When Darkness Falls (a standalone supernatural suspense novel)

The Tower Formerly Known As Sears And Two Other Tales Of Urban Horror

As L.M. Lilly:

Happiness, Anxiety, and Writing: Using Your Creativity To Live A Calmer, Happier Life

Super Simple Story Structure: A Quick Guide to Plotting and Writing Your Novel

Creating Compelling Characters From The Inside Out.

The One-Year Novelist: A Week-By-Week Guide To Writing Your Novel In One Year

How To Write A Novel, Grades 6-8

How The Virgin Mary Influenced The United States Supreme Court: Catholics, Contraceptives, and Burwell v. Hobby Lobby, Inc

Buffy and the Art of Story Season One: Writing Better Fiction by Watching Buffy

Buffy and the Art of Story Season Two Part I: Threats, Lies, and Surprises in Episodes I-II

CPSIA information can be obtained
at www.ICGtesting.com
Printed in the USA
LVHW010601240821
695792LV00004B/27